PURSUIT

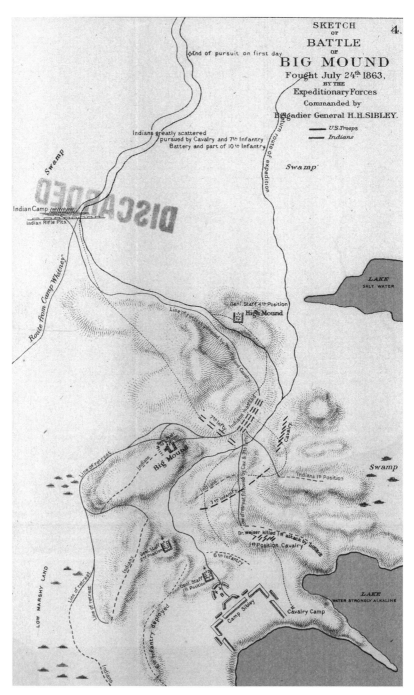

Sketch of the Battle of Big Mound. (John Koblas's collection. Used with permission)

Pursuit

A Novel

by

Dean Urdahl

NORTH STAR PRESS OF ST. CLOUD, INC.
St. Cloud, Minnesota

Cover Art: "The Sioux War-Cavalry Charge of Sully's Brigade at the Battle of White Stone Hill, September 3, 1863." From *Harper's Weekly*. New York: October 21, 1863.

ISBN: 0-87839-421-4
ISBN-13: 978-0-87839-421-0

First Edition, May 2011

Printed in the United States of America

Published by
North Star Press of St. Cloud, Inc.
P.O. Box 451
St. Cloud, Minnesota 56302

www.northstarpress.com

Dedication

To my family: my wife, Karen, sons Chad, Brent, and Troy, daughter-in-law Rebecca, Grandchildren: Alicia Kraft, Violet, Lincoln, Calvin, and Mason Urdahl

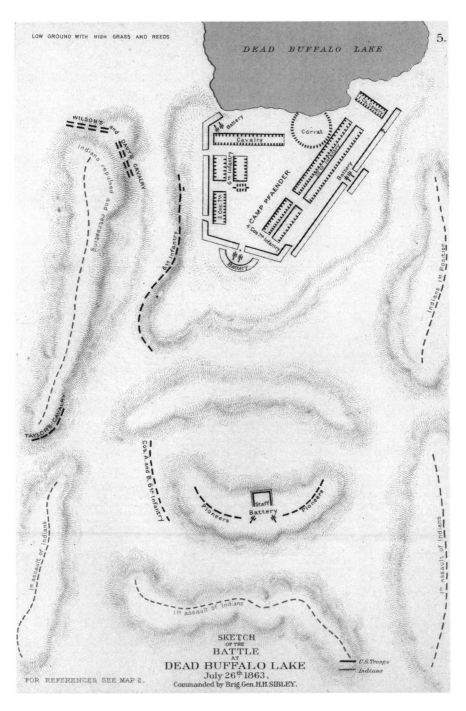

Sketch of the Battle of Dead Buffalo Lake. (John Koblas's collection. Used with permission)

Expeditions into the Dakota Territory in 1863-1864. (Map by Alan Ominsky. Courtesy of the Minnesota Historical Society, appearing in *The Sioux Uprising of 1862* by Kenneth Carley)

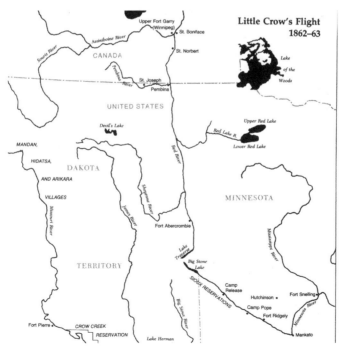

Little Crow's Flight, 1862-1863. (Courtesy the Minnesota Historical Society, appeared in *Little Crow: Spokesman for the Sioux*, by Gary Clayton Anderson)

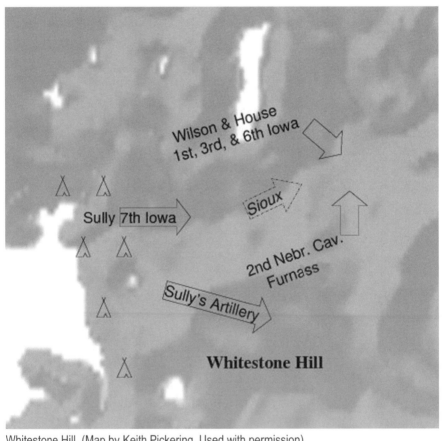

Whitestone Hill. (Map by Keith Pickering. Used with permission)

Ꙙ Preface ꙡ
by Hy Berman

T HE CIVIL WAR AND THE DAKOTA CONFLICT sesquicentennials are almost upon us. Within the next few years we will be inundated with numerous programs, commemorations, public demonstrations, and media overkill on these transformational events in our nation's history. Before we have to overcome the tendency of our popular culture to trivialize these important events by diluting their meaning, it is refreshing for us to turn to the this volume of Dean Urdahl's novel series dealing with the traumatic events surrounding the Dakota conflict and its aftermath.

Pursuit follows both *Uprising* and *Retribution*, the previous two books in the Dakota uprising series and in a readable and understandable way takes us from the hangings in Mankato to the tragic outcome of the attempted genocide of the Dakota people. In this book, the author meticulously follows the course of events of the subsequent wars and expulsions that characterized the most unforgivable chapter in our history and which are still felt with great bitterness by the Dakota descendants.

For anyone who doubted the extent of the brutalities committed has only to read Dean Urdahl's account of the conditions the Dakota faced in the Fort Snelling "concentration camp" after their forced removal to the fort. Or read the author's riveting account of the trek from Fort Snelling to Crow Creek and the establishment of the reservation. The Dakota people did not give up peacefully. The subsequent battles are described graphically, and the roles of generals Sibley and Sully are dramatically explored. Dean Urdahl shows that the battles into which General Sully led his troops were the most bloody of any in the nineteenth-century Indian wars that continued until the end of the century.

The fictional approach the author took in this trilogy does not diminish the power of its historical truths. The author used the best historical sources and the latest scholarship upon which to base his narrative. The fictional approach makes these books more accessible to the ordinary reader and will make it available to a larger audience. This is particularly important if we are to overcome our tragic past and enable us to find reconciliation among our peoples.

The federal law which permanently removed the Dakota people and some other native peoples from Minnesota is still law. Dean Urdahl, as state legislator and as chair of Minnesota's Lincoln Bicentennial Commission, has taken the leadership in getting our state to petition Congress to repeal the Dakota Exclusion Act. By writing this trilogy, he has taken an even more important step in attempting healing closure on one of our most tragic and contentious historical events.

1

NESTLED IN THE SCENIC MINNESOTA RIVER Valley, the frontier town of Mankato was favored with unseasonably mild weather on Saturday, December 27, 1862. A warm front descended upon the valley, bringing with it large, fluffy white snowflakes that tumbled lazily through the afternoon sky.

Jesse Buchanen gazed thoughtfully through an icy window at the distant gallows, which stood starkly empty. The thirty-eight condemned Dakota men who were hanged there one day earlier had been buried and then disinterred by neighboring doctors.

Gay Christmas tunes from a slightly out-of-tune piano rang out from across the parlor in stark contrast to yesterday's mood. Colonel Stephen Miller thought it a good time for a delayed Christmas party. He had invited many of his officers into his home that afternoon.

"Let's put this business behind us," the colonel had urged. "In spite of the tragedies of recent months, we have much to be thankful for. We must remember the spirit of the season and look to the future."

And so they sang, drank wine and ate. JoAnna Miller merrily pounded on yellowed piano keys as young men in blue joyously sang out the songs of the season.

Jesse didn't join in much. The events of the previous day kept dragging down his spirits. But JoAnna was happy, and he was glad for that. A slight smile creased his handsome face as he slowly swirled the red liquid in his glass and gazed at the woman he dearly loved at the piano. Looking at her prompted a wistful daydream about times they had shared and of his longing to have her as his wife.

He had known JoAnna since they were children. Six years younger, JoAnna had been the little kid who tagged along behind her brother, Jimmy, and his friend, Jesse.

Her father Stephen Miller was a businessman in St. Paul. The Buchanens lived down the block in a brick house that doubled as Jesse's father's law office. Jesse had watched JoAnna grow into a gangly teenager. Then he left for the nearby river town of Red Wing to attend Hamline University, Minnesota's very first university, to study law. Returning with his degree, he had found that the skinny Miller girl had been transformed into a fetching young woman with long, dark locks, enchanting blue eyes, glowing skin, and an engaging personality. The immediate attraction was mutual, and as Jesse built his law practice he had also quietly courted JoAnna.

Their relationship soon had blossomed into true love, and they shared brief, dizzying moments of tender kisses and passionate embraces. Although both wanted to marry, Jesse had insisted on waiting, at first because of the Civil War and then because of the war with the Dakota.

"JoAnna, dear," he had explained, "I'm going to enlist in the army. Governor Ramsey has promised volunteers to President Lincoln. It's my duty to go."

"Duty, duty," JoAnna had moaned. "What about us?"

Jesse had folded her hands in his and smiled earnestly into her blue eyes. "This won't change anything about us. I must do this."

"Can't we be married first?" JoAnna had pleaded

"It wouldn't be fair to you," Jesse had responded. "I don't know how long I'll be gone and well. . . anything could happen."

JoAnna had brushed her dark hair from her eyes, wrapped her arms around his neck and commanded, "Don't talk that way! You *will* come back to me."

But much had changed on August 17. A war with the Dakota in Minnesota had preempted plans to go east to put down the rebellion. Jesse had found himself fighting Indians, not Confederate rebels.

Four young Santee braves, empty-handed from a failed hunt and frustrated by their people's treatment by the white government on the reservation, had killed five white people near Acton, some forty miles north of the Redwood Agency on the Minnesota River.

Jesse had been sent to the western Minnesota frontier. General Sibley had been slow to move, claiming that untrained troops and a lack of horses left him ill-equipped to mount a campaign.

Sibley had marched from St. Paul to relieve the beleaguered garrison at Fort Ridgely. Barely 100 soldiers at the fort had endured two attacks from the

Santee. They were tenuously holding on when Sibley's army marched into the wall-less position.

Under ridicule as the "state undertaker," the general had sent a detachment up the Minnesota River to bury dead, seek survivors, and verify the whereabouts of the Indians. It had been a disaster as the troops were attacked at Birch Coulee. They had lost seventeen men and were in danger of being swept from the field when reinforcements from Ridgely arrived.

Sibley had delayed again after that battle, owing to the loss of more horses. When he'd finally moved in mid-September, his goal was to smash the Santee Dakota forever. An accidental battle at Wood Lake, where two of Sibley's regiments engaged the Dakota without his orders, had started when two wagons with troopers headed out looking for garden vegetables for breakfast. They stumbled upon Santee braves waiting to ambush Sibley's column when it marched. Without waiting to hear from Sibley, the two regiments had joined the fight and pushed the Dakota back.

In fact, Sibley had tried to recall the men occupied in the fight. But their blood was up and they would not retreat. The result was the smashing victory Sibley had promised. Only it had happened without his command or active participation. Nevertheless, the result had made him a general.

Jesse Buchanen had fought in the battle. He had even helped a soldier and a one-armed civilian rescue a wounded Indian boy before he returned to the fray. Wood Lake had been the last battle.

Chief Little Crow and most other war leaders had fled. Over 200 white hostages were freed, and other Dakota "war criminals" were rounded up for trial. That path had led Jesse to Mankato this December. It was a journey he wished he hadn't been set upon.

He knew he should hate the Santee Dakota for what they had done, yet he felt more pity than hatred for them. The Santee were one of three great divisions of the Dakota Nation; the Teton and Yankton were in the Dakota Territory.

The Santee had lost their vast land holdings in two treaties. Their reservation had shrunk to a strip of land ten miles wide and 150 miles long on the south side of the Minnesota.

Two agencies, located on either end of the reservation, had administered the reservation as they tried to turn the Dakota into farmers. Poor harvests, delayed government payments, and mistrust of the white traders in the agencies had led to resentment and hatred.

The four young Indian men had set a match to fire-ready tinder by murdering the five whites in Acton, but they had not created the underlying problem. Still they had unleashed a firestorm that wouldn't stop until it led to the destruction of their people and devastation on the frontier.

After about six weeks, the war with the Dakota had ended in Minnesota, with nearly 800 Minnesotans killed. In the aftermath, over 400 Indians had been put on trial as war criminals. Jesse and a missionary, Reverend Stephen Riggs, had been given the task of weighing evidence and acting as a quasi-grand jury. So Jesse had helped with the trials of Dakota warriors at the Lower Sioux Agency.

Meanwhile, JoAnna had accompanied a supply detail from St. Paul in an attempt to join Jesse on the frontier. When the detail was ambushed, JoAnna had found herself abandoned on the prairie. Her sole protection was a pistol she'd alertly picked up after her escort was killed in the attack.

The girl had matured into a woman in the week she wandered alone. After holing up in a deserted dugout cabin, she'd fought off a small party of Dakota using that pistol. As the Indians closed in and death seemed imminent, Jesse arrived, leading a search party looking for her. He had galloped onto the scene just in time and saved her life.

The soldiers had dealt with punishing the Dakota and had prepared for executions. JoAnna, who had miraculously achieved her goal of joining Jesse on the frontier, worked as a nurse and administered to the captives under the guidance of Dr. Weiser.

Jesse had briefly considered marriage after coming so close to losing his beloved. But, while deeply in love, the two had agreed that postponing their wedding was best until hostilities ceased and a semblance of normalcy returned to their lives.

ഇ 2 ൭

Jesse remained lost in his thoughts despite the sounds of the piano and laughter that drifted dimly across the smoky room. He stared without really seeing through the frosty window. Then a nearby voice intruded.

"Come on, Jesse, this is supposed to be a joyous occasion, and you're about as gloomy a Gus as you can be. What's wrong?" The voice belonged to Captain Tim Sheehan of the Fifth Minnesota, commandant of Fort Ridgely while it was besieged, and a bona fide hero of the uprising.

With him was Captain John Jones, perhaps the most famous defender of the fort. He had fired a cannon through the open doors of the head-quarters building and into the Indian-occupied stables beyond. A sergeant at the time, he had been promoted to his present rank of captain. Captain William Duley stood just behind the two from Ridgely.

Jesse looked hard at the three before he spoke. Captain Sheehan was the epitome of an officer. Tall and handsome, he wore a short, sandy-colored beard, and his curly hair just touched his ears. Captain Jones was solidly built and stocky. A full, dark beard hid much of his face below piercing blue eyes. Captain Duley was dark and sullen. Jesse didn't know him very well. Lines like tiny crevices etched Duley's face ahead of his years. Gray flecked his dark hair. His body was slender and sinewy like a clock spring wound too tightly. Jesse had heard of Duley's tragic loss and tried to understand the relish with which he had swung the axe that dropped the gallows the day before.

Jesse wore his blonde hair short. His beardless face portrayed honesty with bright blue eyes, high cheekbones, and a strong chin. Broad shoulders tapered to a narrow waist on a six-foot, one-inch body supported by gangly legs.

He tried a weak smile and then said, "Well, Tim, I guess I just can't shake what happened yesterday."

Sheehan nodded solemnly.

"It was a spectacle," Jones agreed.

Duley pulled himself up hard. "I'm just glad that God was able to use me as his instrument of revenge," he said crisply.

Jesse shook his head ruefully. "That's what bothers me. I don't know that all those poor souls deserved to die. Certainly not Chaska. He saved Mrs. Wakefield. Rdainyanka was Chief Wabasha's son-in-law and simply fought as a soldier in his army. Should all our soldiers fighting in the South be hanged if captured? Shakopee, Medicine Bottle, Red Middle Voice, and his Rice Creek bunch. Where were they? The four who started it all with the murders at Acton, and of course Little Crow, together with many others who are documented to have committed atrocities. Where are they? They weren't on the gallows."

Jesse sighed, then added, "This was revenge for the sake of revenge. No one really cared who died as long as they were Indian."

"Damn right, they didn't care!" Duley's voice rose, and spittle formed at the corners of his mouth. "All the red devils deserved to die! They were all out there killin' whites who were just workin' in their fields and sittin' in their cabins." He leaned over the table toward Jesse. "You weren't at Lake Shetek. I was. You weren't lured into an ambush. I was. You were safe with your law books in St. Paul. You didn't see part of your family killed before your eyes and watch your wife and the two children you had left carried away!"

Jesse knew he'd never convince this man. He probably shouldn't have said anything. "I'm sorry for your loss, Captain Duley. I really am. But does killing the innocent make up for it?"

"There are no innocent savages," Duley snapped, his voice loud enough to draw heads from nearby tables.

Sheehan rested a hand on Duley's arm. "Surely you don't think Round Wing should have been killed? He was miles away from the murder he was accused of. If Jesse hadn't stepped in, thirty-nine would have hung yesterday."

Duley shook off Sheehan's hand and glared at Jesse. "You saved that murdering devil! My neighbors say he *was* at Shetek."

"No one could positively place him there," Jesse said patiently.

"Who needs positive placement?" Duley thundered. "I *know* he was there. I can't believe you helped let him go!"

The disturbance had reached the rest of the room. The music stopped. Other officers pushed closer toward Jesse and Duley.

"Now, Will," Sheehan calmed, "let it go. It's over. Patrols'll be goin' out to finish the job we started yesterday."

"I will *not* let it go. Not until Pawn, the son of a bitch who hauled off my wife, is dead, too." Duley's face was nearly purple with outrage. "And you're not any better, Sheehan. Agent Galbraith says you undermined his authority when the Sioux broke into the agency warehouse and stole food."

Enraged, Sheehan flushed as he retorted loudly, "If I hadn't acted and forced the dispersal of food, nearly 100 soldiers and every civilian at Yellow Medicine Agency would have been slaughtered. And for what? Just because Galbraith was too big a fool to give the Sioux what was rightfully theirs, warehouses full of provisions? Food to feed a starving people. People our government made promises to and didn't keep."

Duley snorted. "It's Indian lovers like you and Buchanen that started this whole thing in the first place. If the savages hadn't been coddled and had been kept in their place, this never would have happened."

Sheehan gaped at the man. "I can't believe what you're saying. We took their land, promised them next to nothin' in return and didn't even give them that. We tried to force woodland people to become farmers. We took their way of life away from them."

Duley pointed an accusing finger. "You're apologizing for 'em?"

"No, just facts, Captain. The murders the Santee committed were wrong. Jesse and I both fought them for that. The uprising was a horrible disaster and had to be put down. But Jesse was right to seek release of an innocent man and to be upset that murderers have escaped punishment while we hung thirty-eight. Some of 'em died under the weight of questionable evidence."

Will Duley stared with hatred at Jesse and Sheehan. A hush enveloped the room. The frail form of Colonel Stephen Miller stood just outside the circle of officers crowding ever closer to the three men. His daughter stood at his side.

Through clenched teeth Duley growled, "I repeat, there were no innocents hung. Two of my kids are dead, my wife was held captive two months with two more of my babies. Now she's back but with . . . with only half a mind. God knows what they did to her. I blame people like you two for what happened. You Indian lovin' sons o' bitches think you can save mankind with a good deed and a law book. Your thinking left hundreds dead and hundreds more missing. Still you're making excuses for 'em! You make me sick. Thank God I got to cut the rope that sent 'em all ta Hell yesterday." With that, Captain Duley turned on his heels and stomped through the knot of onlooking officers, past the colonel, and out the door.

"Well," Miller broke the silence with strained levity. "Let's get back to the piano and some refreshments. JoAnna has more music to play, and we've more songs to sing."

Sheehan looked at Jesse and shook his head. "I'm afraid we've made a bit of an enemy."

"It's a big army," Jesse replied with a shrug and lightness to his voice he didn't feel. "I'll stay clear of him. He farmed at Shetek, you know. The attitudes of people living out there are naturally less forgiving. He went through a lot. Maybe we'll get sent south and not have to worry about him."

The party started up again, but at a subdued level. No one said anything to Sheehan or Jesse about the incident with Duley.

๑ 3 ๑

TWO DAYS LATER THE OFFICERS SERVING under Henry Hastings Sibley gathered in the headquarters building in Mankato for a morning meeting. The large hall was crowded with blue-clad men as their commander strode proudly into the room.

Sibley—the Long Trader, as the Indians called him—looked crisp and confident in his freshly-laundered uniform. New brigadier general bars sparkled on his shoulders. His black hair was neatly combed and his mustache closely trimmed. After serving as the first governor of Minnesota on the heels of a career with the American Fur Company, during which he had worked closely with the Dakota, he now served in the army.

Governor Ramsey had placed him in command of the expedition to rescue Fort Ridgely and put down the uprising. After reaching the fort, Sibley had waited, trained, sent out burial details and otherwise delayed until public pressure and his own sense of timing set his army in motion.

Circumstance and luck had led to a chance encounter with the Dakota at Wood Lake. The resulting battle had been the death knell for the hostiles. Now that the uprising had been put down, hostages freed, and thousands of Dakota rounded up, imprisoned and otherwise punished, the next stage of General Pope's plan was to be put into effect.

Sibley called his officers together two days after the thirty-eight Santee Dakota had paid with their lives for the deaths of hundreds of whites. Sibley cleared his throat and clasped his hands behind his back. His clear brown eyes focused on his colonels seated in the front row. Then he looked to the back where the junior officers stood. *All eager*, he thought. *They'd rather be fighting rebels than Indians but, either way, they want action. Well, it's almost time to give some to them, but not quite yet.*

"Gentlemen," Sibley said with purpose, but then paused and cleared his throat as all eyes turned to him. "The remainder of this winter and early spring we'll train, plan and maintain existing garrisons. In the spring, I'll lay out the plan of operations for you. I think it is safe to say that it'll involve a punitive mission in pursuit of the Sioux who have fled Minnesota for the Dakota Territory.

"In the meantime, I want troops to train for the hardships of a Dakota campaign by marching from post to post across our western Minnesota frontier. The weather will be harsh. There are numerous stockades built throughout settlements in central Minnesota: Forest City, Hutchinson, Sauk Centre, Long Lake, and many more. We'll maintain garrisons in them throughout the winter and spring. Then we'll strip them down to skeleton forces and combine most of the troops for the Dakota campaign. In the meantime we'll prepare."

From the front row, Colonel Stephen Miller rose to his feet. He stretched his slender body to his full five-foot-eight height, and brushed a shock of heavy dark hair from his forehead. "Sir, we get reports of small bands still within our borders holding white captives. Just this morning word came of a white woman held captive by Sioux near Sauk Centre."

Sibley straightened his back and looked down at Miller. "Since it won't be possible for our armies to move until after the spring thaw, I'll leave it up to regimental commanders to determine the advisability of rescue missions. I would suggest that you not commit more than a company for such a detail."

"General," Captain Tim Sheehan cried from near the back, "if we're not moving until spring, how can we expect the Sioux just to be waiting for us when we're ready to march?"

"Captain, winter campaigns are not practical," Sibley answered. "Just as it would not be prudent for us to march against the Indians in snow, it would be disastrous for the Sioux. They'd be moving not just their men, but also families of women and children. No, Captain, I think they'll stay put until it's too late. When they do move, we'll be close enough to run them down."

Finished, the Long Trader turned to leave the room. Stephen Miller stood up from his chair and waited. He knew what was coming. Several of his officers would have interest in his report from Sauk Centre.

Captain Will Duley was first to reach him. "What's this about a white woman held near Sauk Centre? I want to lead that expedition immediately! Why didn't you tell me? Pawn might be there."

Sheehan, Jones, and Jesse also gathered nearby. "Colonel Miller," Jesse pleaded, "please let me go. Tim and John are eager as well."

Miller gazed thoughtfully at his anxious officers, considering before answering. "One company, not over fifty men," he answered. "Captain Duley, you'll command an expedition to Sauk Centre. Lieutenant Buchanen, you'll be second in command. Your mission is two-fold: train your men as General Sibley instructed and ascertain the whereabouts of the white woman, if indeed she exists. Captain, meet with me in the morning."

Sheehan cleared his throat and asked deferentially, "Sir, may I have permission to speak privately with you?"

"Certainly, Tim." He looked toward the other officers and said crisply, "Excuse us, gentlemen."

Miller and Sheehan were left alone in a corner of the room.

"Sir," Sheehan began, "do you think it's a good idea to send Duley and Buchanen out together? There's been bad blood since the Christmas party."

"I'm aware of what happened, Tim. But these men are both good soldiers. They need to learn to get along. When we begin the campaign in the Dakotas, cooperation will be key. I can't have officers at each other's throats then. Duley and Buchanen will learn more about each other on this mission. I think they'll come to some form of mutual respect. Tough jobs under adverse conditions, as this will be, tend to bring men closer together. That's my hope for these two men."

Sheehan looked unconvinced. "I understand your thinking, sir, but I still don't think it's a good idea."

Miller smiled and slapped him on the back. "Don't worry so much, Tim. It'll work out fine. You're just out of sorts because you'd like to be with them."

"I would," Sheehan agreed.

"Not this time," Miller chuckled softly. "But don't worry. There'll be lots of Indians to fight this summer."

As Sheehan and Miller conferred, William Duley left the meeting hall. Jesse's eyes followed the captain as he strode out the door.

"Of all men in this command, I draw an assignment with him. He's so filled with hate he's dangerous, to himself and his men," Jesse contemplated in a low voice.

"Take it easy, boy-o," John Jones murmured as he stroked his dark beard. "Just do what you're told and don't put yer nose where it dinna belong. Ya might come to be needin' that man more than ya think."

HENRY SIBLEY SLUMPED INTO A CHAIR at the desk in his office. The room was Spartanly furnished, a wooden desk and a few chairs. A sharp rap upon the closed door grabbed his attention. "Come in!" he called.

Reverend Stephen Riggs, longtime Episcopal missionary to the Dakota Santee, entered.

"Stephen, thank you for coming. I need to talk to someone."

"We've been through a lot, sir, I didn't need to be told twice that you wanted to see me." Riggs had spent decades as a missionary to the Dakota people. His mission at Hazelwood had been near the Upper Sioux Agency and had been burned in the war. The pastor had served Sibley as an interpreter, confidant, diplomat and grand jury in the fall and winter of 1862.

Slight of stature with a head of curly white hair and wearing a black frock coat, Riggs took a seat across from Sibley.

"Stephen," the general began, "I'm not really a soldier. You know that. Not much of a politician either, even if I was governor." He smiled ruefully. "But I was a pretty good fur trader. At least I made a lot of money for the American Fur Company. But now it's getting all tangled together, and it wears on me."

"I can see that. What's going on?"

"Political infighting, for one thing. I've got Governor Ramsey poking at me, saying, 'Conquer the savages at the least possible cost.' It's so much more complicated than that. I feel the conquest is divinely ordained, and my duty is a sacred obligation.

"I worked with the Indian people for years as a trader. I know there was government duplicity in the treatment of the Santee. They were mistreated. I love this land, yet it's changing. It troubles me."

"Just as the role you gave me troubled me, Henry," Riggs said solemnly. "Determining who should come to trial before the commission after the war . . ." He shook his head. "The Dakota were a deeply wronged people. I brought charges against over 400 and sent them before your military panel. I wouldn't want my life set upon by that commission."

Sibley patted the man's shoulder. "You did an admirable job, Stephen, but there was no pleasing anyone. I found that out. Your Bishop Whipple told Lincoln, 'You cannot hang men by the hundreds.' He also argued that the Dakotas had been deeply wronged, that many of them had only reluctantly, if at all, taken part in the outbreak."

Riggs nodded. "Whipple said that the civilized world couldn't justify putting surrendered enemies on trial."

"At the same time," Sibley said, "I had politicians and the press calling for the head of every Indian left alive. Senator Wilkinson declared in Congress that I ought to have killed every one of them as I came to them. I tried to explain to Whipple that, even if Dakota came in under a flag of truce, it made no difference. I made it perfectly clear that the guilty would be punished. Those who resisted made themselves willing accessories to mass murder."

"There were innocents hanged at Mankato," Riggs said softly.

Sibley looked at his friend with exasperation. "A great public crime was committed, not by wild Indians who didn't know better, but by Dakota men who had advantages, even religious teachings."

"But so many were innocent—"

"Do you think I wanted to do what I did?" Sibley snapped. "I had to turn my back on long associations and even personal attachments to some of the condemned. Duty demanded it. The hard fact that every one of them deserved capital punishment . . . of that I have no more doubt than I have of my own existence. Then Lincoln reprieved 265. But I was a good enough soldier to keep my mouth shut."

"You were in a tough spot," Riggs agreed.

"What did it get me? Senator Rice, a Democrat like me, criticizes me, too. He and Wilkinson can only agree on one thing: they don't like me. Now Republicans control the legislature, Ramsey will replace Rice as senator, but my reappointment as a general held. I would've been better off if Lincoln had just cashiered me out of the army."

"Sir . . ."

Sibley pushed himself up from the table and began pacing. "They don't even trust me to maintain order in Minnesota. Stephen, Rice, and Wilkinson got an order from the Secretary of War to raise a force independent of me under Edwin Hatch to protect Minnesota settlers while we're in the Dakotas. Do they think Pope and I are incapable of also protecting this frontier?"

"Henry, I've worked with you a long time, even back when you were a fur trader. We haven't always agreed, but I know you always mean to do what you think is right. I'll be with you now and when you go into the Dakotas after Little Crow. How is your family?"

"My wife's a saint. She stands by after all we've gone through. We've lost two children, you know." He shook his head. "It's been hard on both me and my Sarah."

"You still have . . ." Riggs considered, "five children, don't you?"

"Yes, we were blessed, but I worry about them. Losing children is so hard, especially on Sarah."

"Wasn't there another child . . . before you married Sarah?"

Sibley sat, but shifted uncomfortably in his chair. "Helen. Her mother was Santee. But that was years before I met Sarah. Helen lives with her mother's people."

"I'll pray for your children, Henry."

"Thank you, Stephen. Pray for us all."

◈ 4 ◈

ORNING DAWNED CRISP AND COOL AS the new year approached, but snow was not yet deep in Minnesota. While the temperature had occasionally plunged below zero, the snow banks and drifts that usually blanketed the prairie this time of year were absent.

The air was clear and robust. A thin dusting of snow passed for what everyone knew was coming. Two meetings were taking place that morning. As Captain William Duley strode into the headquarters building to meet with Colonel Miller, Jesse and JoAnna Miller were sitting down to coffee in the colonel's quarters.

"Jesse, why do you have to go off now? The New Year's party is tomorrow night. You'll be here for it, won't you? I've got a new dress and everything."

"I'd love to be with you, JoAnna. But I'll go where and when your father orders me. What choice do I have? There's a white woman out there. We need to find her. You'll be just as dazzling if I'm there or not." He gazed tenderly into her soft blue eyes, her lovely face framed by long black hair.

JoAnna looked down and then smiled coyly. "It's you I want to dazzle, Jesse."

He smiled warmly. "You already have, dear JoAnna. In fact, I was dazzled from the first time I saw you, tagging along behind your brother and me."

"You didn't even notice me. I was a bother," she retorted.

Jesse gently clasped her small hand in his. He let a moment of silence be his response. Then softly, he said, "Bewitched as I am by you, you know that I have to go. We talked about this already when the rebels tried to secede, long before this Indian war changed everything out here."

"But it's over now," JoAnna protested.

He sighed. "It won't be over until we're sure all captives have been turned over and all those who led the uprising are punished. Little Crow is

15

in the Dakotas. Many Santee have gone west with him and other leaders. In the spring an expedition will go after them."

He patted her hand. "Besides, JoAnna, you know if it weren't for the uprising of the Santee, I'd be out east now." He smiled again. "Helping to save the Union for Father Abraham."

A pout returned to JoAnna's youthful face. "Why did all this have to happen?"

"I'm sure a lot of people are bemoaning that," Jesse said, "people who have lost much more than we have, people whose lives will never recover from war. We're lucky. You know that, don't you?"

JoAnna gazed up at Jesse with tears brimming in her blue eyes. "We're lucky as long as you come back to me."

"So, what will you do while I'm gone?"

"I helped Dr. Weiser before. I hear they need nurses and teachers at Fort Snelling. I think I'll go there."

The young lieutenant leaned over and softly kissed her. "I'll be fine," he murmured. "Don't worry. You take care. I don't know if I like the idea of you going to the fort, though. There'll likely be sickness there."

JoAnna wrapped her arms around him and held her fine-figured body tightly to him. Neither spoke. Only the tick-tock of the grandfather clock against the wall broke the silence.

IN HIS OFFICE COLONEL MILLER TRIED TO calm an agitated and impatient Will Duley. "Will, I gave you this detail because you're experienced and I know how you must feel because of what happened to your family. But let me caution you. Do nothing reckless. Lives are at stake. I want you to work well with Lieutenant Buchanen. I know that you've had words with him, but Jesse's a good man and means to do what is right."

"What's right in *his* mind, you mean!" Duley responded. "More people die because of people like him than good soldiers ever kill."

"That's a matter we'll debate some other time, Captain," Miller spoke firmly. "You shall get along on this mission. That's an order. Let me make my other instructions clear. Take the First Mounted Minnesota northwest to Sauk Centre. Bivouac at posts along the way and acclimate your men to the hardships of a campaign. Once you near Sauk Centre, be vigilant for bands of Santee. Don't attack a superior force, although it's doubtful there are any bands as large as fifty Indians out there. If you encounter Santee, try to get them to come in peacefully. Naturally ascertain the possibility of white captives in the area."

"You don't need to tell me that. That's a priority for me."

"This is for the record, Captain. Just so everything is understood."

Duley looked sullenly at his colonel. "Everything is understood, sir. But if we find Indians and they resist, God help 'em because no man, including Buchanen, will be able to hold me back."

"Don't jeopardize any captives, Captain."

For an instant Duley's eyes blazed. "That's the last thing you'll have to worry about, sir. I'll do my job like a soldier. You have my word."

"Good. May God be with you. And, Will, I hope you find what you're looking for."

EARLY THE NEXT MORNING, Company F of the First Minnesota Cavalry, the Mounted Rangers, headed north from the Minnesota River Valley toward Sauk Centre. The journey would be nearly 100 miles. Fifty men hefted themselves onto sturdy army horses and trotted slowly along a frozen trail.

Slate-gray clouds fought the dull sun and won the battle. Saddles creaked from the cold as the men in blue clutched heavy wool coats to their bodies. Will Duley rode at the head of the column of twos, Jesse at his side. The pair had not spoken directly since their argument at the party.

They rode north into a wind that chilled them to the bone. Light snow was driven by the gale, feeling like tiny daggers as it stung exposed skin. Duley wiped his red nose and turned to Jesse.

"Lieutenant," he said, "we've got a long trip and a job to do. I trust you'll do your part like a soldier. I don't care what you think about me or the reds, or anything else. You will follow orders without question."

His icy words hung in the frozen air. Jesse rode with eyes fixed straight ahead. Then, slowly, he turned his head to face Duley. "Captain, I will do my duty as a soldier. There is no question of that."

"Good," Duley snapped, "then we'll get along fine."

"Permission to see to the men, sir," Jesse asked.

"Granted," Duley grunted.

Relieved, Jesse wheeled his horse and rode back to the troopers in the rear. He fell in with them and rode in silence. The jangle of gear, squeaks of leather, and the crunching of hooves in the crusted snow swallowed his thoughts for a time. Jesse resigned himself to a long, unpleasant mission. He only hoped that it would lead to success, that somewhere ahead of them they would find a band of Santee with captive white women and that they could rescue them.

He feared his captain was being eaten up by hatred and consumed by bitterness. Would Sauk Centre lead him to Pawn? Would Duley's wife recover and relieve his tortured mind? Somewhere ahead in the swirling whiteness lay an answer. Duley ordered the pace picked up, and, grumbling, the troops responded.

⁊ 5 ⱳ

LITTLE CROW HUDDLED near a smoky fire in the center of a buffalo hide tipi. He stretched out his arms and held his hands palms outward to warm them. But he couldn't warm his spirit. White Spider and Passing Daylight, his half-brothers, sat across from him in the dim haze. It was late December, and the Minnesota Santee had been on the run since late September. The Dakota leader rose and stretched his cramped fifty-two-year-old legs. His face was lined and leathered beyond his years, his black hair streaked with gray. A long leather shirt concealed wrists long withered and deformed by a bullet that had passed through both arms.

He took a few steps and opened the tipi flap. A cold blast of winter air slapped his face as sharply as a gloved fist. Snow swirled over the plains and the nearby frozen Missouri River. Smoke tendrilled from tipi tops scattered near the river. White emptiness outside filled his heart with sadness.

The man who had led his people in the great Minnesota war returned to his place by the fire and spoke to his brothers. "We came from the Minnesota Valley with 300 Mdewakanton. Now only half are with us. If only the Yankton, Yanktonais, and Teton would join us."

"Brother," White Spider snapped bitterly, "the Yankton and Yantonais are lazy cowards who grow fat on what they get from the whites. They know little of the whites from the few traders they see. They don't know that the whites will soon cover their land like the snows of winter. The Teton are beyond the river and know even less about the whites. But you were right to try to bring all Dakota together to fight against the invaders. We must make them understand."

Little Crow agreed. "We must all stand together, or their land will be lost just as we lost the Minnesota Valley."

"We couldn't even get all the Santee to stand with us," Passing Daylight complained. "Only a few hundred Sisseton and Wahpeton joined us in the fight. Most stood with Little Paul and Red Iron and cried for peace."

Little Crow stirred the fire coals with a stick. "See where it got them. Now they're all penned up at the fort where the rivers join in Minnesota, waiting to be sent to prison or to a worthless reservation to the west. Those thirty-eight hanged at Mankato probably wished they'd left Minnesota with us."

White Spider slowly shook his head. "Now Standing Buffalo and his Sisseton go toward the setting sun too. But he stood against us when we needed him."

"Remember my words," Little Crow said, "during councils I told them that the Long Trader, Sibley, would soon come leading many soldiers and that they would try to rub out all Dakota people, even the Sisseton. After we lost at Wood Lake, while we camped north of Big Stone Lake with Standing Buffalo, he received a message from the Long Trader."

Passing Daylight's face contorted with anger as he remembered. "Don't help Little Crow and surrender, that's what he demanded. But Standing Buffalo only did half of what Sibley asked. He didn't help us."

"I will never forget his words," Little Crow said sadly. "He told us, 'You have already made much trouble for my people. Go to Canada or where you please, but go away from me and off the lands of my people.'"

"Then," White Spider continued, "when Standing Buffalo realized that the young Sisseton who did help us attack at Fort Ridgely and Abercrombie would be punished by Sibley, he moved west, too."

Passing Daylight recalled how the situation had unfolded. "Almost all the Sisseton and Wahpeton, nearly 4,000, went with us to the shores of Devils Lake. But they came to hide, not fight. Why won't the Yankton and Teton help? Don't they see what will happen?"

White Spider sadly shook his head. "As far back as the grandfathers remember, our warfare comes from the village. The young men fight for glory and for their families and bands. Even when we join with other Dakota, it doesn't last. We fight for our band and village, not the bands and villages of others."

Little Crow explained, "Neither the Yankton nor Teton have been much with the whites. They still trust them. The Yankton receive annuities. For almost a month we talked here on the river. They were willing to eat with us, but when I asked that they join in a fight down the river at

Fort Pierre, they grew angry and left us. Some even guarded the fort. West of the river the Teton and Sitting Bull know little of the whites. Maybe when they do, they will help us."

"There are too many maybes!" Passing Daylight cried angrily. "We left the valley in Minnesota for Devils Lake. Then we left there for the Missouri River to plead with the Yankton. When the Yankton left, you moved us up the river to the big bend to ask the Hidatsa, Mandan, and Arikara to help us, even though the Dakota people have fought with these river tribes for many years. 'Maybe they will help,' you said. We held the sacred pipe high in peace. They shot at us and would not talk. Eight of our braves were killed."

"Old wounds were too deep, and they blame us for killing buffalo they say were theirs. We can't sit on this river forever," Little Crow lamented. "We must find help or move on. Standing Buffalo has gone to the Grandmother's Country, Canada. Maybe they'll help us. My grandfather fought for them against the Americans in 1812. They will remember. I know they will. I sent some Mdewakanton with the Sisseton to hear the words of the British and to even speak with the Ojibway. But I chose to stay here. We must keep trying to find friends here among the Indians of the plains. We must find a way to convince them that otherwise they will die and lose their land as we have."

Little Crow paused and considered his words. "If the Ojibway had attacked the whites as we did, it might have been different. Instead all they did was make some noise and scare their agent to death. They would not help. I guess old hatreds run like deep rivers, even when losing everything stares them in the face."

The Santee leader turned morose as he stirred the glowing embers again. "I failed you all," he mumbled, then louder, "Red Middle Voice, Medicine Bottle, and the others, they came to my house after the whites were killed at Acton. Lead us, they cried. I told them I was not their leader. Traveling Hail had been chosen as Speaker over me, and he wanted peace."

Little Crow stared transfixed into the fire. "No, they said. You are our leader. Lead us in this war. So I did. But the young men did as they wished and would not listen. 'Attack Fort Ridgley,' I said, but they foolishly raided New Ulm, and we lost our chance to take the fort. I could not convince enough Sisseton and Wahpeton to join in the fight. Even many of my own band have left me. Still, I must ask others to help when my own people have defied me."

"If the hotheads had listened to you, it would have been different. Lame Bear has joined us." White Spider turned hopeful. "He's a Sisseton. Maybe more will come soon."

"He had nowhere else to go," Passing Daylight commented. "He fled Minnesota with white captives after doing bad things at Shetek. Then he traded the whites to the young Sans Arc men of Two Kettle's band, the Fool Soldiers who risked their lives to help the whites.

"Lame Bear feared the white soldiers will hunt him down. That's why he sought us for the safety of his band. Inkpaduta and his warriors come from Iowa. He comes to fight."

A look of resignation set upon Little Crow's face. "I do not trust Inkpaduta. The whites hate him for his attack at Spirit Lake even before the war in Minnesota started. But at least he's a fighter. I'll keep trying to convince our Indian brothers to join us. I hope that Standing Buffalo has success in Canada. But I swear to you. I will fight the whites to the end no matter how many stand with me. They will never place a rope on my neck like they did to the others at Mankato."

∞ 6 ∞

FORT SNELLING STOOD HIGH ON A BLUFF overlooking the confluence of the Minnesota and Mississippi rivers. Built in 1823 to protect the interests of the fur traders who brought prosperity to the wilderness, it served as a jumping off point in 1862 for soldiers on their way to fight rebels in the South or Indians to the west.

The limestone walls of the fort glistened white in the frigid afternoon sun of January 1863. A sentinel marched in a solitary circle at the top of a stone watchtower. Below the tower, on the river flats between the fort bluff and the river, stood a hovel of roughly 300 tipis surrounded by a sixteen-foot-high wooden stockade fence, a parallelogram 500 feet square resting on three acres.

A mist of smoke shrouded the makeshift village from above. It blanketed the despair that filled the dwellings of the imprisoned. This was most of what remained of the Santee Dakota in Minnesota. About 1,500 souls, mostly women and children, of the four bands of Santee—the Mdewakanton, Wahpekute, Sisseton and Wahpeton—had been moved down the Minnesota from the Redwood and Yellow Medicine agencies to Fort Snelling.

The four bands of the Santee represented the far eastern groups of the Seven Councils of the Sioux. The Yankton and Yanktonais lived on the far western border regions of the Minnesota and Dakota Territory. The Teton, who had seven sub-groups of their own, made their home farther west around the Missouri River.

Thousands of Dakota had fled to the western plains and several hundred were still confined as war prisoners at Mankato. President Lincoln's reprieve of the death sentence for 265 only meant that another prison awaited them in Davenport, Iowa, come spring.

The post doctor, Alfred Muller, and his small staff of nurses and volunteers were kept busy caring for the Dakota and seeing that they survived the harsh Minnesota winter. The doctor's numbers were bolstered by missionaries who strove to save both lives and souls. Dr. Stephen Riggs, Reverend Thomas Williamson, brothers Gideon and Samuel Pond, and Reverend Samuel Hinman dispensed both medicine and the gospel.

Dr. Muller assembled his assistants in a wooden warehouse just outside the compound. Earlier the reverends had used it as a church. Now it doubled as a hospital. Several rows of pallets on the floor were occupied by Santee, their faces marked with the telltale red blotches of smallpox.

Muller gazed with hope at his medical "staff." Riggs and Williamson knew these people well. Both had served as missionaries for decades in the Minnesota River Valley. The Santee trusted them. Hinman, although a young man, had acquitted himself well in the attack on the Redwood Agency. Little Crow had been a member of his church.

The non-church civilians had been solid as rocks, and Dr. Muller knew he was lucky to have them at the fort. His wife, Eliza, had been a heroine of the attack upon Fort Ridgely. Besides tending to wounded and helping to deliver a baby, she had aided an artillery squad in the firing of a cannon. He wasn't as sure of Harriet Bishop, who had come west from Vermont in 1847 at Reverend Williamson's urging. As devoted as she was to spreading Christianity among the Dakota, a growing bitterness was showing through. Muller mentally noted that she would bear watching.

Three young people had been Godsends. There was a brave young man, Nathan Cates, who had been a soldier in the Great War until he lost his arm at Shiloh and came to Minnesota. Cates had fought bravely at Fort Ridgely and courageously rescued four girls held captive by the Dakota. One of the girls, Emily, was now his wife and stood at his side. There was a mysterious side to young Cates, but Muller had decided it didn't merit his concern.

The third was the daughter of a colonel and the fiancée of Lieutenant Jesse Buchanen. Muller considered that her experiences in the war had been as harrowing as anyone's. JoAnna Miller had just arrived at Fort Snelling. Muller had known her family before the war and had watched her transform from an immature girl to a courageous woman.

Foolish impulsiveness had led to a misguided attempt to join her father and fiancé after prematurely supposing that hostilities to the west had ceased. After wandering the prairie and surviving an attack by a war party, she was rescued by Jesse and his men. As surely as a crucible, the experience had changed JoAnna.

Next she had accompanied Dr. Joshua Weiser on a rescue mission of their own into Dakota Territory. Eight survivors of the Lake Shetek massacre had been rescued by a band of young Teton and turned over to soldiers at Fort Randall. Weiser was sent to bring them back. Dr. Weiser, with JoAnna as his nurse, had brought the captives back to Mankato. JoAnna herself had survived a bout of smallpox on the return trip.

A tight-lipped smile peeked through Muller's heavy beard. *This is a horrible spot to be in, but I couldn't ask for better people to be here with*, he thought.

Then he addressed his assistants. "Lieutenant McKusick has been appointed Indian Camp superintendent. He has given us the task of not only caring for these miserable people, but the soldiers as well. Measles doesn't know skin color. We try to save them all. I wish that Dr. Weiser was with us, but we are fortunate that Dr. Wharton is here." He nodded to the portly white-coated man before him.

"Seems to me we should concentrate on those who saved lives in the war, not them that killed whites!" Harriet Bishop snapped.

"Now, Harriet," Stephen Riggs demurred, "these are mostly women and children here, and many of them were instrumental in the protecting of white settlers. Regardless, all deserve our help and the mercy of the Lord."

"They live like animals in a pen," the woman muttered.

"Doctor," JoAnna asked, "when I worked with Dr. Weiser, his treatment for measles was just to keep the sick apart from others, to try to keep them comfortable and maybe give them a sip of whiskey. Is that what you recommend?"

"Well, yes, Miss Miller. I wish we knew what caused measles, but we do know people spread it. We also know that it takes a couple of weeks to show up after first being exposed to an infected person. If someone has had it before, the severity is much less the next time. If there is little history with the disease, as with the Dakota, it spreads more virulently. We can expect eighty-five percent of them to come down with measles and ninety percent of those to have visible symptoms."

Gideon Pond cleared his throat and asked, "Then what, Doctor?"

Muller slowly shook his head. "About fifteen percent will die. Mostly the old and the children."

"That's mostly what we have here," Nathan Cates interjected. Here in Minnesota, Nathan was known by an assumed name, Cates, but to friends and relatives back home in the South, he was Nathan Thomas.

"Yes, Nathan, that's what we have here. Let's try to hold down the numbers that statistics tell us will die."

"We must save their lives before we can save their souls," Hinman commented.

Reverend Riggs smoothed back his thinning white hair and considered the young Episcopal minister. "And, you, as newly appointed chaplain of the Indian Camp, are in a unique position. Much of the soul saving will be up to you. Dr. Williamson and I will divide most of our time between Fort Snelling and those imprisoned in Mankato."

Williamson cleared his throat. "My son, John, will be here to assist you. I'll spend most of my time at Mankato."

"And my brother and I are nearby in Shakopee and Bloomington," Gideon Pond added. "We'll be able to come here regularly."

"Good," Muller concluded. "For now, continue your ministrations in the compound. When practical, the warehouse can be used for preaching and," he nodded at Nathan and Emily, "teaching."

7

HIGH ON THE BLUFF ABOVE THE INDIAN camp, a blustery wind snapped the stars and stripes banner that waved atop the round tower at one end of the fort. At the opposite end of the limestone-walled structure stood the commandant's quarters.

Colonel George Crooks, late of the military commission and newly-named commander of Fort Snelling and the Sixth and Seventh regiments, rubbed his hands together, warming them before a crackling fire in a stone fireplace. He spat onto a hot rock and watched the spittle dance and sizzle. He wiped stray spit from his short black chin-beard with the back of his hand. His back was to Stephen Miller and Bill McKusick, who sat upon wooden chairs in the small office.

Crooks turned to face his officers, his face ruddy from the warmth, his bald forehead glistening with perspiration. "Gentlemen," he drawled, "I need a status report. The last census on December 1 had them at 1,601. That's down fifty-eight from what we had when we left Lower Sioux. God knows how we lost fifty-eight."

"The line of march was over four miles long," Miller answered. "Some maybe ran afoul of revenge-crazed settlers, some maybe had measles and died, and who knows, some may have found a way to escape."

"All right. Tell me, Lieutenant, where are we today?"

"Colonel Crooks, sir," the mid-thirties, red-bearded McKusick replied, "we do a count every day, and the numbers stay 'bout the same. Some get captured and transferred in from out west, but we're losin' some ever' day, too. One day there was forty-some dead of measles. Nelson Givens, Galbraith's assistant at Yellow Medicine, is in charge of the counting."

"What are you doing with the bodies?"

McKusick shifted uncomfortably on his feet. "We dig trenches, adults in first and then the little ones on top."

"Unfortunate," Crooks shook his head. "It could be worse. Sibley kept over 400 in the stockade at Mankato. They could be here. I just heard that come spring they'll be sent to a prison in Davenport. Muller and Wharton, are they doing all they can for the sick here?"

"I think so, but these Indians, they never had the measles before. They ain't used of it. Dr. Muller . . . he's lined up some nurses,"

"My daughter among them," Miller interrupted.

"And the missionaries are there," McKusick continued, "and that one-armed fella and his wife are helping with the teachin.' They work in the camp, but they use the warehouse, too. It's kinda a school, hospital, church, whatever they need it fer. The camp's orderly, enough. There's streets, alleys, even a public square."

"Orderly, but dirty," Marshall rejoined. "The offal from the lodges is thrown into the streets. On warmer days we have barefooted women and children splashing around in filthy snow slush. Just wait until spring when the lowlands flood. Then we'll have a real mess down there."

Crooks sighed. "Do what you can to maintain hygiene, Lieutenant. How many men are there?"

"About fifty adult full bloods and maybe a hundred or so half-breed men. The rest are women and children. They's nine leaders inside the fence. They kinda live together in their own groups."

"Is the troop strength sufficient?"

"Yessir, Colonel, I got men on twenty-four-hour guard. They got orders to keep the reds in and the white townsfolk out. I got details gettin' firewood and givin' food to 'em. Hell," McKusick reddened, "'scuse my language, but they eat as good as the soldiers and it's gonna take 1,400 cords o' wood for their fires."

"They cost us a dollar a day each. I hope they get decent food. Bread, crackers, and some beef, I suppose," Crooks added.

"They'd rather eat buffalo," McKusick replied, "but they gotta be happy with the beef we give 'em. Ya know, an ox weighs 1,500 pounds. It'd be nice if that's what we could feed 'em. But dressed out they's only 'bout 450 pounds o' meat and dried just a little over a hundred. We gotta ration purty careful. Still, I get letters complainin' that we treat 'em too well."

"I'm guessing the Sioux aren't the ones complaining," Miller commented sardonically.

"What about mistreatment of the women? I've heard rumors," Crooks inquired.

"It's my opinion that stories of murders and rapes are unfounded," Miller replied.

"Let's keep it that way," the commander concluded. "Let's just get through to spring with no blowups and these people alive so we can get them out of here."

"To where?" Miller wondered.

"Somewhere beyond the borders of Minnesota, that's for sure. Wherever it is, it's our job to see that they're alive to be sent there."

8

NINE TIRED AND WORN DAKOTA LEADERS huddled in a circle for warmth around a struggling little fire in the hovel of a tipi. They were Wabasha, Passing Hail, Red Legs, Simon, Black Dog, Wakute, Taopi, Good Road, and Eagle Head. Each had followers and a jurisdiction in the camp.

"Once the fires blazed enough to keep us sweating in our lodges. Now we are barely given enough wood to warm our hands," Wabasha complained.

Black Dog grimaced in pain from an arthritic hip. "We should have followed Little Crow to the west. At least he's free. You fought the whites, Wabasha. You were our leader before Little Crow became our war chief. But you stayed when Crow went west. Do you wish that you were free today as Crow is?"

Wabasha silently shook his head, his long gray hair swaying from side to side. "I rode with Little Crow, but my heart was never in the fight. I contacted the Long Trader to save the people."

"For how long will Crow be free?" Taopi countered. "We hear that the Teton and Yankton will not help the Santee. It's only a matter of time before the white army hunts him down like a sick buffalo. Already as many as the leaves of a small tree have left him and come here."

Red Legs looked at a newly-smoothed plot of fresh earth in the center of the tipi. "But Haza has left us," he said in a melancholy tone.

"It was good to bury her here," Wabasha replied. "The red marks killed her, and the whites would have thrown her in a ditch with all the others. People from town dig them up and cut them. Her spirit can rest because of what you have done for her, Red Legs."

"More die each day," Good Road added. "Before the whites came there were no red marks. Our people never knew of them and never died because of them."

Passing Hail nodded with sorrow. "The black coats and the doctors try to help, and many of the people live. But others do not."

"Even with the sickness," Wabasha's face screwed up with bitterness, "the whites come to look at us like we are animals in a pen. Some are not satisfied to walk around the tipis. They enter without asking. Yesterday as I sat in my lodge, a black-coat pastor opened the door flap and walked in. When I challenged him, he said, 'You must be seen in your wigwam to be appreciated.'"

Eagle Head snapped at Wabasha, "If they enter my lodge like that, they will leave with a knife in their ribs."

"No," Wabasha said firmly, "the soldiers would kill you and many others. That is their way. Where is Wacouta?"

"He has come, but he stays to himself with his family," said Red Legs. "He is much bitter over how he has been treated since he opposed Little Crow in the war."

"There is much for all of us to be bitter about," Wabasha replied.

Simon stretched his palms nearer the flickering bluish flame. "What of the men who walked around with the black boxes that captured our images?"

"They are called photographers," Wabasha answered. "Maybe what they do is good, maybe some day people will look at these images and know what these people have done to us."

Black Dog poked at the flame with a stick. "Many of the people are turning to the white man's God. Before the war the people listened to the black coats and turned to their God like the trickle of a small stream, now they are coming to Him like the rush of a mighty river."

"Our gods have failed us," Eagle Head countered, "they did not help us in the war. Many of our brothers, sisters, aunties, uncles, mothers, and fathers have died or are gone from us to the west. Thirty-eight of our brothers were hanged at Mankato, hundreds more are in prison there. Now the people here die of the red marks. The people think that our gods have left us. Maybe the white man's God is stronger. He has helped them, and so they come to Him."

"I heard the black coats talking," Black Dog responded. "The older Williamson said to Riggs that in twenty-five years only sixty Dakota had come to their God. Now, he said, that happens in one day. Hundreds have been baptized, he said."

The lines in Wabasha's face creased more deeply as he considered Black Dog's words. "It comes from fear and hope, and that is all we have left."

Black Dog offered another viewpoint, "Many turn to the white man's God because the black coats say that they will be saved. This offers hope to those who fear the hangman's rope. Many do not understand that the white men mean to save souls for the hereafter, not lives for today."

Wabasha sighed deeply, "I get letters from Mankato in the marks Dr. Riggs created for Dakota words that we may read. A prisoner wrote that some young men disappear when they refuse to become Christians. No one ever sees them again. This is a bad thing."

"Hau. Hau," the others mumbled in agreement.

A SQUAD OF SOLDIERS LINED UP FOR TARGET practice on the river flats between the stockade and the warehouse. The targets were V's cut into tree rounds some fifty yards distant. A shot that hit near the intersecting point of the V "cut the V," in frontier parlance, and was a bull's-eye.

Private Terrance O'Reilly brushed a couple inches of snow from the ground and then knelt to aim his percussion-shot Springfield.

"Careful," Private Willie Johnson urged as he unbuttoned his dark-blue woolen overcoat, "there be women just to the left gatherin' firewood."

O'Reilly gazed at Johnson with a sly grin and aimed at the wooden target. Then, just before he squeezed the trigger, O'Reilly swung the rifle to the left and fired. An Indian woman shrieked, threw her arms into the air and crumbled like a rag doll upon a pile of sticks.

"My God!" Johnson exclaimed. "What have you done?"

"Gittin' even, muh boy," the private answered. "Father Abraham seen fit ta spare 'bout 265 of the 303. I cut it down to 264."

"You murdered a woman!"

"They kilt near 800 whites in the war. Most was women and children. They dint care who they kilt. Neither do I."

Sergeant Wood confronted Private O'Reilly. "What happened here?" he demanded.

O'Reilly feigned contrite sorrow. "Don't know, Sergeant, I jest missed. I feel horrible bad."

Private Johnson shook his head in amazement and turned away.

Sergeant Wood turned back to the others in his squad, his face flushed scarlet. He spoke with even determination. His words hung like ice in the frosty air. "There will be no more mistakes. I repeat, THERE . . . WILL . . . BE . . . NO . . . MORE . . . MISTAKES! I have also heard of outrages committed by soldiers against the Indian women. No one has come forward with any proof. But I say again, THIS . . . WILL . . . STOP. I don't care if you think you can do what you want because they're Indians. The nooses that fit the necks at Mankato will fit white necks, too! Spread the word!"

In the distance Wabasha and the eight other leaders gathered around a young woman as her blood turned the snow crimson. Red Legs fingered his knife and started toward the soldiers. Wabasha reached out and seized his arm in a vise grip. "No, it would do no good. Stay here," he ordered. "Your blood would stain the earth next. We must find other ways to save these people."

A tear formed in the corner of Wabasha's eye and slowly rolled down his worn cheek as Red Legs sheathed his knife.

9

COMPANY F OF THE FIRST MINNESOTA Cavalry made fifteen miles the first day out from Mankato. The next day they made even better time until late afternoon, when a storm blew up from the northeast.

Duley ordered camp in a low ravine by a frozen creek. Corporal Oscar Wall and Private Willie Sturgis, both defenders of Fort Ridgely, chewed on salt pork and hardtack as they huddled against the bank of the ravine with wind whistling over their heads.

Wall held the hardtack close to his eyes and peered closely at the cracker. "Can't see no bugs. It looks like it's fit ta eat."

"Ya kain't be sure, Oscar," Willie drawled laconically. "Ya gotta dip them crackers in purty hot water ta make the bugs crawl out."

"Well, Willie, in this wind we ain't gonna be boiling no water. Looks like if there be any beetles in the hardtack it's just extra meat fer me."

Sturgis held tight to his heavy blue tunic coat, then spread a rubber blanket upon the frozen ground before laying a woolen blanket on top. The wind and snow pellets stung his eyes as he looked up.

"Tarnation!" Willie rubbed his eyes. "Everyone else's goin' out come March and April. Why'd we git so lucky as ta git sent out here this time o' year."

"Trainin', Willie. That and savin' some white woman."

"If this is trainin' ta make us better, we're gonna be the best there is, Oscar. Git yer beddin' down so's we can git the tent over it."

The sun set as the men of Company F lay upon rubber and wool blankets and pulled more woolen blankets over themselves. The two-person tents provided some shelter, but not much comfort from the howling gale outside.

"Oscar," Willie complained, "jes remember, last night we wuz warm and dry in barracks bunks. I'll never say nothin' bad 'bout bedbugs agin."

Breakfast was prepared in a blinding snowstorm as the wind screeched like a banshee. There was no shelter for the fires and nothing with which to make a shelter. Coffee could not be brought to a boiling point and was tepid at best.

Willie took a sip and spat it out. "Cold coffee. I'd rather drink pee. At least that's warm."

Bob Hutchinson, another private, smiled and made to unbutton his trousers. "I kin oblige ya, Willie."

Sturgis grinned back, "No, thanks, Bobby. I'll jes haf'ta suffer with cold coffee."

Will Duley strode into the midst of his troopers, his cheeks ruddy as he wiped his nose. "Men," he cried, "I know it's tough duty. But the faster we move, the quicker we'll be at Sauk Centre and a warm bed. Strike camp and git mounted. It's time to move."

The sun was just rising as the First Minnesota Cavalry hit the trail north. A pelting storm continued throughout the day's ride as sleet and then snow alternated attacks. The men pulled their fur hats down, yanked up their woolen collars and hunkered down in their saddles. Numbing cold chilled the soldiers to the bone.

Jesse turned his thoughts to JoAnna, hoping the distraction would warm him against the frigid air. He shut his eyes and envisioned her enchanting blue eyes, raven hair, and soft-skinned beauty. He recalled the scent of her perfume, her tender touch, how very much she wanted them to be married.

Maybe getting married now would have been better, he thought. She had changed from being marooned on the prairie and fighting off a war party. Thank God, he had rescued her just as the Sioux were closing in. He shuddered even more as he remembered how close he had come to losing her.

Now JoAnna was working as a nurse at Fort Snelling. She'd be around sickness and rough men. Jesse didn't like it, but that's how it was going to be with the newly independent woman he loved. Jesse tugged his collar higher and settled in for the rest of the miserable ride. Hours passed as they endured mile after bone chilling mile.

"Lieutenant!" Duley reined in alongside Jesse. "Look there, up ahead. That's St. Joseph. We'll spend the night there. Hopefully inside some buildings. See ta the men. Ask the town folk for help."

Through the swirling maelstrom of ice and snow, distant buildings showed dimly. The sparkle of lamps through frosted windows provided a surer sign of direction.

The troops rode through the blustery wind and snow into a small frontier village of German ancestry.

A well-lit tavern in the center of the settlement attracted Jesse's attention. He rode ahead, dismounted and entered. Kerosene lamps illuminated the room. A half-dozen men stood alongside a bar made of planks resting upon wooden barrels. A bearded bartender looked up as he poured a drink into a dirty tin cup.

Jesse welcomed the wall of warmth from a potbellied stove as it defrosted his snow-covered eyebrows and face. He slapped the snow from his coat as the seven men eyed him with cool curiosity.

The bartender leaned over the bar and spat a brown stream of tobacco into a spittoon on the floor. He didn't bother to wipe away the spittle that clung to his red beard. Then he asked Jesse, "Whacha doin' out here on such a night? Ain't Father Abraham got more sense then ta send fools out in a snowstorm?"

Jesse shook his head ruefully. "President Lincoln didn't send us. General Sibley did, to rescue a white woman held by the Sioux near Sauk Centre. We need your help. I've got fifty men outside who need shelter for the night."

A large barrel-chested man at the end of the bar lifted his leg and farted loudly. "That's what we thinka ya and the resta yer blue-bellied friends," he slurred. "Leave us 'lone an' go fight for the nigras."

A slender middle-aged man cleared his throat. "Ya see, Lieutenant, mosta us come here ta git away from fightin' and wars. We don' take too kindly ta sendin' our boys ta fight in a war jest fer nigras. Let them rebs go. We don' give a damn up here."

Jesse's face hardened as the red from his temper blended with his ruddy, cold cheeks. "I'm not here to debate politics with you. We are just wrapping up an Indian war that cost about 800 lives of *white* Minnesotans. You should care about that. There's another thing I won't debate. Where in this town will my men lodge tonight?"

"Out on da street under yer horses," the bartender sneered as his friends snickered agreement.

Jesse snapped to attention, placed his right toe behind his left heel and wheeled an about-face. Without a sound other than the sharp rap of booted feet on the wooden floor, he strode out the door into the windswept night.

The men grinned at each other and laughed heartily as they watched Jesse depart.

"Guess we showed 'im," a short chubby man cried. He gave a mock salute to the bartender. "Ya really gave 'im what fer, Linneman."

An instant later the door crashed open. The wind whistled through the doorway, causing the yellow flames of the lamps to flicker wildly. Jesse reentered the room followed by eight soldiers, splotches of blue showing through snow-covered overcoats.

"Rows of four!" the young lieutenant commanded. Four men formed a line with another four falling in behind them. "READY!" Jesse commanded. The eight snapped their frosted Springfield rifles before themselves. "AIM," Jesse commanded. As the soldiers brought their weapons to eye level, the men behind sighted over the shoulders of the soldiers in front and pointed at the drinkers.

Jesse stepped forward as he riveted an icy stare at the seven men by the bar. Their faces blanched white with terror. Then Jesse spoke evenly and precisely. "I will not risk my men outside in this storm. We commandeer this dwelling and all others that may be needed to accommodate these soldiers. Do you have any objections?"

"No, s . . s . . sir," Linneman stuttered. "These fellas were all jest leavin' annaways. Ya kin stay here. Jes take it easy. We wuz jes funnin' ya."

"We are not in a mood for joking tonight. Detail, shoulder arms. Corporal Sturgis, you and these men stay here for the night after tending to your horses. There are barns in this town, fit for men and animals. We'll take them for the night."

Word quickly spread of the soldiers' presence in St. Joseph. Some townsfolk scurried to bar the troopers from their stables. They were swept aside by wet, shivering men who were desperate for whatever shelter they could find and would tolerate no refusal of a reasonable request.

The January storm raged through the night and the following day. Travel was impossible. The First Minnesota struggled to maintain any fire to cook or heat. They huddled in the haymows and miserably bit off cold rations as they waited for the storm to quiet. Finally the morning dawned still with the sun illuminating a brilliant whiteness.

Will Duley assembled his men on the road in the center of town and shielded his eyes from the sun's glare as he gazed at the snow-drifted trail leading to Sauk Centre. The streets were empty, save the soldiers.

"Lieutenant Buchanen," he snapped, "move 'em out."

Jesse extended his right arm down the trail and shouted, "Forward, march!"

As the men and animals trudged out of town through drifted snow, the people of St. Joseph peered through frost-covered windows. Adults scraped openings clear with their fingernails to catch sight of the retreating troops. The hot breath of children melted little circles on the panes of glass so that small blue eyes could stare at the invaders leaving their village.

℘ 10 ℂ

LITTLE CROW AND HIS DWINDLING band moved up the Missouri River and crossed into the northern part of the Dakota Territory. They had crisscrossed the Dakotas from Devils Lake to Fort Pierre and then followed the Missouri River back up north again.

Everywhere Little Crow's efforts at forming an alliance were rebuffed. His natural allies, the other Dakota bands, considered the Santee trouble and wanted no part of them. The river tribes had been victims of Dakota raids as long as any could remember and would offer no aid to their former tormentors.

As Little Crow moved his followers across the prairie back toward Devils Lake, envoys from the Sisseton and Wahpeton bands of Santee were heading northeast to begin talks with the British in Canada. A dozen Mdewakanton, led by Little Crow's son-in-law Heyoka, made the journey as well to learn what the British had to say.

Eighty men and six women rode horseback or walked alongside horses dragging supply-laden travois as they followed the Red River into Canada. They were led by Sisseton chief Standing Buffalo, who had resisted war with the soldiers and had spoken out against the killing of white settlers.

Late December found the northern plains snow-swept and drifted. The river was frozen solid and easily crossed. The tipi poles that formed the bases of the travois cut shallow ruts into the snow as the horses dragged them.

Heyoka rode his pony to the front of the procession, his long, lean legs more suited to a larger animal. His mount trotted up to Standing Buffalo, whose horse plodded at a slow pace as the chief clutched a woven robe around his shoulders. The Sisseton leader wore eleven eagle feathers in a band around his head. Brown eyes in his handsome face reflected intelligence and sensitivity.

"Hiya," the young warrior called, "is Fort Garry near?"

Standing Buffalo squinted into the distance. "Two, maybe three days' travel. But we will meet the British halfway there, at St. Norbert."

"Little Crow wishes me to meet the whites with you. If there is hope of help, he must know it."

Standing Buffalo's response was defiant. "Crow brought this upon us. Now he begs for help. We should be warm in our lodges in the valley of the Minnesota. When I heard of the killings at Acton, I felt like the earth had been taken from us. I was out hunting when I heard five whites had been killed by Dakota. I felt dead as well. I knew that all was lost when I first heard what had happened. I was right.

"Now we are left with little choice but to beg for help. There are metis, mixed bloods, here. Maybe they will aid us. You may hear the words the British tell us. We go to them, but I have little hope."

"Why would they not help us?" Heyoka responded. "The Mdewakanton helped them in their war against the Americans. The British once promised to help."

"That was long ago," Standing Buffalo answered. "Like many whites, the British forget what was once said. Why were you sent? Why didn't Little Crow come?"

"He still talks with the Missouri River bands. He thinks they are more likely to fight with us than the British are."

"Little Crow is right. But his number of followers grows small. No bands or tribes come to join him. Now we are left to seek mixed bloods and whites."

The next day, December 27, 1862, the Santee delegation reached St. Norbert, south of Fort Garry. The fort was called Winnipeg by some. There they counseled with Governor William McTavish of the Red River Colony and Alexander Grant Dallas, the governor of the Hudson's Bay Company.

The leaders gathered in a log building warmed by a smoky fireplace. The Dakota cleared chairs and furniture to the side and sat upon the floor. The portly, short, red-haired governor of the colony bent down with arthritic difficulty to join them.

McTavish urged Standing Buffalo to end their trip at St. Norbert and return to the Dakotas. "This is not a good time for us to help you even if we could," McTavish explained. "Talks are going on with the Grand-mother, Queen Victoria, to make Canada an independent country."

"We have always been friends with the Grandmother's people," Standing Buffalo retorted. "We fought with you against the Americans in your last war with them. Now we need your help. Send us soldiers or let us stay in Canada with you. That is what we ask."

McTavish uncomfortably shifted from one buttock to the other as he met the stares from the black eyes in the circle. "Please, understand. We don't have soldiers here to send to you. We thank you for your friendship, but we can't support you here. Do you ask for support from the metis? They have expressed concern about your visit. I saw them display weapons to use on you, but nothing has come of it yet. They want you to leave as well."

"Cowards!" Heyoka angrily shouted. "If all Indians had come to us last summer, we could have beaten the Americans."

"Metis are not cowards!" Governor Dallas rejoined sternly. "They're people of mixed French-Cree and Ojibway. They headquarter at Pembina and consider themselves citizens of no country. They move freely over the border. You would be wise to be friends with them."

"We must be reasonable," a black-robed, bearded white man began slowly. "I'm Bishop Tache, a pastor to this colony. Considering the metis . . . they do little farming, and food in this colony is precious. We can feed you for a little while, but we don't have the resources to sustain you long term.

"Governor McTavish knows more, but I'm told he has not the men to protect you if the metis or the Cree or Ojibway choose to make war on you. Leave this place. Go back to the other Santee."

Standing Buffalo stared at the fire and all were silent. The chief tried another approach. "Will you, Governor McTavish, intercede for us with the Long Trader, General Sibley? My Sisseton band was divided over the war. We still are. Many refused to fight and wanted peace. I fear that if we surrender, many will swing from ropes like those at Mankato."

Resolution swept over McTavish's face as he replied, "I will write a letter to Sibley. I urge you to return south, but you may remain here at least until the weather improves. Speak to the other tribes and bands, form alliances with them. It's your best chance."

The Santee left the warmth of the building and returned to the chill of Canadian winter. As they walked to lodges erected in the snow, Heyoka asked Standing Buffalo, "What will you do? I must return to Little Crow. But I'll stay here a little while. There still is much to learn."

"We will stay here as long as we can. I'll try to build good relations with the metis, the Cree, and the Ojibway."

"The Ojibway have long been our enemies. They killed Little Crow's father, and they didn't help us in the war. Why should they help now?"

Standing Buffalo gave a small smile to the younger man. "Maybe they have grown smarter. We bring plunder from the war with the whites. Maybe presents will cause them to become friends. We have women to offer them to unite our people. I don't ask them to fight the whites, only to let us live here in peace."

Weeks later Heyoka left his Mdewakanton and the Sisseton to return to Little Crow. Standing Buffalo began to create meaningful ties of kinship with neighboring Indian tribes. Presents were accepted and intermarriage occurred as friendly bonds were established. The Santee built a camp in the shadows of Fort Garry.

Traders feared the worst if an alliance flourished. James Whitehead, a trader at Leech Lake in Minnesota, wrote about his concerns to Dallas of the Hudson Bay Company. "Whites might be driven out of northern Minnesota and southern Canada, and trade between the two regions severed."

Heyoka continued a solitary ride south. It was February as he neared the Pembina River north of a border town also called St. Joseph. On the Canadian side Heyoka rode into a cluster of fifteen Dakota lodges. Dusk was near, and howling dogs alerted the village of the approaching rider. An older man strode through the snow to meet him.

"Hiya, I am Running Bear. These are my people, Mdewakanton, like you."

"Hiya, I'm Heyoka, husband to Little Crow's daughter. What brings you to the north?"

"To avoid the white army when it comes. We come in a good way and ask the metis of St. Joseph for help. They are good to us. Father Andre of the town comes each day. There was fear that we would take from them, but now they know that we only want to trade for food."

"I go to Little Crow. I will tell him of you. More will come."

"The town will be good to us as long as there is food. Father Andre already is concerned that they will run out if more come. Stay with us tonight. My lodge is warm and dog stew boils over the fire."

Heyoka gladly spent the night with his newfound friends on the Pembina. He stayed with them a week to confer with the metis and learn more about St. Joseph.

$\mathfrak{so}$ 11 $\mathfrak{cs}$

IN THE DISTANCE, A HASTILY CONSTRUCTED wooden stockade stood shrouded by frozen clouds of snow. It had been built for refuge during the uprising. Now it housed a troop of Union soldiers, lonely sentinels on a prairie devoid of white people. From the bend of a nearby river the watchers were being watched.

Two Santee peered from brush that lined the ice-covered stream. One was tall and muscular, his long, dark hair braided. The other was older, his face leathered, his black hair streaked with gray.

"Round Wind, are you sure they're coming?" the older man asked.

"Yes, Pawn. Before I left Mankato, I heard that the Long Trader ordered a patrol. The long knives will come. They will join those in the fort and look for us. Duley from Shetek leads them. He looks for you with hate in his heart. You should have stayed with Lame Bear on the Missouri."

Pawn snorted derisively. "Lame Bear is a weak old man. He traded away the Shetek captives to a band of Sans Arc boys, Fool Soldiers the boys are called by their own people. Some follow Little Crow. Some bands like mine choose a different path. We have returned to Minnesota."

"Duley will not rest until he finds you, Pawn. He's crazy with hate. He came to the prison when I was held there. He whipped us, demanding knowledge of where you were. No one could tell because no one knew."

Pawn peered ahead as he answered. "We traveled with the white captives to the big bend in the Missouri. Lame Bear was scared that the soldiers would follow. He asked the Teton and Yankton to help. They kept away from us like we had a sickness. I left Lame Bear after he surrendered the captives. Duley's woman was alive when I left.

"Round Wind, when we saw you walking alone on the prairie, it was as if Wakan had sent you to us. We heard you were to die with the others. You were to be hanged, too."

Relief flickered in Round Wind's eyes as he explained, "The white father, Lincoln, crossed my name off the death list. I did not kill the woman they claimed I killed. At the last, another white came forward and told the whites that I had told the truth. They let me go the day before the hangings. I waited to see the thirty-eight murdered,and then I began my journey to the northwest, to Devils Lake, where I heard Little Crow is. That's why I was on the road you traveled. How many warriors are with you?"

"Only about four hands of fingers, as many as we had when we raided the Ojibway in the night of the tree-popping moon. We found a white woman alone in a cabin and took her with us. She'll take the place of the woman I had that Lame Bear gave away. Help us fight them."

Round Wind measured Pawn's words before he replied. "They will not rest until they find you. Especially now that you have a white woman. You took Duley's woman to the west. He has her now but will use this other woman to take his revenge on you. I did not fight the whites in the war, and I will not fight them now. I go west to Devils Lake."

Disappointment flashed across Pawn's face. Then he pointed into the distance. "It may be too late for you to run. Look, there, see the blue line in the snow. The soldiers come."

A short time later Will Duley led fifty men of the First Minnesota Cavalry through the gates of the Sauk Centre stockade. A wide-horned elk skull hung from the upper beam of the entrance. An American flag waved and snapped briskly against the stark blue sky where clouds had parted.

Just outside the gate, to the right, was a single log cabin. Within the fort smoke meandered from the chimneys of two larger cabins. Smaller one-room structures lined the walls of the enclosure on three sides.

From the large center building, a young lieutenant, hastily wrapped in a woolen blue overcoat, strode briskly toward Duley. Will stepped down from his horse and returned the lieutenant's salute.

"Lieutenant Ramson, sir," said the soldier. "We heard you was comin'. Welcome to Sauk Centre, sir."

"Lieutenant Ramson, I'm Captain Duley. We're here to relieve you. But first, see to my men. Then I'd like a briefing."

Ramson turned to a bearded man hurrying to his side. "Sergeant, find quarters for the men and tend to their horses. Captain, please join me in the headquarters building."

As the cavalry was quartered, Duley and Jesse followed Ramson into the center building. The large room had a desk near a back wall, but chairs ringed a potbellied stove in the middle of the room.

"Sit here, if you will." Ramson gestured to the chairs. "It's a little informal but it's a lot warmer."

Duley held his hands toward the warmth of the stove and leaned forward. He asked, "What can you tell me about this place, Lieutenant?"

"Built last fall during the uprisin'. It went up in one day. Tamarack logs. At first there was only 'bout fifty-five men." He hesitated. "Some was really just boys. Fifteen to seventy was the ages. I'm scairt ta think what wudda happened if the reds attacked. Alls we had fer guns was muzzle loaders, old guns and singled-barreled shotguns that were as dangerous behind the gun as in fronta it. We din't have ten rounds of ammunition to the man. But ah guess they din't know how weak we was, cuz they never attacked."

"Are there Dakota about?" Jesse inquired.

"Some's been spotted up the Sauk River. There's a camp up there."

Duley's face steeled and his eyes turned an icy blue as he asked, "How many?"

"Not many," Ramson answered, "jest four, five lodges. That'd be fifteen, twenty men at the most."

"Why didn't you attack, I heard there was a white woman with them?"

"Well, Captain, we was told to wait for you. These men here's pretty green. Me too, when you come down to it," Ramson admitted. "We've been keepin' track. If they'd started movin' we wudda done something' 'bout it. But now yer here to take charge. Orders said when you got here, we was to leave. Tomorra we march southeast. The Abercrombie Trail that connects Fort Snelling with Abercrombie passes right in front. We'll be on it for Snelling."

Duley rose, but Ramson said quickly, "Oh, but there's one fella that's asked to stay with you. He jes joined up with the cavalry but he's bin fightin' reds since it started. Name's Solomon Foot."

"I've heard of him, 'Daniel Boone of Kandiyohi County' he's called. Stood off a band of Sioux when they attacked his cabin. He's welcome with us. Lieutenant Buchanen, see to the men. We'll hit the village at dawn."

ON THE BANKS OF THE SAUK RIVER, Pawn, Round Wind and several other Dakota men huddled around a fire in the center of a hastily erected tipi. A white woman in a dirty, tattered dress ladled stew from a bubbling pot into containers and handed them to the men.

Pawn grimaced as he stretched his legs before him. "The soldiers know we're here. These aren't rabbit soldiers like those in the fort. Duley leads them, and he'll come for us in the morning. I know how these men fight."

"What should we do?" Round Wind wondered. "If they attack here, you can't hold them. They'll ride through us as if we're not even here."

Pawn stood and walked stiffly to the tipi flap and looked out into the twilight. Big white snowflakes drifted thickly through the darkening sky.

"The snow is coming faster. The storm is here," Pawn considered thoughtfully. "They will not attack in a storm. At first light we'll take down the lodges and leave. We have some women and children. It's best to wait."

"Pawn," Round Wind interrupted, "you should go now. Leave the white woman behind."

"No, she's mine. I'll take her with me."

"Pawn, don't be a fool. She's what will make the whites pursue us. She's why they come. Leave her, or whatever chance we have is lost. We must go now, in the snowstorm."

Pawn angrily kicked at a bundle of goods on the ground. "Go if you must. We will stay until morning. Take a horse. I don't care."

A half hour later, Round Wind left the little village, his pony trudging through the falling snow. He rode off into the stormy night. A northwest wind whipped fresh snow into his face. Round Wind wrapped himself in a blanket and peered ahead looking like a cocoon.

"I go to Little Crow," he mumbled as he looked back over his shoulder at the disappearing village, "may Wakan be with them."

Before dawn Pawn crawled from beneath a warm buffalo robe and stirred the embers in the fire. He placed some wood on them and blew gently until a yellow flame greeted him. Pawn looked at the lump under a robe that was Jane Wyatt, the white woman. She was very plump and not handsome of face, he thought, but a good cook and worth keeping around for a while. He would take her with him. Round Wind was wrong.

Pawn stepped through the flap into the chill of early morning. The snow had nearly stopped. He moved tipi to tipi and told his people, "Eat fast and take down the lodge. It's time to move on."

Looking at a nearby hill to the west, Pawn left instructions for the dismantling of his own tipi and proclaimed that he would go to the highest point available to pray that the Spirits would be with them. He mounted a spotted horse and rode alone up the hill.

℘ 12 ℠

SNOW HAD FALLEN THROUGH THE NIGHT, leaving a thick new carpet of white on the prairie. A pinkish glow low on the eastern horizon heralded the new day as two troops of soldiers assembled in the Sauk Centre stockade. Their horses stomped and snorted frosty breath into the early morning air.

Jim Ramson trotted to Will Duley, who sat expectantly astride his house as his mounted men gathered into rows of four. "Sir, are ya sure ya don't need us?" the lieutenant asked. "We can start out for Fort Snelling later."

Duley turned a sharp gaze at the mixture of men, some too young and some too old, that sat ahorse before him. *They'll just get in the way,* he thought. "No, Lieutenant, my men are more experienced, most of 'em fought at Wood Lake. I'm leaving two squads, ten men, behind to maintain the post. Even with that, we outnumber the bastards two to one. See you this summer when we move out to the west."

Duley dismissed the lieutenant by snapping a salute that Ramson returned before wheeling his horse around. Then Ramson shouted, "Forward!" and pointed out the open stockade gates. In moments the former garrison faded into the early morning light as they headed southeast down the Abercrombie Trail. Soon only the faint clanking of their gear as they disappeared into the snow signaled that they had ever been there at all.

"You sure we won't need them?" Jesse asked pointedly.

"Not them," Duley replied directly. "If the Sioux had attacked this post, I don't think they could've held it. Even with superior numbers. They're pretty poor excuses for soldiers."

"What about him?" Jesse pointed to a solitary horseman approaching from the barn. A wide-brimmed black hat concealed the rider's face, and his long black coat showed snowflakes that had swirled down from a cabin roof.

He reined in before Duley and Jesse. Raising his head, his clear blue eyes looked directly at the captain. "I think I can be of use to you," he said simply. "My name's Foot, Solomon Foot."

For once Duley looked impressed. He took in the solidly-built man before him and extended a gloved hand to firmly grasp Solomon's. "They tell stories about you, fightin' off the reds in the Kandiyohi lakes, rescuin' four white women with a one-armed fella and shootin' up their war party."

Jesse cleared his throat. "I met you at Wood Lake. That one-armed fella, Nathan Cates, and me brought Major Welch back to you when Welch was wounded. You were too shot up to fight that day."

"I'm better now," Solomon responded. "My family's safe in St. Cloud. I'm joining up with the cavalry, and you need a scout. Let's move out."

"Glad to have you, Mr. Foot." Duley turned his mount toward the gate, swiveled in his saddle and cried, "First Minnesota Cavalry, forward ho!"

FORTY-TWO MEN RODE OUT FROM THE stockade toward the Sauk River and then west. "When we reach the village, we'll divide," Duley instructed. "Lieutenant Buchanen, take half the men and go to the north end of the village. I'll take the rest to the south, and we'll smash them between us."

"What about women and children?"

Duley sighed and looked skyward. With resignation he replied, "Tell your men to spare any women and children." He paused and added, "Unless they get in the way."

"Remember, Captain, we're here to rescue a white woman. What if she's in the crossfire?"

This time the irritation was more evident in Duley's voice. "Watch out for her, too. Now move!"

They had traveled just a couple of miles when Foot informed Duley, "See that low hill up ahead? The Indian camp is just below it on the other side."

The captain raised his hand to signal a halt. The soldiers silently reined in. Bits of cloth wrapped around metal for the mission deadened the sound of clanking and clinking. "Lieutenant," Duley turned to Jesse, "you know your orders. Take the north end. I'll go south. Once you hear the bugle, pitch into 'em. Leave some men behind to run down any that try to escape."

A few minutes later both detachments were in position. Duley and Buchanen watched from low elevations as Dakota men and women busily dismantled their tipis in the gathering daylight.

Solomon sat silently and expectantly next to Jesse. "He gonna give 'em a chance to give up first?" the frontiersman wondered.

"Not likely, Solomon. This'll be shoot first and ask questions later. Sturgis, Wall, take three others and watch for escapees."

"You want us ta shoot 'em?" Willie asked.

"Not unless your life is in peril. Just stop 'em. Men," Jesse raised his voice, "spare any women and children. Fight like soldiers against soldiers fighting you."

An instant later a bugle blast sounded from the other end of the camp. "Follow me!" Jesse shouted. His horse bolted forward through the light snow as his spurs dug into the animal's sides. The command followed at a gallop as their mounts kicked up a cloud of snow behind them.

As Duley's and Buchanen's men converged upon the camp, Dakota men scrambled wildly to arm and protect themselves. Fear and astonishment blanched the faces of the few women in the camp. Several children stood wide-eyed in terror at the thundering peril.

With drawn sabers and Maynard carbines uncased, the soldiers slammed into the Dakota. Duley grabbed the reins with his teeth and swung his curved officer's sword with his left hand as he fired the carbine with the other. The Maynards, only about half the size of an infantry musket, could be fired with one arm.

Several Indian men were bounced by shot onto the frozen ground, staining the pure white of the snow crimson. A few tried to return fire as they huddled behind their bundled belongings. They quickly realized the futility of their predicament.

A Dakota stood, dropped his rifle and folded his arms stoically across his chest in surrender. Jesse watched in horror as one of Duley's men fired his pistol point blank into the man's chest.

Jesse galloped his horse to his captain and wrenched the animal's neck to bring it to a skidding halt before Duley. At that moment a long-haired blanketed figure raced away. Duley brought his pistol to eye level to fire.

Jesse brought the flat of his sword blade down on Duley's arm just as a shot blasted from the barrel. The figure tumbled face-first to the ground.

Fire blazed from Duley's eyes as he leveled the weapon at Jesse. "You Indian lovin' bastard. I'll put one between your eyes and they'll give me a medal for it."

Coolly and evenly Jesse replied, "I don't think they give medals for murdering Dakota men and killing the white woman you were sent here to save, and that is what you may have done."

"Whaddya mean?" Duley inquired as he stared at the lump in the snow. Flecks of spit formed at his trembling lips. "That's not her!"

The shooting stopped. A deadly silence fell over the killing ground. No Indian man was left standing. One woman huddled with two pitifully whimpering children. Sturgis and Wall looked down from the north. They had never moved. None had been able even to try to escape.

Duley, Foot, and Jesse dismounted and walked to the form of the fleeing figure shot by the captain. Tenderly Jesse rolled the body over. It was a white woman. She groaned and opened her blue eyes, then winced sharply as she grabbed her upper arm.

"You're lucky, ma'am," Solomon said gently. "It just got your shoulder."

In spite of himself, Will Duley sighed in relief. "Sergeant," he looked up at a mounted soldier, "see to the survivors and wounded. Then let's get back to the fort."

The men of the First Minnesota rode in silence back to Sauk Centre. Some were smug in the satisfaction brought by revenge, others dumbstruck by the slaughter they had witnessed, had been part of.

Solomon rode alongside Jesse. "Fifteen killed at Lake Shetek and Slaughter Slough. Duley lived through it and swore retribution. He got his fifteen and more today."

"Two slaughters don't make either one right," Jesse replied grimly.

From the hilltop to the west, Pawn watched in anguish. He had observed the scene with hopeless despair, knowing that there was nothing he could do to change the outcome. Pawn knew he should have listened to Round Wind. Now he must find him and together they would go west. The Dakota licked his lip and tasted the salt of grief.

◦ 13 ◦

ESPAIR FROM HUNGER, SICKNESS AND the desolation of defeat hung over the Dakota compound at Fort Snelling as surely as fog on a spring morning. Crooks and Givens continued a daily count that fluctuated because of deaths and the influx of more prisoners brought in from the west.

Missionaries and teachers formed the nucleus of leadership for the Dakota people. Rev. Hinman, Rev. John Williamson, Dr. Thomas Williamson, Rev. Riggs, Father Augustin Ravoux, and Gideon and Samuel Pond worked tirelessly to save lives and souls at both Snelling and the prison in Mankato. Nathan and Emily taught English and writing with the assistance of JoAnna, who divided her time between the teachers and Drs. Weiser and Wharton.

The large building between the fort and the camp continued to serve as hospital, church, and school, but the missionaries continued to minister in the camp as well. Rev. John Williamson, son of Thomas, clutched the collar of his black coat tightly around his neck as he plodded through the snow-tramped village. Flakes from a light snow collected on top of his thick dark hair and drifted into his pleasant, angular face. As Williamson passed lodges, the muffled sounds of whimpering, crying children captured his ears.

He neared the tipi of Good Star Woman and looked at the ground by the opening flap. No crossed sticks prohibiting entrance were there. John cleared his throat and entered. Inside it was smoky and dim. A woman squatted by the fire and stirred a pot of weak broth.

"How are you?" the pastor inquired tentatively.

The woman looked up at him with dark eyes devoid of hope. "Too many die, blackcoat. Sometimes many in one day." She paused, then added, "My little sister is one of them. They are buried in the trench, not in the way of the Dakota. But the priest, he brought a box for each body and says in the spring he'll bury them right."

"Father Ravoux will not forget you, Good Star, are you well?"

"I did not eat the crackers and bread that came with the wagons. I think that is what caused the red spots."

Williamson shook his head grimly. "The people are sick, measles, dysentery, and diphtheria, but bread and crackers didn't cause it. If you begin to feel sick, you must let us know right away."

"This broth should have meat in it," the woman mumbled. "We had horses and oxen when we came here. Now the whites from the town have stolen almost all of them. The wagons, yokes and harnesses too. They leave us with nothing, and the soldiers do not stop them."

The pastor turned and started out the tipi flap. Then he paused, turned and said simply, "I'm sorry," before heading back into the hovel of a camp.

The religious leaders were holding a meeting in the warehouse, and Williamson's visits in the village had made him late. He picked up his pace and hurried along the path to the log building.

Hinman, Riggs, the Ponds and Bishop Whipple sat around a potbellied stove in the middle of a spacious room. All wore the black frock coats of their profession. Father Ravoux and John's father were at the prison camp in Mankato.

Whipple, the Episcopal bishop of Minnesota, was paying an infrequent visit. As Williamson slid into an empty chair between Hinman and Riggs, Whipple smiled broadly. "Welcome John. We were about to begin. I'm most curious about what's transpiring here."

"It's a sad place, Bishop, very sad," John replied. "I just came from the camp."

Riggs, who had been a one-man grand jury for the commission that tried the Santee, looked intently at Whipple. "Bishop, this is a strange winter. I preach in the camp among the dying and the dead. Then I leave there and preach the Word of Life to the spirits in prison. Sickness is there as well.

"Remember, I had to communicate the death sentence to a whole room of human beings. I've been sent to the frontier to hunt up and minister to the wants of the refugees along the border, to allay their feelings of retribution against all Indians.

"Last Sabbath I spent down at Fort Snelling with the Indians in the camp. It's very tragic. The crying hardly ever stops. From five to ten die daily."

Gideon Pond smoothed back his hair and added, "I read that only one in 100 Americans reaches sixty-five years, and the life expectancy averages only thirty-three years. With the Dakota it's even less, especially with the squalor they live in here."

"My father wrote me recently," John Williamson began. "He raises an interesting point about the mortality suffered at Fort Snelling and Mankato. He suggests that about 300 wicked men caused this war and that most of them escaped to the Dakotas. Because of them, Congress will declare the lands and annuities of the entire population of 6,000 souls forfeited, that 2,000 are prisoners, and two to three hundred will die of disease."

"The army is trying to care for the sick," Samuel Pond added. "I think they're doing whatever modern medicine is capable of. Each regiment has a surgeon and assistant surgeon. They're bringing sick to the hospital and seeing that nutrition improves in the camp."

Whipple rubbed his bald forehead, his dark hair still long on top and in back. "Interesting and dismaying. But for some I found hope. I've been able to arrange for a small number to leave this place."

"How so?" Hinman asked. He was the youngest present at twenty-four, newly ordained, slender, with full dark hair. He had escaped the attack at the Redwood Agency on August 18 and was now chaplain of the Fort Snelling camp.

"Gabriel Renville, the agent's mixed-blood son, convinced General Sibley that mixed bloods should be enlisted as scouts and sent to the Redwood Agency and points west. The Renvilles, Gabriel, Michael, Daniel, Isaac, John Moore, Thomas Robinson, and four full-bloods were included in the first group. By now there are sixty Dakotas and mixed bloods scouting for Sibley in the west, some in Dakota."

Williamson nodded. "I've heard that Taopi, Iron Shield, His Thunder, and Yellow Pigeon Hawk have joined them."

"The families of these men were confined here at Snelling," Whipple continued. "Alexander Faribault has land to the south. He's a good man. I convinced General Sibley that the families of those Dakota enlisted as scouts should be sent to Faribault. He agreed to shelter them on his land and has created a community for them."

"Good for him!" Hinman exclaimed. "At least there's some charity left in this state."

"The cry for retribution still resounds," Whipple continued. "President Lincoln spared 265 from the hangman's noose. But the demand is great for removal."

"To where?" Samuel Pond wondered.

"Out of Minnesota, that's certain," Whipple answered.

John Williamson slowly shook his head. "It'll be decided by the Indian Department and Congress. Eighty miles west of Lac Qui Parle, in Dakota Territory, is the coteau, a land of rolling hills. There's plenty of wood, water, and nice land to cultivate. Wide prairies on either side would discourage white settlement. It would be a good place for them.

"Many of the children in this camp were at the boarding school on the reservation. I pity what has become of them here. Many are sick and will forget what they learned in school about truth and virtue. Mr. Cunningham in Minneapolis wants to start a boarding school here. The coteau would be a good place for a school if they are moved there. Maybe even Nakota and Lakota would come to the school."

"If it's so good for the Dakota to go there, then I'm certain they won't be sent there," Gideon Pond murmured. "Why couldn't they have been left alone on the prairie?"

"Because it would have been death to them, Gideon, you know that," Riggs replied. "I talked to Sibley about this after Camp Release. He had two options: free the women and children and non-combatants onto the prairie, or bring them here. What do you suppose would have happened to them had they been left to their own designs?"

Pond considered Riggs' words for just a moment and then responded, "They would have been murdered. The retribution of the settlers referenced earlier would have been realized."

Riggs sighed. "At least they're coming to our savior in numbers like we've never seen before. Here and at Mankato, hundreds are being baptized and confirmed."

"Stephen," Whipple commented, "they're desperate people. Their gods have failed them. They look to our God and hope He will lead them to a better way."

"Bishop, we've had bonfires of their medicine bundles, the tokens that bind them to the past and their old ways. The Dakota dispose of them willingly."

Hinman's face wore a perplexed look. "This shows my inexperience and ignorance, but I keep hearing about Dakota, Nakota and Lakota. I know they are all related Sioux tribes, but what makes them different and separate?"

Riggs cleared his throat. "Samuel, all of us could explain, but I'll try. It's all about language and the letters L and D. In the Teton dialect, the L is generally used instead of the D. So Tetons call themselves Lakota. The Yankton and Yanktonais make up the Nakota and use the D instead of the L, as do the Dakota, or Santee."

"All these divisions are confusing." Hinman shook his head. "I understand there are four bands of the Santee. I worked with them. But what of the others?"

"There are three great divisions: the Teton, Yankton, and Santee, or Lakota, Nakota, and Dakota. All once lived in Minnesota. Wars with the Chippewa, also called Ojibway, resulted in the Santee remaining in the southern half of Minnesota while the other two moved west. The Yankton to just beyond the southwestern border of Minnesota, and the Teton farther west to the Missouri."

"I see," Hinman ruminated, "but I hear of other tribes like the Oglala or Sans Arc. How do they fit in?"

Riggs smiled. "I know, it's a lot of names to take in at once, but let me try to help you. Just as there are Seven Council Fires—the four in Minnesota, the two Yankton over our border and the Teton to the far west—there are seven subtribes of the Teton. They are Oglala, Brule, Hunkpapa, Minneconjou, Two Kettle, Blackfeet, and Sans Arc. In a nutshell, that's it, the cultural and political makeup of the Sioux Nation. By the way, Sioux is a derogatory term, it means snake, or something like it. Dakota means ally."

Gideon Pond interjected, "Most whites don't try to figure all this out. They just call them Sioux."

"Thank you," Hinman replied, "I might have to write this all down to remember, but it is helpful."

"End of history lesson," Riggs concluded.

"So here we sit," John Williamson summarized, "trying to save lives and redeem their souls, whatever division they come from."

Whipple stood before his seated comrades and intoned, "Let us bow our heads in prayer."

As the others folded their hands and bowed their heads, Whipple entreated, "Be with us, Father, as we try to help these people. Guide our hearts, hands, and minds that we may do what is right in Your sight. Amen."

Looking up, Whipple was startled to see an ugly red gash atop Hinman's head. Several stitches held the jagged wound on his scalp together.

"Samuel!" the bishop said with alarm. "What happened to your head?"

"It's nothing. Some white ruffians broke into the stockade last night. I'm afraid they resented the attention I was giving to the Indians."

"They beat him senseless," Williamson noted. "I took him to the fort for medical attention."

"I asked that nothing be made of it," Hinman said, "I'll be fine."

Concern swept over Whipple's face. "I'll talk to fort officials about this. You all are providing a great service here. The government owes it to you to keep you safe. Samuel, all of you, please be careful. Try to go about in pairs whenever possible."

ಖ 14 ಜ

JoAnna Miller sat in the dim shadows of an adjoining warehouse room, the sick room. One window permitted light from a gray, darkening sky to filter onto the dusty floor.

A dozen cots were occupied by measles-ravaged Dakota. Most of the sick were children or elderly. JoAnna squeezed the water from a cloth and placed the cool, damp rag on the forehead of a feverish little Indian girl.

A pained moan escaped the child's lips. "Now, now," JoAnna cooed, "this will cool you. Sleep, sleep."

The nurse silently thanked God for the dim dinginess of the room. Bright sunlight hurt the eyes of the sick. "Not much chance of bright sun in here, at least there's one good thing," she whispered to herself.

"What did you say?" Nathan Cates gently asked.

"Nothing," JoAnna replied as she smiled wanly up at the tall, handsome young man before her. He stood straight like the soldier he had been before he lost his left arm at Shiloh. His dark hair strayed over his ears as he smiled at her with even white teeth. It made her think of Jesse. Emily, Nathan's wife, was tending to the sick across the room.

"I was just thanking God for small things, like a dim room for pained eyes. You and Emily are teachers, not nurses, thank you for helping out here."

"The time for teaching will come, we've got to get them well first. Besides, we don't have much for teaching materials. We lack paper, pencils, books. But Reverend Riggs is scrounging. I hear he has stashes of books that he's hidden away and will deliver to us."

"Nathan, it's odd, isn't it? You leave one war and come to another and now this. Don't you just hate what's happened?"

Nathan glanced down at Emily, who had joined them. Fatigue couldn't hide the strength and beauty that lay inside her. She swept a damp, blonde curl from her forehead, straightened her slight frame and smiled at her husband.

"So, Nathan, do you have regrets?" Emily asked.

"None." He gently touched her soft cheek with his hand. "Even here, you are beautiful. Circumstances no matter how horrible brought me here and to you. I regret the killing, in both wars."

"Yes," JoAnna said, "but think of the noble causes you fought for, to free slaves, to protect the settlers from massacre and now you fight to save these poor, miserable wretches from disease. You should be proud."

Nathan's face paled slightly as he closed his blue eyes in remembrance and nodded his head. Then he looked at JoAnna and replied, "Pride is a funny thing and it takes different forms. What seems right, might be wrong."

Confusion flashed across JoAnna's face as Nathan and Emily crossed the room to tend to other children.

Emily grasped Nathan's hand in hers and said softly, "A strange answer, but the truth might be harder for her."

"Only you know that I was a captain in the Confederacy and that Jeff Davis sent me here to start an Indian war, only you and Little Crow know."

"But you had a change of heart, fought the Dakota and rescued white captives. Many call you a hero."

"Emily, they wouldn't care about that if they knew the rest. They'd string me up just like the thirty-eight at Mankato or like Meeds, my contact in Minneapolis. They found him out and showed no mercy. I'm out of war now, I just want to be with you. We can serve by teaching, caring for these sick and helping the Dakota people."

The door opened with a bustle as several men strode brusquely into the room. All wore long, white dirt-stained coats. Dr. Wharton, his assistant Dr. Potter, and another aide moved through the rows of cots. Wharton and Potter stopped briefly at each, touching the foreheads of the sick, sometimes peeling back a blanket and examining abdomens for red splotches or distension.

Wharton shook his head and said to Potter, "I just received a letter from Muller. He says that measles has been rampant at Fort Ridgely since

February. It seems two soldiers brought it in when they returned from furlough in the Minnesota Valley. He says most of the patients pulled through all right even though many were children.

"Muller says the best treatment was to keep them from exposure to the cold. That's not easy to do in this drafty place. Another thing, seems that anyone who had the measles before didn't get it this time. That's good, I guess."

"Sure," Potter answered, "'cept the Indians hardly ever got it in the first place. If they never had multiple exposures, they won't have any immunity. That's why most of them in the encampment are gonna come down with measles. At least smallpox and diphtheria cases are few."

"And so, Doctor, we do the best we can with what we have. There are cases of diphtheria in St. Paul and surrounding counties. We must keep the sick isolated, comfortable and as warm as we can."

"Yes," Potter replied as he adjusted a damp cloth to a young boy's forehead, "that and pray."

∞ 15 ∞

THE MISSIONARIES, INCLUDING FATHER Augustin Ravoux, Riggs, and John Williamson, traveled regularly between Fort Snelling and Mankato. Occasionally other religious leaders or medical personal made the journey as well. They were happy to bring news and messages up and down the river from one camp to the other.

At Mankato, disease outbreaks were fewer and the opportunity for salvation and education greater. Riggs and Ravoux waited patiently at the Dakota log prison as guards unlocked the chains that secured the door. The missionaries each supported one end of a large, heavy box.

Days were lengthening as spring neared, but inside the jail was still dingy. The three stoves spread throughout the expansive single room were smoky, yet the welcome warmth attracted the convicted Dakota.

Ravoux wore the black robe of a priest and had a full, dark beard. Riggs, clean shaven, was slight of build. His waves of graying hair formed a widow's peak on his forehead. The sight that greeted them warmed the clerics' hearts more than the wood stoves could. The inmates were huddled together in groups of eight or ten. John Williamson stood amongst them pointing at words on a slate before a small group. Others were reading or studying books, writing on slates or paper. Some were reading or writing letters.

Riggs let out a loud sigh. "I don't believe it. Colonel Marshall claimed that we would see a reformation here, but I didn't expect this."

Williamson's face lit up it spite of the shadows in the room. He strode briskly to his two friends and slapped each soundly on the shoulders. "Welcome. Do you have what I think you have in the box?"

"If you are suggesting books, John, you are correct. I have 100 copies of the new ABC book. I meant to have 200, but these are all that were stitched."

"That's good for some, Stephen," Williamson responded, "but many of these are beyond that. It's amazing how much they have learned."

"We also brought more than 100 copies of Bunyan. I took them out of a cache on our way up to Camp Release last September. John Renville had buried them for preservation."

"It was like finding buried treasure," Ravoux interjected.

"Some are learning English," Williamson continued, "but praise God for the work of the Ponds and you, Stephen, in creating a Dakota alphabet and translating books into it. You should hear them sing hymns in Dakota. The avenues of Heaven must echo with them."

Riggs beamed. "John, it's been a winter of great advancement. There's never been such a time for them to read, learn and study. Thousands of letters have been written."

"What about Fort Snelling?" Williamson wondered. "How goes it there?"

Ravoux placed a hand on John's shoulder. "It does not go as well. Many more are sick. The children miss the structure of the boarding schools. But we do our best, and advancements are made. Totems of their past gods and medicine bundles are burned in bonfires as they turn to the One True God. Reverend Riggs managed to convince the Indians that there was no magic in the charms they clung to and that they could not accept Jesus while clinging to symbols of paganism. Stephen did amazing work. Baptisms and confirmations are occurring in numbers that surpass the totals of all decades past."

"How many of these conversions are of pure motive and how many are of convenience? How many are out of desperation?" John Williamson inquired.

Riggs sighed as he considered the question of the young pastor. "The whole work is a very wonderful reformation and a most amazing work of God's Spirit. But my view is different than that of your father and Gideon Pond. In his several letters to the Evangelist, the Reverend Pond asserts that very few were guilty of the murders and outrages on the frontier. I wish that I thought so as well. But I can't. I went through the weeks of trials with them.

"My point of observation is different. There were many bloody hands there, and I wondered how could I place into such hands the emblems of the body and blood of a dying Christ. But if Peter preached that the sinners who crucified Christ could be washed clean of sin, can't Dakota sinners be washed clean by the blood of Christ?

"They are a mixed multitude and have mixed motives. If these men live to get out of prison and are again with their friends, some of them will not be true to their profession of religion. But they won't go back to where they were before. The meetings, singing, talking and the reality of this place will influence them forever."

"Well said, Stephen," Ravoux nodded.

"Reverend Pond and my father were here recently," Williamson said. "When they entered the prison, fifty men requested that they be baptized. Gideon was glad to accommodate them. He told them that before they were friends, but now they are brothers."

"I'm not as liberal," John continued. "When I was at Fort Snelling, I found requests for baptism were becoming more abundant. But I'm more selective than Gideon and my father. Father suited the covenants to the circumstances.

"I made the converts at Snelling come before a session of the church and be subjected to an examination as to piety and knowledge as thorough as I was accustomed to in any of our churches. We had 140 admissions, but I believe them sincere. There would have been hundreds of others had my father and Gideon been ministering to them. But I don't want backsliders."

"We all have our methods to bring souls to Christ. I won't place one over the other," Riggs added.

"How do you handle polygamy? Many still cling to more than one wife," Williamson wondered.

Riggs answered, "Before they are baptized, those who had two wives entered into an agreement to put one away. Many had agreed to this when they received the sacrament here at Mankato before they were sent to Fort Snelling. But many did not do it. In some cases at the camp, we made both wives promise to be willing to be put away.

"Then we called the men in and told them that they must finish what they had begun at Mankato. They could only have one wife."

"I did something similar here, Stephen. I can show you a list of eighteen men who set aside one of their wives and listed who they would keep."

Father Ravoux recalled, "It was hard at Fort Snelling, John. When the wives were told that their husbands must make a selection, there was much consternation."

"And for some, relief," Riggs suggested.

"Many of these wives were sisters," the priest continued. "They had been living together in the same tipis. Hearts were broken whether they were selected or discarded."

The clinking of ankle chains sounded behind Riggs. He turned to find a slender, scraggly Dakota man behind him. The man shakily held a sheet of paper to Riggs.

"Black Coat, this is for my daughter, Two Stars. Give it to her, please."

Stephen glanced down at the letter with cramped handwriting scrawled across it. "Certainly. I will see she gets it."

A small smile of gratitude creased the Indian's face as he turned away while Riggs folded the paper and put it in his pocket.

The men of God immersed themselves in the huddle of Dakota and began to distribute books.

ॐ 16 ॐ

IND SWEPT SNOW AND ICE OVER THE frozen Dakota plains and into Minnesota with no regard to skin color or band. At Fort Abercrombie on the Dakota side of the Red River, white and red shivered together in the cold.

A white sergeant stood near a breastwork of the unwalled fort alongside an Indian man. "What's that comin' our way?" He pointed to a snowy white haze kicked up by a galloping horse.

The Indian, named Taopi, narrowed his eyes into the stark blue horizon and answered slowly, "I think it is His Thunder. He was sent to the west to find Mdewakanton trying to return to Minnesota."

"Whatcha gonna do 'bout it?"

Taopi answered by turning to another Indian several yards away. "Good Thunder, let the people know. I believe that Santee come and must be turned back. Our people are waiting by the river."

The Dakota leader left to alert Indians on the Red River.

The sergeant questioned Taopi. "What do ya aim ta do? Yer not gonna shoot 'em, are ya? Them's yer people."

Taopi looked sadly to the west. "The Long Trader sent us here to keep Mdewakanton from coming back to Minnesota. There are sixty of us along the border to do just that."

"Yer gonna shoot yer own people? What about yer families?"

"It is because of our families that we do this. They have been moved from Fort Snelling and are cared for by a man named Faribault. They live on his land and are better off than those at the fort. Besides, these are bad Indians who started the war. We will keep them away."

Minutes later His Thunder galloped into the fort compound. He shouted at Taopi, "They come, not many, about as much as a basket half-full of rocks."

"We are ready," Taopi responded as he pointed. "See the riverbank."

As a couple dozen Mdewakanton approached the Red River, dozens more riflemen opened fire. Several of the approaching band fell mortally wounded. The others scattered and turned back to the west.

The sergeant watched with Taopi and shivered under his heavy blue coat. It wasn't the cold that made him shiver but the reality of death. "I still don't see how ya kin do this ta yer own kind."

"We do what we must. It is for our families. They are looked after if we scout and protect the border. You fight your own people, too. You are doing it now in the South."

"Yep." The sergeant's face reddened in the cold as he spat a stream of tobacco, staining a white snowbank. "But I don't think that's right, neither."

๑ 17 ๙

EYOKA LEFT THE FAR NORTH VILLAGE at St. Joseph with renewed hope. Little Crow would be pleased to know that traders and the people of the town were not hostile to the Dakota who camped nearby. Trading three captive white boys they had captured in Minnesota showed good will. Father Andre had said it would help them with the British in Canada.

A few days later brought the solitary horseman to Devils Lake in the north central Dakota Territory. An early spring thaw had reduced the snow to patches on the prairie, and Heyoka had made good time. He narrowed his eyes and squinted into bright sunlight as three riders galloped their ponies toward him.

Mdewakanton, he realized, I know these people. They are from Little Crow. The riders wrenched their horses' necks to the side and pulled up abruptly before Heyoka.

"Hiya," one exclaimed. "We have been watching for you. Little Crow is camped on the lake at a place where the water is on all sides but one."

"He left the big river?" Heyoka asked incredulously.

"A moon ago. There was no help for us on the river. Word came that the Mdewakanton were welcome in the Grandmother's Country. The path was good and buffalo many. But for some the journey was still hard."

Heyoka's horse snorted a frosty mist into the air as it pawed the frozen ground with a front hoof. His rider steadied the animal and replied, "You traveled in the month of the tree-popping moon. It must have been cold and hard."

"Yes," a second horseman answered, "but our lodges were warm when we got here, and British traders gave us food for the things we took from the white Americans."

"Didn't you have buffalo to eat?" Heyoka asked.

"Yes, but not those other things we need, like flour, salt, tobacco, coffee, and ammunition."

"Take me to my father-in-law. Take me to Little Crow."

The Mdewakanton leader's lodge was near the center of the camp. The frozen ice of Devils Lake reflected bright sunshine, and Heyoka shielded his eyes with his hands as he looked for his father-in-law. A man stood alongside a young boy in front of a large buffalo-hide tipi. He bent and guided the boy's hands, positioning them on a bow. Then the man drew the young one's hand and the leather bowstring back and let an arrow fly. It thudded into the soft bark of a nearby tree.

The man, who was Little Crow, stood and grinned down at the boy. "Well done," he smiled, "keep on and you will kill a big buffalo some day."

At the crunching sound of horse hooves on hard-packed snow, Little Crow turned to find Heyoka approaching.

"Hiya, it is good to see you back safe, Heyoka. What have you found?"

"Hiya, father." The rider slid easily from his mount and strode to the older man.

"I have much to tell you."

"Come," Little Crow gestured to his lodge, "we will eat and talk."

The wailing sound of an infant crying in the distance gave Heyoka pause. "A warning cry?" he asked.

"No, it is Crow Woman's young one. He is hung from a tree in his cradleboard. He will cry until he stops. She will do nothing for him until he stops. The young ones must learn that crying does no good. They must not be allowed to scare game away or alert enemies as to where we are. They must learn. Come with me."

Heyoka followed Little Crow toward his dwelling. They walked through women busily working at various tasks in the camp. Food preparation, mending and sewing clothing, preparing hides, child care, all were done by women. The camp was their domain, including the raising and dismantling of the tipis. Men were warriors and hunters. The definition of roles was carefully observed.

The interior of Little Crow's buffalo-hide tipi was warm but smoky. Little Crow sliced off a chunk of dried venison and handed it to Heyoka.

Then both sat upon robes of buffalo hide near the fire in the center of the lodge. The smoke slowly tendrilled up through an opening at the apex of the lodge poles.

The younger man ripped off a hunk of meat with his teeth. "As I rode in, it seemed there were fewer lodges than before. Is this true?"

"There are about 100 men remaining, along with women and children. Some have left us. The journey here was hard and some feared that there would not be food enough for so many on the plains in winter. Tell me about the Grandmother's Country. Where is Standing Buffalo?"

"He stays in Canada. At least until it is warm. At St. Joseph on the Pembina there were fifteen lodges of Mdewakanton. The town has many mixed bloods. They are good to the people and trade with them. The British say they do not have soldiers to fight the Americans but will send a letter to the Long Trader to try to help. Why did you leave the big river?"

"The river tribes turned on us, the Teton and Yankton offered no help. We heard that the British offered at least some hope for the people. We moved to be closer to the Grandmother's Country. Should I go to speak with the British?" Little Crow asked. "They are friendly here, many have come south to trade with us."

"Standing Buffalo's Sisseton have started to intermarry with the Ojibway. The mixed bloods show friendship but worry that food will not last. The British act like friends but hold us away from them. They cannot be trusted to help us."

"Still," Little Crow rubbed his cheek as he thought, "the British are not hunting us to kill us. They want to trade with us and know that we have much that we took from the whites in Minnesota. The Ojibway marry our women. There are important things that tie us to both Indians and whites. Maybe an alliance can happen.

"When it becomes warm and the game and food more plentiful, I will go to St. Joseph. I will go to the Pembina to talk to the British and the Ojibway," Little Crow decided.

≈ 18 ≈

ALONG WINTER FINALLY GAVE WAY TO A slushy spring in central Minnesota. Sibley's plan to rotate troops from fort to fort went into effect. Duley and his men were ordered to Fort Ridgely.

There had been little activity in the stockade at Sauk Centre after the attack upon Pawn's camp. Company F of the First Minnesota Cavalry Mounted Rangers had simply endured the boredom that comes with being assigned to a frontier post.

Occasionally they received news and dispatches from Sven Swenson, the Norwegian driver of the stagecoach that traveled the trail from Fort Snelling to Fort Abercrombie. He became their window on the rest of the world.

Duley had ordered occasional patrols to reconnoiter the surrounding area, but generally post life consisted of drilling and waiting. Solomon Foot was mustered in and assigned to the Mounted Rangers. On a mid-April night, Solomon and Jesse sat around the shimmering glow of a kerosene lamp in one of the Sauk Centre stockade's single-room cabins.

The room was stark and sparsely furnished. A small table, two chairs and a cot in the corner were the only furniture. Thunder rolled outside like a continuous roll of drums, and occasional streaks of lightning reflected off big drops of rain that thudded on the cabin roof. A steady *drip, drip, drip* plopped onto the dirt floor through a leak in the cabin ceiling.

"Well, Jesse," Solomon drawled, "quite a castle you've got here. It'll be hard ta leave it. I'm sure you'll miss it."

Jesse smiled broadly. "I've never been happier to leave any place in my life. Going to Ridgely doesn't get me any closer to JoAnna, but it gets me out of here and, I hope, assigned to another commander."

"After that little incident when we raided the camp and rescued Mrs. Wyatt, we needed more stoves around here just ta melt the ice every time Duley came around you. Has he talked to you since?"

71

"Only if he has to, Solomon. Usually he just sends me orders through corporals or sergeants."

"You saved him, Jesse. If you hadn't hit his arm, that woman would be dead today. Doesn't he realize what woulda happened to him then?"

"Oh, I think he does, and he resents me more for it. Tomorrow, we leave this God forsaken place and the devil take it."

Solomon smiled. "Don't be too hard on Sauk Centre. My brother Silas plans to spend some time here this summer. He's kinda an entrepreneur and plans to round up some abandoned cattle."

"Good luck to him, Mr. Foot, I hope he does well. After the winter I've spent here, I just want to move."

Early the next morning a bugle blast assembled the troops on the parade ground. Duley, mounted on a spirited black gelding, rode before them. Facing his men, he shouted, "We go to Fort Ridgely by way of Forest City and Hutchinson. The last dispatch I received said that the roads are terrible bad owing to heavy spring rains and not enough drainage and bridges. Much of what we gotta go through is like a bog.

"This will be a real test for men and horses both. I'm sure you'll be up to it." He swiveled his mount around and pointed ahead. "Column of twos, forward!"

Jesse rode in back with the men. Solomon rode uneasily alongside him. "I know this is how we gotta travel," the older man complained, "but I never feel right on a horse."

"Ride in the wagons, the mules pull real gentle," Jesse laughed.

"I'd as soon have my bones crunched by some Sioux than bounced around in them boxes." Foot removed his broad-brimmed hat and wiped sweat from his broad forehead.

"Solomon, by the looks of this road you'll do more sinking than bouncing."

In places the road was a quagmire. Mule teams became virtually useless and, even without their riders the cavalry horses struggled through the muck that sucked at their hooves.

Men and wagons continually bogged down with wagon wheels up to their hubs. The troops pried with levers, pushed and strained to free a wagon only to have it bog down again.

Foot and Willie Sturgis watched a struggling detail try to pry loose a wagon from a particularly gooey soup of mud.

Solomon scratched the stubble of his beard and reasoned laconically, "Ya know, Willie, neither the men, nor the teams can get any footholds in that stuff. Get longer lines, put the animals up ahead where the footin' is better, and then have men help push the wagons. They just might be able ta drag 'em through."

Sturgis was pensive and then brightened. "Mr. Foot, I think ya might be onta somethin' there. I'll tell the lieutenant."

The gangly young corporal hurried off to pass Solomon's strategy on to Jesse. A short time later the crossing was modified. When the troops encountered a soft spot that was more than fifteen yards wide, the teams were unhitched and led to drier ground the best way possible. Then a long line was attached to the wagon and the whole troop of fifty men would pull the conveyance through the mud.

At times sloughs were one to two hundred yards across, but by using the longer lines, men and animals were able to find decent enough footing to get the wagons through one at a time.

The hours of backbreaking toil took a heavy toll on the Mounted Rangers, and a trip that should have taken days took two weeks. Finally, in early May, Duley's troops reached Fort Ridgely to join the army assembling in the valley of the Minnesota.

ɛɔ 19 ʗʂ

STANDING BUFFALO AND HIS SISSETON returned from Canada to the banks of Devils Lake in April. They were joined by Sweet Corn, the Sisseton leader who had led an attack on Fort Abercrombie.

Yankton from the south had also come to the lake in north-central Dakota. But soon they found themselves quarreling with the Mdewakanton, blaming them for bringing trouble to all Dakota people.

Bad blood bubbled over, leading the Yankton to angrily cut up several Mdewakanton tipis and leave to return to the south. Standing Buffalo and Sweet Corn caught up with their southern brothers and rode alongside their leader, Bone Necklace.

Standing Buffalo explained, "You were right to leave Crow. The Long Trader will come soon. We know this is true. He will try to rub out all of us. It won't matter if they fought in Minnesota or not."

"Bad things will happen on the lake," Bone Necklace replied. "It was not safe to stay. Little Crow has brought this on us all. You are right, the whites will not try to separate Minnesota Dakota from the rest. They will kill everyone. Young men from my band rescued the Shetek women and children. But the white soldiers will not care."

"That is why we want to ask Sibley for peace," Sweet Corn offered.

"Ask if you want, my Yankton do not wish to fight him," Bone Necklace insisted. "We go to our homeland, far from the Mdewakanton, and even though you do not wish to fight, we want to be far from you as well. You said it yourself. Whites don't care. They will rub us all out if they can."

Disconsolately, Standing Buffalo and Sweet Corn rode back toward Devils Lake.

"All must leave Little Crow," Standing Buffalo told his companion. "Mdewakanton, Sisseton, Wahpeton, all. If they don't, they will die. The blue-coat soldiers will come."

Sweet Corn rode silently and made a clicking sound when his horse stopped and pawed the dirt. The animal resumed on the trail as his rider spoke. "Little Crow says he will get behind the blue coats. He says they move like a turtle and will be strung out on the road like a snake. He will attack them in Minnesota before they get here."

"He has only a hundred men. Thousands will come with the Long Trader, as many as the leaves that fall from the trees when the air turns cold. No one will join Little Crow to die, and many of the Mdewakanton who are still with him will leave. They know the end is coming."

Meanwhile, Little Crow had made a decision. He would go to Canada and negotiate personally with the British. He left Devils Lake with sixty men and twenty women.

His son Wowinape, Heyoka, and brother White Spider rode beside Little Crow on the soggy prairie. A misty rain dampened the earth and matched the spirits of the Dakota. Each man wore a sodden blanket draped over his shoulders.

Little Crow swiveled on his horse and looked back at the procession that followed. Dozens of horses pulled travois, carving muddy slits in the prairie. Women, children, and older men trudged along beside them. Some younger children rode atop bundles in the travois. His warriors rode amongst them.

"Too few," the chief mumbled, "less than half what we had when we left Minnesota."

"Inkpaduta stays with us," White Spider encouraged.

"Trickles come to us when we need rivers. The Teton, the Yankton, Santee who left us or were never with us, the river tribes, all will find that they were fools not to fight the whites with us. They will have to fight the Americans soon, whether they want to or not, and it will be too late to stop them. Inkpaduta may be with us now, but where was he when we fought the whites? He was in the land of the Yanktoni hiding."

"Not hiding, brother," White Spider corrected. "No one can question Inkpaduta's courage after Spirit Lake."

Little Crow stared to the rear where Inkpaduta rode with his band of Wahpekuta. "He fought for his people and family," Little Crow agreed. "The trader Lott killed his brother and eight family members with an axe. Inkpaduta made him and many more pay for the murders."

"Then they crossed from Spirit Lake into Minnesota. Why did you lead a hunt to find him?" asked Heyoka.

Little Crow shifted uncomfortably on his horse. "The whites said to help find Inkpaduta, or the Wahpekute and the Mdewakanton would be held responsible for the Iowa killings, and our annuities would not be paid until he was captured."

"But he escaped to the Dakota Territory," said White Spider.

"Our hunt for him was for show, not for real. But he did much that has led to our fight with the whites," Little Crow concluded. "At least he is with us now. Pawn should have stayed with us, too. A raid back into Minnesota was foolish. But maybe he will learn something to help us."

"Will the British help us?" Heyoka fingered a round brass medallion that hung by a leather strap around his neck. His fingertip circled the worn impression of King George III on the medal.

Many of the Dakota men wore similar ornaments. They had been given to Little Crow's father and his warriors as symbols of peace and in recognition of their support of the British in the War of 1812. It was Little Crow's intent that when they arrived in Canada, the British would see the medals and remember.

"We have little else to hope for," the leader replied. "An alliance with the British will give us the support we need. But our time is getting short. The Long Trader will come. But he can't get us if we are in Canada."

White Spider looked hopefully at his brother. "Standing Buffalo says that the Ojibway were friendly, they married some of our women. Maybe they will join us now."

Little Crow's face screwed up like he had tasted a sour lemon. "They had their chance. If they had moved against the Americans from the north, our war would have been different. Hole-in-the-Day tried, but his people wouldn't listen then, and they won't listen now, either. But I will try. The days of fighting our longtime enemy are over. We must be allies of the Ojibway."

Wowinape was hopeful. "Medicine Bottle and Shakopee are in St. Joseph with the mixed bloods. They will help us."

"They are only two, my son. We need many two's. When we reach the north we must meet with the Ojibway and British and seek their help."

The shrinking band of Mdewakanton reached Pembina just south of the Canadian border on May 24. They camped near the Hudson's Bay

Company post and met in council with the Red Lake, Lake of the Woods and Pembina Ojibway.

Over 200 men from the three bands plus sixty Mdewakanton gathered around the leaders who sat upon the prairie in a circle. A pipe passed from hand to hand around the loop of a dozen leaders. Each blew sacred smoke into the air.

Pembina chief Red Bear gazed across at his traditional enemies, the Dakota. "I speak for my people," he stated with authority. "Why do you come to the land of the Ojibway?"

Little Crow spread his arms wide to either side. The stained cotton shirt he wore pulled up, revealing wrists withered from bullet wounds in his youth. "We come to honor our brothers and to give them food and objects we took from the Americans. We wish to show you that we come in a good way."

Red Bear grunted and replied, "Not so long ago you were trying to rub us out."

"Yes," Little Crow concurred, "once we fought each other, and our fathers fought and their fathers fought. But a greater enemy is coming, and if we don't stand together against them we will all be swallowed up by them. Stand with us and give us sanctuary."

Red Bear was not persuaded. "Because you know the Americans will come for you. Because there is no place for you to go, you come to us. Even your own kind, the Teton and Yankton, send you away from them."

Little Crow silently gathered himself and spoke with the dignified voice of a proud chief. "We do not come to beg. We come as warriors who have fought a war that all Indians should have joined in. Now we ask that you provide us with a safe place until a time when we are ready to move on and fight again."

Red Bear sighed deeply and looked at the other Ojibway leaders. "We have smoked and talked about this. Go to the north, to Fort Garry. If the British will have you, there will be no trouble from the Ojibway. They will set the boundaries. We will not fight you, but we will not fight the Americans with you, either."

With that, Chief Red Bear reached down and gathered a garment around his shoulders. It was a faded, tattered American flag. As he rose to his feet, the stars and stripes hung from his body in silent testimony to his sentiment and loyalty.

The Mdewakanton left the gathering knowing that they could expect no help from the Ojibway. On May 27, Little Crow led his followers from Pembina up the Red River to Fort Garry.

"We must make a fine impression," the Santee leader advised his people as they neared Fort Garry.

They were determined not to disappoint. The procession was a spectacle to behold when the Mdewakanton rode into the Canadian city two days later. The Minnesota Indians paraded into Fort Garry, riding horses and aboard mule-drawn wagons.

Little Crow had insisted that they wear their finest clothing. The men wore fine broadcloth coats and pants taken from white settlers in the prairie war. Many hung the King George III medallions from their necks. Women were resplendent in silk dresses and leather leggings. They shaded their copper faces with fancy parasols.

But the most impressive spectacle was Little Crow himself. The war chief wore a black coat with a velvet collar, a breechcloth of broadcloth and deerskin leggings. A fine shawl draped around his neck, while another encircled his waist as a sash. A "seven shooter" pistol was tucked into it.

Governor Dallas, short and stocky, strode purposefully from the log government house to greet the Santee.

Little Crow dismounted from his spotted horse and stood before the British official. "I am Little Crow of the Mdewakanton Santee Dakota. I wish to speak with the man who leads the British people."

Dallas, obviously impressed, extended his hand. As he and Little Crow exchanged a handshake, Dallas offered, "I'm the governor of this province. What does the chief of the Santee want with me?"

Other officials gathered behind him while he asked his question, including several with pads of paper. These were newspaper reporters who had gathered in expectation of Little Crow's arrival.

Inkpaduta and White Spider stood beside their leader as he responded. Little Crow was direct to the point of seeming arrogant. "We come to offer peace and friendship to all in the Grandmother's Country. But to the Americans we will fight to the death. Me and my people are fighting with ropes around our necks now.

"When you needed the help of the Dakota people as you fought the Americans, we came to help you. Now it is the Dakota who need help. Maybe you have a place where we can be safe."

Dallas straightened his round form as best he could and answered Little Crow. "The Queen is most grateful for the help our red friends provided. But I do not know what we can do to help you. There is," he searched for the right words, then extended his hands palms-up and slightly shifted them up and down, "a delicate balance that we face with the Americans.

"There are those in Minnesota who wish to expand by annexing land controlled by the Hudson's Bay Company in Canada. There is even an American Party in Fort Garry which desires to see it happen. We cannot give them a reason to move into Canada. Pursuing you here would give them an excuse. They may come and never leave."

Little Crow looked hard at Dallas. "Then give us ammunition and guns," he demanded.

The governor was resolute. "Now, we can't do that for the same reasons I just outlined. It would give them a reason to invade us. Little Crow, surely you must understand our predicament."

A haughty expression spread over the Santee's face. "We don't need it anyway." He glanced at the newspapermen scribbling frantically on their pads. "We have more than enough with us to kill all Americans who come against us. We will stay at St. Joseph if we wish."

"Then you don't need us," Dallas said decisively as he turned and strode back into the government house.

The newspapermen crowded around the Indian leaders.

"What do you think about what's been happening in Minnesota to your people?" a short, bespectacled, gray-haired man inquired.

"They all should have left with me," Little Crow answered, clearly enjoying the attention now afforded him. "The Santee who stayed behind are in prisons and cages or they were hung from ropes like pieces of meat in the street. Thirty-eight of my brothers were murdered because they dared to fight the white man. They were soldiers, not criminals. Soon all will be sent from our homeland, to pens in the west where the Teton and Yankton long ago decided no one could live. Other warriors will go to a prison in the land of Inkpaduta." He nodded to the man at his side. "I cry salt tears for what will happen to my people."

Another reporter held up a hand marked by ink-stained fingertips. "Little Crow," he wondered, "what should be done with the Sioux held by Sibley?"

"I surrendered the captives we took in the war. We killed none of them. The Long Trader, Sibley should do the same. He should free his prisoners."

The gray-haired, bespectacled man stepped onto a raised platform near Little Crow to jockey into better position and resumed his questioning. "What about how you started the war? Aren't you getting what you deserve?"

"Being a little harsh, aren't you, Stan?" the man next to him commented.

Little Crow smiled grimly. "That is not how it was. But I will not defend my people with facts. It appears that they would not change Stan's opinion anyway."

Governor Dallas had returned to the large cabin that served as the seat of government. A large man, six-foot-three and nearly 300 pounds, pushed himself upright from a creaking wooden chair with effort. The man's face was framed by a heavy, coal-black beard. His equally dark, bushy hair brushed his collar. He wore a gray Confederate uniform with the gold bars of a brigadier general on his shoulders.

He extended a large, ham-like hand to Dallas, towering over the governor as he enveloped the smaller hand with his own. "Excellent, Governor. Send them back to the border. Little Crow will have little choice but to return to Minnesota. The Union will be preoccupied, just as we planned. Letting him escape to Canada would have taken the heat off Lincoln."

Dallas seemed distressed. "General Pike, I don't like getting involved in this, dealing with spies and such."

Albert Pike chuckled. "I'm not a spy, Governor. I'm Chief of Covert Operations for the Confederate States of America. That sounds more official, doesn't it?"

Dallas ruefully shook his head. "Titles don't change the mission. Stir up the Indians, get wars started along the frontier . . . isn't that your charge?"

"Innovative, isn't it?" Pike laughed. "We got off to a pretty good start in Minnesota. It might have even been better, but our agent there got cold feet. That's what we get for using the nephew of a Yankee general.

"I told Jeff Davis to get someone else, but no, he insisted this one-armed fellow, Nathan Thomas, would serve very well. He believed in the 'cause.' He broke with his Union Uncle George long ago. Well, we did have a good beginning in Minnesota, but our Captain Thomas got friendly with some Yankees. Then the fool fell in love with a school marm and wound up fighting for the blue bellies.

"But at least it got us this far. Soldiers were kept in Minnesota to fight Indians, and others were called away from fighting us and sent back to Minnesota."

"Where do you go next?" Dallas inquired.

"South and west, there are Indians there who need encouragement, too. You might hear of incidents in Missouri, maybe even Texas, Oklahoma. You never know."

Dallas reddened slightly and cleared his throat. "People say things about you, General Pike."

The general smiled. "What kinds of things?"

"Well . . . that you worship Satan. That you belong to something called the Illuminati, that you talk about something called the 'One World Order.'"

"My, you've heard so many things." Pike chuckled and then, as if someone had wiped his face clean with a rag, a stony expression replaced the humor, and he leaned close toward Governor Dallas. "It would be best," he warned grimly, his dark face growing darker, "if you did not take such talk seriously. It might not be . . . healthy." Then he stood and stretched tall his towering, powerful frame.

A cold sweat erupted upon Dallas's forehead as he absorbed the sinister meaning of Pike's words. "Just s-s-saying," he mumbled, feeling small and vulnerable. "I didn't m-m-mean anything."

Pike laughed and picked up a satchel from the floor. "Well, Governor, I must head off to the sunny south. Remember, no help for Little Crow here. Is that understood?"

"Yes, General," Dallas nodded too eagerly, "yes, I most certainly understand."

LITTLE CROW HAD WORN HAUGHTY INSOLENCE as a mask. When he and his advisors returned to their camp outside of Fort Garry, haggard despair replaced boldness.

"You got nothing!" Inkpaduta challenged. "You spoke big words, true words, but nothing came of it."

"I knew they wouldn't keep the words they gave to our fathers." White Spider spat the words. "They are white, and they all lie."

"What will you do? Sibley will come," said Heyoka.

Little Crow considered the comments and then replied slowly, "I will eat and smoke and think. Then I will see the governor again."

A commotion alerted Little Crow that someone was approaching. A small knot of his band was shouting enthusiastically while crowding around two men who strode toward Little Crow. The cadre parted before their chief, revealing Medicine Bottle and Shakopee, two of the most involved and most wanted refugees of the Dakota War.

Little Crow restrained the impulse to be direct. Instead he played homage to custom. "Let us enter my lodge and smoke," he said. "Do you want to eat?"

The Mdewakanton chief, his primary lieutenants and the two visitors sat in a circle in Little Crow's tipi, passing the sacred pipe and blowing its smoke into the air. Then Little Crow opened their discussion. "Have you come to join us? We need more great warriors like Medicine Bottle and Shakopee. You stood with me when we fought in Minnesota. Fight with us again. Do not hide in the Grandmother's Country."

Shakopee, at about fifty, was nearly twenty years senior to Medicine Bottle. Also known as Little Six, he had been a leader of the Soldiers' Lodge, the faction of Mdewakanton that had conducted much of the war. Sarah Wakefield, a hostage, testified that Chaska had saved her life from Shakopee.

Medicine Bottle had been with Little Crow when the fighting began in earnest at the Lower Sioux Agency on August 18. He had attacked the Forbes Trading Post and was thought to have killed government employee Philander Prescott.

Both Shakopee and Medicine Bottle had escaped to Canada after the Battle of Wood Lake. Now they stared stoically into the flickering flames of Little Crow's fire. Shakopee answered first. "We came to urge you to stay in the north. It's not safe for you or your people where Americans can find you."

Medicine Bottle pushed two long black braids behind his head. The advice he gave supported his friend. "Shakopee speaks the truth. We won't follow you to our deaths. The Americans can't come to Canada to take us. We're safe here. You would be as well."

Little Crow spat into the fire and paused as his spittle sizzled on a hot rock. "Even if I wanted to, we can't stay here. The Grandmother's governor said that we must leave, that they won't help us. You are only two. They don't care about you. We are not many, but are still too many for them. Come with us."

Shakopee stared into the fire a moment. "We fought at your side in Minnesota. We were not afraid to die with you then. It was time to be brave, to be a warrior. We were fighting to keep our land free of intruders. It's different now. We won't follow you just to die."

Little Crow raised himself to his feet. "Then we have nothing to say. Stay here and hide. We will return to Devils Lake."

Shakopee stood and looked directly into Little Crow's eyes. "We each travel upon a road we do not know. The next time we meet will not be in this world."

Their chief nodded slowly and then dismissively waved the two men away.

"Now what will you do?" Inkpaduta asked.

"See the governor one more time," Little Crow replied.

TWO DAYS LATER, WITH A MORE CONTRITE ATTITUDE, the Mdewakanton again stood before Governor Dallas. "I ask that you help my people," he said directly.

"How?" the governor asked. "I already told you our situation."

"Write a letter to Sibley, see if you can bring about a peace between us. We gave up our prisoners. Let him give up his."

Dallas rubbed a hollow cheek with his left hand and turned to the assistant alongside him. "Well, Brimley, I think we can do that, and we can report to our superiors that there have been no disturbances while Little Crow was here. Hmmm . . . you are leaving, aren't you?"

"Write the letter and we will leave," Little Crow concluded.

"Done," Dallas replied quickly. "I'm not just concerned about the Americans. The Ojibway, Cree, and the metis mixed-breeds might start a general war with you as well. We have been giving their men presents to keep them quiet. It's best you leave now." *And Pike shall be happy, too*, he thought.

The letter was a small consolation. Bitterness burned like gall in the stomachs of the Santee as they left to follow the Red River to Pembina, just inside Dakota Territory at St. Joseph.

ℬ 20 ℭ

ATE WINTER AND EARLY SPRING BROUGHT continued misery and bad news for the captives at Fort Snelling. Unseasonable warmth began to bake the soggy mush from the parade grounds. True to the fears of missionaries and soldiers alike, the flood plain below the fort bluff had filled with water. Colonel Crooks ordered the Indian camp to be moved back atop the bluff near the fort.

Then word came from Washington regarding the fate of the Santee. The United States Congress had passed a bill on February 16 abrogating and annulling all past treaties with the Sioux. Remaining annuity money was re-appropriated for a fund to reimburse the white victims of the Dakota War.

Next, on March 3, President Lincoln validated the concerns of Minnesota officials by signing the Indian Removal Act. This law ordered the transfer of all Dakota and Winnebago to land outside the boundaries of any state.

The measles epidemic had run its course. Somewhere between two and three hundred Dakota had succumbed to the disease. It was difficult to determine the exact number of deaths because few records were kept and some families buried their dead inside their tipis to spare them from the indignity of being buried in a mass burial pit.

And, while religious conversions continued at both Fort Snelling and Mankato at a high rate, the populace of Minneapolis and St. Paul did not greet the advent of new converts with Christian joy and gratitude.

The *News* and the *St. Paul Pioneer* regularly reported on the mass baptisms and confirmations held at Fort Snelling and at the prison in Mankato.

The *St. Paul Daily News* reported, "The murderers who raped and killed across western Minnesota now try to cheat their due retribution by turning to Christian baptism and confirmation. May God have mercy on the missionaries who aid these heathens and are cheating the hangman and Satan of their just reward in Hell."

The news brought forth ire from citizens and soldiers alike.

REVEREND STEPHEN RIGGS STARED STRAIGHT ahead as he briskly strode past townspeople and soldiers toward the fort beside the newly-constructed prison camp. While his eyes could focus on the distant enclosure, he couldn't shut off the catcalls and jeers that flooded over him.

"See, it's that man that saves Indians!" "Indian lover!" "He helps murderers!" "You mock God!"

As Riggs turned up an incline on the path to the fort, he heard a hawking sound and felt a juicy glob splat his crimson cheek. He pulled a handkerchief from his pocket and scrubbed his cheek as if he were scouring a frying pan. Keeping his eyes focused forward, the minister continued into Fort Snelling.

Once inside the limestone walls, Riggs turned toward the foot of the Round Tower, where Lieutenant McKusick and his colleagues had gathered. Hinman, John Williamson, Gideon Pond, and Father Ravoux were engaged in conversation. A bright morning sun shone down upon them, promising a pleasant day in spite of the chill in the early morning breeze.

"Reverend Riggs," McKusick greeted, "good to see you! We were just getting started. I see you made it through the gauntlet of our citizens all right."

"Mostly unscathed," Riggs answered as he rubbed his cheek again.

"Good." Then the lieutenant turned businesslike. "I've asked you to join me this morning to update you on some things that will concern you. I've been informed by Adjutant General Baker that the reprieved Indians at Mankato are to be transferred to Davenport, Iowa, for safe keeping. To turn them loose in Minnesota is deemed to be sure death for them at the hands of people like those you passed through on the way here."

"When will this happen?" Hinman asked.

"Soon, within the month, by the end of April for sure. It depends on steamboat availability and the status of the rivers. The Mississippi is still rising, owing to late-winter rains. When it and the Minnesota can be navigated, the steamboat will go to Mankato and pick up the red devils."

Riggs shifted uncomfortably at the insulting term. "What about the forty-eight found not guilty?" he wondered.

"They will be dropped off here to rejoin their families," McKusick answered. "The rest go on to Iowa."

"How many?" Riggs asked.

"About 270-some."

"What about the thirteen hundred or so we still have here?"

"Sometime in early May, they will be moved out as well. Somewhere near Fort Randall in Dakota Territory. Oh, by the way, we're rounding up the Winnebago to send there as well."

"Winnebago!" Riggs exclaimed with alarm. "Only a few can be proved to have participated at all in the war. They live peaceably south of the valley. Why them? This is wrong."

"A few here is too many. This is a good time to remove all Indians in southern Minnesota. The time has come for them to stop roving, to settle down and farm. They were included in the removal act signed by Lincoln."

"Because of the war or because they live on some of the richest farmland in North America?" Pond replied, sarcasm oozing from his voice.

"That's not for you to worry about," McKusick snapped. "Your task is humanitarian."

NATHAN AND EMILY STOOD ATOP THE round tower. They gazed down at the small cluster of men below as a solitary soldier watched the river flats from his post on the opposite side of the tower. Emily clutched a woolen shawl around her shoulders to fend off the chilly breeze that stretched icy fingers toward her.

"I've heard that the Santee will be moved soon," Nathan said. "I think that's what they're talking about down there."

"To Dakota Territory?" Emily wondered.

"It looks like it. Emily, what should we do?"

"I'll go wherever you want," she answered. "But we have a connection to these people. I think we should go with them into the Dakotas."

"Are you certain? It'll be rough out there. At least here civilization is nearby. Your parents live in Minneapolis. You could teach here."

"Nathan, remember that I previously gave this up for the frontier. I didn't have to go to the Lower Sioux Agency to teach. I could have stayed at home. I chose to go. I could choose to go again, if that's what you want."

Nathan smiled at his wife. "Then we'll go. I feel an attachment to the Santee. Because of what has happened to them. I still feel that somehow I'm partly responsible."

Emily reached out and clasped Nathan's hand. "You know that it would've all happened anyway. President Davis sent you here, but destiny had already set the course. The war would have come even if you had stayed in Virginia. Your coming here saved lives. It didn't cost them. And look at all you have done for Johnny."

She spoke of the teenaged Santee boy, the former student also known as Traveling Star. Johnny had lost his parents in the war and was under the care of Nathan and Emily.

"You saved his life, Nathan."

"After he saved yours," her husband said gently.

"He only has us. Even his uncles were killed."

"He can stay with us, Emily. When the Santee are sent out, we'll go with them. If you're sure?"

"I am most sure, Nathan. We need to finish what we've started with them."

"The teaching part or the killing?" Nathan asked grimly.

"The killing is past."

"Don't be so sure about that. It isn't over yet, Emily. The soldier in me feels it."

⚘ 21 ⚘

N EARLY APRIL THE MINNESOTA AND Mississippi rivers continued to rise steadily as spring rains washed through streams like faucets into the rivers. The long awaited time for successful steamboat navigation was at hand. For much of the year, steamboat travel was possible from St. Paul to Chaska. But travel up the river to Redwood and Yellow Medicine was possible only during high water, typically only in the spring. On April 13, after a spring thaw had filled the river, boat captain Asa Hutchinson maneuvered the *Favorite* alongside the wharf on the flats below Fort Snelling.

The steamboat was met by dozens of Dakota men and women. Under the watchful eyes of Fort Snelling guards, the prisoners unloaded 2,600 sacks of corn before the steamer pushed off to deliver military supplies at Yellow Medicine and then to pick up a far different cargo for the return trip.

At Mankato, Reverend Thomas Williamson sat inside the stockade's prison walls with an open Bible in his lap. The walls were of logs, and its sparse windows kept the room dim and starved for sunlight.

A couple hundred Dakota men huddled together in small groups. Some clutched red blankets around their shoulders to warm against the spring morning chill. A young Indian man sat alongside the cleric and followed Williamson's finger intently as it moved from word to word.

"Valley," the minister pronounced slowly, "V-A-L-L-E-Y. Now you." He nodded appreciatively as his student hesitantly pronounced and spelled the word. "Good, Red Fox, very good. Soon you'll be reading better than me." He smiled and patted the boy on the back.

A sudden shaft of bright light splashed like spilled paint upon the hard-packed earthen floor. Colonel Stephen Miller and two guards had pushed a door open and strode into the large space. Miller paced crisply to Williamson and beckoned him to rise.

"Reverend," the colonel said, "come here. I wish to speak with you." He stepped away from the others as Williamson stood.

"Keep practicing, Red Fox. I'll be back with you in a moment," the minister called over his shoulder as he joined Miller.

"Thomas," the colonel spoke softly, almost in a whisper, "the time has come. Soon the *Favorite* will arrive, and everyone here will be taken away."

"To where, Colonel?"

"Davenport, Iowa."

"All of them?" Williamson was incredulous. "What about those found innocent?"

"At first all were to be sent to Iowa. Reverend Riggs has intervened. The forty-eight acquitted Dakota will disembark at Fort Snelling to join the others there who will be sent to the Dakotas. The couple of dozen women and children who have been helping out here can go to Davenport if they wish."

"By my count, that means a little over 200 men will be imprisoned at Davenport."

"That's what we expect." Miller answered.

"When will the *Favorite* arrive?"

Miller paused thoughtfully before replying. "Hmmm, this is the twentieth. I expect the steamer tomorrow. Let the Indians know. My men will prepare them. I don't want any fuss from the citizens of Mankato, so we'll board after dark tomorrow night."

Williamson stood in the center of the prison floor and called for the Dakota to come to him. Soon they surrounded the pastor, leaving a circular space around him so that from above it looked as though he was standing in the middle of a large doughnut.

As Williamson explained what fate awaited them, the Dakota reacted in various ways. Many stood emotionless and stoic. Some, particularly the women, wailed in despair. A few began mournful chants.

A pretty young woman stood to the side and sobbed into a shawl. Williamson walked to her and gently placed a hand on her shoulder. "Don't fear what lies ahead. It'll be better than staying here."

"You don't understand, Reverend," the girl answered, "I cry for joy."

"What do you mean?"

"These soldiers, these guards, I'll be free of them. Never again will they abuse me and the other women. At least not here."

"How . . . what did they do?"

"Many nights the guards took us," she turned to hide the shame in her face, "they did whatever they wanted with us."

"I'm so sorry," Williamson offered, "I know words are not enough. But you'll leave here," conviction grew in his voice, "and I'll work to protect you and the others from the animals that prey on you."

As John walked from her, a guard smirked at the girl, "Hey, Little Bird, gonna miss me?"

Impulsively the pastor balled up his fist and smashed it directly into the soldier's face. The man tumbled backward and stared up with stunned surprise.

"Never," Williamson commanded, "will you touch Little Bird or any of these women again. Spread the word that the truth is out about scum like you."

John Williamson strode with purpose from the prison and reported directly to Colonel Miller. The colonel covered his eyes with one hand as if trying to wipe away the image of abuse. "Thank you, John. This is a damn shame. I'll try to stop it from happening again. I'll let the camp commanders at Fort Snelling and Davenport know to be alert for abuse there as well. But, John, you know that I can't make any guarantees. I can only try."

The next morning, shafts of cheerful pink sunlight danced through cracks in the prison's log walls. But the mood inside was somber. Blue-clad soldiers were busy shackling leg irons onto paired-up prisoners.

Among them was Joe Godfrey, the half-Indian, half-black refugee from the hangman's noose who had avoided execution by agreeing to help convict others. Many of the thirty-eight hanged at Mankato died as a result of his testimony. Thus, Godfrey escaped charges of murdering eighteen and was sentenced to ten years in prison. He was chained to another French-Indian mixed blood, Antoine Proicilli.

When dusk finally arrived, they trudged in awkward coordination, more than 100 pairs of men, over the gangplank and onto the steamer. On the way they passed through a gauntlet of soldiers who lined both sides of the path from the prison to the river.

Several lit torches held by the troopers revealed the gamut of emotions on the faces of the condemned as they passed by. Anguish, fear, apprehension, pride, and solemn acceptance were all evident. Many clutched red blankets sent to them by friends and relatives at Fort Snelling. Sixteen Indian women, two babies, and the forty-eight acquitted men accompanied the prisoners and shared their uncertainty.

Colonel Miller and the men of the Seventh Minnesota followed them up the gangplank and onto the steamboat.

That afternoon at Fort Snelling, Reverend Stephen Riggs preached to a mass gathering in the concentration camp near the fort. Dressed in a black frock coat and white shirt, he stood on a low rise in the ground before hundreds of Dakota people. Small droplets of sweat beaded upon his ample forehead as Riggs began to preach.

"I am so glad to see so many of you here today. I believe this is the largest gathering of Dakota people that I have spoken to. Today's text is on suffering. You know of how our Savior, Jesus Christ, suffered and died for you. How He was whipped and stabbed with a spear, how the crown of thorns ripped into His flesh. You know how He hung on the cross and endured great pain that you might have eternal life.

"Just last Sunday sixty-five more Dakota souls came to Christ through Holy Baptism. This is a great and wonderful thing. There are benefits that can be derived from suffering. Good can be found in bad. My fellow brothers in Christ and I have long been trying to decide how we could get the Gospel to the Yankton Dakota. Through your suffering, I now see a way. Through the example you set and by the witnessing that you can do, the message of the Gospel will reach the Yankton Dakota. By your trial and tribulation, good can come, and the souls of countless Yankton can receive salvation through our Savior, Jesus Christ."

Riggs continued speaking in the bright April sunshine. He elaborated on what he called "the Dakota mission of salvation," and supported his goals by reading lessons from the Bible. His listeners stood before him quietly absorbing his words. Some shifted from side to side on the soggy soil.

They were a disheveled-looking assemblage. Indian people customarily washed each day in available water. This was not possible within the confines of the stockade, and both the Dakota and their clothing showed the effects of months of imprisonment.

They were apprehensive, not only for themselves but also for their brothers at Mankato. Rumors had reached the Snelling Dakota that the Mankato prisoners would be moved, but they had no idea that at that very moment the *Favorite* was bringing them closer with each turn of the paddle.

༄ 22 ༅

THE *FAVORITE* WAS TYPICAL OF OTHER steamboats that plied the Mississippi. It was double-decked with a large side paddlewheel in the rear third. Atop the second deck, a high, black smokestack protruded near the stern. Just behind it, over the second deck, a small cabin stretched to nearly the center of the boat. A smaller steering cabin rested above the other structure, like a thimble resting on a cheese box.

Nearly 300 Dakota—the 207 convicts who were shackled together, the forty-eight acquitted, and numerous women—were crammed into the lower deck. Seventy-four soldiers were on the second deck when they weren't standing guard duty over the Dakota. Placed in charge of the prisoners by Colonel Miller was Major Joe Brown, formerly a government agent at the Lower Sioux Agency, and the husband of Harriet Brown, a Dakota woman who had been held captive by Little Crow until she was freed at Camp Release.

The Dakota men sat in sullen silence with heads bowed. Red blankets were draped over many shoulders. Private Silas Nordstrom walked among them with his musket held across his chest. Nordstrom was a big, burly, blonde Norwegian. His brother Ole and Ole's family had been killed in Kandiyohi County as they left a church service.

The burly private sharply kicked a chained foot out of his way as he walked before the Dakota. Staring over them with a malevolent sneer, he spat a brown stream of tobacco through his yellow-stained teeth. It splatted on the head of a middle-aged man, who glared up at Nordstrom with hate-filled eyes.

The soldier wiped the spittle from his short blonde beard and taunted, "Don't like a little spit, huh? Yust vait till ya get ta Ioway!"

When he was sure that all eyes were focused on him, Nordstrom smiled sardonically, made a jerking motion with his hand alongside his neck, and then snapped his neck down with his tongue hanging out. "Dat's vat's vaiting fer ya." Then, to make sure the Indians understood, he slowly drew his index finger across his throat in a cutting motion.

An angry clamor arose from the captive Dakota. Chains clanked as the men scrambled to their feet. Other guards, muskets cocked and ready, rushed to support Nordstrom. Women began to wail in terror. Suddenly a pistol shot blasted twice, and silence reigned as Joe Brown strode through the acrid, black smoke of the weapon he had fired.

"What in the name of God is going on here!" he demanded.

No one spoke. Only the eyes of the soldiers moved as they turned to Nordstrom. The big Norwegian shuffled his feet and explained sheepishly, "Aw, I vuz yust funnin' vit dem a little."

Brown glared daggers at the soldier. "I can imagine how you were having fun! There'll be no more of it. You," his eyes swept the faces of the dozen soldiers on the deck, "will not taunt these people again. Do you understand? You will not provoke them."

Next Brown turned his attention to the Dakota themselves. In their language he explained to them, "You have nothing to fear. No harm will come to you on this boat. When you get to Iowa, you will be confined. You will not be killed."

His words quieted the huddled captives, but apprehension still hung like a cloud of doom growing with each thump of the paddle.

The next day, two Santee men, Watca and Tawipe, tossed fishing lines into the Minnesota River below Fort Snelling. Several other men scattered along the riverbank were also fishing. In the distance a mournful, low whistle signaled the approach of a steamboat. Suddenly a company of soldiers appeared on the river levee.

Watca turned to Tawipe with questioning eyes. Then he peered intently at the nearing boat. "Look," he cried, "red blankets! It's our brothers from Mankato!"

"I see Dakota headdresses!" Tawipe answered. "You're right!"

Word spread like a bolt of lightening along the shore and up the bank to the fort and camp. In minutes a mass of Indian men, women, and children swarmed down the bank to the river flats and the levee. There they encountered a rocklike barrier of soldiers holding fast between the river and the crush of Indians.

A sergeant cried, "Bayonets at the ready!" The company lowered their Springfield rifles, and bayonets glistened in the sunlight. "Hold, men, hold!" he shouted.

Colonel Crooks himself appeared as the *Favorite* neared the wharf. Women screamed as the names of sons, husbands, fathers, and brothers rang out from the throng. The steamboat docked, and the gangplank slammed onto the wharf with a thud. The prisoners crammed against the boat railings, desperately seeking faces of their loved ones, waving frantically when they found one.

Forty-eight Indian men were hurried down the plank onto the levee. Then, to the consternation of the gathering on the bank, the plank was quickly withdrawn and the paddles began to churn the boat away.

Wails again pierced the air, and the crowd turned menacing as it shoved forward. Crooks stood atop the levee, pistol in hand. Two quick shots blasted from his weapon. The Indians fell silent.

"Those found not guilty are freed!" he shouted. "The others are not to be hanged. Nothing will happen to them! They are being taken downriver to another place, another guard. They will not be killed!

While his assurance served to calm some of the Indians, cries of fear and lamentation followed the *Favorite* down the river, cries usually reserved for the dead.

∞ 23 ≪

HENRY SIBLEY RODE INTO FORT SNELLING upon a prancing black horse. Bugles and drumbeats signaled his arrival as grandly as if he were a Roman emperor. He rode directly to the far end of the compound to the commander's quarters. McKusick, Crooks, and Riggs stepped from the building's white-pillared porch and stood at attention in the frosty morning sunshine.

Sibley reined his horse before them, dismounted and returned the salutes of the two who were soldiers. "Gentlemen," he relayed crisply, "things are coming to a head here. I've come to inform you."

"My quarters are open for you," Crooks replied as he gestured to the open front door.

Sibley took the offer and was followed into the building by the three others. The general took the liberty of standing behind Crooks desk as he gestured to the men to be seated.

"I'll get right to the point. The Pierre Chouteau, Jr., and Company have been awarded a contract. The United States Government will pay twenty-five dollars per person to transport each Dakota, with food provided for each at ten cents per day. The Winnebago will be moved as well."

"The Winnebago?" Riggs questioned. "I still insist they played little or no role in the uprising."

"No matter," Sibley snapped. "It's time to move them all. For their own safety."

"When? How?" Crooks asked.

"Soon. In the first week of May the *Northerner* and the *Davenport* will arrive. They will transport all Dakota by two different routes. The *Davenport* will travel down the Mississippi to St. Louis, where the cargo will be transferred to the *Florence* for the journey up the Missouri. The *Northerner* will go down the Mississippi to Hannibal, Missouri. From there they'll traverse Missouri by train to St. Joseph. At St. Joseph, they'll rendezvous with the *Florence* and join the other Indians on the steamboat. They will all be transported to Crow Creek Reservation in Dakota Territory."

Crooks pulled at the dark beard on his chin. "Thirteen hundred Dakota on a steamboat built to take about half that many. How will that work?"

"They'll just have to crowd together a little. It'll be a short trip from St. Joseph."

Crooks considered this a moment and then replied, "If you call about sixteen hundred miles a short trip, I guess you're right."

"Colonel, you said thirteen hundred Indians. I thought there were sixteen hundred here."

"Well, General, it seems we lost about 300. Measles and other sickness took them."

"Pity. One more thing, Crooks," Sibley concluded, "you'll still have some to watch over here. A few dozen have signed up for the expedition after Little Crow. Their families will remain here, under your care. Also, it's likely more will be rounded up and sent to Fort Snelling."

WORD OF THE IMPENDING DEPARTURE SWEPT like a flood through the fort and the camp. For many, hope mixed with apprehension. Wabasha addressed the council of his band leaders. They sat in a circle around a smoldering fire.

"Soon, we go to Crow Creek. Keep your bands together," Wabasha advised. "Tell them wherever we go, it'll be better than here."

"They'll make us all into farmers," Passing Hail said. "I hope the land is good."

Red Legs complained. "There will still be guards. We'll still be in a prison."

Sadness crept over Wabasha's wrinkled face. "At least the prison will be large, and we'll have room."

"For what?" Good Road wondered. "We have few men. Most are women and children."

"Children grow," Wabasha answered. "We have a new life before us. It must be better than this."

THE MINISTERS AND TEACHERS OF FORT SNELLING also had decisions to make. They met in the warehouse alongside the fort. Reverend Thomas Williamson, the Pond brothers, Hinman, Riggs, John Williamson and Father Ravoux were joined by Nathan and Emily Cates. They sat at a long wooden table. Shadows flickered in yellow candlelight as the setting sun rested like a disc on the western horizon.

Thomas Williamson spoke first. "The Dakota will be moved out soon. I'm sure that eventually all of us will spend some time at Crow Creek. I'll be leaving shortly for Davenport, where the reprieved from Mankato are still incarcerated. My son, John, will be leaving on the *Northerner* to make the trip to Dakota Territory. Who else intends to go?"

"General Sibley has asked me to accompany his expedition into the Dakotas. I have agreed," Riggs answered. "I'll go with the army."

Young Samuel Hinman, pastor at Lower Sioux when the attack came there, rubbed his bare cheeks thoughtfully, his jawline framed by a dark beard. "I'll go. I felt like my mission at Lower Sioux was cut short. There must be something more."

"Go on the *Davenport*," Riggs suggested.

"Anyone else?" Williamson wondered. Silence prevailed as the minister looked over the small group.

Nathan cleared his throat and looked at Emily. She nodded yes and smiled.

"Emily and I will go. They'll need teachers there."

Thomas Williamson smiled. "Good, I was hoping you'd come with us. You've done marvels here, and you'll be needed at Crow Creek. Does anyone know about Miss Miller?"

Nathan had the answer. "I believe that Dr. Wharton's going and that Miss Miller plans to go, too."

"We shall be well represented. Let us pray."

Thomas Williamson prayed over the heads bowed around the table, asking for guidance in the tasks before them. They knew a new life was beginning for many, both red and white.

✂ 24 ✃

MAY 4 DAWNED DARK AND OVERCAST. Clouds laden heavily with moisture hung menacingly over the Minnesota River. JoAnna, Nathan, and Emily stood on the levee near the wharf. The gangplank from the *Davenport* was down and ready for cargo to be loaded.

The three peered with anticipation up the bluff toward Fort Snelling and the camp.

The two women held their long gray capes tightly at their necks as the garments flapped in the early morning breeze. Nathan placed his arm around Emily's shoulder and held her close to comfort as well as warm her.

"Have you written Jesse?" Emily asked JoAnna.

"I sent a letter to Fort Ridgely. I think he'll be there soon."

"I'm guessing he won't like what you've written very much," Nathan commented. "He won't like that you're going to Crow Creek. When are you getting married?"

JoAnna sighed softly, her eyes moist. "Once I was eager to marry right away. Jesse cautioned against it until the war was over. The War Between the States, he meant. I didn't want to wait, but I agreed. Now he wants to marry soon, but he was right before, whether he wants to admit it or not.

"Both of us have our own tasks before us until the war is over. Then will be the time to marry. But Nathan, you're right. He won't like this."

Emily gently placed her hand on JoAnna's shoulder. "It's too bad that Jesse can't go with you, like Nathan is with me."

"I'm a nurse. Jesse is a soldier. I know that Nathan was a soldier, but now you both can serve together by teaching. Jesse's determined to see this war through by staying in the middle of the fight."

A camp holding several hundred former black slaves, now considered contraband in the war, had been established the day before. The former slave status put them in a no-man's-land category. They had escaped from states currently engaged in the rebellion, but they had not been given free status. Considered contraband of war, they were paid eight dollars a month if they served the Union. These men had been brought north to serve as mule drivers for Sibley's coming expedition west.

The strains of a low, mournful song emanating from the former slaves in the camp echoed up to the three friends. "Swing low, sweet char-i-ot, comin' fo' to carry me home."

"Pretty, isn't it?" Emily remarked.

"Yes, poor devils," Nathan answered. "Yesterday when they got here off the *Davenport* some of the Dakota passed by their camp. It was kind of funny. The blacks and the reds stared wide-eyed at each other. I think the former slaves thought that their people were about the most mistreated and degraded people on Earth. Then they got a good look at the Indians and re-alized that some have it even worse."

JoAnna added, "I imagine that many Indians were surprised to see that there are those with darker skin than theirs."

"Look!" Nathan pointed up the path leading from the fort. "Here they come!"

The lodges in the Indian camp had been struck. Everything the Dakota had in the world was slung over the backs of the Indian women and held in place by straps around their foreheads.

Seven hundred and seventy, the first to be shipped to Crow Creek, trudged in military order toward the waiting steamboat. Wabasha took the lead. His band was followed by the bands of Good Road, Wacouta, Passing Hail, and Red Legs. A high percentage of them were women and children. The total number of men in the camp was 176. Some would leave on the next steamboat.

Forty men of the Tenth Regiment, Company G, Minnesota Volun-teers, were led by Captain Saunders to the wharf. Reverend Hinman walked alongside the soldiers until he spied Nathan, Emily, and JoAnna.

The pastor bounded over to them and tried to contain the excitement in his voice. "Are you ready?"

Nathan reached down and picked up a full satchel. "Yes, Reverend, Emily and I are ready to board. JoAnna leaves tomorrow with John Williamson on the *Northerner*."

Emily and JoAnna embraced quickly in farewell. Then JoAnna reached up around Nathan's neck. As he bent down, she impulsively brushed her lips to his cheek.

"Take care," she said. "I'll see you at St. Joseph. That's where we meet again for the last leg of the trip, isn't it?"

"Yes," Nathan smiled, "you take care, too. We'll see you in St. Joseph."

He and Emily fell in with Samuel Hinman behind the disconsolate file of Dakota people.

The two main decks of the *Davenport* were soon filled with Indians and their forty-man army escort. Hinman shook his head sadly as he stood with the Cates by a railing.

"It already seems crowded," the pastor marveled. "How can they expect to cram over 500 more on here at St. Joseph?"

"They'll find a way," Nathan answered, "and if a few die along the way, I'm afraid the attitude will be, 'good riddance, more room for the others.' It's four days to St. Louis. I don't think they'll all make it."

Emily shook her head in dismay. "And these are the good Indians. What have they done to deserve this?"

"They were born Indians. That's enough for the State of Minnesota right now," Hinman replied.

The first stop was only a few miles away. The *Davenport* made a scheduled half-hour stop in St. Paul to take on cargo. A crowd of soldiers had formed on the levee. Soon they were buoyed by townspeople, who began to push toward the steamboat.

One man dressed in a blue soldier's blouse struggled to climb upon a crate. Two men helped him up. He had struggled in part because of a lame leg.

The man perched on the crate and waved a crutch in the air. He shouted at the growing mass. "I lost the use of my leg at Birch Coulee. Now these red devils are gettin' away! They killed 800 of our friends and relatives, and what'd we do for 'em. We took care of 'em all winter and even gave 'em religion. Now our guv'ment sends 'em to the Dakotas and gives 'em more land. Not so fast, I say. Not so fast! I've got a little piece of Minnesota right here in my hand." He held up a rock. "Let's send more of our state with 'em!" With those words, the man heaved the rock toward the mass of Indians on the steamer.

Instantly a barrage of rocks and stones filled the slate-gray sky and rained down onto the Santee. Women and children screamed in agony and fear as the missiles found their marks. On the closely-packed boiler deck, several women crumbled like rag dolls as rocks cracked onto their heads.

Nathan pushed soldiers and Indians alike aside as he searched for

Captain Saunders. Finally he found the young red-haired soldier. "Captain, you must stop this!" Nathan shouted.

"H-h-how?" stuttered the obviously shaken officer.

"Form your men, fix bayonets and threaten to charge into the crowd. They're cowards. They'll disperse at a show of force."

"I'm not sure."

"Do it!" Nathan commanded. "NOW!"

Saunders swallowed a gulp and yelled, "Company G, form at the gang-plank, fix bayonets and advance. DO NOT CHARGE UNLESS ORDERED."

As the troops gathered at the gangplank, Captain Saunders stood before them. "Advance slowly. Form a line and push them back."

The captain drew his sword and strode before his men onto the wharf. "DISPERSE!" he screamed at the crowd. Then he dodged a rock that whizzed by his head.

"MEN, FORM A LINE AND FIRE A VOLLEY OVER THEIR HEADS." Saunders waited a moment until men formed, and then shouted, "READY, AIM, FIRE!"

A ragged volley from Springfield muskets blasted into the air. A strained silence hung above them as if by a precarious thread. The faces of the mob of soldiers and citizens on the levee contorted with ugly hatred.

Saunders shouted at them, "LEAVE NOW OR THE NEXT VOL-LEY WON'T BE OVER YOUR HEADS!"

For a moment no one moved. Tension filled the air. No one knew which side would give first. Then the soldiers reloaded, and the mob froze, some clenching rocks in their hands. The man on the crate broke the stalemate.

"Let's go!" he cried. "We made our point!"

With that the crowd retreated off the levee and dispersed.

Nathan, standing next to Saunders commented, "Good job, Captain. The courage of cowards is only paper thin. You did the right thing."

"You knew what to do. Thank you," the young officer replied. "How . . . ?"

Nathan's answer was brief. "Experience." He walked back to the steamboat, and a short time later they were churning down the Mississippi, away from St. Paul and Minnesota, to a new life and uncertainty.

The next day the *Northerner*, carrying John Williamson, JoAnna, Dr. Wharton, a military escort ,and 547 Santee Dakota, also departed Fort Snelling bound for Crow Creek.

ᔣ 25 ᔥ

THE MOUNTED RANGERS RODE INTO Fort Ridgely on May 6. The fort was made up of a rectangle of gray stone buildings. The long barracks comprised most of the south end and was the largest building.

The fort stood high above the Minnesota River and had withstood two attacks during the war in August. The Santees' failure to take the fort had slammed the door shut on taking the valley, and the Indians had sealed their ultimate defeat.

Major Duley rode at the head of a column of twos. Solomon Foot and Jesse rode several horse lengths behind.

"Hasn't changed much," Solomon said as he scanned the fort. "I see they still have the barricades and breastworks up in the spaces between the walls."

"They won't be taking them down anytime soon. The war might be over, but attacks are still happening."

"Sure they are, Jesse. A few Indians here and there might kill a lone white man or two. But the real fighting's over. They won't make another massed attack like they did here."

"Not as long as we're ready for them, Solomon."

The column passed to the north end of the rectangle where the headquarters building stood. A large barn stood beyond the headquarters, just outside the fort proper. The troops rode on ahead to the barn while Jesse, Solomon, and Major Duley dismounted at the white-porched building that served as headquarters.

A dark-haired, mustached young man strode down the porch steps. He wore a wide grin as he greeted the three men. "Solomon, Jesse! How good to see you. Major Duley, I met you once last winter." His face turned solemn. "You were at Shetek, weren't you."

"Yes," was Duley's clipped response.

"I'm Lieutenant Timothy Gere, temporarily in charge here. At least until I go south to fight rebs."

"This young man was a real hero here last August," Solomon explained to Duley. "Twenty-some soldiers was all that was left in here. Four hundred Sioux outside, and Tim here held them off."

"Only because reinforcements came. And then I got sick." Gere looked at Duley and touched himself under the chin. "Mumps, and I couldn't have got them at a worse time. Lucky Sheehan got here to take over. The reds had twice as many in the second attack."

"From what I hear, it was lucky that Sergeant Jones had cannon-firing drills. The big guns drove 'em off."

"We had a lot of luck. Remember, we lost Captain Marsh and twenty-four men at Redwood Ferry just two days before the attack here."

"Fool!" Duley snapped. "He thought he could go to Lower Sioux and reason with them."

An awkward silence hung in the air before Gere replied evenly, "Captain Marsh was a good man." Then he brightened, patted his shirt and pulled out a letter, and handed it over to Jesse.

"It came yesterday. It's for you. I knew you were near and kept it for you." The young lieutenant made an exaggerated swipe of the envelope past his nose and exclaimed, "Sure smells good! This didn't come from no stable hand."

Jesse grinned sheepishly as he took the letter from Gere and eagerly glanced down at the envelope. "It's from JoAnna. Excuse me." Hurrying to the headquarters porch, he roosted on a step and anxiously ripped the envelope open. His breath caught at the familiar sight of JoAnna's elegant handwriting.

Dearest Jesse,

I hope this letter finds you well. I know you've been on the move from Sauk Centre. I will be going as well. Jesse, dear, I'm going to Crow Creek with the Sioux. Dr. Wharton has asked me to be his nurse there. Don't fear for me. The hostiles will be far away. I know that we could not be together anyway, that you are going with General Sibley to the Dakota Territory in pursuit of Little Crow and those who committed atrocities in Minnesota.

I hate war. When it is all over we will be together as God intends.

Maybe your travels with Sibley will take you near Crow Creek. It would be so wonderful if we could see each other there.

I will love you always.

Your JoAnna

Jesse sat in numbed silence, his head in his hands. Solomon walked to him. "Somethin' wrong, boy?"

Jesse wordlessly handed him the letter.

The older man read the note and placed his hand on Jesse's shoulder. "I've seen worse. She wants you. It's just taking a little more time. What with you traipsing all over the Dakotas, you weren't going to be with her anyhow."

"But at least she would have been safe, at home."

"Jesse, in this world we never know what's safe and what isn't. We're in God's hands, boy. That's the way it is."

Jesse called to Gere, "Tim, have the boats left for Crow Creek yet?"

"One left yesterday and one the day before."

Jesse buried his head in his hands again. "So close! If only I could have gotten to St. Paul."

Solomon looked sympathetically at his young friend. "It wouldn't have done you any good, boy. Some things are meant to be, and they have their own way of working out for the best. You'll see."

"I hope you're right, Solomon, I really do. Tim, when do you think we'll be moving out?"

"I've heard that General Sibley is assembling his army in early June. The rendezvous camp will be near Redwood Agency. I know that companies of the Sixth, Seventh, and Tenth Minnesota have been ordered there. Plus a lot more, like you. Sibley named it Camp Pope after our commander. You're to go there and work with other early arrivals to establish the starting point for the expedition. By mid-June you should be on the way to Dakota Territory."

"The sooner, the better!" Jesse proclaimed. "I want this to end, and it won't until we hunt the Sioux down and finish it."

Camp Pope had been established about four miles from where the Redwood River emptied into the Minnesota. The First Minnesota Mounted Cavalry joined a few other early arriving companies. Over the next few days, the trickle of arrivals turned into a steady stream, and a sea of tents swelled on the prairie.

∽ 26 ∾

ONCE ON THE RIVER, WITH THE STEAMER paddling away from St. Paul, the Santee quieted. Pastor Hinman tried to help pass time by leading them in hymn sings. For much of the journey to St. Louis, people stood along the riverbanks and gazed with curiosity as songs of praise drifted over the water from the steamboat.

A deathly silence enveloped the decks as they passed the stockade at Davenport, where the Mankato prisoners were now kept. The passengers peered hard into the distance, hoping to catch a glimpse of someone they knew. But it was too far to recognize anyone.

Hinman turned to Emily and Nathan. "I've heard that Dr. Thomas Williamson asked Reverend Riggs to join him in the Davenport confinement. Word is that they have songbooks, and Stephen is teaching them to sing. I'm told they are organized into tribal clans and belt out the tunes enthusiastically."

"Apparently it offers some comfort." Nathan paused as strains of "The Old Rugged Cross" reverberated around them from the deck below.

"They need comfort," Emily added. "Look what they are given to eat and drink, dirty water, musty hardtack, and briny pork."

"Will it be better at Crow Creek?" Nathan wondered.

Hinman sighed. "We can hope. At least they'll be able to produce their own food."

Two days later dissatisfaction boiled over. While soldiers were distributing food, one Indian indignantly fired back a moldy green piece of salt pork at a soldier. Other Dakota men rose to their feet and moved on the blue coats. Pushing and shoving led to shouts to desist and finally to gunfire. Three Dakota men were killed. There were no more disruptions.

The *Davenport* reached St. Louis on May 8. There the Indian "cargo" was transferred to another paddleboat, the *Florence*, for the journey up the Missouri River. At St. Joseph, Missouri, they would pick up the second group of Santee passengers from Minnesota.

THE *NORTHERNER* HAD LEFT FORT SNELLING several days earlier, on May 5. JoAnna, Dr. Wharton and John Williamson, along with a company of soldier escorts and 547 Dakota people, had an uneventful four-day voyage to Hannibal, Missouri. There the Indians were herded into boxcars, sixty per car, for the trip across Missouri to St. Joseph and the rendezvous with the *Florence*.

Reverend Williamson complained to Dr. Wharton. "Can't you do something about this? They're crammed worse than cattle into those cars. No sanitary facilities, horrible food, and they'll bake in there in the hot sun. This is inhumane."

"Yes, you're right, but there isn't much I can do about it. I've already lodged a protest. We do have one silver lining. Look." Wharton pointed to a growing cloudbank in the west. "Those clouds will bring rain and cool things off. If we're lucky, it'll stay with us awhile."

Luck was indeed with them as the clouds and moisture lasted a couple of days. The party arrived at St. Joseph before the *Florence*. The Santee were herded into a stockyard to await their fellow tribesmen and their women.

In mid-May the *Florence* docked at St. Joseph. Soldiers squeezed over 500 more people onto the hurricane and boiler decks, which were now packed closer than a canister of sardines.

John Williamson and JoAnna were overjoyed to rejoin Hinman and the Cates. But their happy reunion was quickly replaced by the solemn despair before them. From the bow of the boat they watched as soldiers poked and prodded the Dakota people into position.

Nathan stared in sad disbelief. "There isn't even room for all to sit at the same time. They'll have to sleep in shifts."

"Or just sleep standing up. They'd be held upright by other bodies even while sleeping," Hinman suggested.

"I watched closely as we left Minnesota," Williamson remarked. "As they gazed at their native hills for the last time, it was if a dark cloud, a huge weight, was crushing their hearts. Things will get better, they were told, but this brings no relief. The shock, the anxiety, the confinement . . . and the pitiful diet brings sickness."

JoAnna asked, "Were those on the *Davenport* treated the same? Stale hardtack and briny pork, with no chance to cook?"

"Yes," Emily answered, "and diseases are becoming rampant. Especially for the elderly and the babies." She paused and wiped a tear from her eye. "We stopped several times along the way for burials."

"Maybe Crow Creek will provide some relief, a better life," Williamson hoped.

Nathan gazed unwaveringly at the massed throng before him. "Don't count on it, Reverend. I don't think our government is turning any Garden of Eden over to these people."

The five watched as the Dakota seemed to be straining, pushing, to open a pathway through the crush. By turning sideways and shuffling forward, Wabasha managed to reach the small party of whites. He made no attempt to brush away the tears that traced the deep wrinkles of his face.

"What are you doing to my people?" he demanded in a voice thick with emotion. "Every day it is worse. Now for 800 miles more we must live like this. Can you do nothing?"

"We are here," Williamson said softly and sadly. "But until we reach Crow Creek, I don't know what we can do. I agree that the boat and food supplies are horribly inadequate. I've spoken with Captain Saunders and the boat pilot, Hutchinson. They'll get us to Crow Creek as quickly as possible."

Anger flashed like hot embers in Wabasha's dark eyes. "So the only way for more room is for people to die. That will happen. You will have more room soon."

With those words, the Indian leader returned to his people. The whites watched sadly as Wabasha was engulfed by the human sea of agony.

"It only gets worse," Williamson commented. "Soon the Winnebago will depart Minnesota for Crow Creek as well."

The days blurred together as the paddleboat navigated the twists and turns of the Missouri River. Hinman and Williamson tried to break the monotony with hymns, but with each day, the enthusiasm for singing died a little more. Eventually the hungry cries of sick children and the moans of the elderly drowned out the songs.

The green of Minnesota became a cherished memory as the beloved lakes and hills gave way to a sun-scorched, treeless brown. But the Santee got temporary relief from their miserable crowding when the *Florence* docked at Fort Randall in the southern Dakota Territory on the afternoon of May 28. They were herded to an open space alongside the fort. Nathan and Emily walked nearby.

"Emily, no trees anywhere. The land above the fort is all barren and worthless. I've heard it hardly rains in the summer. Crow Creek can't be much different."

"How does anyone expect them to live here, much less to farm and grow crops?" Emily pondered.

"They can't live here, not the way the government wants, anyway."

"Oh, Nathan, it'll be better farther north. I know it will. It has to be."

Nathan peered intently to the northwest and the brown bluffs that lined the side of the wide river. "Don't count on it, Emily."

***

THE *FLORENCE* FINALLY REACHED Fort Thompson, site of the Crow Creek Reservation, on June 1. The cluster of whites from Minnesota stood on a nearby hill and watched as the Santee were dumped from the boat onto their new home.

The Indians hunched their shoulders as furious gusts of hot wind stung their skin with little missiles of sand. Williamson reached down and clutched a handful of the sandy earth. When he held it out in his open palm, the wind instantly swept it away. "This dry, parched ground will grow nothing!" he exclaimed.

"My God!" Hinman agreed. "We have brought them to a living Hell!"

JoAnna squinted her eyes into slits against the wind. Tears traced muddy rivulets down her wind-dirtied face. "May God help us all," she whispered.

~ 27 ~

A S THE MINNESOTA SANTEE WERE arriving at Crow Creek, Little Crow was preparing to leave St. Joseph for Devils Lake. Disturbing news reached him before he departed. Pawn had sent a rider to deliver a message. The young man told the disheartened leader, "Pawn greets Little Crow. He says to tell you that the Long Trader is massing an army on the upper Minnesota not far from Yellow Medicine. Pawn says that a great army is being formed and that they are coming for you. Pawn is continuing to raid by the Big Woods, and his band, though few in number, has many kills of whites. He says he will meet you at Devils Lake."

"I think maybe he shouldn't have left us in the first place. Take down the lodge poles!" cried Little Crow. "We go back to Devils Lake."

With that, Towacin, a young man who had followed Little Crow from Minnesota, lost his final scrap of patience. He strode to the war chief and spoke respectfully but directly. "Little Crow is a great leader in war. But that time is past. There are many of us who will follow you no more."

Little Crow glared sharply at Towacin. "Don't be a fool. What would you do? Surrender to Sibley? Stay with me. It is your only chance to live free."

The young rebel gathered himself and replied resolutely, "Your days of living free are done and so are ours. We will give ourselves up rather than get caught and die in a trap with you."

Little Crow turned south while nearly half of those who had gone north with him stayed behind. Twenty lodges and almost forty people remained on the Pembina River. It was June 5, 1862.

More trouble awaited the returning Mdewakanton at Devils Lake. Standing Buffalo greeted Little Crow as he entered their village. The Sisseton leader met the Mdewakanton with a stony glare and then motioned for him to walk to the point of a peninsula that stretched into the lake.

Sisseton and Wahpeton leaders sat in a circle around a lively campfire as they awaited the Mdewakanton. Little Crow, White Spider, and

Inkpaduta sat on the ground with the others. A bright June sun hung in the noontime sky. Standing Buffalo narrowed his eyes as he peered at the yellow globe. Then he turned a face like worn granite to Little Crow and handed him a long-stemmed pipe fashioned from red stone.

"Smoke," he said. "Then we talk."

Each man in turn puffed from the sacred pipe and then passed it on until all in the circle had smoked. Then Standing Buffalo stood with the circle and spoke.

"I was not for your war." He looked hard at Little Crow. "When I heard of the killings at Acton and the agency, it made my heart sick and sad. I knew that our lives would never be the same. Yet, I came to you with my warriors."

"Not all of them!" Little Crow snapped disgustedly. "If all had fought, it would have been different."

"It is true the Sisseton and Wahpeton were divided about the war. Red Iron and Little Paul and many others stayed out of the fighting."

"Red Iron blocked our escape route from Sibley. He would have fought us if we passed over his land." Little Crow spat out the words as he rose to his feet.

Shouting, he turned to the circle of Dakota. "Join me now! It is not too late! There are horses and much of value in Minnesota. Follow me. We will raid into their land, land that is really ours!"

He gazed down and was met by a circle of faces devoid of expression. Standing Buffalo faced Little Crow and responded, "Only fools would follow you now. Because of you, we can never return to Minnesota. We've lost our annuity payments forever. We're in danger, too, because the Long Trader will come hunting you and may find us. Sibley will take the war beyond the Minnesota River Valley. He'll take it to us, and we'll never be able to plant our maize and live by the big stone lake again. It's because of you, and we won't follow you again. Leave us."

Little Crow's face clouded over like a gathering storm. He motioned to White Spider and Inkpaduta, who scrambled to their feet. As they angrily stomped away from the circle, Little Crow turned and yelled over his shoulder, "Fools!"

When they arrived at their camp, the Mdewakanton chief was heartened to see Pawn, who stood by as women erected a tipi.

"My heart is glad to see you," Little Crow greeted. "What can you tell me of Minnesota?"

"I have much to say. Let us talk," Pawn answered.

"Stop," the chief commanded the women. "We won't camp here anymore. Soon we'll leave. Talk to me, Pawn."

"Sibley's army will march soon. He has many men. They will come looking for you and all who fought the whites in the valley. Will no one help us?"

The haughty demeanor that Little Crow had tried to hold collapsed. He hung his head and confessed, "No, there's no one. The Grandmother's Country turned us away. The Ojibway grow fat in the north and will not leave. The Sisseton and Wahpeton are frightened women and only want to make peace with Sibley. The Yankton hide in their brown hills and the Teton stay away to the west. Now even my Mdewakanton are afraid to stand against the whites. There will be no alliance. We are alone."

"What will you do?" Pawn asked.

"I will go into Minnesota, and we will raid! Who will go with me? Who is yet a warrior?"

White Spider, Heyoka, and Wowinape stepped forward to stand with their leader. "More will follow," White Spider predicted. "What of you, Inkpaduta, and you, Pawn?"

Inkpaduta had stood hesitantly in the background. Now when called upon he spoke. "I'm not a woman, and I'm not a coward. But I won't fight with you, Little Crow. I don't wish to return to Minnesota. Our life is not there anymore. I'll fight, but I'll fight Sibley as he comes to the Dakotas. We'll kill him as he comes to us."

"Pawn?" Little Crow questioned, astonished.

"I'll go with Inkpaduta. I've been back to Minnesota. It's not for me anymore. We did attack, we killed whites north of the valley. A soldier and another man were driving cattle to Fort Abercrombie. We attacked their camp and killed them. The man's name was Silas Foot." Pawn's chest expanded with pride like a puffed-up rooster.

"You killed the brother of Solomon Foot of the Kandiyohi lakes? It is *washta*, good," Little Crow murmured. "Solomon was not a friend of the Santee."

"I left a raven on his chest," Pawn said proudly, "as you left a dead crow on the bodies of whites you killed. It's my sign. I left ravens on the chests of those I killed at Shetek as well. I let all know what I have done by my sign."

"By your sign, you have told the whites who killed Silas Foot. His brother will come for you now."

"And so will Duley and the others. I don't care. I'll kill all who come for me, just as we did at Shetek."

"Most of those were women and children. This will be different. But, both of you do what you want, go where you want," Little Crow said with resignation. "One last time, I'll go back to Minnesota. I have six children left. I'll get a horse for each of them."

"Be careful and trust no one," Pawn warned. "The whites offer money for Indian scalps. They'll pay much for yours."

Little Crow reached on top of his head and tugged a handful of gray-black hair. "It will not be easy to take, let them try!" the chief proclaimed. He turned to White Spider.

"Brother, go west to the Mandan, they are our last hope for help. Send word of what they say. I will not continue into Minnesota if the Mandan will help us against the whites."

Within the hour, Little Crow turned to the east. Only seventeen men followed him. The man who had commanded 800 at the attack on Fort Ridgely and had led thousands of Santee was down to a handful. Inkpaduta and Pawn rode west.

⁊ 28 ⱦ

C AMP POPE SWELLED IN SIZE DURING the first weeks of June as companies that had been traversing the Minnesota frontier now flowed to the launching point of the Sibley Expedition to the Dakotas.

The camp was located on the Redwood River about four miles from where it entered the Minnesota. The tents were erected in the midst of destruction wrought by the war the previous summer. Charred ruins stood as lonely testaments to the 1862 rampage. Grass and wildflowers grew over fresh graves.

General Sibley arrived on June 10 to oversee the final stages of preparation before the expedition west began. He reached Camp Pope with a heavy cloud of impending doom over him. His seven-year-old daughter, Mary, was deathly ill. Three days after his arrival, Sibley's worst fears were realized. Word came that his dear daughter, his Mamie, had died.

Stephen Riggs brought the tragic news and offered counsel to his friend. Tears formed in the general's eyes as he slumped against a tree. He kept mumbling, "My dear lamblike little Mamie."

Riggs put his hand on his friend's shoulder. "It was God's will. It's hard, I know, but it's beyond us. She's in Paradise now."

"She was my favorite, you know," Sibley moaned softly, "and poor Sarah, alone in Mendota. I should be with her. I've left her alone to bury our child, the third one we've lost. And," his voice cracked, "she's pregnant again. This notice came from our doctor. I've received no letter from Sarah."

"She's mourning, too. You'll hear from her soon."

"Stephen, I've endured much since I left Ohio, but nothing is as bad as this, not war, not deprivation, nothing."

SOLOMON FOOT SAT ON A TREE STUMP HOLDING a steaming tin cup of coffee. He blew gently over the top of the fluid and cautiously took a sip.

"Whew! A mite too hot," he winced as he looked at Jesse, who sat on a nearby log.

"Be careful, Solomon, we're moving out soon. We'd hate to leave you behind with an injured mouth."

"No chance of that." Solomon gazed beyond the camp at a ruined building in the distance. "It's good so many are showing up. This place was too quiet, burned buildings, graves here and there—it seemed more like a sepulcher than a camp."

"It's lively now," Jesse remarked. He paused and listened to the sounds of whinnying horses, sergeants barking orders as men drilled, gunshots as soldiers fired weapons, and pots and pans clanging.

"Have you heard when we leave, Jesse?"

"We were told mid-June. Today's the fourteenth. Can't leave too early. We have a lot of horses and cattle that need forage, and it takes longer for grass to grow in the Dakotas. We have officers' call shortly. I'll know more then."

Corporal Willie Sturgis approached with an envelope in his hand. His long, angular body seemed apprehensive as he held the message to Solomon. "Mista Foot," he said, "this here came fer ya."

When Solomon took the paper, Willie, who was usually gregarious, turned and left.

Foot looked at the envelope. "It's from my wife, Adeline. She's back in Sauk Centre with the little Foots." He ripped it open and unfolded a sheet of paper which he read silently, his face expressionless. When he was finished, Solomon looked at Jesse and said tonelessly, "My brother Silas is dead. He was herding cattle by Fort Abercrombie with a soldier. Indians killed him. There was a dead raven on his chest."

"Pawn did it! I'm sorry, Solomon."

"Silas was a good man. I have many great memories, especially deer huntin' with him. I want Pawn."

"You may get your chance. I've got to get to officers' call, Solomon. Are you okay?"

"Just tell Sibley I'm ready."

HENRY HASTINGS SIBLEY, FIRST GOVERNOR of Minnesota and now the general of the state's army, stood beneath a leafy green cottonwood tree near the bank of the Redwood River. His dark hair and mustache were neatly trimmed. In spite of the hot June day, he looked crisp in his freshly laundered blue uniform.

But his eyes looked incredibly sad, Jesse detected, like something was wrong. Only Stephen Riggs knew what troubled their general so deeply. Jesse stood near the front. William Duley waited nearby.

Several dozen men stood before the general. All wore the various gold epaulets of officers' ranks on their shoulders. Sibley braced himself, determined to keep his emotions in check, convinced that his men needed a show of strength, not tears, from their leader. Four men stood behind Sibley, all in blue coats: Colonel Marshall, R.C. Olin, Riggs, and Quartermaster Anthony Corning.

"Gentlemen," he began, "in conjunction with our commander, General Pope, we have developed a plan to capture Little Crow and the renegade Sioux who fled Minnesota for the prairies of Dakota Territory. This campaign will be arduous. Our soldiers have been selected largely for their general fitness for the duties to be performed and the hardships endured. Your training and service along the border and patrolling the frontier forts will serve us in good stead.

"To the best of our knowledge, Little Crow and some of the more dastardly of the Sioux murderers are gathering near Devils Lake. Yes, we hanged thirty-eight. But that was just the tip of the iceberg. We have beaten the red man and driven him from our borders. Those who were captured and imprisoned at Fort Snelling have been delivered to Crow Creek. Those remaining at large must be punished and their power forever destroyed. We must make sure that they are never able to return to Minnesota to rampage and violate again. We must prevent them from joining the Teton or other western bands where they could do mischief in the future. To that end, gentlemen," Sibley said, then paused and briefly stroked his mustache, "this is what we will do. Eight thousand troopers will be sent west. Four thousand, under my command, have gathered here. Another 4,000, led by General Alfred Sully, will gather on the Missouri in northwest Iowa. We will proceed up the Red River to a point east of Devils Lake. General Sully will come up the Missouri supported by steamboat until they are west of the lake. At that point, we should have Little Crow between us. We will then swing together and smash the Sioux in a pincher maneuver. Sully should be in position to cut off any possible escape as well. We shall kill or capture them all. We will depart from Camp Pope on the sixteenth, the day after tomorrow."

Sibley paused and looked at Adjutant General Olin, who had been a lieutenant during the outbreak and had served as a member of the commission that had sentenced the 303 to die. "Mr. Olin, please review the roster of organizations with us."

Olin stepped forward and removed a sheet of paper from a breast pocket. He unfolded it and began to read: "Under General Sibley's command are the Sixth Minnesota under Colonel William Crooks, nine companies of the Seventh Minnesota under Lieutenant Colonel William R. Marshall, eight companies of the Tenth Minnesota under Colonel James H. Baker, one company of Pioneers under Captain Jonathan Chase, and nine companies of the First Minnesota Cavalry, or Mounted Rangers, under Colonel Samuel McPhail. Eight pieces of artillery with 148 men are under Captain John Jones. Seventy-five Indian scouts are under Major Joseph R. Brown, George McLeod, and Major Duley. In all, sir, there are 4,075 soldiers. We also have nearly 2,000 civilian support personnel, including 250 black contraband mule drivers."

"Thank you," Sibley nodded at Olin. "Since this is an all-summer campaign and there is nowhere from which our supplies can be replenished, we have quite an extensive supply train with us. We have 225 six-mule teams, artillery caissons, ambulances, other wagons, and a large herd of beef cattle to supply the army. We are on our own. The only settlement with a sizable number of white citizens is Yankton. We are moving into a territory nearly devoid of whites. The people we will encounter are to be considered hostiles. Let me say this." He straightened his shoulders as the politician in the general rose to the forefront. "If your men need a reminder about why we are doing this, tell them to look around as we march up the river valley. Let them see the burned-out ruins of homes where families once tried to build something out of this wilderness, see the ruined and abandoned fields, the graves and, worst yet, remember the blackened and mutilated corpses of men, women, and children left to rot on the prairie.

"These crimes and wickedness must be atoned for, and it is for this that we ride west! We ride for retribution!"

Sibley turned away as cries of, "Huzzah! Huzzah!" burst from the assembled officers.

ℬ 29 ℛ

WHEN JESSE RETURNED TO HIS CAMPSITE, Solomon was still seated on a log. He looked sad and pensive, older than his forty years. His wide-brimmed black hat lay by his side as he wiped his widening forehead with a handkerchief.

"It's a hot one," he said. "Any news?"

"We leave on the sixteenth. Everything's ready to go. You all right?"

"I'll be better when we're on the move. Sitting around here, there's too much time to think. I'll miss my brother. But, enough, I'll grieve in my own way. Who heads the scouts?"

"Brown, McLeod, and Duley."

"Well, so it's more of Duley, is it. At least we have something in common now. We'd both walk through Hell to get Pawn."

Jesse considered a moment and then replied, "From what I've heard of the Dakotas, I think you'll find him and plenty more."

A detachment of infantry moved out on the westward highlands on the night of June 15 to take the advance the following morning. A day of furnace-like heat had given way to a serene night. The fragrance of wild-flowers wafted through the camp on a gentle breeze. Above, the sky was star-bedecked except for on the southwestern horizon, where lightning flashes twisted and bolted through a cloud embankment.

In the camp, men played cards under lamplights, and songs echoed from around campfires. But the tranquility of the night was broken as a rumor spread through the camp like wildfire. Dr. Weiser had diagnosed a case of smallpox!

The men had signed up with Sibley expecting hardship. The possi-bility of being wounded or killed by the enemy was accepted as part of the risk. But an invisible, silent killer like smallpox was another matter.

The rumor was true, Dr. Weiser had identified a well-defined case of smallpox in an infantryman. The soldier would be left behind. No other cases were reported.

At 3:00 the next morning, as the eastern horizon was revealing the first pink hues of dawn, a bugle blast sounded through Camp Pope. Jesse stumbled out of his tent and found Solomon already sipping from a coffee cup.

"Well, Solomon, I heard Sibley was a man of defined habits. Apparently being an early riser is one of them."

"It's a beautiful morning, Jesse. It's good to start early, easier on the horses and mules. We'll move fifteen to twenty miles by mid-day and then make camp. The animals will have time to forage, and the men will avoid marching in the heat of the day. Not a bad plan."

"I guess I'll get used to it. At least we're finally going. The great Sibley Expedition is underway."

By four o'clock that morning the pageantry of the march was, in fact, underway. The column wound its way up the Minnesota River Valley, passing near huge granite boulders before ascending the rolling hills to the west.

The scouts leading the way were six miles into the journey before the rear guard could set out. The artillery, ambulances, and wagon train covered a distance of nearly four miles, led by 4,000 soldiers marching or riding before them. It created a magnificent sight to behold. But there was no one in the valley to see it, only the soldiers themselves.

The morning grew hot as the sun turned into a blazing ball above. A great cloud of dust from animals and marching feet enveloped the procession like a dense fog. No wind blew to push the dust away, so it simply hung in the air and coated everything that passed through it. Purple-hued prairie grass, sometimes six-feet high, parted before the advancing army as if a ship's prow were slicing through an ocean.

While the expedition started with song, drumbeat and bugle blasts, the tone turned somber as the day wore on. Ruins were scattered along the march. Not just the ruins of buildings, but the ruins of hopes, dreams, and lives of Minnesota pioneers.

Most of the men in the line of march had lost friends or relatives in the war, and every burned-out building was a reminder. Even worse was the fact that to these soldiers, murderers had escaped, leaving only emptiness and destruction in their wake. It was their task to even the score for their dead. That was what the expedition was all about.

Solomon was right. A halt was called in mid-afternoon to take advantage of abundant water and grass. A white city of tents soon sprang up over the purple plain. The camp covered more than one square mile of prairie.

On the second day of the expedition, the order to march came at five o'clock in the morning. The forward units of the procession were three hours out before the rear guard hit the trail. Jesse trotted forward to ride with Solomon and the scouts.

"Beautiful, isn't it, Jesse?" Foot observed. "Lush green grass lying atop the hills like a carpet. Look at the blades of grass heavy with dew. They sparkle like diamonds."

"And rose bushes throughout, lotsa pretty red blossoms."

"Right, Jesse, and think, if we weren't passin' through here today, no human eye would ever see 'em. Only God above would appreciate this beauty."

General Sibley had announced that it would be a short march. Camp would be at Wood Lake, site of the final battle of the September 23 outbreak the previous year.

One of the reasons Jesse rode with the scouts was to observe the battlefield site with Solomon. By mid-day they approached Wood Lake.

Solomon scanned the plain and lake before him and commented to Jesse, "Don't take much imagination to see this as it was. Indians over there," he pointed, "soldiers movin' into the gulley."

Jesse gestured. "There's where Marshall and the Seventh made the charge that saved the day, and there's where Major Welch was shot, and Nathan Cates and I carried him back to camp. That's where I met you for the first time."

"I wuz too shot up to fight. Nathan and me had just got back from Abercrombie and freeing the four white girls from White Dog."

"Nathan shot him, didn't he?"

"Right between the eyes while the Indian held a knife to Emily's throat."

"Quite a shot."

"Nathan's quite a man. I'll bet he was a great officer before he lost his arm at Shiloh." Solomon paused. "Let me change that a little. Nathan was a great officer. He would be one still, one arm or not. But the outbreak took the fight out of him. He married Emily and wants to teach. So, that's why he's gone to Crow Creek."

"Who knows, Solomon, we might wind up at Crow Creek ourselves."

"If we do, we'll be huntin' something, not teachin'."

The next morning brought the procession to the Upper Sioux Agency. It appeared nothing like the lively little settlement it had been less than a year before. The buildings looked sad and abandoned. Those spared the flames stood neglected, with windows smashed and doors shattered. Weeds grew on once well-worn pathways.

Stephen Riggs joined Jesse and Solomon for this part of the journey to share his particular memories. "See there," he gestured to a ruined building, "about 5,000 Santee gathered around it last July demanding food. If Lieutenant Sheehan hadn't stood his ground with his company and convinced Agent Galbraith to distribute food, there would have been chaos here. The war would have started right on that spot."

Solomon made a sucking sound through his teeth. "Instead they came and burned it a month later."

"Yes, but with much less loss of life than if had they attacked in July. Those of us who were here were led to safety, thanks to John Otherday."

"That didn't endear him to the other Santee," Jesse commented.

"No, certainly not to the Mdewakanton, but remember, most of the Sisseton and Wahpeton did not fight us. Otherday was a Sisseton."

"And now he scouts for Sibley." Solomon nodded up ahead where the Indian scout rode with the Renville brothers.

"Too bad about Sibley's little girl," Jesse offered sympathetically.

"Yes," Riggs agreed, "it's hard on him. It was hard, too, that it took his wife awhile to write him. Three days in a row when Sibley saw me, the first words out of his mouth were, 'No letter from Sarah.' Thank God she finally wrote him."

Each day of the march brought more landmarks and memories flooding back to those who already remembered all too well. On June 20 they passed Camp Release, where Little Crow's 265 captives had been given up to Sibley by Chief Red Iron after Little Crow had lost at Wood Lake and fled to the west.

It was also where Riggs had begun his questioning of accused Santee and the trials had started. As they marched west, the party traversed the Lac Qui Parle River, then Big Stone Lake, where hidden caches of Santee plunder were discovered. Dishes, tin ware, harnesses, chains, straps, pails, some furniture, and even a supply of corn were found. Much of it was still useable.

June 25 was the nineteenth birthday of Corporal Oscar Wall of the Mounted Rangers. His company of cavalry rode on the right flank of the procession and was in the saddle by four in the morning.

The bright sunny morning buoyed Wall's spirits even more considering his birthday, and his excitement rose to an even higher level when he spotted a sea of black spots in the distance. "Buffalo!" he cried.

Sibley had discouraged hunting forays during the expedition, but Wall enthusiastically approached his officer. "Lieutenant Beaver, it's my birthday today. How about letting me get some buffalo steaks for mess tonight?" He pointed hopefully to the distant herd.

"Well, Corporal, we're not supposed . . . oh, what the hell, take a couple of troops with you and go for a hunt."

"Really, sir?" Wall had expected a negative response. "Thank you, sir. We'll save a good slice of steak for you!"

Then he looked to Willie Sturgis and Sven Svenson and exclaimed excitedly, "He said it's okay. Let's go!"

With that the three soldiers galloped down into a ravine, following it toward the herd. Leaving the depression, they rode up onto the plain to find the buffalo again. They quickened their pace until they were near where the herd munched prairie grass.

Sturgis pointed the barrel of his carbine. "Look at that big bull. He's huge!"

"So, vat do vee do?" Svenson wondered.

Oscar thought a moment, then replied, "We cut him out from the rest and shoot him."

The three horsemen rode into the herd and approached the bull. The rest of the animals paid no attention and continued to chew, oblivious to the riders. By crowding their prey on horseback, they caused the bull to move and then to trot some distance away.

Oscar lowered his voice and just above a whisper commanded, "Now! Let's shoot!"

The three men raised their carbines and opened fire. It took repeated shots to bring down the massive animal. In short order the soldiers fell upon the beast with hunting knives and soon had their haversacks filled with choice cuts of buffalo meat.

"Where's da army? Dey must be quite a few miles away by now," Sven wondered.

"Up ahead, look." Oscar squinted. "See that cloud of dust. That's them."

After a few miles the cloud disappeared.

"Looks like they musta made camp." Willie observed.

"And our company will be hungry. Let's bring supper," Oscar grinned.

That evening every man in their company had a hunk of buffalo steak. Oscar decided to parcel some out to officers.

"Is this a bribe?" Jesse deadpanned, trying not to smile.

"No, sir," Oscar answered, "I'd never do that. I just thought you 'n' Mr. Foot might like some fresh meat." *Of course,* Wall thought, *it never hurts to have someone on yer side if ya need help.*

The next day's camp was south of Big Stone Lake near the site of an old trading post. A practice had arisen to name the camps after officers on the expedition. This was called Camp Jennison in honor of Colonel S.P. Jennison of the Tenth Minnesota.

Soldiers looking for firewood happened upon a grisly sight. The bleached skeletons of six men lay on a hillside, silent witnesses to a tragedy thirteen months earlier.

Sibley himself rode to the scene with Colonel Marshall. "What do you make of it, General?" Marshall asked.

"It's known that a half dozen or so men were killed near the Myrick Store, which was near here. I heard they were even warned by an Indian that danger was near. But it was August 21, and word of the massacres in the valley hadn't reached here yet. These men didn't pay any heed to the warning and it cost them."

"Was there a witness?" Marshall wondered. "You seem to know a lot about this."

"A man named Manderfeldt got away, made his way to settlements down the river after twelve days of horrible conditions and hardship. The story of what happened here comes from him."

Sibley stood tall in his stirrups and shouted to a sergeant. "Gather these bones and bury them. Put up a marker. Somebody will put the names on later."

Early the next day, Sibley's men were on the move again. They entered a region that had endured a lengthy drought. The hot, baked earth led to suffocating dust. Burned grass was stunted and dry. Water was scarce.

The troops were grateful to camp between Big Stone and Traverse lakes. In spite of the drought, a luxurious growth of red-top grew between the lakes.

The site was remarkable for another feature. The nearby lakes flowed in opposite directions. Lake Traverse flowed into the Red River of the North and on to Hudson's Bay, while Big Stone dumped into the Minnesota and on to the Gulf of Mexico.

Camp McLaren was the expedition's home for three days. On June 30, Sibley sent a detachment north to Fort Abercrombie for supplies. Then he led the main column to the northwest, out of the Minnesota River Valley and onto the hot, dusty Dakota plains toward Devils Lake.

Minnesota was at their backs now, their homes well behind them. A vast treeless prairie stretched before the army. They pounded over earth that couldn't have been harder had it been baked in an oven. The surface was ripped open by great cracks, an inch or two in width and a foot or more in depth, stretching for yards. The Sibley Expedition had entered a strange, almost unknown world.

ʂ๐ 30 ൭

L ITTLE CROW'S DREAM OF A GREAT Indian alliance was a faded memory, a lost, last hope for his cause. He had sent White Spider to the Mandan to make a final appeal for help. When word came back that his brother had failed and been driven away by the Mandan by force, Little Crow determined that it was time for him to go home.

The great war chief who had led thousands now led seventeen men, mostly family and close friends, back into Minnesota. Among them were his young son, Wowinape, and son-in-law, Heyoka. Inkpaduta and Pawn had pledged to remain in the west.

Inkpaduta urged Little Crow to stay with them. "Why return to Minnesota? There's nothing there for you now."

Little Crow's answer had been unsatisfactory. "I raid to kill Americans."

As they backtracked toward the land of their births, Wowinape sought a more realistic answer. "Father, we cannot fight the whites with so few. Why do you go back to Minnesota?"

He looked symphathetically into the eyes of the slight sixteen-year-old boy. "My son, if the Dakota hope to stay on the high plains and hunt buffalo, they must have horses. Almost all of the horses we took with us a year ago have perished. I have six children left, and I will steal a horse for each one of them before I die. The horses are in Minnesota."

The chief continued on in silence, but his mind echoed with the memories of a conversation held nearly one year earlier. Susan Brown was the mixed-blood wife of former Indian agent Joe Brown, the very man currently leading Sibley's scouts in Dakota. Susan had been captured near Upper Sioux and had traveled with Little Crow's band throughout the war.

She had many conversations with the Mdewakanton leader. One lingered in his mind as if it were trapped in a maze and couldn't get out. It had occurred when Little Crow was depressed after failing to take Fort

126

Ridgely and being repulsed at Forest City and Hutchinson. Sibley was closing in, and Little Crow could sense the end was near.

He had entered the lodge where Susan was kept and had sat cross-legged before a smoldering fire. Wiping a sheen of sweat from her brown-toned face, Susan had asked her captor sympathetically, "What will you do, Little Crow, when this is over? You can't win. You know that now. What will become of you?"

Resignation in his eyes, he had looked up at Susan Brown. "I will take my people to the west where we will join the Yankton and the Teton. The Santee will be welcomed by them, I'm sure of it. But of me? Someday I will return to the Big Woods. There is much good that I remember of my life there."

"The whites will kill you if you go back."

Little Crow had smiled at Susan. "That doesn't concern me. A better life awaits me. If my death can serve to benefit my people, then it is all good."

Susan had answered angrily. "You Indians and your self-sacrifice. Dying does not help your people."

"I'm blamed for the war by many, Indian and white. I'm a source of division among my people. The destiny that made me a leader will demand that I sacrifice my life."

Gazing at him with sadness in her eyes, Susan Brown had slowly shaken her head. "Just free me and the others before you set out on killing yourself."

Little Crow recalled how he had brightened with false bravado. "It may all be different. This war is not over yet. But, if we have to go to the Teton and Yankton they will ally with us and fight the whites. There is much to do before I go back to Minnesota."

Nothing had worked as Little Crow had planned, and now he was back in his homeland, stuck with relentless memories of that prophetic conversation.

The chief put a hand on his son's shoulder and turned Wowinape to face him. Then he took a leather pouch from a strap around his shoulder and handed it to the boy. "Here. It is my medicine bundle. Guard it for me."

"But, Father, medicine bundles ensure happiness and long life. A warrior gives it up only when he is about to . . . no! You will not die. Not now!"

Little Crow laughed and said, "Just take care of it for me. I won't die, don't worry."

By late June the party had traveled east of Yellow Medicine. They divided into two groups.

Little Crow advised, "Be warriors, take horses and meet back here, north of Hutchinson."

Heyoka rode farther to the east with a half-dozen men. Little Crow headed north. Two days later Heyoka and his little band came upon a family traveling southeast of Smith Lake in Wright County.

Two oxen trudged across the prairie pulling a lumber wagon driven by Amos Dustin. His wife, Kate, mother, Jeanette, and their three children bounced and jolted over the uneven terrain.

The Dakota descended without warning. Armed with bows and arrows, clubs and knives, they first clubbed and shot Amos. Little six-year-old Alma slid under the front wagon seat to hide. Her dress grew soaked with her father's blood as it seeped through cracks in the bench and onto her clothing.

Kate was felled by an arrow that entered her back and passed through her body, the tip protruding below her right breast bone. Jeanette Dustin, fifty-one and seated in the back of the wagon, seized her son's walking stick and began swinging it at her attackers. Heyoka split her skull with a blow from his hatchet.

Four-year-old Robert screamed, "Oh, Papa!" He was quickly cut down by an arrow in his neck. A Dakota brave wrenched two-year-old Leon from the wagon and poised a club above him.

"Stop!" Heyoka commanded. "We've done enough. Leave him. There's a girl under the wagon seat. Leave her, too. Take what you want. Then we go."

A short time later the Dakota left the macabre massacre scene. Miraculously, Kate was not dead. But she found it impossible to walk. She dragged herself along as Alma carried Leon. They became mired in a marsh until they were found the next day by a search party alerted by the return of the Dustins' oxen. Kate died of her wounds several days later on July 3.

Little Crow, with Wowinape and others, passed by Forest City and continued beyond Kingston. Between there and the settlement of Fairhaven, they fell upon a man who had unwisely returned to his farm to see to his cattle. They killed him on the spot but found no horses. The Dakota returned to their rendezvous point north of Hutchinson without the prizes they sought, horses.

Heyoka presented Little Crow with a coat from a lone traveler they had killed.

"I will take the coat," his leader said, "but where are the horses?"

"I see no new horses with you, either," his son-in-law responded.

"We'll try again tomorrow. I think we'll do better if we stay together," Little Crow urged.

"No, Father, I'm done. I'll join Medicine Bottle and Shakopee in Canada."

"I say we must all stay here. Who's with me?" Little Crow cried.

"We must leave this place!" another warrior shouted. "We go south!"

"You are fools. We're nothing if we separate."

"Father, we're very little if we stay together," Heyoka countered.

Eight men went south. Seven others followed Heyoka north to Canada. Little Crow refused to go with either group. He stood disconsolately within the Big Woods with only Wowinape by his side.

The father and son gazed into a smoky camp fire that night. Little Crow turned nostalgic and philosophical.

"My son, I want you to understand some things. Listen carefully that you will remember. The whites think I am a savage who caused the war. Yet, I had spent my entire life trying to avoid just such a war. Change was coming, and I knew that our people must change as well. I could see what would happen, and I understood the white man as few others did. I knew the futility of war with the whites.

"When war threatened years before, I spoke and worked against it. I led men to find Inkpaduta to stop him when he killed whites in Iowa. Remember when they came to me after the killings at Acton? I told them that war was wrong."

"But you led them anyway," Wowinape reminded his father.

"It was my destiny. I was chosen to lead our people. I had been their speaker, their voice. I kept the old ways as much as I could and took from the white world whatever seemed necessary to survive."

Wowinape stirred the fire with a stick, sending red sparks and embers into the air. "But when you had to choose between the two worlds, you chose our ancestors."

"Yes, and I knew that many of my friends and relatives and other Santee would oppose my decision and oppose the war. But for me there was never a choice." Little Crow paused. His head down, he whispered more to himself than to his son, "It started here, and it will end here."

The next afternoon the two happened upon bushes lushly heavy and ripe with raspberries. The solemnity of the previous night was forgotten as Little Crow and Wowinape spent several hours happily picking berries and remembering the pleasant days of their past life in the Minnesota River Valley.

As the sun neared the western horizon, the idyllic moment was shattered by the blast of a rifle. Little Crow winced and grabbed his upper leg. Shocked, he looked at his son, who stared wide-eyed in surprise and fear.

"Go," the father gasped. "You are small and unarmed. Do not fight. Hide in the brush."

As he spoke, Little Crow grabbed his rifle lying on the ground beside him and returned fire. He quickly raised another weapon and fired a second shot. An instant later a bullet struck his rifle and buried itself in his chest. He fell backward into a raspberry patch.

Nathan Lamson and his son Chauncey had been traveling north to look after stock at their home five miles north of Hutchinson. The sight of Indians and the knowledge that a bounty would be paid for their scalps caused sixty-year-old Nathan to fire at Little Crow. The Indian fired back.

Chauncey pulled the trigger on his rifle just as Little Crow's second shot struck the elder Lamson, rendering him unconscious. Chauncey, assuming his father dead and fearing other Indians were nearby, ran back to Hutchinson with the news.

Wowinape crept cautiously to his father's side. Little Crow knew his wound was mortal. Through labored breaths he told his son, "Take my weapons, and my medicine bundle, and go to your mother at Devils Lake." Then he died.

His son dressed him in new moccasins for his trip into the afterlife, wrapped his body in a blanket, and then left for Devils Lake. He would travel at night. He knew it would take a month to reach his destination. It was July 3.

Chauncey reached Hutchinson at about 10:00 that night. He and his desperate mother begged the men of the town to go in search of Nathan. Several citizens and soldiers from the stockade volunteered to organize a party to investigate.

After a ride into the darkness, they reached the Lamson cabin, where they rested for three hours. At daybreak they reached the site of the shooting. They found Nathan Lamson's bloody white shirt on the ground but no sign of the man.

Little Crow lay where his son had left him, dead in a patch of berries. The soldiers tied a rope to the chief's legs and dragged his body back to Hutchinson. To their amazement they were met by Nathan Lamson as they rode into town. He smiled broadly in spite of the bullet wound in his hip.

It was the Fourth of July, and Hutchinson was ready to celebrate. Citizens filled the ears and nostrils of the Dakota chief with firecrackers and set them off. Someone sliced off the scalp and handed it to Lamson. An officer drew his sword and hacked off the head. Men jammed a fence rail into the skull and carried it through town at the front of a procession as they sang patriotic songs.

Then they went to a refuse pit where slaughtered animals were disposed and threw the body in. The head was heaved in after it. No one knew it was Little Crow.

ᏸ31Ꮬ

REVEREND JOHN WILLIAMSON AND Colonel Thompson, the agent at Crow Creek, stood on opposite sides of the Santee procession and counted as the Santee disembarked from the *Florence*. Their counts matched: 1,300 was the agreed upon number.

Fort Thompson was an ambitious name for the new reservation. It had no fort, no buildings, nothing that would indicate any type of settlement. There was also nothing green. A succession of hot, dry summers had burned even the roots of the grass, leaving a bare gumbo.

The landscape to the west featured only two colors, the blue of the sky and the wide river, and the brown of everything else. The east side of the Missouri, the reservation side, dropped into a flat flood plain, where the only trees grew. Across the river, bluffs and rolling hills met the riverbank more abruptly as they rose over the Missouri.

Williamson joined his white friends from Minnesota on a hilltop and watched as the soldiers and Dakota people erected crude shelters of hide and canvas. "We need to build as well," he offered. "Not just shelters for ourselves but a large structure, a place for the Dakota to gather."

"Like a church or a school?" Emily asked.

"Yes, but we don't have enough wood or the means to construct buildings that large. Especially since Colonel Thompson intends to build a fort here."

Nathan pondered thoughtfully and then brightened. "An arbor!" he exclaimed.

"That might work!" Williamson agreed. "There are plenty of willows and brush by the river and some cottonwoods. We can use the big trees to set up a framework and then string the branches overhead for a roof."

"If it's big enough, we can use it for worship and school," Emily added.

"It has to serve at least a thousand people," Williamson continued.

Captain Saunders and Colonel Thompson had joined the little group.

"I've got a small sawmill," Thompson offered. "I brought it for constructing a fort and agency buildings. We can give you some help on the arbor. We need to keep the Indians busy. Idle hands are the devil's workshop."

"Remember," Saunders added, "these people are to be considered in the same class as prisoners of war, no travel off the reservation, not for hunting or for gathering nuts and berries."

Dr. Wharton's concern regarded physical sustenance. "What about the food? We have some pork and flour, but not enough to last more than a few months."

"A contract has been approved for food. It's coming on a steamboat from Mankato," Thompson answered. "In the meantime, we'll have to stretch the rations out. I've got some ideas."

The next weeks were a beehive of activity at the camp. A large arbor was constructed. Cottonwood trees were brought from the river bottom, and Colonel Thompson oversaw the building of a fort and various other structures. A little town on the banks of the Missouri was rapidly taking shape. There were no other houses within fifty miles.

Pastors Williamson and Hinman held daily meetings, instructing people in religion. Hymns echoed through the new village from beneath the arbor. Twelve of the leading Dakota women were appointed as deaconesses or Bible women and conducted women's prayer meetings.

Williamson and Samuel Hinman watched with pride as the women moved individually from tent to tent to teach and read the Bible.

"Amazing, isn't it," Hinman remarked, "in such a desolate place, God's seeds are taking root."

"Yes, Samuel, we're feeding their souls, but not their stomachs. Hunger is rampant."

Hinman sighed. "Colonel Thompson has implemented one of his 'ideas'. I hope it helps."

"Cottonwood soup will just prolong the inevitable," Williamson lamented. "The food rations from Mankato must arrive soon, or these people must be allowed to leave the reservation to hunt and gather."

A whistle sounded, and the two men watched as a mass of Dakota began to file toward a large tank in the center of the village. Thompson had conceived the idea that by cooking the rations together, they could make them go farther and furnish more nourishment.

Hence, he had a large tank constructed of green cottonwood boards. The tank was filled with eight to ten barrels of water. The day's flour ration was mixed in a barrel with a little water and then stirred into the tank. A small piece of pork was added but nothing else. The steam was turned into the tank. It could be heard puffing and sputtering all night.

Each morning the Indians came when the whistle blew. They brought pails to the tank and received a ladleful for each member of the family. The brew was strongly flavored with green cottonwood and quite thin.

It was almost unpalatable, but it was their food for the day and all they had. The Santee called it cottonwood soup.

Nathan and Emily worked with children and adults both, teaching them to speak, read and write English. It helped that some of the younger ones had been Emily's students at the Lower Sioux Agency school.

One of those students, Traveling Star—or "Johnny" as most whites called him—was invaluable in helping to translate between Dakota and English. Johnny had saved Emily's life during the attack at Lower Sioux, and Nathan had saved him from being killed at Wood Lake. Johnny's family had been wiped out in the war. Nathan and Emily had taken the teen-aged boy under their wing.

Nathan smiled at Emily as they moved beneath the arbor to examine alphabet letters written on slate tablets by children. A young Indian man was doing likewise nearby.

"I'm proud of Johnny," Nathan beamed. "He's really catching on to this."

"He's smart, Nathan. He can read, speak and write in both languages. His English is better than our Dakota."

"The more they learn, the better their chances of surviving."

Emily sighed and brushed a damp blonde curl from her eye. "But what are we preparing them for, Nathan? They can't leave here."

"I know, Emily, but it keeps them occupied, and it does prepare them for the future. Whatever that future holds, it must be better than this."

JoAnna Miller and Dr. Wharton were kept busy in a small shed that provided a poor substitute for a hospital. The wooden structure had cracks in the walls through which slanted rays of sunlight brightened the dirt floor. In places flies also squeezed in to torment the sick as they lay on makeshift beds.

"Three miserable cots, if you can call them that," Dr. Wharton complained to JoAnna. "If we had a hundred beds in here, they'd be full, and we'd still have more needing to get in. We just bring the worst of the sick in here and wait for 'em to die."

"While the rest suffer in miserable hovels they call tents," JoAnna added, "and how can we help them? They need food. They get scant nourishment from what the government provides them."

"I've been talking to Thompson. If they won't feed them, they need to let them leave and get their own food. I told the colonel, 'What do you expect? Pitiable diet, shock, anxiety, confinement in close quarters. Naturally all that must be followed by sickness, and it is.' We came here with 1,300; now 2,000 Winnebago have been brought in just to the north, and Thompson keeps saying not to worry, that food is coming from Mankato. I say, when! Hundreds will die and for no reason unless they let them leave the reservation for food.

"But Thompson and Saunders say no," Wharton continued with biting sarcasm. "They might lose one or two of them. Better to lose them by dying than let 'em run away?"

JoAnna and Wharton heard shouts and a commotion outside. They opened a rickety door and stepped into bright sunshine.

A young Santee brave was running through the camp waving his arms and yelling, "Tatanka has come! Tatanka is near! The people are saved!"

Buffalo had come to Fort Thompson.

∂ 32 ∞

SOLOMON FOOT RODE ALONGSIDE Gabriel Renville at the head of Sibley's column as they left camp on the morning of July 1. The northwestern sky was still draped in black and dotted with sparkling specks of white light. Behind them the bright hues of morning crept over the eastern horizon.

"It's a big country, Gabe," Solomon observed.

"Many places to hide. Many places to look," Renville replied.

"And your Uncle Joe is leading us on the search." Foot pointed a few riders ahead where Joseph Brown led the column.

"Gabe, your father, Joe, was a trader. Your mother was a Santee, right?"

"A Sisseton Santee," Renville corrected.

"And your half-sister is Susan, Joe Brown's wife, held captive by Little Crow. You didn't join in the war, but you were livin' as an Indian. How'd you decide?"

"Most Sisseton and Wahpeton stayed out of the war. I was raised Indian, not white. I stood with Little Paul, Red Iron, and Standing Buffalo. Little Crow brought ruin to our people. When word came to us of the murders at the agency, we knew that the end of our ways was near. It's because of Little Crow that we've lost all we had. He must die for what he's done. My heart will be full of joy when we find him."

"Frankly, it's Pawn I want to get my hands on. He kills without reason."

"Solomon, they all have reasons. You just don't understand them or can't justify them. Some, you might just call murderers, but even they may reason with you by saying that the whites are invaders. If invaders bring their families with them, then all suffer the consequences."

"You're right, Gabe. I can't justify killing women and children."

"You're not Dakota, Solomon. Many feel that whites killed Indian children by withholding food when the people were starving. But I won't justify the killing, either. The war was wrong because of what it's done to my people, and Little Crow knew what the outcome would be."

The rising sun lifted the curtain on the vast baked plain before them. Open wagons rolled along the flanks of the column as soldiers stuck their bayonets through thin eight- to ten-inch rounds and slid the dry, skewered discs off their weapons and into the wagons.

Solomon looked back at the fuel gatherers and at the vast splotches of buffalo chips littering the ground everywhere. "I read that there were once sixty million buffalo on the Great Plains."

Gabriel sighed. "In Minnesota, too, and now there are none to be found there. Soon they will be gone from here, too. White people will kill them or drive them away. We use all of Tatanka," he added sadly. "Your people kill for sport, leave the carcass to rot."

The waste of the buffalo, the chips, had become the fuel of the expedition. The scarcity of wood was expected, and the dried leavings of millions of buffalo were scattered all over the plains. Each night the chips provided cook fires for the entire command of soldiers and civilian workers.

A few miles behind the scouts, Sibley rode disconsolately, his shoulders slumping forward in the saddle. The anguish of his daughter's death still weighed heavily on him. His burden was deepened by news that his ten-year-old son, Frank, was also ill.

Stephen Riggs had become an almost constant companion and confidant for his friend. He rode beside Sibley and counseled, "Frank is a strong little boy. Surely he's getting better."

"No word, Stephen. I hope you're right. The last I heard was that it wasn't too serious. I wish I had more time to write longer letters to Sarah. But keeping abreast of this massive supply train consumes all my time."

"You didn't expect problems with the mules, did you."

Sibley smiled in spite of himself. "Contraband drivers and unbroken young mules from Missouri." He chuckled softly. "The blacks chasing after bucking and twisting mules, trying to hitch them to the wagons. I couldn't help but laugh."

Quartermaster Corning trotted alongside Sibley and Riggs. "Sir," Corning said, saluting, "word from a couple of wagons back a ways. They hit a rut and busted some barrels. We've got hardtack falling out."

"Damn the blasted barrels." Sibley looked apologetically at Riggs. "Sorry, Stephen. Call a halt, Mr. Corning, get the barrels fixed and tell the drivers to stay out of ruts. Captain, tell the men to fall out and rest. Forage the animals. We have sufficient grass here."

They waited for an hour while men repaired the damaged barrels. Then they were on the move again.

Soon afterward, Duley rode back to Sibley and asked, "Can you smell it, sir?"

The general rode on as he sniffed the air. "Fire!"

Duley pointed. "It's over there, see the smoke a ways off." Far to the west a gray smudge blemished the bright blue sky.

"We got to keep moving. Order the pace picked up!" Sibley ordered. "With the wind blowing from the northwest, it should push this behind us. But we can't take chances."

Riggs peered intently to the west. "Henry, I saw lightening out there last night. A strike must have ignited the fire. Fire . . . it is the awesome cleanser of the plains. It brings rebirth."

"How so, Reverend?"

"It burns off the litter and dead growth, enriches the soil and cleans it for new growth. The growing point of grass is below the surface. Untouched, it rejuvenates, and the plain is reborn."

"That's fine as long as we aren't in the way."

Late that afternoon camp was made. Sibley had begun the practice of ordering the construction of defensive fortifications each night. Details were ordered to work on trenches and two-foot-high breastworks.

When a junior officer had questioned the need, Sibley had replied, "I never worry about what the enemy might do. I'll prepare myself beforehand and let the enemy do the worrying."

The air grew fuller and more acrid from smoke. With the searing sun and strong breeze driving it, the prairie fire roared like a blast furnace. Jesse and Solomon stood together and watched with relief as a now-visible flaming red line raged behind them, clearing the ground like a living scythe and continuing to the southeast.

"Solomon, that's not the first fire we've dodged, and it won't be the last either."

"One came by my place in Kandiyohi. Addy and me and the little Foots had to dive into a lake for safety. We stayed there while the fire swept by us."

"Was your house wood or sod?"

"Wood. Addy wouldn't have a soddy. But sod don't burn."

ON JULY 1 THE SIBLEY EXPEDITION MARCHED eighteen miles. They made sixteen miles the next day and another sixteen on July 3rd. They covered eighteen miles on the Fourth of July after nine hours of marching. At 1:00 p.m. Sibley ordered camp made at a big bend in the lush green valley of the Sheyenne River.

The green along the river was a stark contrast to the dusty brown to which they had become accustomed. Oscar Wall and Willie Sturgis walked out from the camp to remember the holiday in their own way.

"Great place for the Fourth, ain't it, Oscar? We got trees by the river. It's the first o' annathin' green I seen since we left Minnesota."

"Nice place for the Fourth, but no bands, Willie," Oscar noted. "No best girl, no red lemonade, no big shots in carriages, no speeches, no reading of the Declaration of Independence. Just this," he gestured outward with both arms, "this great wonderful emptiness."

They stood in silent reflection for a moment gazing at the high, wide-arched blue sky and the boundless plains. There was nothing else, save herds of buffalo visible in every direction.

"Jest think, Oscar, hardly any white people has ever seen this. Nobody ever surveyed it. It's just a big, quiet nothing."

"A magnificent nothing, Willie."

"It's a great Fourth! But I think I know what I miss the most."

"What's that, Willie?"

"The best girl."

SIBLEY GATHERED A LARGE GROUP OF HIS officers beside the river. The water flowed by lazily as if reluctant to join the Missouri. Sibley's voice rose as he addressed his men.

"We have much to consider today. We should be grateful that we are in a place with plenty of wood, water, and grass. That we have lost no one since we left Camp Pope. The detachment that I sent to Fort Abercrombie for supplies five days ago is to rendezvous with us here. We'll wait for them.

"We've received dispatches and mail from Abercrombie. Two great battles are being fought. Lee has invaded Pennsylvania, and it looks as if Grant has about starved out Vicksburg. It will fall soon. The great Civil War is reaching a climax. I pray that God will soon end this unnatural, brutal war and reunite the country. The great war between our states is fought for freedom. Let us remember that this is our Independence Day."

A barrel of liquor brought for "special" occasions had been opened, and the officers had filled their tin cups from it. As Sibley concluded his remarks, John Jones raised his cup and shouted, "Huzzah for General Grant!" The men toasted enthusiastically.

A moment later, R.C. Olin cried, "Huzzah for President Lincoln!" With a boisterous cheer, they toasted again.

Lieutenant Beaver, a wealthy young adventurer from England, had become a favorite of Sibley's. He raised his cup high. "As a citizen of the land from which you obtained your freedom, I congratulate you. Your country is wonderful!" Another round of drinks was enthusiastically consumed.

Jesse looked into his cup. Room for one more toast, he considered and then lifted his cup high. The others followed suit. "Huzzah for our general, Henry Hastings Sibley!"

Sibley nodded appreciatively at the loudest cheer of all. Yet when he turned away, Stephen Riggs could sense an air of gloom in the commander.

"What's wrong, Henry?" he asked.

"Thoughts of war and death, Reverend. It's such a waste. I read somewhere that Lee said that if war wasn't so horrible, we'd grow to love it too much. I'm not really a soldier. There's nothing about war for me to love. Death troubles me. I think of my little girl, and I worry about Frank."

"Nothing in the dispatches about Frank?"

"No, Stephen, nothing. But I'm filled with foreboding and I dream, agonizing dreams that I can't shake."

"About what?"

"Death, Stephen, death."

১৩ ৩৩ ৫০

SIBLEY'S ARMY REMAINED CAMPED on the Sheyenne River for nearly a week after the Fourth of July. Scouts and cavalry explored the surrounding countryside. During these sorties, buffalo and antelope were spotted in abundance.

Hunting was strictly forbidden now, for the sound of gunshots would alert nearby Indians or reveal their presence. But men hungry for fresh meat frequently found such an order not to their liking and easy to disobey. Many a choice bison or antelope steak found its way into camp.

July 9 brought a hot wind sweeping from the south, blasting tiny beads of sand over the parched prairie. The canvas tents provided shelter from wind and sand, but they heated up like bake ovens, nearly suffocating the soldiers within. The next day the wind shifted to the northeast, but any relief was short-lived. A bank of thick smoke descended upon the camp from the north.

Jesse's eyes stung from the acrid smoke that filled his nostrils as well. Captain John Jones walked by Jesse's tent. He paused, poured some water from a canteen into a yellow kerchief, and wiped his face and eyes.

"Lieutenant," he called, "as an artilleryman I've been in fights where the smoke was thick and hurt the eyes. This is almost as bad."

"Another prairie fire," Jesse commented.

"No, I dinna think so. I smell pine in the smoke. My guess is that the fire we're smellin' be many miles north. Mebbe even in Canada."

"Well, it's sure bad. Look," he pointed toward the river, "the Sheyenne is barely fifty yards from us and we can't see it from here."

"I hear that we're pulling out in a coupla days. The Abercrombie detachment is near."

"Maybe the weather will be more conducive for a march, Captain."

When reveille sounded early on the morning of the eleventh, the weather had another surprise in store for Sibley. A chilling wind from the north bore down on the men. The smoke was much less dense than it had been, but the cold penetrated like little pins into the men's skin and drove them into overcoats. But Sibley's Expedition was on the road again moving northwest.

Heat returned with a vengeance the following days. Solomon rode out front of the column with the Renville brothers. His black slouch hat was dirty and sweat-stained, and he kept a kerchief around his neck to keep the sun from broiling the back of his neck.

"What's that?" Foot pointed into the horizon. "Green groves and a lake. I hope we can camp there tonight."

His companions laughed and Gabriel shook his head at Solomon. "What you see is not really there. It is what you call a mirage."

"A mirage! That can't be. It's only a few miles away."

"Watch, Solomon. After we have ridden a few more miles, tell me what you see."

The image grew from a tiny dot to a vast landscape as the vertical rays of the sun revived memories of cooling shades and refreshing waters. But, like the end of the rainbow, the haunting landscape was not real. It would fade away gradually, hour by hour, leaving the impression that they were descending into a low area. Like a carrot held before a mule, the apparition was always just before them, providing men with certainty that once they climbed out of the low spot they would find the ideal camping spot. It was never there.

Solomon Foot witnessed the quivering, vanishing Garden of Eden firsthand, day after day, as the army marched across the treeless plains with the hot sun beating down on them. After time, even the most deluded accepted the mirage for what it was. Yet, even with that knowledge, there were men who convinced themselves that this time it was real.

"Lookee there," Willie Sturgis squinted ahead through the bright sunlight. "That lake is real."

Oscar Wall shielded his eyes with a hand and replied, "Sure looks real, but it isn't."

"It *is* real," Willie retorted. "How much ya wanna bet? I'll bet ya half a month's pay."

"I don't wanna bet. This is like taking candy from a baby. That's a mirage."

"No, it ain't, not this time. Put yer money where yer mouth is."

"Okay, Willie, you asked for it."

"Look, by the lake!" Willie cried. "That's one of them there castles, like in a picture book I saw, and there's a cloud rolling on the ground to the castle."

Oscar's mouth dropped open and then he sounded a low whistle. "It's still a mirage, that must be a herd of buffalo running along, that's the cloud. But it is an amazing sight, real or not."

That night as they camped on the hot prairie, Willie scrawled out an IOU and dropped it into Oscar's lap.

The next day they camped between three small real lakes. The men rejoiced that the lakes afforded clear, cool, real water. Dank and alkali water had been common in most of the lakes encountered during the march. This was a much appreciated exception.

They marched through dust and the haze of another northern fire on July 15. Stephen Riggs held a white handkerchief to his face as he rode beside Sibley. He pointed with astonishment at an approaching cloud.

"Henry, look, I've never seen a cloud move like that before, so fast and turning left and right."

Sibley studied it for a moment. "It glistens, and they look like snowflakes. But Stephen, that is a swarm of grasshoppers. This is all we need. Our horses and mules are about played out from the heat, and now we have to compete with insects and fires for what little grass there is. Pray for us, Stephen. We need help from heaven."

The swarm swept down upon the men and animals, who fought them off by swinging rifle butts, shovels and tails at them. Finding nothing worthy to eat in the procession, the grasshoppers left as quickly as they came.

The expedition crossed over the Sheyenne on July 16, and two days later they camped within thirty-five miles of Devils Lake. A drenching rain fell on the morning of July 18. But the downpour did not halt the march. In fact, it was a welcome break from days on end of unrelenting heat. The sun returned that afternoon and baked dry the clothing and blankets of the men.

Toward evening Sibley rode near a small lake to inspect campsites along the shore. His horse slipped in mud and fell. The animal landed on its side, wrenching Sibley's knee and hip beneath it.

Dr. Weiser was quickly on the scene and helped the general to his campsite. Sibley sat on a campstool with his leg stretched out before him as Weiser probed and inspected it for damage. But the pain in his leg was nothing like the pain in his heart that was soon to come.

Stephen Riggs strode to Sibley and handed him an envelope. Through the flickering flames of the campfire, Riggs read the look of deep despair on his friend's face.

"What is it, Henry?" the pastor asked with alarm.

"Frank, he's dead, too. Oh, my poor Sarah, two children to bury while I'm away out here. And a baby coming. I should never have gone. I should be home."

"No one could have known, Henry, only God."

"God doesn't have to be so damned tight-lipped."

Riggs and Weiser stood in silence. The pastor placed his hand on Sibley's shoulder, whispered a short prayer, and left with the doctor. Sibley wanted to grieve alone, left to his thoughts.

The next day Henry awoke with a stiff, aching knee and sharp pains in his hip. Thoughts of his two dead children and grieving pregnant wife hung over him like a cloud ready to burst.

Then his chief scout, Joe Brown, approached with Will Duley and several metis, mixed-blood hunters. Brown was tentative. "Sorry to bother you, sir, I heard . . ."

"Thank you, Mr. Brown," Sibley finished, "the point of your visit, please."

"These men are hunters, they were at Devils Lake just a few days ago. Tell him what you told me," he nodded to the eldest.

"General," a tall, bronze-complected man said, "the Sioux you seek. They're gone. Weeks ago they went west to the big, muddy river."

"You sure?" Sibley struggled to rise from his stool and then collapsed back into it. "This changes everything."

"There is no doubt. The Sioux have left. They look for the Teton."

"Little Crow? Is he with them?"

"They're led by Standing Buffalo. They have also split off into several smaller bands. I'm told that Little Crow went back to Minnesota with very few warriors."

"If that's true, Hatch will have to take care of him. We have to hunt down their warriors here. I want an officers' call. Duley, see to it."

Duley snapped a salute and then asked, "Sir, may I ask one question?"

"Ask."

He turned to the metis. "Pawn. Did you see Pawn? Was he with them?"

"I don't know. Some say that he's gone to the west with Inkpaduta."

"We're goin' west, aren't we, General?" Duley asked.

"Yes, now get my officers."

Sibley stood between Weiser and Riggs. They supported him while his officers gathered. Then the pained and weary leader made his announcement.

"Gentlemen, there's a change of plans. We'll rest here the next two days to prepare for what's coming. The Sioux have left Devils Lake and are heading west. We'll run them down. But we can't do it with our cumbersome supply train and slower troops, even though the Indians will be slowed by women and children. We'll establish a supply camp and leave the slower units here. The rest of the expedition will push ahead with great speed until we come upon the Indians and subdue them."

Sibley turned his men from their northwest pursuit on July 20 and headed directly west.

❧ 34 ❧

OUNDING HEAVEN'S NEWS OF NEARBY buffalo was met by great excitement at Fort Thompson. The young Indian was known to be an excellent hunter. Villagers crowded around as he dismounted from a horse and handed sacks of buffalo meat to a man standing nearby.

"Give to grandfathers, grandmothers, and children. There will be more for the others later."

John Williamson hurried to the young brave. "Sounding Heaven, how did you do this? Where did you get a horse and rifle?"

He quickly wrapped a blanket around his gun and handed it to a man behind him.

"Tell no one, I took my rifle apart and hid the pieces. I put it back together when I got here. I shot two Tatanka, then Teton came. They wanted hides. I traded them for a horse. I now have the only horse in the village," he added proudly.

Another Dakota man shouted, "Where is Tatanka? We all must hunt!"

A frenzy swept over the mass of Indians as they joined in the call to hunt Tatanka.

Williamson shouted, "Don't do anything foolish! The agent forbids you from leaving Crow Creek. Let me talk to him first."

"Talk to the agent," someone shouted, "but we must hunt!"

The missionary left for the stockade, known as Fort Thompson after the agent who built it. Nathan hurried alongside him.

"I heard you. I don't know much Dakota, but I've picked up enough to understand you're going to Thompson. Do you need help?" Nathan wondered.

Williamson smiled at him. "You're welcome to help me try to make the agent see reason."

"John, you speak Dakota better than any white man I've ever heard. Better than your father or Riggs. How'd you pick it up so well?"

146

"I was raised at my father's mission. From my earliest days I remember learning English from my parents and Dakota from the children I played with each day. I naturally learned two languages at the same time. It has served me well."

A few minutes later the two men were in the stark office of Colonel Thompson.

"Colonel," Williamson explained, "you know very well the shortages the Dakota face. They're on a starvation diet. Buffalo have been spotted nearby. You must allow the Indians to hunt them."

"John, you know I can't do that. My orders are to not let them leave the camp here at Crow Creek. Why, they'd have my head back in Washington if anything happened."

Nathan's reply was immediate. "You were also told that food would arrive by steamboat to feed them. Where is it?"

Thompson walked back behind his desk and picked up a sheet of paper. He glanced at it and then waved it at John and Nathan.

"Do you know what this says?" The agent balled the paper up and tossed it onto the floor. "It says that the company with the contract to ship food to us from Mankato has waited too long. The Minnesota River is now too shallow and with the drought, the Missouri isn't navigable in places, either. The supplies are now going to be shipped overland. But it's going to take them months to get here."

"You mean they won't even get underway until late summer or early fall?" Nathan was exasperated. "What if we get an early snow? They won't get here until half of these people are dead of starvation."

"Colonel, in the name of all that's holy, you've got to let them hunt," the missionary implored.

Thompson stared down at the rough wood of his bare desk and slowly nodded. "You're right. I wasn't sent here to starve women and children. They can go on one condition: I want you two to go with them. You'll be under my direction, and if this goes bad, it's on your heads. Don't let them desert to the hostiles."

Williamson looked at Nathan, who nodded. "Thank you, Colonel. It's the right thing to do. Nathan and I will go on the hunt with the Dakota, and we'll bring them back to you here."

The next morning Thompson issued half a dozen guns, some ammunition, a little flour and salt pork, and watched as 800 Dakota disappeared over the hills north of Crow Creek. The Indians brought their household utensils and tents with them. They had to be prepared for possibly spending months on the plains.

The tents were threadbare and almost as thin as the ragged clothing of the Dakota. An onslaught of cold or freezing rain, let alone an early snowfall, would be disastrous to them. Even the strong among the Dakota were enfeebled by hunger. Adding to their burden were the many children who had to be carried. But in spite of all the obstacles before them, they were buoyed by the knowledge that buffalo, Tatanka, was near. Tatanka would save the people as he had for centuries.

John and Nathan had horses and rifles, making a total of three animals for the hunt. The two white men walked and carried their own equipment packs while letting the elderly, sick and children share the use of their horses.

Tatanka had moved away from Crow Creek, and the hunters could find no trace. Sounding Heaven insisted that he knew the direction that the buffalo must have taken. He led the people over what seemed an endless plain. The sun burned hot each day, glowing brightly in a vivid blue canopy that didn't end until it reached the horizon. Each night he ordered camp set up on the leeward side of where he felt their prey must be so that man scent would not alert the herd.

John and Nathan soon learned to adapt themselves to the "Indian way." The camp took no morning breakfast. Hunters would leave early in the morning and have an informal lunch as they rested at mid-day. The main meal would be toward evening when the men returned with game.

The Dakota did make some concessions to their white companions. Pastor Williamson held morning and evening religious meetings consisting of a hymn, a short scripture reading and a prayer.

Napesni, an elder leader, spoke to John and Nathan after the band of hunters left in search of buffalo one morning. Word had come back that three separate herds of buffalo had been spotted.

"It's better that they are apart. Tatanka might scatter all at once if they were shot at in one large group."

"Kind of like divide and conquer," Nathan said to John, "and they are already divided."

"It was good of you to loan out your horses and rifles." Napensi's smile deepened the creases in his furrowed face. He was dressed in a cotton shirt and buckskin pants. His mostly white hair hung in braids.

"Better riders and better shots could make better use of them," John replied.

"Horses, the God Dogs, they changed how we hunt. It was much better once the horse came. Without them our life was much harder. Even our lodges became bigger. Horses can pull longer lodge poles than dogs."

"How did you hunt before the horse?" Nathan asked.

"If there were cliffs, we would drive them over and kill those who did not die in the fall. Many times we would light fires to keep Tatanka from water. They would come to drink, crazed with thirst, late in the day. Then men would crawl near them covered by wolf or coyote furs and shoot them with arrows. You've seen that we use all of Tatanka. He provides our food, our tools, our weapons. Life without him is very sad."

"Like Crow Creek," John agreed.

Late in the afternoon amid shouts and tremolos of joy, the hunting party entered the village with great quantities of buffalo.

Sounding Heaven announced, "We have had a big hunt. Women, come to take your part."

Dakota women rushed forward to receive a portion of the meat. It was all equitably divided. Many of the women had been on the hunt and had butchered the animals. As the men rested and smoked, some women prepared a feast while others scraped the hides free of fat and meat and prepared them for tanning.

AT CROW CREEK, SAMUEL HINMAN AND EMILY worked tirelessly to educate young and old alike. They received assistance from Edward Pond, a son of Gideon, and occasionally from JoAnna.

Wabasha encouraged his people to learn from the teachers and missionaries. In council he reasoned, "Life is hard here. If the whites insist we must live like them, we must learn to survive."

Colonel Thompson had provided lumber from cottonwood trees, and a large building had been constructed. Gaps between the boards allowed inclement weather into the room, so Williamson and the others had lined the interior with adobe before John left.

The shortage of paper needed for school work was solved by using old newspapers. John and Hinman mixed lampblack with oil and brushed the words of lessons and songs on the old newspapers. Then they used them as charts and papered the walls with them.

"Make the words large and plain," John had instructed. "The students have to be able to read this from across the room."

"We still have only a few teachers, and so much to teach to so many," Samuel complained.

Emily's face animated with an idea. "We have many very bright students, Johnny among them. Let's have them help us."

"Pupil-teachers," Samuel mused, "do we have enough qualified?"

"We can soon," Emily answered. "Especially now that Sam Brown has joined us. He interprets very well."

"Let's get them ready. They must be proficient enough to read the Bible well. Then we can put them in charge of less advanced groups. I agree, young Sam is a welcome addition."

Sam was the nineteen-year-old son of Joe Brown. He had declined to follow his father on the Sibley Expedition and had decided to aid his mother's people at Crow Creek.

Along with his mother, Sam had been held captive by the Santee for nearly the entire six weeks of the conflict. His life had been spared by Little Crow when many around him were killed. Sam saw the despair in the concentration camp at Fort Snelling and vowed to go to the Dakota Territory and try to help the Santee adapt.

Each morning an old Indian man acted as "town crier" and walked through the village announcing the start of school. The school building became a bustling center of activity as the teachers and pupil-teachers taught reading and English to dozens of willing students.

Emily and JoAnna watched as their pupils traced the letters of the alphabet on sheets of newsprint.

"They catch on fast," JoAnna noted.

"Thanks for the help. How is your work with Dr. Wharton?"

"We lose some," JoAnna replied quietly. "The horrible condition of what food there is, exposure to the elements—it's hard on them, especially the elderly and the very young." She looked sadly at the children and then brightened as another thought came to her. "Have you heard from Nathan? It's been weeks."

"A runner came with news of the hunt and a note for me. Nathan and John are well. They are doing some teaching and conducting services in the camp."

"Do they hunt?"

Emily laughed. "I don't think so. Apparently they've given their horses and rifles to the Indians. John says the Sioux are better shots, but he obviously doesn't know Nathan very well."

"He killed White Dog, didn't he? When he rescued you and the other girls?"

"Solomon and Nathan saved our lives. White Dog and his band had taken us almost all the way to Fort Abercrombie. Then our two saviors caught up with them. It was horrible. In an instant Solomon and Nathan had killed six men. White Dog held me as a shield with a knife to my throat, but Nathan simply raised his pistol and shot him dead. He saved my life. But you had a close call, too."

"I guess both of our men came to the rescue. I had been separated from my cavalry escort during an attack. I was wandering, lost on the prairie. I was lucky to find an old soddy for shelter. The Indians attacked me, I . . . I . . . actually shot and killed one. But then I had only one bullet left. I actually think I would have used it on myself if Jesse and his troop hadn't ridden in to save me."

"We have been fortunate, JoAnna, to have survived with so much evil and destruction around us."

"Yes, Emily, and a bit strange and ironic that both of us have chosen to try to help these people. People who were trying to kill us."

Emily looked over the collection of women, children, and elderly men that sat before them. "It wasn't these people. It was those who followed Little Crow, and hardly any of them are here."

"Jesse is looking for them with Sibley. Maybe his search will bring him here."

"Perhaps, JoAnna. But he's following dangerous men. If Jesse is near, danger might be near as well."

∞ 35 ∞

SIBLEY LEFT A PERMANENT CAMP BEHIND him as he headed west. Fort Atchison was on the banks of a lake which was also named for Ordinance Officer Atchison. It was within two miles of Lake Jessie, named for his wife by General John C. Fremont, who had explored this region nearly two decades earlier.

About half of the expedition, or 2,056 men, embarked on the forced march toward the Missouri River with Sibley. They consisted of 1,436 infantry, 520 cavalry, and 100 artillery. The best teams of mules were hitched to wagons carrying necessary ammunition and twenty-five days of rations.

Left behind in Camp Atchison were nearly 2,000 men, two-thirds of the cumbersome train of wagons, and all disabled men and animals.

As Oscar Wall rode beside Willie Sturgis, he sympathized with those back in camp. "They've put up breastworks and barricades. Now what do they do?"

"Jes sit around, I guess," Willie answered. "I'm glad I'm still on the march. Those poor souls are cut off. They's no other civilized folk for hundreds o' miles, no trees, cut off from everbody."

"And nothing to do, 'cept dig latrines and drill. They might be safe there, but at least we've got somethin' to look forward to, Willie. There's nothing worse than being a soldier and just sittin' around waitin' for something to happen."

"And we're gonna move fast. No more lollygaggin'. Oscar, one thing I git confused about. Officers talk about squads and comp'nies. I git that, but what's all these other things, reg'ments and such. How many are in 'em?"

Wall smiled, "Well, Willie, I read up on that once. Numbers are given for each, but don't mean that much. A squad's 'bout eight to ten men. Companies are supposed to be a hundred. But we call fifty men a company out here. Regiments are supposed to be ten companies. Then we get to brigades.

They're four to six regiments. In other words four to six thousand men. Next is a division, three brigades or about 12,000 soldiers. A corps is two divisions and the whole thing is . . . an army. Out here we don't concern ourselves with much above company and, like I said, troop numbers still vary. That, Willie, is your military lesson for the day."

"Oscar, you know a lot. You should write a book someday."

"Maybe I will, Willie, and you'll be in it if I do."

Near the front of the cavalry column, Colonel McPhail reined his horse in alongside Jesse. "Lieutenant," he said, "I want you to ride with the scouts, you seem to get on well with that Foot fella, and well. . .I want you to keep an eye on Duley. Something's about to happen. I can feel it. Duley is a loose wheel. I don't want him goin' off half-cocked and causin' trouble."

"I'm not sure I can help much. Duley and I aren't exactly friends."

"Lieutenant, you don't have to be his friend. Just watch over him. You already saved his butt once at Sauk Centre."

"He would've killed the woman we were sent to save."

"That's the type of thing I want you to save him from."

"I'll try, Colonel."

The next morning, July 20th, reveille broke over the camp at two o'clock with the blare of bugles rousing the bone-weary army. Sibley entered the neighboring tent and gently shook Stephen Riggs's shoulder. "Rise and shine, Stephen. We want to be moving out by 3:00."

"Must you impose your personal habits so completely upon this army?" a grumpy, sleepy voice rejoined. "The rest of the world doesn't arise every day before sunrise, and you do, army or not."

"Oh, come now," Sibley laughed, "this is the best part of the day. Man is at his mental and physical peak before sunrise."

"There might be many good reasons for getting an early start, General, but I can't accept that adjusting to your inner clock is one of them."

Sibley laughed harder and repeated, "Rise and shine, Reverend."

By 3:00 a.m. the expedition was indeed winding to the southwest. Jesse Buchanen rode out with the scouts, seeking signs of Indians. The march was uneventful. No hostile Dakota were spotted. The army was able to make twenty miles and set up camp at noon.

The scouts continued to survey the surrounding countryside. Solomon, Jesse, Daniel, and Isaac Renville rode with Duley to the north. Suddenly a large party of Indians came over a rise. Duley instinctively raised his rifle and pulled back the hammer. "Duley, don't be a fool!" Solomon barked. "Those are Chippewa, friendlies."

"You're right. They are Ojibway, or like you say Chippewa, not Dakota," Isaac Renville confirmed.

The large band rode to the scouts. They were mostly mixed-bloods with some full bloods among them. They were robust, all mounted and well-armed. A full-bearded white man rode out from the others and approached Duley. He wore a long black robe and seemed out of place among his buck-skin-clad companions.

"I'm Father Andre. I minister to these people. We hunt buffalo. Is Sibley near?"

Duley eyed the assemblage suspiciously. "And why do you want to know?"

"I have information for him."

"About what?"

"About the enemy he holds in common with these people, the Dakota."

"General Sibley is below the rise behind us. Follow and we'll take you to him."

It created quite a stir in camp when Duley and the scouts rode in at the head of 300 Indians. Men scrambled for their rifles and bugles sounded the alert until Duley shouted, "These men are Chippewa. They have news for the general! Don't be alarmed!"

Jesse and Duley brought Father Andre to Sibley's tent. The general and Riggs had been sitting on camp stools talking when his visitors rode up. The priest shook Sibley's hand and introduced himself.

Then he began, "I have news for you. There are many Dakota just miles west of the James River. You're near. We were hunting buffalo. So were they."

"How many are there?" Sibley wondered.

"I would say four to five thousand."

Sibley whistled. "Maybe I shouldn't have left 2,000 men at Camp Atchison."

Duley interjected emphatically, "Don't let their numbers bother you, General. It's been proven that a trained force of soldiers can beat a force of red savages many times their number. We can do it. We don't need any more."

"I think some want to fight you," Father Andre said, "maybe some do not. I guess you will find out."

"What about the Chippewa?" Sibley asked.

"They don't like the Dakota. There's much bad blood through their history. They wanted me to find you and tell you this. But they won't fight. Tomorrow we hunt again."

"Thank you, Father. Tomorrow we look for the Dakota Sioux."

COME MORNING THE MINNESOTA ARMY was once again underway well before dawn. The terrain was somewhat rough. Rolling hills stretched toward the James River, and when daylight came, the soldiers spotted alkaline lakes here and there, glistening like dirty diamonds where the landscape dipped into potholes.

Scout Tom Robinson trotted over to Jesse and Solomon. "Major Brown is breaking the scouts into many smaller groups to spread out and cover more territory. The hostiles are near, and we've got to find them. John Moore and me are to go with you to the north."

"Then let's get lookin'," Solomon replied.

The four rode for a couple of hours and saw nothing. From time to time Tom Robinson would dismount, kneel down and examine the ground.

"Watcha lookin' for?" Solomon asked.

"Signs. Horse tracks, travois marks, signs of horses eating or waste. Whatever tells me that they came this way. There's nothing here yet."

Robinson swung easily back onto his horse and made a clicking sound that started his horse off at a slow trot.

"Tom," Jesse asked, "you were a go-between with Sibley and Little Crow. You brought messages back and forth between them. How'd you get that duty? Did you fight?"

"I never fired a shot at a white man. I'm a mixed-blood Mdewakanton. Little Crow needed someone who could read and write in the white man's tongue. That was me."

"Look there." Moore pointed at scrapes crossing the path before them. "Lodge poles from travois. They've passed through here."

Robinson knelt, then touched and smelled the earth. "Less than a day, the Ojibway are right. The Dakota are close. Tomorrow, I think we find them."

THE DAKOTA WERE CAMPED LESS THAN twenty miles away. Inkpaduta and Pawn had joined up with Standing Buffalo and his Sisseton after they had moved west from Devils Lake. Heyoka had rejoined his companions after his brief sojourn into Canada.

Four thousand Dakota had erected their tipis on a range of low hills. One hill more prominent than the others dominated the landscape. To the north of the hills was a large brackish lake.

The lodge of Standing Buffalo stood ten feet tall. Buffalo robes lay on the ground around a crackling fire. Smoke wafted up through an opening in the tipi. Sweet Corn, Standing Buffalo, Pawn, Inkpaduta, Heyoka, and several other leaders sat around the fire. Each in turn breathed in smoke from the sacred red pipe.

When all had finished, Standing Buffalo spoke. "The Long Trader, Sibley, is near. Many blue coats are with him. We have many women and children. When the snows come, we'll have no food. The people are tired. I think we should give ourselves over to the Long Trader."

"No!" Inkpaduta's eyes flashed with hot sparks. "We have many soldiers, too. We must stand and fight. I have not come this long to give up."

Sweet Corn's face reddened deeply in agitation. "You were not even with us when we fought in Minnesota. You hid in Sioux Falls after the white men left!"

Inkpaduta scrambled to his feet. "Do not question my courage. Remember that I and my Wahpekute first fought the whites at Spirit Lake. Remember that a white man murdered members of my family eight years before you fought the whites.

"We did not attack the whites first in Iowa. They came after us first and why?" He spat out the words. "Because we shot a white man's dog that had bitten a Wahpekute. For that they killed us, they took our weapons that we hunt with and left us to starve."

He glared at Sweet Corn. "You had annuities to fall back on, we had nothing. But we rose up and killed dozens of the whites by Spirit Lake and into Minnesota. We were first to kill whites, and what did the Mdewakanton do? Little Crow came after me. That is why we left for the Dakota Territory."

"Little Crow had no choice," Standing Buffalo defended his former chief. "The whites would cut have off our annuities and blamed us all for the killings in Iowa if Little Crow had not tried to find you." He paused. "And you know that he would have found you if he had wanted to. Little Crow did not try."

Pawn shouted his support for Inkpaduta. "We must not give up. Not while there are so many of us. Let us rub the whites out and leave them like greasy spots in the dirt."

Standing Buffalo sighed. "I have smoked and talked with my elders. They agree that I should talk to the Long Trader and that we should give up to him."

Inkpaduta, Pawn, and Heyoka angrily stomped out of the lodge.

Pawn turned to Inkpaduta. "We will fight tomorrow, no matter what the women who are our leaders want. I will make sure of it."

∽ 36 ∾

THE SIBLEY EXPEDITION CONTINUED its steady progress covering another twenty miles by noon on the morning of July 24. Head scout Joe Brown galloped to where Sibley's column was gathering on the banks of a large, shallow salt lake.

"General!" he shouted. "Indians are everywhere! Look at the hills!"

The lake to his back, Sibley shielded his eyes from the bright sunlight and surveyed the scene before him. A high hill rose in the distance. To the right of the "big mound," as Sibley came to call it, spread a series of lower, rolling hills, some quite long. The first hills were to the southwest about 200 yards away. Big Mound was directly to his front several hundred more yards away.

It was the most beautiful spot they had encountered on the expedition. It was the population on the hills that was disconcerting.

"My God, look at them!" Colonel Olin exclaimed. "The hills are covered with Indians, like so many red ants."

Sibley calmly turned to his adjutant. "See that the wagons form a circle out from the lakeshore. Throw up earthworks and be ready for an attack."

"Who's attacking, General? Us or them?"

"That remains to be seen, Mr. Brown. Get a flag of truce. Take some scouts with you and head out to that first hill on the right. See what they want."

"General," Dr. Josiah Weiser interjected, "some of those Indians may be friends of mine. Many lived by me in Shakopee. I was their physician. Let me go with Brown."

Sibley thought a moment and then replied, "All right, Doctor, maybe you can help. But be careful."

Brown saluted, wheeled his horse around and selected a detachment of scouts to ride to the hill with him. Jesse, Solomon, Will Duley, and four

Renville brothers, plus Weiser trotted over the couple hundred yards of flat ground toward the rise to their right. Brown held his saber high, a white cloth tied to it and waving in a breeze.

The Dakota waved and smiled as the scouts rode up the hill into their midst. Some appeared particularly happy to see Dr. Weiser.

"Doctor," a young man cried, "it's good to see a friend!"

Weiser dismounted and shook hands all around. The other scouts gathered near the doctor.

"Go ahead and see what they want," Brown whispered. "They seem to like you."

"Who leads you?" Weiser asked the young warrior as dozens more Indians gathered behind him.

"Standing Buffalo."

"What's your intention? We want you to go to the reservation at Crow Creek."

The young man smiled. "We won't resist. Standing Buffalo will come and give up his people to the Long Trader. Tell General Sibley to come up here, and Standing Buffalo will come to him."

Another Dakota warrior sidled up to Solomon Foot and said in a low voice, "White man, there are bad Indians here. It's not safe. Tell Sibley."

Foot nodded almost imperceptibly without looking at his informant.

After more friendly conversation, with Weiser meeting more friends from Shakopee, the little band rode back to Sibley's camp. Some Dakota had come down from the hills and were talking to soldiers just yards from the camp.

"Looks like old home week," Jesse laughed. "This will be easier than we thought."

"Not so fast, boy, " Solomon cautioned, "I got a warning back there."

Leaving Jesse looking perplexed, Foot rode ahead to tell Brown what he had heard. A cloud bank darkened the western horizon as they approached the soldiers' camp. Breastworks had been thrown up, tents pitched, and men were digging wells.

As soon as his scout detail entered the camp, the general approached to learn their findings. "What do they want?"

"General," Weiser beamed, "they want to give up. Standing Buffalo wants to meet you on that hill to surrender."

"Well, if they intend to lay down their arms, I suppose I will go up—"

"That might not be wise, General," Brown interrupted, "Mr. Foot here had a warning whispered in his ear. It seems that not every Indian wants peace."

"What do you mean?" Sibley looked sharply at Solomon.

"Just somethin' one of 'em said. Just a warning. I think you'd be wise to heed it."

"Let's be sure," Sibley considered. "You men go back up there. Take another scout with you, Stevens. Dr. Weiser, if it looks like Standing Buffalo is really coming to surrender, send me word."

Once again the small band of scouts ascended the hill. More Dakota had gathered on the rise, and Weiser greeted more of his friends. A small entourage rode with Standing Buffalo in the distance as he came to surrender. Standing in the midst of Indians on the hill was Pawn.

Pawn clutched a rifle tightly beneath a blanket to hide it from view. Dr. Weiser passed before him, happily shaking hands with another Dakota friend. Pawn stepped from the crowd and quickly fired his rifle. The bullet struck Weiser in the back. The doctor crumpled to the ground, killed instantly.

Solomon snapped a quick shot a Pawn, but the murderer escaped into the mass of Indians. Shock and confusion swept over the hill. Urgently the scouts tried to catch Pawn, but he eluded them unscathed.

From the camp, Sibley clearly saw a puff of blue smoke and watched Weiser fall. The report of the rifle reached his ears a moment later.

Standing Buffalo also witnessed the scene as he neared the hill. Some Dakota on the hill began to fire at the scouts. Stevens was hit. The rest galloped back to Sibley amidst a hail of gunshots.

Duley, McPhail, and Marshall rushed to Sibley.

"Weiser's dead!" Marshall exclaimed. "Let's pitch into the red devils now!"

"Not so fast," Sibley cautioned, "Standing Buffalo is out there. On his way to surrender. Maybe he still will."

Sibley and his officers stood a moment and watched as Standing Buffalo turned around and rode back up to Big Mound.

"All right," Sibley became decisive, "I want the Sixth under Crooks and your Seventh, Marshall, along with McPhail's cavalry to sweep in a long battle front up that hill. Once you gain the hill, wheel toward the southeast and keep pushing until you get to the Big Mound. Jones and Whipple's artillery will offer support."

"What about the Tenth Infantry, General?" Marshall inquired.

"Baker and the Tenth will support this camp. We can't leave it defenseless. Now, go get them. They have women and children. Spare them."

The Dakota had fallen back to another high plateau just to the southwest of the one where Weiser had been killed. Standing Buffalo watched with Sweet Corn as men, women, and children scrambled up the hills.

Standing Buffalo spoke first. "I feel as I did when the war started in Minnesota. This is bad for our people."

"Pawn killed the white man," Sweet Corn said.

"I'll deal with him later. Our warriors must take a stand on the hills as long as they can. See that the women and children retreat behind the high ground. Sweet Corn, they must escape to the southwest."

"We hold good ground," Sweet Corn offered with some hope. "We are above the whites. We can hold them off."

"They have more guns, and they have the big guns. Hear the thunder they make."

A blast from Jones's cannon whistled above the crashing hooves of the cavalry horses and blasted into the hillside, hurtling dirt and rock into the air.

Sibley raised binoculars and watched from his lakeside camp as his men pressed forward up the hills. They faced fierce resistance. The Dakota warriors desperately tried to hold their position.

"Stephen," he turned to Riggs, "there must be fifteen hundred of them out there. They can hold awhile, but not long. We'll push them off the hills, just wait."

His words were prophetic. The Indians retreated from hill to hill, crossing a mile-long plateau and massing once again at the brow of a hill just off the southwest end of Big Mound.

McPhail shouted at Solomon, "They wanna take shelter below the crest of that southwestern slope! We can block their escape to the west! Tell Lieutenant Buchanen to take Company F and charge the savages at the extreme left."

Foot jerked his horse's head around and slapped its flank. The horse and rider bounded down the hill to where Jesse waited with his troops.

McPhail turned to another nearby officer and screamed over the din of gunfire, "Captain Austin, take Company B and charge those Indians taking shelter farther to the right."

Both companies of cavalry launched at full speed. Sabers glistened in the afternoon sun. The short Maynard carbines blazed fire as the troops galloped headlong toward their foes.

The Dakota warriors waited. The earth trembled beneath the horses' hooves as they thundered over the hard-packed parched earth.

"Wait!" Inkpaduta screamed. "Wait until they come close! Fire when I fire!"

As the soldiers neared the crest of the hill, a furious volley cut loose from the Indians' rifles. The Dakota then scampered down the backside of the hill in retreat. The cavalry horses strained mightily and slowed to a walk when the slope of the hill became too steep.

"Fire at will," Jesse yelled. "Bring them down!" Several of the fleeing Indians tumbled to the grass as a rain of bullets thudded into them.

The blare of a bugle rose above the bedlam of screams, shots, and horses. It was a call from McPhail for both companies to join him on the right. Instantly the men galloped their horses to the colonel.

Half a mile away at the foot of a long hill, Indian men, women, children, dogs, and ponies were squeezed into a narrow escape route between two lakes. Like a small stream feeding a river, they came off Big Mound and the high ground to the south until they joined in flight between the lakes. Cries of children, barking dogs, and the sharp whinnies of horses added to the melee of gunshots and hooves.

From the hilltop, McPhail impatiently watched the Indians stream away. Solomon galloped up and wrenched his horse to a stop.

"Colonel," Foot cried, "a column thrown around the western end of the lakes will stop them! We can capture them all right there!"

"I know, but I have orders not to pursue beyond this point. I must wait until Sibley sends another order."

"Colonel," Solomon pointed and shouted urgently over the clamor, "they're getting away."

"Sibley knows what's happening. There might be warriors beyond the next rise waiting for us."

"No, Colonel, we have the most advanced position. We have the best view of the retreat. I'll bet you all the land in Kandiyohi County that there's nobody hidin' out there to ambush us."

"We wait, Mr. Foot," McPhail said in a loud, controlled voice.

The cavalry gathered in formation and waited. Horses pawed nervously and scarred the earth. Will Duley's eyes blazed as he looked back to Sibley's camp.

"Damn old woman," he yelled at Jesse, "this is our chance to smash 'em, and he makes us sit here!"

"Wait, Captain Duley. Right or wrong we have orders!"

The dark cloud bank that had been gathering in the west now rolled over the battlefield. A lightening bolt seared through the blackened sky, and a crash of thunder resounded and echoed over the gunfire and battle sounds.

Then the sky above them opened up, and a driving rainstorm poured down, pelting soldiers and Indians alike with sheets of water. McPhail raised his sword and pointed to the south. A blinding flash of lightening struck nearby, and the sword flew from the colonel's hand. Horses reared in fear while Private John Murphy launched from his stumbling horse as if he had been catapulted. His smoking body hit the leaden earth and trembled just an instant before he died.

"Lightening hit 'im!" Willie Sturgis yelled as he scrambled to the side of his dead comrade.

Oscar Wall looked down from his horse. "Don't touch him, Willie. You can't help him now. Look, there's a messenger coming for McPhail. Mount up!"

The colonel wiped the rain from his eyes and eagerly glanced at the crumbled bit of paper. One word was scribbled on it: "Attack."

"Bugler!" he screamed, "sound the charge!"

At the first note, the two companies of cavalry bolted down the hill. The Indians had passed by the lake and were a mile away in the open, heading to the southwest. The troopers also had to slow at the narrow gap between the lakes, but the column formed into units of fours and passed through.

Beyond the lakes, McPhail ordered, "Form a line of battle and sweep the plains until we get them all!"

Sibley ordered up a supporting column of the Seventh and part of the Tenth infantry as well as artillery under Lieutenant Whipple. But they found it impossible to keep up with the fleeing Indians and racing cavalry.

Standing Buffalo stood on a hillside with Sweet Corn watching his people pass by. Women, children, and some of the older warriors raced by, eyes wide in near panic. A soggy blanket was draped over his shoulders. The rain had lessened, but it hadn't stopped.

"Have you told the young men what they must do?" Standing Buffalo asked.

"Yes, Inkpaduta and his sons lead all who can fight. They will stay to the rear and protect the others as they flee."

"They must fight, hold and then fall back. They must repeat that many times until we reach safety."

"Yes," Sweet Corn agreed, "they have been told. But look, the whites come at us like devils. How can we hold them?"

"By fighting and running, fighting and running. It's our only hope."

The two men watched the Dakota warriors stubbornly shoot at the onrushing soldiers, then fall back, take another position and fire again. Inkpaduta, with Pawn at his side, frantically marshaled his warriors to defend the retreating mass of Indians.

Rising Star, tall and muscular and once a friend of John Williamson at the Yellow Medicine Agency, strode to Inkpaduta. "I know some of these people. I'll talk to them. Maybe they'll listen. Standing Buffalo wanted to give up. This is all wrong. Our women and children will be run down and killed."

"Fool," Pawn growled, "they'll kill us anyway. You can't stop them."

"Watch me try," Rising Star said. He took a bundle out of a bag, unrolled it and wrapped it around his body. It was a large American flag. The Indian strode purposefully toward the oncoming soldiers.

Duley, with Jesse behind him, sighted Rising Star. The rain had stopped and a rainbow formed a crescent around the flag-draped figure.

"What's he doin'?" Will snapped.

"Surrendering?" Jesse offered.

"More likely a trick." Duley raised his carbine, sighted and fired.

Dozens of other soldiers opened fire as well. Jesse watched helplessly. There was nothing he could do for the lone man walking toward them. The troopers spurred their horses on, firing at him and ignoring his flag.

Rising Star realized that talk was hopeless and that sure death awaited. He whispered to himself, "If this is my fate, I will bring others with me. It is a good day to die."

He winced as several bullets found their mark on his body. Still with the flag around his shoulders, Rising Star knelt and fired back. His double-barreled shotgun spat both loads into the soldiers. With his mouth full of buckshot, Rising Star poured powder into the muzzle and spat a charge of bullets into the barrel. There was no time for wadding. He quickly slipped a percussion cap onto the gun's nipple as six riders descended upon him. They were ten feet away. The Dakota frantically pulled the trigger. A blast of fire and smoke exploded from the barrel. At such close range the buckshot could not scatter. Instead, it buried itself in a coat rolled up on the pommel of Private Ezra Green's saddle, knocking the soldier from his horse but not injuring him.

Rising Star rose to his feet and swung his gun like a club. The butt end caught Andrias Carlson in the chest and swept him off his horse. The Indian, now with over a dozen wounds in his body, whirled around and swung his gun again and again.

Then Will Duley charged. Hanging low in his saddle, he fired a shot from under his horse's neck. The bullet lodged in Rising Star's head and sent him crashing to the rain-soaked earth. The warrior fell on top of the flag, staining it with his bright red blood.

The cavalry charged on after the desperate Santee Dakota. Another solitary figure appeared before them. This time, it was an old white-haired man. He looked to be at least eighty years old and had no weapon. The man had tried to keep up with his people's exodus, but his frail body left him farther and farther behind.

Exhausted, he kept up a faltering trot. He looked back when he heard the approach of a young soldier on horseback. In fear or acceptance of his fate, the old man covered his head with a blanket and continued on. The young soldier raised his saber to strike.

Jesse watched with alarm from twenty yards away and shrieked, "NO!"

The soldier took a quick glance at Jesse and, ignoring his shout, delivered a slicing blow to the back of the Indian's neck, nearly beheading him.

The cavalry horses galloped over the bodies of others who were shot down in flight. Many of the bodies were scalped by soldiers seeking bloody trophies and the bounty offered in Minnesota.

The Dakota continued fighting their stubborn holding action until darkness fell and wrapped itself around red and white, dead and alive without discrimination. McPhail tried to continue the pursuit in the ink-black night. Only the bright flashes of gunfire revealed the location of combatants.

"Press on," Will Duley urged, "we can find them. Light or not. I can smell 'em."

"It's ten o'clock, Captain," McPhail considered, "the men are wet, tired and hungry. If we camp here tonight, we'll be in position to run them down tomorrow."

"Colonel?" A voice penetrated out of the darkness. "You there? It's me, Lieutenant Beaver. I've got a message from the general."

"Here!" McPhail called.

Beaver rode alongside but still could be heard rather than seen. "General Sibley orders all forces to return to Big Mound."

"Even us?" Duley asked incredulously. "We've got the enemy where we want them. We can take them all tomorrow. Right, Colonel?"

"It does seem curious to order us to Big Mound. Are you sure he meant us?"

"I lost the note, but I know it said *all* forces."

"All right," McPhail sighed. "Bugler, sound recall. We're going back. Lieutenant, we seem to have lost our bearings in the chase and darkness. Will you lead us back?"

"Well, Colonel, that's going to be a bit hard for me, too. I only found you by following the sounds of battle. I'm lost, too."

"Colonel," Duley implored, "this is all wrong. We can't give up the fight now."

"We have orders from our general, Captain Duley. We will go to Big Mound."

The two companies of cavalry retraced their approach as best they could. About five miles back they encountered the infantry and artillery that had been deployed after the first charge. They had been bivouacked for about an hour and were somewhat rested.

McPhail's cavalry was exhausted and disgusted. To a man they believed that the enemy was in their grasp, only to have it released by their own general. The night continued to be murkily dark under the dense cloud cover.

The fatigued horses moved slowly, their heads bowed nearly to the ground. Whipple's artillery and the infantry managed to keep pace with the bedraggled cavalry. Still they lost their way.

Frustrated, McPhail called to Whipple, "Lieutenant, fire some cannon shots. Maybe someone will hear us and fire back." Several cannon blasts into the night were met by silence. The troops continued wandering through the darkness, occasionally firing blasts, hoping for a response.

Just at daylight, around 4:00 a.m., Whipple's cannon shot was met by a distant answer. By 7:00 a.m. McPhail led his column into Camp Sibley.

"Much as I wudda liked ta have kep' up after 'em, I'm glad ta be back in camp," Willie Sturgis said.

"It's been quite a ride, Willie," Oscar Wall replied, "I added it up. We've been in the saddle for twenty-eight hours. For a considerable time, we were actively engaged in fighting. We've had nothing to eat and no water since yesterday morning."

"Our horses fared no better, Oscar. Hey, lookey this. They broke camp. No tents up, no food cookin', nothing."

"Don't worry, Willie, McPhail will see we're cared for."

While their colonel met with Sibley, most of the exhausted soldiers picketed their horses and then, too tired to prepare food, simply collapsed without shelter onto the soggy plain.

Sibley was surprised to see the cavalry return. "What are you doing here?" he exclaimed to McPhail. "Did you lose them? How did they get away?"

McPhail looked perplexed. "We had them, General. It was dark, but I had a pretty good idea where they were. We were going to attack in the morning. Then we received an order from you. All forces return to Big Mound."

"That wasn't for you!" Sibley snapped. "This was your order: bivouac where night overtakes you if you can hold your ground. Return to camp if you can't. That was your order. The other was for everyone else, not you."

"Well, General," McPhail rubbed his forehead, "apparently there was a mix-up. We received a message to return."

Sibley slapped his thigh with his cap. "Damn! So they got away! We had them, and they got away."

"They've got women and children and they're still close. We'll get them, General. Don't worry. We'll finish them off."

"By God, I hope so!"

Most of the day the dog-tired soldiers slept in the broiling hot sun. Late in the afternoon, a bugler sounded assembly, and the men staggered to their feet in a stupor that resembled a mob of drunks.

They made a march of five miles and then camped. Many had their first food and first cup of coffee in forty hours. But more than fatigue troubled Jesse as he drank the hot brew with Solomon.

"I heard we lost Lieutenant Freeman, along with the beef contractor, Brackett. They went out looking for buffalo before the shooting started. Freeman was found dead and Brackett's missing. Hell can't be much worse than what we just went through, old man."

"It was an endurance test, for man and beast."

"That's only part of it, Solomon. I signed on to be a soldier, to fight other soldiers. I planned on those being Confederates. We're fighting old men, women, and children. Did you see the man in the American flag? We shot him down. He had something to say to us. But no one cared. I close my eyes and I can still see the old man being run down and having his head nearly sliced off. Then, the scalps our men took. I thought we were fighting savages, not *being* savages."

"War is an ugly business, Jesse, they killed my brother, they tried to kill me and my family. You might feel different if they had killed your JoAnna."

"Maybe, but I hope that even that wouldn't turn me into a barbarian. It's eating up Duley alive."

Solomon gazed at the bubbling pot of coffee hanging over the flickering fire and spoke softly. "War brings out the best and the worst in men. Doesn't matter what your side is."

That night they buried Dr. Josiah Weiser and Private John Murphy with full military honors. A drizzling rain and northeast wind brought a chilly night to Sibley's men. But curled up in their tents, the fatigued army slept well for the first time in forty-eight hours.

ဆ 37 ஓ

URING THE CHASE, THE DAKOTA HAD cast off any impediments to their flight. Buffalo hunts throughout the summer had resulted in a large supply of dried meat and buffalo robes. Some were left behind in their camp near Big Mound, and more was cast off as they were pursued.

The soldiers reveled in their new-found dietary bounty and stuffed their haversacks for lunch on the march and for evening mess. Many of the Dakota, having lost their food supply, resorted to digging roots for sustenance.

Standing Buffalo gathered his people to rest several miles from Sibley's camp. The cold drizzle outside matched the disconsolate mood of the leaders huddled in the chief's tipi. Inkpaduta, Pawn, and Heyoka sat together while Standing Buffalo, Sweet Corn, and other Sisseton leaders completed the circle.

Standing Buffalo looked hard at each of them before he spoke. His voice was sad and slow. "Many young men were killed by the whites. It did not need to be. It was time for us to give ourselves up to Sibley. We can't last through another winter on the run."

His voice grew sharper as his eyes blazed at Pawn. "You caused this! You killed the doctor! Now they won't rest until we're all dead."

Pawn scoffed at Standing Buffalo. "You think it's better to live in a cage. We're still free here. We can go to the big river and join the Teton."

"You go to them!" Sweet Corn snapped. "I fought the white soldiers at Abercrombie while you were killing women and children at Shetek. I know what real war is like. The Teton would not join Little Crow. Go to them! See if they help you fight women and children. My time to fight is over."

Standing Bull continued, "Sweet Corn speaks true. We will fight no more. Those who think differently," he looked directly at Inkpaduta, Pawn, and Heyoka, "should leave us now. You are not welcome here anymore."

The three angrily rose to their feet.

"Keep running or give up!" Inkpaduta cried. "Hunkpapa are near. We'll join warriors who want to stand against the invaders. You do what you want."

FARTHER TO THE SOUTH, THE CROW CREEK Santee continued their hunt. Successful buffalo harvests dramatically transformed them. John Williamson enthused about the apparent changes.

"Nathan, look at how much better they look! Their faces were emaciated, their eyes hollow. Now their forms are round and sleek."

"They seem happy and contented," Nathan agreed. "If it weren't for you, John, many more would be dead at Crow Creek. The Santee realize it, too."

"God used me as his instrument to help them."

"But before winter they must return to Crow Creek. A good supply of buffalo will help. But eventually they'll be back as they were, malnourished with a pitiful supply of government food."

"We'll find a way to deal with it, Nathan. Oh, while you were out hunting with the Santee yesterday, one of Sibley's border patrol scouts came by."

"The ones on the Coteau des Prairies?"

"Yes, the Indian scouts Sibley sent to the high eastern Dakota table land, to keep Lakota and Dakota from coming into western Minnesota. Many brought their families with them and established Camp Scout. Most are Christian, and I think I should pay them a visit. When it's time to return to Crow Creek, perhaps you can continue with the Santee, and I'll pay a visit to Camp Scout."

"Sure, John. That should work. There are few problems with these people. They handle their own discipline quite well. The Soldiers' Lodge tipi seems to offer a deterrent to bad behavior."

"They have their own methods and a very low rate of crime. I pray to God that we bring back a bounty of buffalo meat to Crow Creek."

AT CROW CREEK, SAMUEL HINMAN, Emily and JoAnna continued to conduct classes in the cottonwood schoolhouse. More and more pupil teachers were prepared, and the number of Santee capable of reading their own language continued to rise.

The students received some instruction in arithmetic and history of western civilization. They were drilled to memorize Biblical passages and instructed in morals and religion. Santee of all ages came regularly. The more advanced students began to read and write English.

Infrequent mail deliveries were a source of excitement and anticipation for the white population of Crow Creek. Hinman beamed and held an envelope in his hand as Emily entered the school.

"Mail just came, Emily. This one is addressed to me and John. It's from his father. Dr. Williamson is at Davenport." He ripped the envelope open and began to read. Then he stopped and looked to Emily.

"This is all right, isn't it? It's from John's father, but it's addressed to both of us."

Emily smiled brightly. "Read it. John won't mind."

Samuel read silently for a moment and then summarized, "He's at the prison in Davenport. Conditions are poor. He hopes to get one-third of them and their families freed and sent here soon. Dr. Williamson says it's a hard fight. Minnesota politicians want to keep the Dakota locked up forever. He says he can accomplish nothing without prayer, patience, and perseverance."

Emily noted, "If they send more people, then they better send more food and medical supplies. JoAnna and Dr. Wharton are doing all they can. But the deaths keep happening."

"Sickness and despair is a way of life here, Emily."

A young Indian burst through the open doorway and cried excitedly, "It's time. They're all ready!"

Pastor Hinman spread his hands expansively. "Nothing like a wedding, or in this case weddings, to create a festive mood. Come, Emily."

In the camp arbor a large number of Dakota had gathered. Samuel stood before them wearing black pants and a white shirt. He preached a sermon on Christian marriage and then asked, "How many have come prepared to be married?" At least two dozen stepped forward.

Hinman laughed. "Emily, help me sort this out. Who matches with who?"

Emily happily sorted the pairs. Somewhat perplexed, she turned to the pastor, "Samuel, there are sixteen men and fifteen women. Someone is literally the odd man out."

A middle-aged man stood sheepishly apart from the others.

"Where's your bride?" Samuel asked.

"She's not here. She's in the tent. She doesn't wish to get married, but I do."

Samuel placed his hand sympathetically on the man's shoulder. "I'm sorry, but it takes two to consummate a marriage."

"You can't just declare that we are married?"

"No, I can't marry you without her willing presence."

"With my people, if I brought enough horses the woman's father could declare that we were married, no matter what she thought."

"That's not the way it is in the world you now live in."

The Indian man dejectedly turned away and left. Pastor Hinman then married fifteen happy couples.

38

AFTER MOST OF A DAY'S REST, THE SIBLEY Expedition moved out early on the morning of July 26th. They followed the trail over which the cavalry had fought its running battle with the Dakota just two days earlier. Indians were sighted periodically in the distance throughout the march.

Duley turned to Joe Brown. "Should we go after 'em?"

"I think they'd like that, Captain, but, no, they're just watching us. They're staying out of rifle range. I'll let Sibley know that we see them, but riding out there would cut us off from the main body, and we'd be easy pickings."

"I'll at least let them know we know they're out there." Duley raised his carbine and snapped off a couple of harmless shots.

"Hold on, Captain," Brown cautioned. "This isn't the time or place. Sibley is a couple of miles behind us, and I don't like our odds. It looks like they outnumber us significantly."

"I don't care how many there are. It's just more to shoot."

"Later, you'll get your chance again. Not this moment."

Jesse's head swiveled at the sound of shots nearby. "What's that?"

"Just Duley takin' potshots at some Indians," Solomon answered. "He'll get us all in trouble some day."

Foot gnawed on a dried strip of buffalo meat as he rode with the other scouts.

"A good, quick breakfast. Want some?" he asked Jesse.

"Already had some. It's a shame we had to waste so much of it."

Solomon nodded. "The Sioux left behind more than we could carry. But we took what we could."

"Still it was sad to burn the rest or leave it to rot."

Solomon took another bite. "It was their whole winter supply. It puts them in a real pickle. When hard weather comes, they'll be hungry."

"And more likely to give up if they haven't already. I guess eliminating their food supply is part of Sibley's plan." Jesse looked to where distant Dakota warriors watched from a hilltop. "I just hope they don't try to take it back."

"Well, Jesse, I read once where Napoleon said that an army travels on its stomach. No food, no army. I think the Sioux will discover that Napoleon was right."

Around 2:00 p.m. the scout detail came upon a small lake. Joe Brown looked it over and nodded approvingly at Gabriel Renville. "Ride back and let the general know that we've got a good campsite for bivouac here. Water, good grass, the lake offers some protection from attack, we can see in all directions. It's a lot better than Birch Coulee."

The head scout remembered the disastrous site picked for the Birch Coulee camp back in Renville County, Minnesota. A burial detail sent out from Fort Ridgely had camped on a table-top prairie with ravines or tall grass on all sides. Brown was there and had witnessed the near total destruction of the troop.

"You led the men at Birch Coulee," Gabriel affirmed.

"We had too many leaders there," Brown replied. "Captain Grant chose the site. I disagreed with it, but not strenuously enough. I firmly believed that no Sioux were near. But they came." Brown shook his head. "Seventeen dead, near fifty men wounded, eighty-five horses killed. Losing the horses nearly wiped out our cavalry and made Sibley delay his march up the Minnesota even more. It was a disaster on many levels. If a relief column from the fort hadn't arrived, we all would have been killed.

"But enough of that. I've learned about campsites. This one is good. Tom," he called to Robinson, "picket the horses by the lake. The mules, too, once they get here."

As the horses grazed in the thick grass, Solomon and Jesse walked to the lakeshore to fill canteens. Near the muddy shore a buffalo had become mired and lay dead.

Michael Renville approached and smiled. "Many names have been given to places on our journey, Big Mound, Lake Jessie, Camp this and Camp that. I'll name this one 'Dead Buffalo Lake.'"

Solomon smiled and nodded. "Seems to fit pretty good, don't ya think, Jesse?"

"I'll tell the general. Dead Buffalo Lake it is."

A camp was established along the lakeshore. As more and more Indians were sighted, a perimeter of breastworks and barricades was built out from the lake. Hills rose in front of the camp and to either side. A particularly long hill lay on the right.

Sibley and his officers waited expectantly within their protective conclave.

INKPADUTA AND HIS BAND OF DAKOTA dissidents wandered to the west after the Battle of Big Mound. They urgently sought support from whatever source offered to help. Crossing the treeless plains toward the Missouri River, they suddenly found themselves surrounded.

Indians, painted for war, had materialized all around them as if out of thin air. Inkpaduta, with Pawn at his side, froze his body. But his eyes moved rapidly, taking in everything around him. "Hundreds," he whispered to Pawn, "there are hundreds of them."

"Who are they?" Pawn answered.

"They must be Hunkpapa."

A younger man, barely thirty, rode alone toward the Santee leaders. His hair was straight, but of a reddish-brown color. His head was large and his features were more Anglican in form than those of most Indians.

The horse stopped before Inkpaduta and the horseman spoke. "I'm Tataka Iyoutake, Sitting Bull, of the Hunkpapa. Are you Santee from Minnesota?"

"Yes, I'm Inkpaduta. With Standing Buffalo we fought the whites two days ago to the east."

"Where is Standing Buffalo?"

"Like the old woman he is, he makes ready to give up to Sibley, the Long Trader. We wish to keep fighting. Are you the war chief?"

"He is a holy man, a *wichasa waka*," another rider, a few years older, answered for Sitting Bull. "He dreams of buffalo and thunderbirds. He has many powers to help his people. He is young," the rider said proudly, "but he can heal and understands all about our life and the spirits who guide us."

"But can he fight?" Pawn asked defiantly.

"He counted coup on a Crow when he was not yet a man."

"Will he fight now?" Pawn rejoined.

Sitting Bull slipped easily from his horse. He walked to the Santee with a slight limp of his left foot. He noticed Inkpaduta watching his foot.

"A Crow shot me. I killed him. Come, let us meet and smoke in a circle." Sitting Bull and four of his leaders sat on the prairie grass. Inkpaduta, Pawn, Heyoka, and Grey Eagle joined them.

"This is Gall." Sitting Bull introduced the man who had previously spoken for him. "He's my friend and a war chief."

After each had smoked from the sacred red pipe, the young Hunkpapa spoke. "The Lakota and Nakota stayed out of your war in Minnesota. When Lame Bear and others came seeking our help, we turned them away. It was not our war. We had seen few white people, and they did not bother us. A band of young Sans Arc even rescued white captives brought from Minnesota.

"Many feared that by helping the Dakota Santee, we would bring trouble from the white soldiers on ourselves. So we did nothing. Now it's true, you have brought the soldiers to us. Today soldiers shot at some of my braves hunting buffalo.

"I have had a dream. Hunkpapa were fighting the white soldiers. It is meant to happen, and now the whites have come. They ride across our hunting grounds. They shoot Tatanka. The whites do not care who are Teton or who are Santee. They take our land. They take our food. They come to kill Indians. My warriors are watching the soldiers' camp now. We will join you in killing them."

At Dead Buffalo Lake, Sibley and his soldiers watched the movements of Indian riders on the distant hills. Mule drivers sweated in the afternoon heat, cutting hay-grass with scythes near the picketed animals. It was past mid-afternoon when the idyllic scene exploded into violence.

To the camp's right on a long hill, hundreds of Indians appeared as if by magic. On horseback and dressed only in war paint and breech clouts, they poised on the hill crest.

Sibley turned to Olin. "They were using the hill as cover. We've got hundreds of horses, mules, and their drivers exposed by the lake. Whose horses are the closest?"

"Taylor's Mounted Rangers' and the scouts."

"Tell them to get to their mounts and get ready for action. Bugler," he called, "sound assembly. Get more cavalry deployed as soon as possible."

Tim Kelly, an Irish mule skinner, paused from swinging his scythe and wiped sweat from his forehead. He gazed at the nearby hill and was startled to see it overrun by Indians.

"Lookey there, boyo," he called to a young driver, "the hill be crawlin' with the red divils. What we be lookin' for has found us."

Kelly watched as a rider moved forward from the others. He wore an eagle headdress and held a lance in one hand, his horse eagerly prancing ahead. It was Sitting Bull.

The Irishman sneered and picked up his bullwhip. He pointed at Sitting Bull and then whirled the whip above his head before snapping it with a loud, crackling pop.

"Ya, want som'ma this? Come 'n' git it!" Kelly screamed.

Sitting Bull didn't understand the words, but their meaning was clear. Like a hurricane, the Hunkpapa warriors descended the hill toward the mules and horses. Jesse and Solomon galloped frantically with the other scouts, followed by the Rangers.

Captain Taylor shouted, "Head 'em off, boys! They're tryin' to flank our right. Don't let 'em get to the animals and drivers!"

Solomon grabbed his reins with his mouth to better fire his carbine as he thundered nearer the charging Lakota. Jesse bent low in his saddle, firing his pistol from alongside his horse's neck. About halfway between the hill and the lakeshore the two forces crashed together. A soldier next to Jesse took an arrow in the chest and bounced on the prairie sod as he fell.

Jesse ducked as a lance whizzed by his head. A fiercely-painted warrior kicked his horse's sides, and it bolted at Jesse. The Indian raised his tomahawk as he charged toward the young officer. Jesse aimed and fired. An empty click sounded. The barrel was empty.

The warrior urged his steed alongside Jesse. He took a mighty swing with his sharp-bladed weapon. Instinctively Jesse bent backward in his saddle so that his head rested on his horse's rump. The hatchet sliced through the air just above him. Jesse drew his saber from its scabbard. The Indian's momentum had taken him past the young lieutenant. He turned his horse back toward the soldier and made another run, tomahawk held high.

As the warrior started to bring it crashing into Jesse's skull, Jesse thrust his sword upward into the attacker's belly. Surprise flashed over the Indian's face. Then he tumbled to the ground.

Sitting Bull, realizing that he faced too much firepower, broke off the attack and moved back toward the hill. Duley and a few others tried to follow.

Captain Taylor yelled after him, "Duley, get back here! What you're doing is suicide!"

He turned to Jesse. "Lieutenant, stop him. Our orders are to protect the mule drivers, not chase Indians."

Jesse galloped after Duley. Shouting at the man to stop did no good, so he raced alongside and reached down to snare the bridle of Duley's horse. Jesse held tight and tried to wrench the animal to a stop.

"Damn you!" Duley cried. He pulled his pistol from his holster and took aim at Jesse. Then Duley crumbled in his saddle and fell to the earth as Solomon cracked his head from behind with a rifle butt.

Foot immediately dropped to the ground and hoisted up the dazed officer. Over the commotion of war whoops and gunfire, he called to one of the men who had been following Duley. "Get 'im on your saddle and get back to camp!"

In moments they all were galloping back to Sibley.

Meanwhile, the Indians had launched a general attack on all sides, save from the lake behind the soldiers. Gray Eagle led the assault. Sibley sent the Sixth Minnesota under Colonel Averill, along with artillery under Whipple and Jones, to forward positions to his front and left.

Dust swirled from the hooves of the indians' horses as they sped onward. The cloud created by the galloping animals led to faulty aim on both sides. The Indians dropped back, leaving their dead behind.

The battle lasted over two hours. After the initial action, most shooting occurred from long range as the attackers fired at well-entrenched soldiers.

The camp remained on the alert through the night, but Sitting Bull had pulled his men back. Sibley asked Olin for a report on the battle.

Olin relayed to the general, "Our scouts say that sixteen Indians were killed, a Santee, Gray Eagle among them. We lost one cavalryman. Another thing."

"Yes, Mr. Olin, what else?"

"Our Indian scouts say that most of the dead weren't Santee. They are Hunkpapa, Teton. It seems they've joined forces with the Santee."

Concern swept over Sibley's face. "That's something we don't need. I wonder where Sully is. We're supposed to meet on the Missouri. We're getting close to the river. If Sully were near, the Teton should be to the west, following him and not coming after us. Anything else?"

"Just this, General. The scouts found an old man out there. It appears that the Hunkpapa were a hunting party, not looking to fight until they came upon Inkpaduta. They have a new leader, someone called Sitting Bull."

"Indian leaders come and go. Maybe Inkpaduta is on the way out. He certainly failed the Dakota at Big Mound. What did the old man say about this Sitting Bull?"

"Quite a lot, really. He's about thirty, his name was Slow, until he changed it after killing a buffalo."

"Slow," Sibley considered, "like a slow runner or feeble minded?"

"No, slow like he takes things in and thinks before he decides. Apparently he's held in quite high regard by his people and is growing in esteem with the other Teton bands as well. He's a holy man. They say he has intense spirituality and administers the complex religious rituals and beliefs of the Sioux people. Sitting Bull can heal, they say, and he carries medicinal herbs."

"So he's a medicine man," Sibley concluded.

"He's much more than that, General. He's a warrior and is known for his prowess in battle. Also, and this is kind of interesting, the old man says that Sitting Bull dreams and that his dreams come true."

"So we have a prophet Indian. Well, I haven't heard of him until now, and we just ran him off. I'm not worried, but I'll keep this Sitting Bull in mind."

"Oh, we almost lost Duley today."

"How's that?"

"He was riding hell bent for leather after the Indians on our right. Taylor had called the pursuit off, and Duley just kept going. He would have ridden over the hill into hundreds of Indians with just a few men. Buchanen pulled up his horse and Foot clubbed him over the head to settle him down."

"Hate gets in the way of reason. Watch him."

"Watchers have been assigned."

"Good, see that the men rest well. I want to make twenty miles tomorrow."

↢ 39 ↣

THE EXPEDITION DID MARCH HARD ON July 27 and covered twenty miles over rolling country. Sibley brought his officers together to outline his current plans. He stood on the bank of a small alkaline body of water. The plentiful supply of rocks littering the countryside earned it the name Stony Lake.

The assembled officers stood in the brown-tinged grassland as Sibley looked over them, his hands clasped behind his back. Behind the general the afternoon sun sparkled in the green-tinted lake.

"Gentlemen," he began, "you've done hot work the past few days. We have engaged the enemy twice in battle. By our count the Indians have lost close to sixty men killed and, more importantly, a large amount of their winter supply of meat. We have lost five dead. I'm thankful that our horses and mules were spared in the attack and that we were able to rest them.

"I am, however, indignant to find that the slain Indians at Dead Buffalo Lake were scalped. I don't care if our State offers a bounty. Shame upon such brutality. God's image should not be thus mistreated and disfigured.

"It remains our goal to subdue the Sisseton, Wahpeton and any Mde-wakanton remaining with them. We will place them at Crow Creek and punish those among them who committed crimes against the people of Minnesota. General Sully is to rendezvous with us at the mouth of Apple Creek on the Missouri. We will be on the east side of the river and Sully on the west. The Dakota will be crushed between us.

"Tomorrow we shall set forth directly for the Missouri River and push all Dakota before us toward the river. The Missouri is only about thirty miles away. There Sully will be waiting. Our rendezvous with Sully was to be on the twenty-fifth. We will be a little late."

Sibley set out on July 28, unaware he'd been given two pieces of misinformation. Because of low water on the Missouri, Sully had trouble moving his supply barges and was delayed. He was camped near Fort Pierre at least one week's march from the rendezvous point.

The general also didn't realize that Standing Buffalo had completely separated from Inkpaduta and that it was mostly Wapekute and Teton that he was pursuing.

Dawn brought a sight of magnificent natural beauty. The early morning sunlight reflected upon air tinged with a smoky, ruddy hue. The contrast of natural colors of green-brown grass, blue lakes, yellow sunlight and a bright azure sky was surreal.

About one-half mile out from Stony Lake, the idyllic scene was shattered by war whoops and thundering hooves. Lakota warriors sprang from the earth all around the soldiers' column as if they were part of the soil.

Naked except for breech clouts, their black hair streaming in the wind as they bent forward urging their ponies on, they swarmed down a ridge toward the army.

"Keep moving!" Sibley ordered. "They're after the train of wagons. Lieutenant Beaver," his aide de camp appeared at the general's side, "tell McPhail I want two regiments to move forward on either side of the column. Get Whipple's six pounder in front and Jones' guns in the rear."

Solomon Foot rode in the forefront with Joe Brown. Jesse was farther back keeping an eye on Will Duley. Solomon's jaw dropped in amazement as the scene developed.

"Look at 'em," he murmured to Brown. "I never saw anybody ride like that before. It's like them and the horse are one animal. This looks like what you'd see in a picture book."

"Right, Solomon, but picture books don't shoot at you. Don't become a prize on some lodge pole."

Foot took off his wide-brimmed black hat and rubbed a hand over his thinning hair. "Not much of a trophy."

In spite of the moment, Brown chuckled. "Just the same, be careful."

Sitting Bull and his forces galloped in a great circle around the wagons and the column of soldiers. Nearly 3,000 warriors surrounded the procession in a wide loop, searching for an opening, firing mostly at long range.

Whipple opened fire near the front with two cannons.

Jesse watched as a distant Indian waved a blanket, corresponding with renewed attacks.

"Signals," he pointed for Duley to see, "this attack is actually being orchestrated."

Occasionally Lakota would foray closer trying to break the army line. Without orders, men began to fix bayonets, expecting close-order fighting. Indians tried to slice into both flanks of the column and then massed at the rear, where the Lakota were met by blasts from Jones' cannons.

The sun's rays reflecting through the smoky atmosphere cast an eerie glow on the attackers. The rattle of musketry mingled with crashing cannon and war cries lasted for two hours. Then, as mysteriously as they had appeared, the Indians were gone, leaving five dead on the grass of the plain.

It was all over by mid-morning. No soldier was hit. The lines were re-formed as the army continued westward. Seven fresh Indian graves were found along the way. After twenty-two miles over rough country, camp was made. The bivouac was on the site of a hastily abandoned Sioux camp whose fires were still burning.

THE FINAL PUSH TO THE MISSOURI RIVER began at 4:00 a.m. on July 29. Sporadic gunshots kept the expedition alert as the scouts, cavalry and artillery paved the way. On distant hilltops, clusters of Indian warriors were periodically detected watching the progress of the advancing army.

Before noon scouts spotted the Missouri River about eight miles distant. They led the expedition down into the river valley. Heavy timber lie before them on the east side of the Missouri, while bluffs rose on the opposite side. Joe Brown, Solomon Foot, Will Duley and Jesse rode at the head of the column.

"Look at the bluffs," Brown pointed, "crawlin' with Indians, on top and up the sides."

"They knew we were close. They must have crossed over last night and this morning," Solomon observed.

"We need to find where they crossed. They might have left some behind," Duley pointed out.

"Lieutenant Buchanen," Brown ordered, "go back to Sibley and find out what he wants to do. Tell him it looks like they crossed Apple Creek and went downriver to cross the Missouri."

Sibley himself wanted to view the scene and, after Jesse delivered the message, the general rode to the front of the column with Stephen Rigg and Lieutenant Beaver. "Where's Sully?" Sibley cried. "He should have been there waiting for the Sioux on the other side."

"Apparently delayed, Sir," Beaver answered.

"What do you want us to do?" Brown questioned.

"I'll send McPhail and his cavalry up here. You'll lead the descent to the river with them."

Brown wiped the back of his neck with a yellow bandanna and gazed up at the broiling sun. "The men will be anxious to get to the river and cool off."

"No one can go to the river until it has been reconnoitered to be sure it's safe. Indians may be waiting in the timber down there. We will cross at Apple Creek and try to find their crossing."

Traveling north of Long Lake, the forces reached the mouth of Apple Creek on the Missouri at about 11:00 on the morning of July 29. Lieutenant Beaver delivered a dispatch from Sibley to Colonel Crooks. The colonel had wrapped a kerchief over his sweaty bald head and secured it with a wide-brimmed hat. He opened the envelope and unfolded Sibley's message.

"Tell the general we'll start out immediately."

Crooks turned to his adjutant. "We're to take some scouts and the Sixth Minnesota and explore the woods and the place of crossing on the east side of the Missouri. It's heavily timbered and we may face the enemy. Get me some scouts and we'll move out."

Solomon and Jesse, along with Michael and Gabriel Renville, joined Crooks and they pushed across Apple Creek. They meandered and picked their way through the thick trees and brush.

"Men," Solomon began, "they're out there, the short hairs on the back of my neck are standing up. I can feel it."

"We better not get too far out front," Jesse responded, "we'd be cut off." Behind them the expedition had begun its own crossing of the creek, which was about twenty-five yards wide and muddy. Ropes were tied to the wagons, and men helped the mules by pulling the wagons. It would take three hours to get the army over the creek.

A rattle of musketry echoed through the woods to Sibley where he watched the crossing. Then the roar of cannon resounded to the north. Warriors, concealed in the timber, had opened fire on Crooks' men.

"Fall back," Crooks ordered. "Form a skirmish line and volley fire. Cannon will drive them out like smoke in a beehive." Arrows and gunshots thudded into trees all around as the soldiers took cover behind fallen logs and trees and returned fire.

Sibley, miles from the fighting, scribbled a message and handed it to Beaver. "Well, young man, when you were back home in England last year did you ever think you'd be fighting Indians in Minnesota?"

Beaver smiled. "It's a great adventure."

"Take this to Crooks and be careful. This is more than adventure. Take a cavalryman with you." Sibley paused and then called as Beaver turned to leave, "Lieutenant, you've been a comfort to me this summer. What with my family. . .I just. . ." Sibley steeled himself as he checked his emotions and finished, "Like I said, be careful."

Private Nicholas Miller joined Beaver as they galloped in the direction of the gunfire. Beaver found Crooks to the rear of his skirmish line and handed him Sibley's dispatch.

"Tell General Sibley that the cannon have driven the Sioux back. I suspect that they are trying to delay us while their people are crossing the Missouri. I will advance soon."

Jesse and Solomon huddled in blistering heat behind a fallen cotton-wood tree. Several arrows protruded from the opposite side.

"Keep your head down, boy," Solomon cautioned, "they're movin' toward the river, but they're still out there."

The precautionary note was cast aside when the order came. "Move out! Push 'em to the river!"

"All right, Jesse, officers always know better. Let's go."

The army moved forward as opposition before them dissolved. Soon they were near the riverbank. An epic sight greeted the soldiers. A ragged line of Indians faced the army and fired rifles at them. The ground all around was littered by abandoned wagons and camp equipment.

The river was filled with makeshift rafts loaded with Indians desperate to reach the far side of the Missouri. Many Dakota frantically swam alongside the rafts. Across the river the bluffs were swarming with refugees scrambling up the hillsides.

"Shoot!" Crooks screamed. "Shoot them in the water. Stop as many as you can!"

The soldiers burst through the few warriors who were left in the dwindling line of defense and began to fire at the escaping Indians in the water.

Jesse stood behind the rampaging army and holstered his pistol as he looked at Solomon. "I'll not be party to this. This is murder. Like shooting fish in a barrel. There must be a couple hundred of them in the water."

"It's not just the men being shot, Jesse, they can't tell between men, women or children swimming out there."

Dozens of Indians were shot like sitting ducks in the river. Once they were out of rifle range, the survivors began to reach the bluffs and join their tribesmen. Then a series of hundreds of glittering, blinding spots of light reflected from the far bank.

"What is that?" Solomon wondered.

Jesse peered intently. "Mirrors, they're signaling with mirrors. Probably answering the reflections from our rifles. A strange sight, though. The bluffs look lit up like a Christmas tree."

Once the shooting stopped, Crooks made another order. "Burn the wagons and any equipment the Indians have left. I don't want them coming back for it."

"All the wagons and carts?" a captain inquired. "There must be over a hundred of 'em."

"Burn them all," Crooks confirmed. As flames erupted from the discarded heaps of Indian belongings, the bodies of eight Dakota children washed onto the riverbank.

That night Sibley joined Crooks and other officers while camp was set up near the banks of the Missouri.

"Set off flares," the general ordered, "maybe Sully will see them. I've been warned that the Sioux may come back over the river and launch an attack. We must be vigilant.

"Where is Lieutenant Beaver? I haven't seen him since I sent him with a message to Colonel Crooks."

Crooks answered, "He and the private left me to go back. I haven't seen him since."

"What the Hell is that?" Duley pointed to a pink glow that enveloped the camp.

"Fire!" Colonel Marshall exclaimed. "They're trying to burn us out!"

A gunshot rang out in the distance.

"Keep the men in camp," Sibley commanded. "They can burn all the prairie they want. The green timber will protect us."

McPhail rode toward the assembled officers, accompanied by two other riders who each led a horse with a body draped over the saddle. The colonel dismounted and sadly approached Sibley. "It's Lieutenant Beaver, Sir, and Private Miller, Indians killed them."

"No," Sibley exclaimed, "not another one!"

He walked to the horse and watched as Beaver was laid upon the ground. His short-cropped hair did not appeal to his attackers. They had removed his whiskers instead, leaving red gashes on each side of his face. Sibley shut his eyes tightly as if to erase the image from his mind.

Riggs placed his hand on Sibley's shoulder. "I know it's hard, Henry."

"He came to help us. He came for adventure. Stephen, he became like a son to me. Now I've lost three since I left Minnesota."

"Life is hard, you've suffered more than your share."

Another officer brought a breathless private to Sibley. "General, he's got something to tell you."

"I went ta the river to wash. Indians were comin' from da river ta steal mules, I think. I took a shot at 'em and ran off ta tell ya. They set fires."

"Put the men on alert," Sibley announced wearily, "but the Sioux won't come closer, I'm sure of it."

The Sioux did not approach camp. Over the next two days an occasional volley was fired into the camp and fire was returned. Excited by gunfire, cattle stampeded and the soldiers had to subdue them. Each night signal flares were shot into the air to alert Sully. There was no answer.

Jesse, Tom Robinson and Gabriel Renville listened to chirping bird sounds on the morning of July 31.

"What kind of bird is that?" Jesse wondered.

"I'd say a full-breasted Lakota," Tom returned.

"They are all Lakota, talking to each other with signals like bird calls," Gabriel explained to Jesse. "See the campfires in the distance. But most are far away. Only a few are on this side of the river."

Jesse scratched his blond hair. "General Sibley has called for a dress parade for this afternoon. I wonder what that's for?"

Solomon Foot had joined them. He commented, "I think we're goin' home. But we'll find out soon."

That afternoon the expedition army gathered on the flats by the Missouri River. Officers had tried to make sure that their troops looked presentable. Blue blouse tops were completely buttoned, dust swatted off and the men were as formal as tired, dirty, sweaty men could be.

Sibley stood on the back of a wagon and shouted for soldiers to hear. "You have marched nearly 600 miles from St. Paul, and the powerful bands of the Dakotas have succumbed to your valor and discipline and sought safety in flight.

"We have chased the Dakota to the west of the Missouri River. I hereby declare that our mission is a success. The goals that we were sent here to attain, we have attained. Tomorrow we shall begin our return march to Minnesota.

"One more thing. There is a rumor, as of yet unconfirmed, that Little Crow may have been killed near Hutchinson. I pray to God the rumor is true!"

Cries of "Huzzah, Huzzah!" thundered from the dry throats of 2,000 men.

THAT NIGHT SIBLEY SENT FOR SOLOMON, Jesse and Will Duley. The general sat at a camp stool with a field writing desk before him as the three approached. By the light of a smoky lantern he was writing a message.

"Gentlemen," he addressed the three, "I have a mission for you. General Sully is downriver somewhere. I want this note delivered to him informing him that we have returned to Minnesota after completing our mission on this side of the Missouri."

"Yes, sir," Jesse responded. "If you don't mind my asking, why us?"

"Most of my men are eager to return home. But I know that each of you may have particular interests in attaching to General Sully for the remainder of his campaign. Lieutenant Buchanen, this may take you near Crow Creek. I understand someone waits for you there."

"Yes, General, JoAnna, thank you."

"And for you, Major Duley, and you, Mr. Foot, I've been informed that Pawn is in the area. I thought that would be of interest to you. Will you go to Sully?"

Solomon looked at the others and nodded his head. "I think we all are ready. We'll head out in the morning."

Duley scowled at the others. "It's no secret that I don't like you, Buchanen, and frankly, I don't think much of Foot, either. I don't care if you're some big Indian fighter. As far as I'm concerned, you're both too chummy with the reds. But if hangin' with you two means I get a chance at Pawn, I'll swallow my distaste for you both and go to Sully with you. I'll be ready in the morning."

"So will we, Major," Sibley concluded, " but we'll be going east, we'll be going home."

ဆ 40 ၰ

NATHAN AND JOHN WATCHED WITH satisfaction as the supply of buffalo meat continued to grow. The band of Santee were healthy, happy and free. Only the eventual return to Crow Creek hung over them like a cloud that wouldn't disappear.

Each white man stayed in a separate tipi and was hosted by a Santee. Sounding Heaven shared his lodge with Nathan, while John stayed with Napesni, who had been a friend at Redwood.

Wherever the camp moved, a Soldiers' Lodge was erected in the center. There decisions were made. On August 2nd an excited buzz swept through the camp. Strangers were approaching from the east. Men gathered in the Soldiers' Lodge to discuss how to react. When told by watchers that only three were coming, Sounding Heaven proclaimed his relief. "If there are so few, it doesn't matter. They can do nothing to us. We must welcome them as friends."

Napesni, however, left the lodge with trepidation. He found Nathan and John and explained to them, "Strangers are coming. You must both stay in my tent until we find out what they want."

A few minutes later the three strangers rode spotted ponies into the Santee camp. But they were not strangers to most of the inhabitants, they were Heyoka, Inkpaduta, and Pawn. They were immediately escorted to the Soldiers' Lodge.

John watched through a slit in the tent and relayed to Nathan, "Three men. One's Heyoka, Little Crow's son-in-law. They've got lariats bundled over their shoulders. They're sitting down around the fire and being given food. They look scraggly, dusty and tired."

"I wonder what they're doing here?" Nathan whispered.

"I suspect we'll find out, my friend."

After they ate and smoked, the three visitors explained their presence. Inkpaduta spoke first. "We have come from Devils Lake. We come to find horses."

"What of the white army? Where is the Long Trader?" Sounding Heaven inquired.

"He's east of the big river," Pawn answered. "They fought Teton, but did not cross the river. I think they're going back where they came from."

Napesni had returned and asked, "What of Standing Buffalo? We heard you were with his band."

"They go north toward Canada," Heyoka said. "They try to hide from the white man. But they can't."

"Where are you going?" asked Napesni.

"We will find horses, then return to the Teton," Inkpaduta answered. "They'll still fight the whites. But we ask that we can rest here for a time, maybe hunt buffalo with you."

Sounding Heaven considered and replied, "Yes, our lodges are open to you."

Napesni left the circle in alarm. These men were haters of the whites, any whites. If they knew that whites were in camp, they would kill them. Especially Pawn. He was a *watohda*, a wild one.

Then a look of inspiration flashed over the old Indian's face, and he returned to the circle. "Pawn is welcome to stay in my tipi," he announced.

"Good," Sounding Heaven responded, "Inkpaduta will stay with me, and Heyoka with Little Bird."

A short time later Napesni led Pawn to his lodge. The older man entered first and put a finger to his lips as he motioned Nathan and John to the rear of the dwelling. Pawn entered, and through the dim light saw the two white men. He froze. As his eyes adjusted, he reached for the knife on his belt and snarled at Napesni, "Is this a trap?"

"He *tokeca sni Hekodawaye*. Stay, they are all right. They are my friends."

John stood and walked to Pawn extending his hand. "Ho, *napenayuza*, How do you do? Shake hands."

Pawn stared at the offered hand as if it were poison. His glare swept through the tipi, then rested upon John. Finally, he clasped the minister's hand in his and then retreated out the tent flap.

"He'll come back," Napesni told his guests. "But he won't harm you."

"How can you be sure?" Nathan asked. "That's Pawn. I've seen him at Yellow Medicine. He killed over a dozen people at Lake Shetek."

Napesni looked solemnly at his friends. "He won't harm you because he has such regard for Indian etiquette that he never would break the laws of hospitality by killing a fellow guest. I asked him to be my guest because I knew that he could not hurt you without offending me. If he stayed in another tent, there would be no guarantee."

That night Pawn entered the lodge and slept near the tent flap. He would not go further into the lodge, and he would not speak to John or Nathan.

The three visitors left the next morning to hunt with the other Santee. Pawn left his place silently without waking anyone. Later John awoke, went outside and began to put on his shoes.

Old Napesni, who was already awake, admonished his friend. "You act like a boy who does not know anything. When you sleep out like this, upon awakening you must first look in every direction from where you lay. There might be an enemy in sight and in this way you may see him before he sees you. Or there may be a wild animal or possibly a rattlesnake waiting to jump on you if you move. I see you do not know anything, so I will have to teach you."

True to his word, Napesni devoted much time to explaining Indian customs and etiquette to his white friends.

As they rode in search of Tatanka, the three Indian visitors discussed their plans. "Soon, we must leave these people," Inkpaduta advised. "They will go to Crow Creek, to the reservation pens. I'll go back to Sitting Bull."

"I'll go with you," Pawn added. "Let's find bands that wish to fight and not live in cages."

Heyoka rode silently for a while, considering his words. "I spoke with the black coat, the minister. He wants to go to the southeast, to a place called Scout City. I know of it. It's where Santee warriors block other Indians from returning to Minnesota. I will take John Williamson there."

"Why?" Pawn asked.

"Because I believe it's what I'm supposed to do. It's time for me to leave you."

The next morning Inkpaduta and Pawn were gone. Heyoka remained to guide John Williamson to Scout City. Nathan also stayed, but a few days later his plans changed as well when three soldiers rode into camp.

Jesse Buchanen, Solomon Foot, and Will Duley were surrounded by Indian riders, who escorted them toward the Soldiers' Lodge. Shouts and tremolos created an uproar tinged with greeting and fear. They dismounted and were immediately met by Nathan. Napesni stood in the background.

Jesse and Solomon warmly embraced Nathan. "What a sight for sore eyes!" Foot exclaimed. "Here we are out ridin' in the middle of nowhere, and who do we run across but an old friend."

"In the middle of an Indian camp," Jesse grinned. "How is JoAnna . . . and Emily?"

"Both were just fine when I left nearly a month ago. They're teaching, and JoAnna is nursing as well. There's been a lot of sickness."

"What about these red devils?" Duley snapped. "Have they just been turned loose to do as they want and go where they want?"

Nathan turned soberly to Duley. "It was either let them hunt or watch them starve."

"Watching them starve would have been fine with me."

"See here, Duley . . ." Nathan took a step toward Will, his hand clenched into a fist.

Jesse reached out and held him firmly by the shoulder. "Easy, Nathan. Let it go. We've got things to talk about."

Nathan released his tension and nodded at Jesse. "All right. What are you doing here anyway? I thought you were with Sibley."

"Sibley fought a few battles, made it to the Missouri where we waited for Sully to show. When he didn't, Sibley simply declared victory and is heading back to Minnesota. We have the assignment of finding Sully and telling him what happened to Sibley."

"Come with us, Nathan," Solomon urged.

Nathan hesitated. "I'd like to, but I promised John Williamson that I'd stay with the Santee while he went to minister to folks at Scout City. I can't leave them. What if they didn't return to Crow Creek?"

"Then we could hunt them down and kill them," Duley responded.

"One Arm," Napesni said, "if it is your wish to go with these men, do so. You have my word that we will return to Crow Creek. We have nowhere else to go, and our families remain there. We must return to them."

"You have his word, Nathan," Solomon noted. "That's big medicine to an Indian. Besides, after we've seen Sully, you can come back to these folks if you wish."

"You've convinced me."

"Are you hungry? We have buffalo," Napesni offered. "Then leave in the morning."

They sat around an open fire by the Soldiers' Lodge, gnawing buffalo steaks. Juice ran down Solomon's chin, and he wiped it off with the back of his hand. His mouth full of food, he mumbled to Nathan, "They killed my brother Silas, you know."

"When? How?"

"By Abercrombie, last June. He was herding cattle for the government. They found a dead raven on his chest."

Nathan looked inquisitively at his friend.

"Pawn." Duley spat a chunk of fat onto the ground. "Pawn did it. That's his sign."

Nathan looked astonished. "He was just here, with Inkpaduta. They just left a couple of days ago."

Duley scrambled to his feet. "Where? Where did they go?"

"West. All I know is west. They were looking for horses."

Foot looked solemnly at Duley. "Tomorrow we go west, too. Mebbe our paths will cross theirs."

The next morning Nathan bid his Indians friends farewell as he rode off with his friends to find Sully. And Pawn, if they were lucky.

❧ 41 ❧

THE FOUR RIDERS CONTINUED MOVING downriver to the southeast with the wide Missouri River on their right. They knew that Sully must be heading toward them.

"River's down," Solomon observed. "That's what two years of drought will do."

Jesse gazed over the river. "Must be what's kept Sully from us. Low water will slow his barges, and that's his supply line."

"That's all well and good," Duley emphasized. "But if we keep going down the river, we're sure to find him. Three thousand men can't be lost, and their orders were to march up the river to meet Sibley. My bet is they're still coming."

"They better be," Solomon rejoined, "or we're wastin' a trip into the middle of nothing'."

"We'll find Sully," Jesse assured his companions. "We just have to keep moving south."

LAKOTA WARRIORS GAZED FROM THE BLUFFS on the west side of the big river as Sibley's army disappeared to the east.

Gall and Sitting Bull watched intently. "There're leaving," Sitting Bull pronounced.

"Only to return," his friend replied.

"Someday, some others, but not the Long Trader. He takes his people home to Minnesota."

"What do we do?"

"Cross back over the river. Better grass and more buffalo wait for us."

Gall's eyes swept over the river below. "Many died trying to get to this side."

"Many more would have died if we had stayed over there. We must recross."

Thousands of Lakota using rafts and skiffs made the crossing back to the east side of the Missouri. This time they did so safely without trying to shield themselves from a hailstorm of lead.

Sitting Bull led his people downriver from the crossing and set up a camp. On August 5th he rose to meet the sun as it emerged over the eastern horizon. He prayed for his band and waited for a vision. But what he saw coming down the river was real. A large flatboat full of white people was coming his way.

TWENTY-SEVEN MINERS, ONE WOMAN, and two children floated downstream after leaving gold fields near Boise, Idaho. Many of the men wore buckskin belts filled with gold dust.

"Hey, Jake!" one of the men called. "What do ya make o' that up there? Looks like a big Sioux camp."

"See to yer powder," the leader answered. "I don't like the looks o' this."

Sitting Bull shouted the alarm. "Strangers come! To the river with rafts and warriors. They must be stopped!"

Lakota men streamed to the river. Many paddled into the river in rafts blocking the way. Others poured fire at the approaching flatboat from the river bank. From the boat, the miners returned fire.

Some Indians swam toward the boat and tried to impede those who were desperately poling the barge away from danger. The white men slammed the long poles at their attackers and tried to push the swimmers away. Fighting was fierce as screams, gunfire and the sound of thrashing water filled the air.

The river before the flat boat was filled with rafts as Lakota warriors blocked their passage. Miners hugged the deck of the boat and continued desperately to fight back. But one by one, they fell with fatal wounds. Jake, their leader, and ten others were dead and their ammunition exhausted when the little party was overwhelmed. All left on board were killed and the boat sunk.

The victory had been a costly one for the Lakota. Nearly ninety warriors lost their lives as well.

Indian women stripped the white bodies along the river bank. They ripped open the buckskin belts and found a yellow dust. Red Blanket held the gold up for her husband to examine.

"Spoiled gun powder," he said disgustedly. "No good for anything."

The looters dumped the contents of the belts onto the ground. One object held more interest. A coffee pot rescued from the sinking flatboat was a prized find. It became even more valuable when the yellow dust that filled it was dumped out. An Indian speculator scooped up the gold and later traded it for a horse.

After erecting scaffolds to hold the bodies of their dead, the Lakota moved east onto the wide plain. No white soldiers seemed near, but Sitting Bull deemed it wise to move on after the killings.

THE FOLLOWING MORNING THE FOUR messengers to Sully rode onto the site of the previous day's ambush. Strewn on the ground before them were the scalped, mutilated, and mostly-naked bodies of the mining party.

"My God!" Jesse exclaimed. "Look at this!" Anger flashed through him like a hot iron. "Monsters! Have they no decency?"

"You obviously weren't at Lake Shetek. Of course they're monsters!" Bitterness dripped from each word uttered by Duley.

"Hold on a second," Solomon cautioned. "Yes, this is horrible, and we can't excuse it. But crawl inside their red skins for a bit. To them, we stole their land. If thieves bring women and children with them, well . . . they suffer the consequences of being repelled by them that are being robbed."

"Do they have to chop off hands and feet and heads?" Jesse demanded.

"I've spent most of a year working with Indians," Nathan answered. "Many believe that you enter the spirit world as you are immediately after death. A crippled spirit is no danger to the living."

They dismounted and made their way through the carnage searching for survivors. None were found. Duley knelt on one knee and sifted dirt through his fingers.

"What's this?" he wondered. Then Duley's eyes widened in amazement at his discovery. "Gold! There's gold in the dirt!"

Nathan scooped up a handful of dirty gold. "These men were miners. They had gold, and the Indians had no use for it, so they left it behind."

"And neither do we," Solomon spoke firmly. "It belongs to the dead, not to us. Mount up and leave it."

Duley glared up at Foot. "Who put you in charge?"

"You do what you want, Duley. I'm just sayin' what's proper to do."

"He's right," Jesse agreed. "Let's move on."

Duley slipped a handful of dirty gold into his pocket as he stood. "Shouldn't we bury these folks?" he said defiantly.

Solomon shook his head. "No. First off, it'd take awhile to bury this many, but more important if we bury 'em, it'd be like signing our own death warrants. The Sioux would know that we've been here, and they'd come lookin' for us. I don't think you want that. Let's ride. We've got Sully to find. He can make them pay for this if'n he's a mind to."

GENERAL ALFRED SULLY AND 3,000 cavalrymen from Nebraska and Iowa were marching along the Missouri River approaching Fort Thompson from the south. Sully's army had prepared to leave Sioux City, Iowa, while Sibley was marching through western Minnesota.

Delays plagued Sully from the start. General John Crook was to have led the Northwest Expedition but had been removed during the planning stage and replaced by Sully. The Second Nebraska Cavalry, vital to the campaign, reported late to the Sioux City muster site.

But the biggest factor in the tardy departure of Sully's army was the prolonged drought that lowered the level of the Missouri and kept steamboats from supplying the army. General Pope had designed a two-pronged movement into Dakota Territory. Sibley's army, primarily infantry, and Sully's cavalry would squeeze the Indians between them. The steamboats were vital to supply Sully, who did not have the many supply wagons Sibley had.

Sully had ridden from Sioux City to Fort Randall, then up the Missouri toward Crow Creek, astride a bay horse. A riderless iron gray stallion followed tethered to a wagon. The general rode it on special occasions. As they approached Fort Thompson, Sully pulled his wide-brimmed white hat down to shield his eyes from the bright sun reflecting off the water.

The general was forty-three years old, a West Point graduate and Mexican War veteran. He looked sixty. Streaks of gray swept through his short, dark hair as well as the beard whiskers that covered his throat and his bushy mustache. His cheeks were clean-shaven and well-tanned.

Clear and hard, Sully's blue eyes hid a pain buried deep within his soul. Some believed that the loss of his young wife over ten years ago had aged him and left him bitter and unemotional.

A trusted scout, Frank LaFramboise, trotted his horse back to meet the general. Half French and half Dakota, he was slender and clad in buckskin. "Trail looks clear to Fort Thompson, we could make it by late afternoon. Do you want us to find a campsite or will we push on?"

"How far ahead are the scouts?"

"'Bout three miles."

"We'll go on to Fort Thompson. Ride with me."

The general and his scout rode silently for a short while. Then in a low, rumbling voice like distant thunder, LaFramboise asked, "Will she be there? Maria, your wife?"

"Maria Luskanna Skanskan Stirring Stone Sully? Yes, I expect she will. She had a baby, you know."

"Did you meet her at Fort Randall?"

Sully became lost in thoughts and memories before he replied, "Yes, last year. She reminded me very much of Manuela."

"Who was she?"

A crack of emotion flitted for an instant over Sully's usually stoic face. "My first wife. When I was stationed in California after the Mexican War, 1849 to 1853. I met a young lady from a prominent Mexican family."

Sully shook his head. "They wanted nothing to do with me. I was just the quartermaster of a small garrison in Monterey. They were among the richest and most powerful families in California. I was twenty-eight, and Maria was just fifteen. I'm Protestant. She was Catholic. But she loved me, and that was enough. We eloped."

"How did the family take that?" LaFramboise inquired.

"Resentfully at first. But they came around." The general's eyes twinkled. "They gave me servants and the use of a huge tract of land. I came this close," he held his index finger and thumb an inch apart, "to resigning my commission and assuming the pastoral life of a California don. I could have painted landscapes like my father, lived a life of leisure. But it wasn't to be. It all changed."

"What happened to Manuela?"

"We had a baby, a boy. All was beautiful. Then she ate a poisoned fruit and died. Three weeks later our baby accidentally got a cord around his neck and strangled. He was just a month old. Just like that everything was gone. And so I left California and built forts across the west for the better part of ten years. That's what brought me to Fort Ridgely, which led to me becoming a captain of the First Minnesota Volunteer Infantry."

"Life was hard on you, General. You were in Virginia fightin' rebs . . . so how'd ya wind up at Fort Randall?"

Sully's eyes turned to steel. "They said they didn't like how I handled a mutiny of New York infantry. Hogwash! I was too close to McClellan. When he was relieved of command by Lincoln, I was sent west. Just like Pope after he lost at Bull Run, if you do something those in power don't like, you get sent to Minnesota. Even if Pope deserved it, I didn't."

"General, you don't sound too high on the commander of the Northwest District."

Sully looked to the rear. The officers behind him were engaged in their own conversations and paying him no notice. The general snorted derisively, "Pope is an arrogant popinjay. He gave false reports to newspapers about his 'glorious victories' in the west that were gross exaggerations.

"He blundered headlong into the rebs at Second Bull Run, and it was a disaster. Then when he retreated, I saved his butt with rear guard support. I kept his men from being butchered. Pope will never forgive me for saving his hide. That's what Lincoln gets for appointing a mapmaker who spent fourteen years digging wells and serving on lighthouse duty for two years before the war."

La Framboise patted his horse's neck softly and wiped his sweaty brow from the heat. "Ya saw a lot of war, didn't ya?"

Sully contemplated silently and then recited, "Antietam, Savage Station, Glendale, Malvern Hill, Yourktown, West Point, Bull Run, Peach Orchard, Fredericksburg, Chancellorsville, Fair Oaks, all the battles on the peninsula. I watched five commanding generals come and go. I led the First Minnesota."

He shook his head ruefully. "My reward was to be sent back to Minnesota. And now here I am, out here with Pope as my commander again."

"And what about Maria?"

"Enough!" Sully snapped, "I'm going on like an old woman. I've said more than I should already. This isn't my way. Maria belongs with her people, in her world, not in mine."

A few miles from Fort Thompson, the expedition encountered a dilapidated village. It was the Winnebago reservation. Sully called a halt and briefly conferred with tribal elders about the conditions in the camp. Then he quickened his pace to the nearby fort.

❧ 42 ❧

HILE SULLY NEARED FORT THOMPSON, the settlement was approached from the north by Solomon, Nathan, Jesse, and Will Duley. Their pace quickened as the four drew closer to the fort, and Jesse and Nathan grew increasingly anxious to be reunited with the women they had left behind.

A clamor arose as they rode into a growing collection of rough cottonwood structures amongst hundreds of canvas or hide tipis that surrounded the fort. Shouts of welcome greeted Nathan in particular as the little band trotted through the gates of the stockade.

JoAnna and Emily raced across the dusty compound to embrace Jesse and Nathan. Tears of joy streamed down the women's cheeks.

JoAnna squeezed Jesse tightly as she cried, "I had no idea you were so close. We've had word that there'd been fighting. I was so worried about you!"

"It's all right, JoAnna. I had concerns as well. I heard from Nathan that there's been sickness here."

"Mostly malnutrition, nothing contagious yet. Please, Jesse, just hold me tight."

Nearby Nathan wrapped his strong right arm around Emily and kissed her face. "I was with the hunting party," he whispered into her ear. "Solomon and Jesse found us. They'd been sent by Sibley to find Sully, and they asked me to go with them. I went because I knew it would take me back to you."

"Thank God you're safe! Remember, Nathan, you're a teacher now, not a soldier."

He smiled into her bright blue eyes and brushed strands of blonde hair from her face. "I told them I'd help them find Sully. I don't plan to fight."

The sound of a distant bugle echoed from down the river. "Sully!" Foot exclaimed. "Up to the catwalk. Let's see!"

The four men and two women were joined by others on the walkway that ran around the fort's interior walls. They looked down the Missouri and viewed a cloud of dust rolling toward them.

"Look close," Duley barked. "That's not buffalo. See the flags and guidons? That's Sully!"

"There's a troop coming at us," Solomon observed. "The rest will go into camp. I'm guessin' we'll be seein' the general soon."

Within half an hour, General Alfred Sully rode into Fort Thompson with Frank LaFramboise beside him, followed by a company of fifty troopers. Colonel Clark Thompson and Sibley's messengers strode to the general and saluted as Sully dismounted, removed his gloves and slapped trail dust from his shoulders.

"Welcome to Crow Creek, sir, " Thompson greeted.

"I'd say I was happy to be here, but that would be a stretch," Sully replied.

"General Sully," Duley said, stepping forward, "we were sent by General Sibley to find you. He expected you on July 25."

"Yes, well, we were delayed. I'm afraid we'll still have to wait for another steamboat before we can push on much farther. Where's Sibley?"

Duley shifted nervously on his feet. "Heading back to Minnesota, sir. That's what he sent us to tell you."

Sully's cheeks reddened. "What do you mean, he's gone back to Minnesota? We're supposed to squeeze the Indians between us. That takes *two* armies. I have one."

"Sir," Duley continued, "we fought the Sioux in three successful battles. We pushed them across the river where we thought you'd be. You weren't there, and after Sibley waited three days, he decided we'd accomplished our mission and turned east."

"He jes kinda declared victory and headed back," Solomon added. "We didn't have orders to cross the river, and General Sibley had no idea what had happened to you."

"Where are the Sioux?" Sully asked.

"From the ways things look, they've crossed back over the river and are on the east side again," Solomon responded.

"Your evidence?"

"We found a couple dozen miners slaughtered upriver aways. It was recent and on this side o' the river."

Sully contemplated a moment and then concluded, "So we have work to do. We'll get it done without Sibley. Major House, send a message to the encampment. I'll return soon. Colonel Thompson, I'm not accustomed to laying out my plans in public. I'd like the use of your office. Major Duley, Lieutenant," he nodded at Jesse, "join us, please."

Jesse squeezed JoAnna's hand. "This won't take long," he whispered.

"Come," Emily urged JoAnna, "we'll wait for Jesse in the school. Nathan and Solomon will be there, too."

As the four walked outside the stockade toward the school, the officers entered Thompson's sparsely furnished office. Sully sat behind a desk on the only chair in the room. Will Duley and Jesse remained standing with a small collection of officers, including Colonel Furnas of the Second Nebraska Cavalry, Major House of the Sixth Iowa Cavalry, and Colonel Wilson of the Seventh Iowa.

"How far away is Sibley?" Sully asked Duley.

"Probably halfway to Minnesota by now."

Sully mulled possibilities over in his mind and then summarized, "By the time we sent you back to let him know where we are and by the time he joined us, the Sioux could get away from us.

"Gentlemen," he looked to his officers, "we'll continue up the river to the mouth of the Little Cheyenne. We'll wait there until a boat re-supplies us.

"Major Duley, where did General Sibley last engage the Sioux?"

"Upriver to the north at the mouth of Apple Creek."

"I know the spot. I've examined the map. We'll head near there and then turn east.

"Major, I'd like you, Lieutenant Buchanen, and the two who were with you to accompany us."

"Sir," Jesse interjected, "that would be fine with Mr. Foot. He's a soldier. But the one-armed man, Nathan Cates, he teaches here."

"I know of both of them," Sully continued. "Solomon Foot, the Daniel Boone of the Kandiyohi lakes area, successfully defended a cabin against attack, was left for dead and rescued by a neighbor woman who brought him to Forest City. Then there's the mysterious Nathan Cates, the story goes that he lost an arm at Shiloh, came to trade with the Sioux, then got mixed up in the uprising, helped defend Fort Ridgely and, with Foot, went on a daring rescue of four captive women. It seems that he turned up at just about every major engagement of the war. They're both unique men and I want them on this journey with me. Mr. Cates must be convinced to accompany us."

"Good luck with that, sir," Jesse replied.

Sully stood and turned his attention to Clark Thompson. "Colonel Thompson, as I rode through this camp, I found the conditions deplorable. I spoke with some of the Sioux and with the Winnebago as well. They're starving."

Thompson wiped sweat off his brow with the back of his hand. "They're sending food by wagon from Minnesota in the fall. I know it's taking too long, but I allowed the Sioux to go on a buffalo hunt. Nathan Cates was with them. He says the hunt's going well. I'm doing what I can. I think it's important to prove the feasibility of overland travel from Minnesota to Dakota Territory."

"You're not doing enough. It doesn't help the Indians here, not now. They're dying. They can't wait while you test travel conditions. The drought you can do nothing about, but poor planning and the wholesale theft by Indian Department officials are killing these people, and your feeble efforts of remedy are hopeless. Colonel Furnas, see to it that wagons are sent back to Fort Randall." He scribbled a note from a pad on the desk. "This is my order for food supplies to be brought here. Give the Indians what rations we can spare. We'll await re-supply from the next steamboat. See that it happens."

Sully paused, showing consternation. "The Minnesota supplier should have used steamboats. Sure there are delays. We've experienced them. Much as I've cursed waiting, the boats have ferried us across rivers and transported 200 tons of cargo. It would have required 133 six-mule team wagons to carry that amount.

"The food from Minnesota would still get to Fort Thompson sooner by boat than by wagons that aren't even on the trail yet. Why didn't they use boats?"

"It's cheaper by wagon, sir. That's why," Jesse explained.

"Indians are cheap, too," Sully replied. "The way I see it, this is about making a few people rich."

Duley cleared his throat. "General, if I might ask, you have a reputation of having little sympathy for the reds. Why are you helping these savages? They murdered us in Minnesota."

"Major, I've spent much of my adult life fighting wars, mostly against Indians: the Seminole War in Florida, in California and Oregon and now on the Northern Plains. In war, I have little mercy for those fighting and trying to kill my men. These are mostly old men, women, and children here. They've been promised food by our government. I believe in living up to promises. That's all I have. Gentlemen, we'll return to camp. But first, Lieutenant Buchanen, take me to Nathan Cates."

Sully waited until the others had left the office and then followed. He froze in the doorway when a young black-haired Indian woman stepped before him holding a baby at her breast.

"Alfred, did you forget about me?" the woman asked.

"No, Maria, of course not. I was coming to see you."

"Would you like to see your daughter?" She pulled back a blanket to reveal a small, round face. "Her name is Mary."

The others continued away from Sully as he stood in awkward silence with his wife and child. "Maria, I've sent for food to be brought here. But you really should be at Fort Randall."

"You are my husband. I should be with you."

The general shook his head. "You know that won't work. I'm a soldier. I'm always on the move." He sighed. "I'm sorry, Maria. I'm sorry that I took you. Something from my past grabbed hold of me. I should have known better. This can't work."

Tears welled up in the woman's dark eyes. "My people are here. I will stay with them. We were married by Lakota custom. The marriage ends if you choose it to end."

Alfred Sully steeled his expression against the shame that welled within him and nodded. "I want it to end." Then he walked away.

Jesse led his general to the school, where Nathan and Emily sat together before a rough table in quiet conversation. JoAnna wiped tears from her eyes as she stood near Foot.

"What's wrong?" Jesse asked tenderly.

"Solomon told me about Dr. Weiser's death. He saved my life when I had high fever from measles."

Jesse comforted her in his arms as Sully approached Nathan. "Mr. Cates, I'd like you to accompany us for a while."

"No!" Emily pronounced adamantly. "Nathan's not a soldier."

"Maybe not now, Mrs. Cates, but he has been one, and I can use a man like him on this campaign. It won't be long, a month or so."

"General," Emily rejoined, "it's not the time. It's the danger."

Sully cleared his throat and looked to Nathan. "I've heard from General Thomas, Union officer fighting in Virginia. He's been making inquiries about someone that looks quite a bit like you. Except this gentleman was a Confederate officer. I don't know anything about you, and I don't care, especially if I get the help of a man I can use. Will you help?"

Nathan looked at Emily and shrugged. Reluctantly he replied, "All right, General, for a month. Then can I come back here?"

"Then you can come back here. You have my word."

AS DUSK FELL OVER FORT THOMPSON, Sully returned to his encampment beyond the settlement.

Emily demanded of Nathan, "Did you have to agree? We don't know what he knows."

"Probably not much, but Emily, if anyone found out that I was sent by Jefferson Davis to start an Indian war in Minnesota, it would destroy everything. I can't risk Sully trying to find out more than he knows now."

"Doesn't it make any difference that you turned your back on Davis and tried to stop the war?"

"No, it wouldn't make any difference. I'll go with Sully."

"Be careful, Nathan. You just got here and now you leave tomorrow. It's not right."

"At least we have tonight, Emily."

They melted into each other's arms.

JoAnna sat in an empty meeting building with Jesse. "How much longer can this go on?" she asked.

"Which war?"

"This one, that one, either, what does it matter?"

"Well, JoAnna, in order . . . this war will end when we're convinced the Sioux will stay west of the Missouri. That's where we want them, at least for now. We've received word that the Union won two big victories last month at Gettysburg, Pennsylvania, and Vicksburg, Mississippi. The tide has turned against the Confederacy. It's just a matter of time."

"How much time, Jesse?"

"A year, two at the most, for both wars."

"And you?"

"I'm done when the wars are done. Then we can marry."

"It's too long."

"Your father's going to be governor of Minnesota."

"He wrote me. It sounds good for him."

"JoAnna, you should have stayed in St. Paul, with your father. I worry . . ."

She placed a finger over Jesse's lips and answered softly. "There's sickness and danger there, too. What's meant to be is meant to be."

Jesse removed the yellow bandana from his neck and wrapped it around his sweetheart's neck. "Wear it and think of me."

Her dark eyes misted as she whispered softly, "I don't need reminders. I think of you so very many times every single day. But I'll wear the bandana."

The steamboat *Alone* arrived on August 14 with some of the general's provisions. Sully left word that the next steamer should meet him upriver at the mouth of the Little Cheyenne River.

When the Sully Expedition left for its march up the Missouri, three women stood in silent tears on the fort catwalk, watching their men disappear into the horizon. One held a baby at her breast.

❧ 43 ❧

THE NORTHWEST EXPEDITION MARCHED several days up the Missouri River until it reached its destination. There Sully ordered his army into camp.

In an officers' meeting before his tent, he consulted with his three cavalry commanders, House, Furnas, and Wilson. Albert House and David Wilson could have been mistaken for brothers. The younger man, House, and Wilson both had high foreheads and dark hair. House wore a beard and mustache with bare cheeks while Wilson had a full beard and no mustache.

Robert Furnas had been a politician in Nebraska and bore similarities in appearance to his fellow officers. His face was framed by dark hair and a full beard and mustache.

Sully informed them, "We'll wait here until the steamboat comes with supplies. When it gets here, we'll trim down our force. Anything that slows us down gets left. I want to move fast in pursuit of the Sioux. Have the men leave their overcoats and take one blanket and their dog tents."

"What about forage?" House asked.

"Scouts say that it gets better the farther north we go. I don't want to stay here long."

"Any chance of running into Sibley?" Colonel Furnas wondered.

"I don't know where Sibley is now. Probably in eastern Dakota somewhere on his way to Minnesota. He won't be back here. He complains about being ill-supplied."

"Isn't there a risk of losing the Sioux by delaying here?" Furnas inquired.

"We have little choice. We need supplies. The Indians have women, children, and whole villages to move. They'll be slow. We'll catch them."

Sully opened a folded sheet of paper and held it before the officers. "This came with the *Alone*. It's a message from General Pope. It seems he's disappointed with me. Why are we so slow? Why can't we have the success General Sibley is having?"

He balled up the paper and threw it to the ground. "Sibley fights a few skirmishes, chases the Sioux across the river, then leaves, and the Sioux come back across. What kind of victory is that? He's left us to fight them and to settle this, and we will!"

THE BASE CAMP SOLDIERS AT FORT ATCHISON awaited the return of Sibley during August. To relieve boredom, occasional patrols were sent out to reconnoiter the surrounding countryside.

Captain Burt led a company of fifty men to Devils Lake some forty miles to the west of the camp. They rode through tall prairie grass near the site of Little Crow's old camp. Sergeant Connor, riding beside his captain, was alerted by a raucous "caw, caw" from a nearby crow. He saw the bird swoop low over tall grass and then noticed the grass move.

"Captain Burt," Connor pointed, "there's somethin' in the grass over there. I think I saw a man."

"Take three men and check it out. We'll hold our position here."

Connor and three other blue-clad soldiers trotted their horses toward the lake and the rustle in the grass. Connor halted his men and spoke under his breath. "Fan out and surround that spot there in the grass. Slowly close in and keep your wits about ya."

The four men circled and moved in. The grass suddenly parted as a young Indian man rose above the chest-high vegetation with arms held high above his head. "I have no gun!" he shouted. "I give up to you."

The boy was in his teens, wan, emaciated. The dew of early morning grass had soaked his clothing. The soldiers dismounted and pounced upon him, roughly tying his hands behind him.

One saw a rifle in the grass and picked it up to show to Burt. "He was lyin'. He had a gun."

The Indian protested in alarm, "It has no bullets. I used the last one days ago when I shot at a rabbit. I missed."

"He's just a boy," Burt observed. "Looks like a skinny, drowned rat. What you doin' here, boy? Where are your people?"

"My father sent me here to join other Dakota. They were all gone when I got here. I am alone."

"Who is your father? Who are you?"

"I am Wowinape." The boy proudly straightened his scrawny body. "I am son of Little Crow."

"Well, I'll be . . ." the captain said with astonishment. "Rumor has it that he was killed."

The boy nodded sadly. "Little Crow is dead, by Hutchinson."

Burt struggled with emotions of joy over the death of a hated enemy and sympathy for the bedraggled son. He swallowed the impulse to cheer and replied, "You're coming with us. We'll get you some food. You need it."

The boy was brought as a captive into Fort Atchison.

A FEW DAYS LATER, AUGUST 10TH, word reached Fort Atchison that Sibley was near. A mile from the camp, the general called a halt.

Sibley's order spread through the command. "Dust off uniforms, clean off buttons and look as smart and presentable as you can. Step lively. Drummers and buglers, strike up the beat. Look like the victorious army you are."

In the fort, men were ordered to tidy the camp areas, and preparations were begun for a "royal" meal of baked beans, fried hardtack and coffee. A short while later General Sibley rode into Fort Atchison at the head of his army. Shouts of joy and cries of "Huzzah" burst from the throats of over 1,000 men, as drum beats and bugles reverberated throughout the post.

Willie Sturgis and Oscar Wall received congratulatory slaps on the back from their comrades, who demanded stories of their adventure.

But the big news from the fort garrison was relayed to Sibley and spread like wild fire to his men. It struck like a thunderbolt. "Little Crow is dead, and we have his son!"

TWO DAYS LATER, FORT ATCHISON TURNED into a forgotten spot on the plains as Sibley closed the fort and led his entire command to the southwest and home. The march toward Minnesota was uneventful.

Only one day out from Atchison, Sibley called a meeting with his officers. "We will divide the army here," the general announced. "The bulk of the force will return to Fort Snelling by way of Abercrombie, Pomme de Terre, Alexandria, Sauk Centre, and St. Cloud. Colonel McPhail, you'l take companies B, E, F, I, and M of the cavalry and sweep to the southwest of the Sheyenne River and through the Snake River country.

"I want to be sure no Sioux remain in that area. We have Hatch's battalion to the north by Pembina and the southern Missouri coteau patrolled by half-breeds and friendly Santee out of Scout City, but we must be sure of the area between."

"My God, General!" McPhail protested. "The men will be up in arms. They don't even know where the Snake River is. They want to go home! Besides, this is a very perilous undertaking with so small a force."

"I'll send a cannon with you. But, Colonel, you have your orders."

McPhail had not underestimated the wrath that exploded from his undermanned command. "Now, men," he shouted, "I know how you feel, frankly I told General Sibley that this is a bad idea. We're being sent into an area that we know little about with five companies, a cannon, and a wheelbarrow load of provisions."

"We was supposed ta be done!" a man shouted. "We wanna go back home!"

A chorus of voices shouted agreement. McPhail shouted back, "Men, we've been through a lot together. I just stuck up for you with the general. Stick with me a little longer, and I'll get you home."

Resignation and loyalty to their colonel subdued the troopers.

Oscar Wall turned to Willie Sturgis. "Well, Willie, the colonel has been good to us and hasn't led us wrong yet. I guess we have to trust him some more."

"We ain't got much choice, Oscar."

Sibley's main army continued an uneventful journey back to Fort Snelling, Meanwhile, McPhail led his five companies to the south. Eight days later, Sibley reached Fort Abercrombie.

In the rolling hills of the Missouri coteau near the center of the Dakota Territory, Inkpaduta and Pawn roamed in search of another band of Lakota to join and from which to recruit warriors. Some miles east of the James River, they encountered a large band camped on the banks of a small lake.

Hundreds of lodges rimmed the lake. Some were hide tipis, others were more substantial structures with stone foundations.

"This is a longtime camp," Inkpaduta noted. "For many years Yanktonai and others have gathered each year to hunt before going to their winter home. I know of this place. It is called Whitestone."

213

To the east of the lake was a high, flat hill. A ravine traversed the plain to the left, or north, of the hill. White boulders littered the ground from the lake, on top of and past the hill.

In the heat of the afternoon the village's children played a hoop and pole game, and women busily skinned hides as men, fresh from a hunt, rested in the shade of their tipis. Inkpaduta and Pawn rode past the curious glances of Yanktonai tribesman toward the Soldiers' Lodge.

As they approached the large tipi, several leaders rose to meet them. A large man with a burly chest stood before the two visitors and motioned them to dismount.

"I'm Medicine Bear. This is Big Head and Little Soldier. We are Yanktonai. Who are you?"

"I am Inkpaduta of the Wapekute Santee. This is Pawn, a Sisseton."

Medicine Bear motioned to the ground. "Let us sit in a circle and smoke. Do you want to eat? We have much buffalo."

The men sat upon the earth and smoked the red pipe. They gnawed on dried buffalo meat as etiquette was observed.

"We have heard of you," Medicine Bear began. "Inkpaduta killed *wasichu* in Iowa before the great war in Minnesota started."

"Pawn killed them at Shetek," Inkpaduta replied. "We have been with the Teton fighting the Long Trader. He has gone, but others will come. You must stand against them, too."

Little Soldier spoke resolutely. "We have never fought the whites. Pawn, when you came with Lame Bear and the white captives from Shetek, we told you to keep going, that you would only bring the whites and trouble to us. Now you are back, and trouble will come."

"I saw Santee," Inkpaduta proclaimed.

Medicine Bear replied, "There are some but not many who are here from Minnesota. There are also some Hunkpapa, but only a few. Most have never seen *wasichus* and never fought them."

"You must fight them soon," Inkpaduta stated.

"We do not wish to fight the whites," Medicine Bear countered. "If they come, we will talk to them."

Pawn spat and growled disgustedly. "They will talk with bullets."

❧ 44 ❧

THE STEAMER THAT SULLY AWAITED finally arrived on the morning of August 19 at the mouth of the Little Cheyenne. The boat was immediately unloaded under his careful watch.

"Lieutenant Hall," Sully ordered, "see that the battalion commanders receive these instructions. All baggage of the officers and men of the command will be sent back down the river on the steamer. I want them to account for every man who is in the least sick or not well mounted. Anyone not in perfect health should be sent back to Fort Pierre.

"We'll take rations for a few weeks and forage enough to keep these damn wretched mules alive. Hopefully there will be good grass for the cavalry and artillery horses. Our force will be considerably reduced, but we should be able to travel fast. We move out tomorrow."

A FIERCE RAIN AND HAIL STORM EMPTIED from the skies the next morning, and the men remained in camp. Many huddled in their small dog tents as little rocks of ice bounced off the canvas shelters. Some tents were slashed and ripped as chunks of hail nearly the size of small apples sliced through. Chill and dampness clung to the men like a second unwanted skin.

Solomon, Jesse, and Nathan stood beneath the spreading branches of a cottonwood tree and watched as big plops of rain splattered on the surface of the Missouri. Frank LaFramboise and a young Indian joined them.

"Still wet here," Solomon grumbled, "but even worse on the ground in them tents. Frank, when do you think we'll find Indians?"

"Which Indians? I've heard that you fought Teton, not Minnesota Santee."

"Santee were at Big Mound. Our scouts were sure that most of the bodies we found after Dead Buffalo, Stony Lake, and in the woods by Apple

215

Creek were western Indians. I think Standing Buffalo split off after Big Mound. We've bin fightin' somebody called Sitting Bull of the Tetons."

"If we head east, we'll find them," Frank suggested. "Or they'll find us."

"Who's your friend?" Jesse asked.

"His name is Crazy Dog. He is a Fool Soldier."

"Fool Soldier? What's that?"

LaFramboise nodded at his companion. "His English is pretty poor. He helped rescue captives from Minnesota. Traded a horse for a woman. His people called him and his friends fools. They became the Fool Soldiers and formed a lodge."

Jesse's mouth dropped open in astonishment. "You were with those who rescued the Shetek captives! You're a hero! Even Duley will like to meet you. His wife and children were captives."

LaFramboise spoke Lakota to Crazy Dog, who smiled and nodded at the men. Each of the three shook the young Indian's hand and uttered, "Thank you."

ON AUGUST 21 THE ARMY, NOW ABOUT 1,200 in number, was in motion around hills, through ravines and over hilltops. The scouting parties were sent ahead of the main bodies by several miles.

Sully ordered LaFramboise, "Travel in advance of, or off to the side of, the main column. That'll allow you to move faster, cover more territory and submit reports when we camp. I will also place cavalry units on either flank of the army. They'll offer protection and also serve as scouts."

For the next week the Sully Expedition followed the Missouri River to the northwest. Signs of buffalo were found by scouts near a small creek called Bois Cache, or "Hidden Wood," on August 24, and Sully sent out a hunting party. The party was soon disbanded when more horses were disabled than buffalo.

The next day the army traveled twenty-two miles, and a different party was dispatched to hunt. They were much more successful, and the camp feasted on buffalo that night. Scouts reported sighting Indians near the Missouri.

The next morning, Sully ordered a small scouting party to search for other Sioux. Around mid-morning, while the army continued en route up the river, Solomon and Nathan rode back to the general. Each scout led a horse ridden by an Indian woman. Each woman had one child in front and another sitting behind her.

LaFramboise rode beside Sully. "We found them by the river. Seems they got separated from the others somehow," Solomon explained. "Thought you might be able to get somethin' from 'em."

Sully turned to his chief scout. "Frank, see what you can find out."

LaFramboise spoke easily in the Lakota tongue and listened to the women's responses. He asked a couple of questions, listened more and then turned to Sully.

"They say that General Sibley had a fight near the head of Long Lake. That's where Solomon was," he nodded at Foot. "These women say that the Lakota were on the way to Crow Creek, to the agency, when these two got lost and were alone."

"The tracks we saw were going up the river, away from Crow Creek," Solomon commented.

"So the main body of Sioux is east of the Missouri and likely heading onto the coteau. Lieutenant La Boo," Sully motioned for an officer riding behind him to move forward. "Take companies F and K of the Second Nebraska. Go to the Missouri and follow up the trail. Capture any Indians you find, if possible, and bring them in. I need more information. If you can't bring them in, kill them and destroy their camp. We'll continue to march until we get to good water." He gazed into bright sunlight and regarded the brown-singed grass of the prairie. "It's another hot one. Looks like Hell without the fire."

It was nightfall and thirty-five miles further before the hot, weary army found water when they reached Beaver Creek above Lake Oahe on the Missouri. Sully rested his men there, and they got a late start on August 27. After difficulty crossing the creek, they made only five miles before going into camp. Company K of the Second Nebraska rode in as camp was being bivouacked. They had become separated from La Boo and Company F. Concern grew about the fate of the other Nebraskans.

That night several scouts gathered around a buffalo chip fire. The men chewed tobacco and smoked as the western sky's pink blush turned black. La Framboise and Crazy Dog joined them.

"Frank, how far to Long Lake?" Jesse wondered.

"Twenty miles, Lieutenant. We'll have to meander around some sloughs and hills, but we should make it tomorrow."

"Any sign of La Boo?"

"Nothing, maybe tomorrow."

Solomon called to Will Duley, "Major, have you met Frank's friend Crazy Dog yet?"

"No, but I've seen plenty of reds. Is something special about this one?"

"He is a Fool Soldier, Will," Nathan answered. "He went into the territory after the Shetek captives. He's one of those who traded to bring back your wife and children."

Duly slowly rose to his feet as he unfolded his legs like bent pipe cleaners. He walked to where Crazy Dog stood and extended his right hand. The Indian hesitated a moment and then clasped the offered hand.

"It's no secret that I hate the Sioux," Duley said, "especially after what they did to my family. I'll kill any that get in my way. But," his voice softened, "thank you, you did a brave and good thing. It won't be forgotten."

The scouts ranged several miles ahead of the expedition on August 28. Solomon observed markings on the ground and quickly pointed them out to Jesse and Nathan. "Look at the ground. It's all rutted. Many lodges are being pulled through here. And look there, a fresh buffalo carcass. Hoof prints all over. We're followin' a lot of Indians."

"Look!" Jesse pointed his saber at a nearby bush. "That bush is moving. Something's in it."

"Animal?" Nathan asked.

The answer came when the form of an emaciated old man emerged from the brush speaking in rapid Lakota. His gray hair was twisted and matted, and scratches from the undergrowth streaked his face. He walked with a heavy limp.

"Get Frank," Jesse ordered another scout, Jim Atkinson. "I can't make heads or tails of this."

Minutes later La Framboise engaged the elderly Indian in conversation. Then he turned to the other scouts. "I know this man. He's a friendly from down Sioux City way. He says that Sibley fought Indians at the head of Long Lake. You know that," he nodded at Jesse and Solomon. "He talks of the fight at Apple Creek, too. He adds that after building breastworks by the creek, Sibley left after the Indians crossed the Missouri. When he left, they recrossed and attacked and sunk a boat of miners. He says ninety-one Indians were killed there. I guess you fellas know mosta that.

"But he also says that a war party followed Sibley as he went east. He's over the James River now and nearing Minnesota. Some of the Lakota went north, the larger number went toward the head of Long Lake, 'bout fifty miles from here. They've gone east from there. I'm guessin' that General Sully will head after them. They were surprised to find us so close."

"Seems purty clear," Solomon reasoned. "Sibley was gone, and they thought it was safe to head back to their old hunting grounds. They didn't account for us."

La Framboise added, "Crazy Dog says that this time of year they camp on the coteau near the tributaries of the James. Lots o' lakes and springs keep the grass fresh, there's lots o' buffalo and lots o' fish. I'm going back to Sully with what this fella said. I'll tell him that once we turn east, we'll run into Sioux."

IN CAMP THAT EVENING, General Sully concurred with his scout's analysis. "But we can't head east just yet," he cautioned. "I'm still worried about La Boo. I think he's up near Long Lake. We'll head up there first. I'm sending four companies out with Major Pearman to hunt him up. I'm also sending Captain Cram and two companies of the Sixth Iowa to Apple Creek to examine Sibley's camp and the massacre of the miners."

To Sully's relief, the next morning La Boo found his way back to the expedition's camp. He reported to his general, "We saw nothing, sir. Traveled just about 180 miles. We lived on buffalo, and pretty well covered the country to your left.

"We did find the Indian camp you sent us after. There were only ten lodges and no Sioux. We burned them out and came back looking for you."

After Pearman and his detachment returned, Sully was ready to move the army east. He explained to his officers, "Pearman tells me that there's good grass to the east, toward the coteau. No wood but plenty of lakes filled with abominable water. Cram is back from Apple River. They found Sibley's fortifications and his trail east. Interestingly, the boat and the miners could not be found.

"We will march along the south side of Long Lake and then turn southeast," Sully continued. "No sense in heading toward Devils Lake. Sibley's not there, and I don't think the Sioux are, either. Scouting parties will search for Indians each day of our march."

He turned to his scout. "Mr. La Framboise, stay about five miles in front of us and have other scouts on either side of the main column. You've done a good job so far bringing in Indians who either know or verify information important to this march."

OVER THE NEXT SEVERAL DAYS THE EXPEDITION snaked across the Missouri coteau, covering ninety miles of rolling, grassy countryside dotted by dozens of spoiled, salty lakes. Fearing possible Indian attacks, Sully became cautions in his approach. He maintained an advanced guard and flankers. The wagon train proceeded in two lines sixty paces apart, with a column of soldiers on each side. All loose cattle and horses were herded between the wagons.

General Sully rode in the front and center with one company of men and an artillery battery. He dressed in brown corduroy pants, a white shirt, and a white slouch hat, customary campaign apparel for the general. Camp was made in a flat area between hills on the night of September 2. Sully awaited reports from his scouts as he discussed the day with several of his officers.

Solomon, Jesse, and Nathan were hot, tired and sweaty when they rode in to report on their scouting foray.

"Lots of fresh signs," Foot relayed. "Lodge pole trails are spread out all over the country, but they all seem to be movin' toward the same place."

"It's like Crazy Dog says, there's a favorite hunting spot near here, and that's where they're goin'," LaFramboise added. "My scouts saw the same things. Lots of dead buffalo carcasses, too. They be huntin' and feedin' a lot of people."

Sully mentally measured the reports and replied, "Tomorrow I want Major House to take four companies of the Sixth Iowa, about 300 men, and follow the trail you found today. Frank, take your scouts and travel about five miles ahead of House. House, you'll be five miles ahead of me and the main army. Foot and Buchanen, join La Framboise. Cates, you stay with me. Major House, if you see a small band of Indians, feel free to attack them, or take them prisoners. If you should find a large band that's too big for you to successfully cope with, watch the camp at a distance, try to contain them and send word back to me. We'll move out and surround them."

The scouts hit the trail early on the morning of September 3. Crazy Dog rode about midway between the scout detachment and House's cavalry. Ten minutes every hour, House called a halt to allow the horses to graze.

La Framboise bore to the left of the main line of march through a series of low hills. Jesse and Solomon rode with the head scout.

Around 3:00 in the afternoon, Jesse peered into the distance. "Look," he muttered, "is that another mirage or is that a camp?"

LaFramboise shielded his eyes. "It's a camp. By a lake. See behind the lodges."

"We better tell House," Jesse concluded. "How far back is he?"

"Can't be more than two miles," Solomon judged.

La Framboise curtly nodded his head. "Let's go!"

The three horsemen galloped their mounts to where House and the Sixth Iowa were resting men and horses.

"Indian camp!" Frank blurted. "Just up ahead!"

House tensed with excitement. "How many?"

"Hard telling, mebbe twenty . . . thirty lodges. They're at a lake, and it's tough to see."

"Boots and saddles, men!" House cried. "Lieutenant Dayton, tell the men to load carbines and pistols and be ready to fight. We'll head to the Indian camp through the ravines and use the hills as a screen.

"La Framboise, you, Foot, and Buchanen get closer to the Indians. Find out just how big the camp is."

The three spurred their animals and bolted away. Minutes later the Sixth Iowa followed at a gallop.

As the three scouts and their horses flew over a rise near the camp, they twisted their animals' heads around to fiercely jerk them to a halt. Just below them, on the banks of a small lake, was the sprawling village.

Solomon was the first to find words. "My Gawd! How big is it?"

"Sacre bleu," La Framboise whispered, "six to eight hundred lodges."

They watched in silence, interrupted only by the heavy breathing and blowing of their horses. "Must be a few thousand of them," Jesse estimated.

"They've seen us!" Solomon exclaimed as Lakota pointed excitedly toward the rise where they sat. "Let's get back to House!"

When they wheeled their tired animals around to gallop back to the cavalry, the ground around them magically erupted with warriors. Two hundred Indians surrounded the three and closed in. In moments a confining circle blocked the white men's escape.

La Framboise muttered cautiously, "Let me talk. I know some of these people. Just follow my lead."

Then he raised a hand in salute and called, "Little Soldier." He smiled at a smallish man mounted on a spotted pony. "We are scouting for General Sully, looking for bad Indians. Are there any here who fought in Minnesota?"

"Hardly any," the Lakota responded, "there are a small number of Santee here, and only a few of them fought Sibley. What soldier chief are you with?"

"General Sully."

"We thought he was still traveling up the big river. Sibley has gone to Minnesota. You should not come here. Why do you want to fight us unless you are tired of living and want to die? We are here to hunt, not fight. But we will kill soldiers if we have to."

Frank noticed that the skittish ponies had moved and created a small gap between the warriors. He whispered softly to his companions, "Do what I do, stay low and ride like Hell." He shouted, "NOW!" and sharply dug spurs into his horse's side. The animal lunged forward as La Framboise leaned over its neck, and they bolted into the broken opening in the circle. Jesse and Solomon followed on the lead animal's hooves.

As the trio dashed through them, one surprised warrior raised a rifle and fired. The bullet whizzed by Solomon's head, clipping the brim of his hat. They rode frantically as if pursued by demons. Jesse knew their hopes were slim. Their horses were already tired and winded. They couldn't keep up a fast pace long, and the fresh mounts of the Indians would soon over take them.

Shots from behind continued to buzz past like angry hornets. Then Jesse heard more shots, this time from in front. The ragged rattle of gunfire was the most welcome sound he had ever heard. House's cavalry was returning fire and driving the pursuers back to their village.

The scouts mounted a rise and were met by House. "Hundreds of lodges and a few thousand Indians," La Framboise panted.

"Good work!" a red-faced, excited House proclaimed. "Get remounts and ride back to Sully with this message: 'Hurry up. I'll try to watch them and contain them, but if they get serious, our little army of 300 won't be able to stand against them long.'" He handed a scrawled scrap of paper to Frank.

"We have a chance to pitch into them, but we need Sully now."

"How far back?" Solomon asked.

"About ten miles. Be quick."

Fresh horses were led to the scouts, and in moments the three horsemen were bound for Sully and the rest of the army.

≈ 45 ≈

I T WAS 4:00 P.M. AND SULLY'S MAIN force had gone into camp to the west of the Indian village. Horses had been picketed and soldiers were eating their meal.

Three riders burst into camp and sped directly to the headquarters tent. "General," La Framboise gasped, "we found a big village up ahead 'bout ten miles. Major House is tryin' to contain 'em, but he's badly outnumbered. Says he needs you now."

Sully turned to an aide. "Get my officers. Tell the bugler to sound boots and saddles! How many?" he asked the scouts.

"Several thousand at least," Jesse answered. "Could be a thousand or more warriors, I don't know."

"Did they fight in Minnesota? Did they fight Sibley?"

"Well, Gen'rl," Solomon replied, "they say only a few. Most are Yankton."

"Can we believe them?" Sully considered. "No matter, they're Sioux, and we were sent to fight Sioux."

Furnas of the Second Nebraska and Wilson of the Sixth Iowa burst with anticipation into the tent.

"Colonel Furnas," Sully began, his voice rising in excitement, "I'll leave Major Pearman with four companies in the camp. Poorly mounted and sick will stay behind to strike the tents and corral all the wagons. I want the Second Nebraska on the right and the Sixth Iowa on the left. One company of the Seventh Iowa and the battery will be in the center. See to the men!"

In eighteen minutes the army was mounted and in position. Cheers burst from the throats of over 1,000 men as Sully rode his prancing iron-gray stallion before his men. His blue uniform blouse was fastened with shiny gold buttons.

Trooper Mullin turned to Private Caldwell. "He's on the gray. In uniform. Trouble's ahead!"

Sully reined in before his army and shouted, "Boys, you did damned well! Fours to the right, march. Trot march!"

In minutes the army was galloping, horses thundering over the hilly countryside toward the distant village.

Albert House waited. He sent two companies to the left of the encampment to ascertain more closely the number and position of the Sioux on the uneven terrain. After they reported back, House sent another company to the right to learn more about Indian defenses.

Pawn and Inkpaduta watched closely as the troops moved around them. They watched as young warriors raced past them to the lakeshore and began to smear blue clay over their bodies, thinking there wasn't enough time to apply regular war paint. They had dressed for battle in breech clouts and little else. Many slipped feathers into headbands and fastened amulets to their arms.

"We must attack them now!" Pawn urged. "They are few and we are many."

Inkpaduta agreed. "The young men are ready."

"No!" Medicine Bear ordered as he approached with Big Head and Little Soldier. "Many of the people will die. We will go and talk to them. Maybe they will take me and leave the rest."

"You're a fool," Inkpaduta countered. "Let me lead these people. I know how to fight. We must fight."

"Stay where you are," Little Soldier demanded. "We will go to the blue coats."

Big Head held a white flag of truce as the three Indians rode up a rise to the hill where House waited. Medicine Bear gazed at House and said with resignation, "My people do not want to fight. Most have never fought the white man and are not from Minnesota. Take us instead. We will go with you."

Another half French-half Lakota scout, Pierre Bottineau, translated. House responded, "Are there other chiefs in camp?"

"Yes, but take us."

House straightened his back. "Look, how do I know which chiefs are entitled to speak with authority for your people? It might be you, it might be someone else in the camp. I want all chiefs to surrender."

As Bottineau translated, a look of consternation swept over the faces of the three Indians.

"No, we can't do that!" Medicine Bear proclaimed.

"Then we have nothing to talk about."

Sadly the Indians turned and rode back to their camp.

House called to Captain Marsh and Lieutenant Dayton, "We've got to stall until Sully gets here. Shift position occasionally to distract the reds. Tell your men not to fire under any circumstances. I don't want to rile them up. We need to hold them in check until the rest of the command arrives."

"Captain, we don't hold any cards here," Dayton cautioned. "There's 300 of us and over 1,000 of them. Look." He gestured with a wave of his right arm. "They're movin' around us. Pretty soon we'll be surrounded. The men know it, too. Look at them."

House rubbed his short beard and gazed at his battalion. The men looked tense, and worry etched their faces. They knew they were in dire consequences.

"We must be proactive," the major reasoned. "If we show fear, they'll be on us like flies on a dead buffalo. I know the fix we're in, but a little false bravado," he smiled, "just might buy us the time we need for Sully to get here."

He turned to Bottineau. "Curious piece of ground, isn't it?" He looked out at the lake surrounded by tipis and the green space to the east that extended to a high, long hill a few hundred yards from the lake. Smaller hills extended to either side with a ravine to the left of the high hill. Nature had left a litter of white boulders scattered about the hills.

"They call the hill 'Whitestone,'" Bottineau replied.

It was nearly 5:30 when a rising cloud of dust a mile off signaled the arrival of Sully and his men. In the village the sight of the soldiers caused near-panic and a hasty departure.

The women and old men began taking down the tipis and loading the ponies with tent poles on either side with a strap over the back. Possessions were tied to twelve- to fifteen-foot lodge poles, and the travois was complete. Babies were frantically placed in baskets and strapped onto the poles that extended from the ponies' backs to the ground.

Dogs were strapped in similar ways but with smaller poles. The danger that faced them was now apparent, and a dash to the James River a few miles to the east became their only hope.

Inkpaduta chided the young warriors. "Are you women who run? Stay and fight. Pawn and I will show you how if you do not know."

When Sully thundered toward the camp, he found the Lakota in desperate flight. With women, children, ponies, and dogs, the men were fleeing to the left, or north, of Whitestone Hill and down the ravine.

He watched as a woman caught a runaway horse and propped an old woman in the saddle while a younger woman hitched a travois filled with children to the animal. Indians were frantically seeking escape.

"We've got to stop them!" Sully shouted. "Furnas, take the Second Nebraska and join House on the right. Push your horses to the utmost and corral the reds. Wilson, take the rest of the Sixth Iowa and move to the left. I'll follow with the Seventh Iowa and the artillery and ride through their village. Scouts fall in as well. Let's move and pitch into 'em!"

Furnas and the Second Nebraska galloped over a hill to House's position on the right of the fleeing Indians, while to the west the sun was fast sinking toward the horizon.

"Major House," the breathless colonel ordered, "we are to surround the Indians and cut off their retreat in the ravine. I will continue with my battalion on the right flank, the south of the ravine. Take your men and pursue the reds to the left, the north."

"So, Colonel," House smiled, "we corral 'em and rope 'em in."

"Exactly, and here are your scouts." Furnas nodded at Solomon, Jesse, and Nathan as they approached. "They delivered your message, and you get them back. I'm keeping La Framboise with me. Now, move!" He pointed at the desperate melee below. "They're scared and confused. Victory is ripe for the taking!"

House delivered the order, and the Sixth Iowa galloped north of the ravine and continued east along the rim. Sully held the rest of his men on the edge of the village. Much of the site was in chaos. Many lodges had been dismantled but some remained, along with discarded household goods and supplies.

The general watched as the Second Nebraska Cavalry disappeared over the hills in a dust cloud. Then he turned to Colonel Wilson. "See House taking a position there to the left. He'll need help containing the Sioux. Take the First Battalion of the Sixth Iowa and follow House. Furnas will block the head of the ravine with you and him on the sides. I'll ride through the village and establish a position on the highest point. That hill there with all the white stones on it. You'll close the back door."

As Wilson and the Iowa Cavalry dashed to the north, Sully with some cavalry and artillery batteries crashed through the abandoned village. They clamored over the homes and personal property of the Lakota people. Then Sully encountered a small group of Indians who had ceased running and were huddled together.

Gunshots, screams, horses' hooves and whinnies in gathering twilight led to a pandemonium of confusion and terror for the Indians. Little Soldier pleaded, "Do not kill these people. They do not wish to fight. Many are women and children. We did not fight the whites, never. Why are you doing this?"

"Mr. Bottineau, who is this?"

"Little Soldier, General."

Sully thought a moment before commenting. "I've heard of Little Soldier, he has the reputation of being a good Indian and friendly to us. Captain Millard, I'm placing you in charge of prisoners. Keep them under guard. There'll be others."

With the Seventh Iowa, Sully forged ahead. Another small group of men was attempting to elude the onslaught of soldiers. Major Ten Broeck cut them off much as a cowboy turned a herd of cattle. The warriors, dressed for battle, stopped and dropped their weapons.

Sully rode up and recognized their leader. "Big Head, he's a bad one, Major. Send this bunch to Millard with the others."

Once through the village, Sully called a halt to determine the course of battle. About a half-mile ahead, ragged gunfire was becoming more brisk. "Major Ten Broeck, we will take possession of the hillocks over there. Form a line and have Lieutenant Krume place his battery on top of the high knoll. Have him unlimber and be ready to fire."

The Sioux were now contained in the ravine. In their front were the Second Nebraska and the Sixth Iowa's First Battalion. Both battalions extended along either side of the Indians. The Sixth Iowa's Third Battalion covered the rear. Any attempt to flee south was blocked by Whitestone Hill and Sully's artillery.

At this point communication seemed to break down as each battalion began to act independently of the others. House formed a line of battle on the north of the ravine and found that the Second Nebraska was now on his left flank. House's Third Iowa Battalion dismounted and awaited orders to move forward.

Colonel Wilson and the First Iowa Battalion, led by Major Galligen, thundered onto the scene.

"Major House," Wilson bellowed over the pandemonium of battle, "I'll assume command. Why are your men dismounted? Mount up. We're going to charge!"

A moment later the battalion advanced, first at a trot, than a gallop, and finally a full charge. Wilson raced ahead of his men, his saber extended in his right hand and brandished at the Sioux. Heavy fire from both sides blazed in the dimming light. The colonel hurtled farther in advance of his army until his horse stumbled with a shot to the chest. The animal didn't fall but spun around and struggled back to the battalion line thirty yards to the rear. The beast then collapsed dead on the plain.

Wilson scrambled to his feet from the slain horse. "Major House," he cried, "why isn't that company shooting?"

"Colonel, you didn't give the order to load weapons, just to charge. That company followed orders to a 'T.'"

Wilson shook his head in amazement. "We dismount and fight from here!" he ordered. "Everyone load and fire."

Colonel Wilson was on the ravine with House and directly opposite the Second Nebraska. He formed his troops parallel to the Nebraska line. The Indians raced pell mell up the ravine, scattering as they went. Suddenly most stopped and the warriors formed a huge rectangular box around the women and the children in the ravine.

"Hoyka! Hey!" Inkpaduta screamed.

"It is a good day to die!" Pawn answered. "Here we stand and fight!"

Nearly 1,000 warriors waited after forming a protective shield sheltering the old, the women, and children. An eerie silence fell over the ravine as the Indians anticipated the soldiers' next move.

Furnas conferred with Major Taffe as they watched from the south side of the ravine. "Major, it's getting dark and we can't wait for orders. Time is precious. If anything is to be done, it must be done now! Keep the First Nebraska Battalion at the head of the ravine to cut off the retreat. Stay mounted and form an obtuse angle to my line of the Second Battalion. Await my order to advance."

Taffe and his men immediately fell into position as Furnas waited. Then the colonel cried, "Second Battalion, forward!"

As the Nebraskans advanced, Taffe's men moved forward as well. Four hundred yards from the Sioux, Furnas ordered his men to dismount. Every fourth man held the horses of his comrades.

"Forward march!" the colonel commanded. The blue line, now dim in the dusk, moved toward the waiting Indians.

One hundred yards closer came the order, "Fire! Pour into them, boys!" The command sharply echoed down the battle front, and from all around rifle fire poured into the Indians in the ravine.

The Sioux immediately returned fire from their desperate band, while little leaden missiles that knew neither age nor gender ripped mercilessly into their skin.

The soldiers kept advancing, firing repeatedly as they moved forward. Solomon, Jesse, and Nathan sat on their horses and watched as the Iowans dismounted and blasted into the ravine opposite from the Nebraskans. Chaos ruled amid confusion as bullets rained below, finding their marks in women and children as well as warriors.

Inkpaduta ordered attacks to first try to turn Furnas's left flank and then his right. Both times they were driven back by murderous fire.

The three men watching the slaughter left their rifles in their scabbards. Nathan angrily told his friends, "I went through two years of Hell fighting in the East. I've never seen anything like this."

Solomon nodded. "They've shot me. They killed my brother and would have wiped out my whole family. But I just can't raise my gun in this."

An angry officer turned and demanded, "Dismount! Join the fight!"

"We won't participate in this massacre," Jesse replied. "We are still members of Sibley's army. He told us to deliver a message to Sully, not kill innocents."

"Just like I thought," a man near the officer shouted, "Indian lovin', no good . . ."

It was Will Duley, who had ridden out with Wilson. "We should shoot 'em here!" He raised his rifle as if to fire at Jesse.

The officer knocked it aside and yelled at Duley, "We'll deal with them later. Fight Indians!"

The roar of cannons blasting added to the cacophony of sounds. In the gathering darkness the big guns flashed red and yellow into the night. Cavalry horses began to bolt and scream in the din. Taking advantage of the darkness and confusion, the Indians broke from their rectangle and began to scatter toward the north and east and through the Iowans.

Meanwhile, in the darkness the Iowans and Nebraskans closed ever nearer to each other while firing continuously. More Nebraskans began to fall mortally wounded. Lieutenant La Boo frantically grabbed Furnas by the arm. "Colonel, the Iowans, they're shooting *us!*"

Furnas made a quick assessment. "You're right, sound rally. We've got to fall back to get out of range. Damn darkness. Look at 'em running away like rabbits." The dim forms of Indians were heading up the ravine to the north and east past unmanageable horses and bewildered men.

Inkpaduta and Pawn scrambled past a cavalryman. Pawn's tomahawk crashed into his skull as they raced by the soldier. A cannonball arched over and exploded above their heads. It was just light enough to see three horsemen before them.

In the brief flash that illuminated his face, Solomon recognized Pawn. He swiftly brought his rifle from its scabbard, shouted, "Hold!" and leveled his weapon at Pawn's head. Another exploding cannonball cast light on the scene as the three horsemen and the two Indians stood frozen as if nothing else existed but them.

Then the sound of a rifle blasted. Pawn's hands flew to his forehead. Blood spurted between his fingers, and the Indian slumped to the ground. Shock spread over Solomon's face as Inkpaduta instantly disappeared like fading mist into the darkness. Will Duley, from a position behind Solomon, hurried to Pawn's body. The rifle in Duley's hands was still smoking. He knelt with his hunting knife, slit a circle on top of the dead Indian's head and peeled off the scalp.

"You murdering son of Satan!" Duley exclaimed. "Hell's got one more customer. That's for my children and for my wife."

Solomon turned to Jesse and Nathan. "I couldn't pull the trigger. After all he's done, after he killed Silas, I just couldn't shoot him down like a dog."

"But Duley could and he did," Nathan finished.

The Second Nebraska remounted and was ready to move out in pursuit of the disappearing Indians.

La Boo asked, "Colonel, sir, will you give the order? We're ready to go after them."

Furnas peered into the night. "No, I don't think so. It's too dark, and with the Iowans shooting at us, too, I don't think it would be prudent. We'll hold this position. Have the men dismount and lay on their arms holding their horses. We'll finish off the Indians in the morning. It's 8:30 now, just too dark."

The sounds of battle were over, and darkness smothered the ravine. But there was no peace for the soldiers, the wounded or those Indians left in the ravine. Through the night as dogs howled and Indian women wailed, soldiers gathered up their dead and wounded as best they could.

≈ 46 ≪

ARLY THE NEXT MORNING, SOLOMON, Jesse, and Nathan rode down the ravine into the scene of devastation. The blazing yellow ball in the east promised another hot day. Some tipis still stood, some were torn down. On some discarded lodge poles, scalps of enemies still hung. The Indians had fled, leaving everything—tents, meat, cooking utensils, and even a couple dozen children.

From the village and up the ravine, the specter of death was everywhere. Dead soldiers, dead Indians, dead horses, many dead dogs and hundred of others howling for their masters. Some of the dogs still dragged small poles with bundles attached to them. One carried a young baby.

Added to the din of the howling dogs were the cries of children and anguished moans from the wounded. The three scouts came upon Sully, Furnas, and Wilson, who also were surveying the site.

Nathan watched as the general walked to a dead woman lying on her back. A baby clutched a breast, trying to feed. Sully tenderly picked up the whimpering infant and held it against his shoulder, patting its back.

He turned to an aide and spoke softly. "Here, take this one and see that all other children are taken to the captives for care."

Sully turned back to his officers and acknowledged the approach of the three riders. "Good morning. It was a great victory. We have to follow it up."

"Gen'ral," Solomon replied, "this was a massacre. That's all it was. It's not just that women and children were slaughtered here. They left all their winter food supply. Many more will starve to death later."

"War is a nasty business, Mr. Foot. In the Minnesota River Valley the Santee fought a total war against our settlers as well as our soldiers. I've heard them say that whites took their families onto Indian land, and death was the result. These people killed in Minnesota and brought *their* families to this spot. Unfortunately for them, they paid the price, too."

233

"Did these people fight in Minnesota?" Nathan asked.

"We have found some evidence of plunder from Minnesota in the camp."

"It could o' been traded for. Most of these people are Yanktoni, according to Crazy Dog," Solomon retorted.

"To be fair," Jesse added, "last night we encountered Pawn and Inkpaduta. Duley killed Pawn, but Inkpaduta escaped."

"Damn!" Sully exclaimed. "I wish we'd gotten him. Maybe we will yet today."

Furnas spread his arms expansively. "We have scouting parties spread out in all directions looking for the renegades. We'll round up more. If Inkpaduta is out there, we just might nab him, too. Maybe even round up a few horses and mules."

The general's eyes turned steely as he commented to the scouts, "I've been given a negative report on you three from a couple of officers. I choose to ignore it. While I disapprove of your action, or should I say inaction, there was no harm. To discipline you would tarnish this great victory. I won't have that."

Sully slowly turned in a circle as he viewed the wreckage of the camp. He faced his officers again. "We'll set up camp here on the site of the village. Bring any living Indian to Captain Millard, the wounded, too. Doc will see to them.

"I want all Indian equipment and food, buffalo meat, whatever, taken to the hollow by the hill and piled up."

"What do you want done with it?" Colonel Wilson inquired.

"Burn it."

"General, that's their whole supply of food," Solomon repeated. "They can't live without it."

"They left it. We can't haul it all. We burn it. Gentlemen," he nodded at Furnas and Wilson, "see to it." With those instructions, Sully walked away toward his headquarters tent.

"Sir," Jesse asked Furnas, "what's the tally?"

"We lost eighteen dead and thirty-eight wounded. Not bad considering we had 700 troopers engaged and the Indians over 1,000."

"What about the Indians?"

"It looks like about 300 killed and wounded, more or less."

Furnas asked Wilson, "Did you get a count on prisoners?"

"Millard said he's got 156, thirty-two men and 124 women and children. They all go to Crow Creek. What should we do with the Indian bodies?" Wilson wondered.

"Well, we sure as Hell aren't going to bury them," Furnas asserted. "I think we should just leave some lying around as a lesson. Let the wolves and coyotes gnaw on them a bit. The rest, pile them on with the meat and camp supplies. They'll burn good."

Throughout the day, wounded were cared for while the dead soldiers were prepared for burial. Squadrons of soldiers sweated in the relentless sun as they piled load after wagonload of Indian buffalo meat and supplies in a hillside hollow. Tools for tanning hides, beads, paints, porcupine quills, and trinkets of every kind as well as kettles, dishes, robes, and hatchets were stacked. Everything that would burn went onto the pile. The rest was thrown into the lake. Finally the soldiers threw atop the massive heap the bodies of slain Indians.

General Sully sat on a camp stool and sketched the scene of the village and battlefield. Colonel Wilson watched silently from behind as his commander vividly portrayed the scene.

"Capturing history, General?" Wilson asked.

"A family tradition. My father was a great artist, you know. I dabble in it when I have time."

"You draw very well. It's important to leave pictorial accounts."

"I've been in many places, Colonel. I have many pictures. They'll outlive me."

That night Sully received the disappointing news that his scouting parties had returned empty-handed. The fleeing Lakota had vanished from sight. The graves of eleven were found by a lakeside several miles away. But no live Sioux were found.

"Try again tomorrow," Sully ordered Wilson.

"Lieutenant Hall and Company B are ready. I'll send them, General Sully."

Eighteen soldiers were laid to rest on top of Whitestone Hill on September 5. The huge pile of Indian belongings doubled as a funeral pyre for over 200 Indians. It burst into an inferno and grew white hot as flames leapt high above, seeming to lick the clouds. A heavy black cloud of smoke mushroomed over Whitestone Hill.

Solomon watched and called to a soldier, "How much buffalo meat did you fellas throw on this?"

The young man scratched his head before answering. "Hard telling, but I heard one officer say that General Sully figgered that there must be at least 500,000 pounds."

As Foot watched in silence, Nathan muttered, "Such a shame."

"This or the battle?"

"Both."

They returned later with Jesse. The pile had burned down, but the fire still glowed red hot. They noticed a milky flow, like a small stream, twisting away from the blazing pile and down the hillside.

"What's this?" Jesse knelt by the steaming liquid.

Solomon peered at it closely and then back at the burning pile. "Tallow," he muttered. "It's the melted fat from the buffalo," he paused, "and from the Indians."

"Doesn't it make you proud to be part of a great victory," Nathan said, his voice dripping with sarcasm.

"It makes me want to go home," Jesse replied, "or at least to Crow Creek and JoAnna."

That evening Lieutenant Charles Hall reported to General Sully. The tall officer looked tired and bedraggled. A jagged red scratch on his cheek had scabbed over.

"You look like Hell warmed over," Sully observed. "What happened?"

"General, I had twenty-seven men. We rode into 300 about five miles to the south."

Sully eyes focused with alarm. "Again. What happened?"

"We lost two men, and Lieutenant Leavitt is missing. They likely got him, too."

"How did you manage to escape 300 Sioux?"

"The men stood their ground at first. But we were so closely pressed by the enemy that the men increased the rapidity of their retreat, frankly, without my orders."

"In other words, they ran like Hell to save their skins and get back here."

Hall hoped the twilight hid the shame on his face as he answered, "Yes, sir."

Sully stared in contemplation at the glowing, simmering ball of Sioux belongings on the hillside. Then he spoke decisively. "They need to know I mean business. I won't have my men ambushed. Find two dead warriors from the battlefield. Slice their heads off and put them on stakes on the lakeside. Maybe they'll get the message that we mean business."

Hall's eyes swept over the battlefield. "I'd think they got the message yesterday."

"Well, Lieutenant, this will leave no doubt," Sully concluded.

Sully's expedition left Whitestone Hill on September 6 and headed south toward Fort Pierre and the Missouri River.

৯০47৩

T TOOK A WEEK FOR THE ARMY TO REACH Fort Pierre. From there a battalion of the Sixth Iowa escorted the 156 Indian prisoners over the scorching plain to Crow Creek. Solomon, Jesse, and Nathan rode with the escort.

Back in Minnesota, McPhail's cavalry actually got home before Sibley. Willie Sturgis and Oscar Wall rode into Fort Ridgely on September 1. On his return route to Fort Snelling, Sibley called for a halt at the little settlement of Richmond. There his army rested while the general received important guests.

He set up camp on the banks of the Sauk River. Neat rows of white tents with a large headquarters tent in the center greeted new Senator Alexander Ramsey and his party. An American flag snapped in the breeze above Sibley's tent as the senator and his party approached the general.

They found Sibley thinner than before he left Fort Ridgely. His greatly tanned face was etched in deep lines, reflecting pain and sorrow. More gray was flecked in his mustache and hair.

Ramsey shook the hand of his old friend and political opponent. "Henry, I haven't seen you since June. I'm sorry for your losses, two children. And Lieutenant Beaver, I know you were close to him as well."

"Thank you, Alexander." Sibley bowed his head a moment. "What brings you out here?"

"We're bound farther west to make a treaty with the Red Lake and Pembina Ojibwe. We want to nail down the Red River Valley. We'll meet Hatch and his men up there. They'll come from Pembina. Congratulations on your victories, General. You fought what, three-four battles, you chased the Sioux over the Missouri and got back here with few casualties to either men or animals. Remarkable."

Then he motioned to a portly man next to him. "Henry, this is Joe Wheelock, editor of the *St. Paul Press*. He wants to talk with you."

238

The three men went into the large headquarters tent and sat upon camp stools. Wheelock asked Sibley about the campaign, the battles and the failure to link up with Sully. The tone was general and positive.

Then Wheelock became more direct. "But for all of this, General, you really didn't have a decisive battle, did you? In fact, dispatches from the west indicate that as soon as you rode away, the Sioux re-crossed the Missouri and are free to roam the eastern Dakotas."

Sibley smiled grimly and replied, "I did what I could with what I had. Maybe I'm not much of a soldier. Senator, I'm open to being removed at any time."

"No such thought is on anyone's mind," Ramsey assured his friend. "There's more to do, and you are the one to do it."

Sibley finally returned to Fort Snelling on September 13. He arrived just as newspaper accounts of his expedition were hitting the newsstands. Wheelock had written, "As a triumph of organizing and business skill, Sibley's march and return across the dry, parched plains is probably without a parallel in history. But that is all. Praise must stop there. General Sibley is not a soldier."

Sibley turned the pages of the *Minneapolis State Atlas* to read, "The hour for striking the avenging blow had arrived, but the blow was not struck. It was stayed by treason or cowardice on the part of H.H. Sibley."

Then the general opened a letter from General Pope. He read silently and muttered, "They still want me, but do I want them?" He was ordered to headquarters in Milwaukee to discuss the campaign of 1864 with Pope and Sully.

AT FORT PIERRE, ALFRED SULLY ALSO heard from Pope. Near twilight he sat on a stool beside his tent in his army's encampment outside the fort. He opened two envelopes. One was postmarked in mid-August, the other more recently. He read the earlier letter first and was finishing the second as David Wilson approached.

Sully stifled a laugh. "Colonel Wilson, it seems that last month our commanding general ordered us back to the Missouri River to conduct minor raids and to winter on the river. He once again praises the great success of Sibley, much to our denigration. Fortunately, this missive did not reach me." He tossed the letter into a flickering fire before his seat.

"After word of our victory at Whitestone Hill reached Pope, he changed his tune." Wilson pulled up a stool and sat beside his general.

"Sibley washed out, and Pope is using our success to make himself look good. He invites me to winter with him in Milwaukee." Sully smiled sardonically. "Let me read this word for word, 'I trust you will believe my feelings toward you are of the friendliest character, and that nothing I can do shall be wanting which can promote your interests or your pleasure.' The windbag continues, 'Whilst I regret that difficulties and obstacles of a serious character prevented your cooperation with General Sibley at the time hoped, I bear willing testimony to the distinguished conduct of yourself and your command and to the important service you have rendered to yourself and to the Government— to yourself and your command—I tender my thanks and congratulations.'

"He has to compliment me to make himself look good. Pope has a penchant for that, I committed to memory his acceptance of Lincoln's order to command, 'Let us understand each other,' he said, 'I have come to you from the West, where we have always seen the backs of our enemies.' All I saw was Pope's backside at Bull Run."

"The squirming, pompous weasel," Wilson murmured. "Will you go to Milwaukee?"

"Not soon, David, maybe come spring when the plan is being put together."

Wilson absentmindedly stirred the campfire embers with a stick. "What's next, Alfred?"

"We stay here and finish the job. I won't be satisfied until the Sioux are completely destroyed as a fighting force or until they're driven so far from here that they can't return to Minnesota or the Dakota Territory."

"You want to exterminate them?"

"No, and that's where I differ from some of my colleagues like Sheridan and Sherman. I want to end their ability to make war on us, but I would treat them fairly and assign them to reservations."

Wilson stirred the embers again and caused bright sparks to float into the gathering darkness. "The tide of war in the East has turned. It's only a matter of time. Will they call you back?"

Sully snorted derisively. "This is my future. For the present I'm their designated Indian fighter." He paused thoughtfully. "Then when the war against the rebels is over, they'll replace me with their new favored pets."

"Like who, Alfred?"

"Howard maybe. He's actually a pretty good officer. Custer for sure. The arrogant, impetuous fool is like a son to Sheridan. I've already had words with the golden-haired pretty boy."

Wilson considered Sully's words and then spoke carefully. "Alfred, no one has fought Indians better than you. You've fought against great numbers to great effect. However, you must watch how you talk, what you say about others. Praising McClellan when Lincoln was down on him is one of the things that got you here."

Sully stood and laughed. "I know, David, no one likes a soldier with a big mouth. Who knows, you might be back east while I'm still stuck out here, because of my mouth. Tomorrow we'll march down the river a day or so and build another fort. If I've got to stay here over the winter, I want a good shelter for the men."

"We'll build it," Wilson echoed. "Fort Sully, it is."

The bedraggled little caravan of Indian prisoners and their soldier escorts followed the twists and bends of the Missouri River to the southeast and Crow Creek. The sun baked their backs and the dust choked all, red and white, coating their throats and plugging nostrils.

Soldiers had dumped bags of hardtack into wagons full of women and children to provide something for them to eat. Most food had been left behind in the dash to escape Whitestone Hill.

The scouts rode beyond the head of the column. The destination was clear, but lookouts still had to watch for marauding bands of Sioux that might attempt to free their captive friends and family members.

Solomon turned to Jim Atkinson, another scout. "Are you going back to Forest City?"

"Yes," the burly, dark-haired man replied, "there are still garrisons patrolling through Meeker County from Paynesville south. Manannah, Long Lake, Forest City have forts. I'll ride with patrols through the winter, see my family and then come back to ride with Sully next summer."

"I'm going back to Sauk Centre," Solomon commented, "I've got to keep Adaline warm in the cold nights. Then maybe I'll join you here with Sully, too. Nathan, Jesse, what will you do?"

Nathan replied, "Emily and I will stay at Crow Creek. Pastor Williamson and Pastor Hinman need the help. At least that's my short-term plan. One arm limits my options a little, but not much."

"Oliver Howard is a one-armed general," Jesse pointed out. "You could be a soldier again."

Nathan answered slowly, "Not now. If the time is ever right. Well . . . I don't know. What about you, Jesse?"

"Fight a war somewhere. Either out here with Sully or in the East against the Confederacy. Then when it's over, JoAnna and I will be married, and I'll go back to being a lawyer. I've heard Duley has gone back to Lake Shetek. They're having a formal burial there."

The next day brought them to Crow Creek and Fort Thompson. They rode down the east side of the river across from the bluffs on the west. Approaching the settlement, they increasingly traveled past scaffolds holding the dead bodies of Indians from the reservation. For Nathan and Jesse, the grim sights were tempered by thoughts of the reunions they would soon have with their special women.

The scouts led the procession past a small cemetery not far from the fort. As they neared the grave mounds and little wooden crosses, Jesse exclaimed, "My God! No!" He jolted his horse to a halt, leaped from the animal and tumbled to his knees by a fresh grave, where he dissolved into wracking sobs.

Draped over the cross was a yellow bandana. The name etched onto the cross was "JoAnna Miller."

❧ 48 ☙

ORD QUICKLY SPREAD THAT SOLDIERS had brought more captives in the Crow Creek camp and that Jesse, Nathan, and Solomon were with them. Emily waited for the men in front of her cabin. One look at Jesse's stricken face told her that he knew.

Even before greeting Nathan, she wrapped her arms around Jesse.

"What happened?" his broken voice whispered.

"Fever, Jesse. I'm so sorry. Dozens died. Dr. Wharton did everything he could. There was just . . ." Emily's voice trailed off, and her voice choked as her eyes overflowed with tears.

Solomon and Nathan each rested comforting hands on their grief-stricken friend's shoulders.

"We should have married. I should have listened. Oh my dear JoAnna, I wish we'd married," Jesse sobbed plaintively.

"In your hearts you were," Emily consoled.

SOLOMON FOOT AND JIM ATKINSON JOINED Jesse for the ride back to Minnesota. Jesse would continue on to St. Paul, while Solomon would join his family in Sauk Centre and Jim would ride to Forest City. Foot pulled his black slouch hat low and led the way east.

Stephen Miller had been elected governor of Minnesota, but Jesse still thought of him as the man who was to be his father-in-law, even though now he could never be. Together they would mourn their loss.

The hunting party along with John Williamson returned to Crow Creek as promised. The camp was still dismal. Emily and Nathan plunged into teaching once again. The buffalo meat brought from the hunt was helpful, but not enough. Hunger and starvation were very real prospects.

Colonel Thompson reported that the wagons of food and supplies were still coming from Minnesota but that frequent breakdowns and bad weather were slowing the journey to a snail's pace.

Sam Brown, former agent and scout Joe Brown's son, worked at teaching and translating with Emily and Nathan. He learned much from the new residents of Crow Creek, the refugees from Whitestone.

The nineteen-year-old boy was mortified by what he heard about Sully's victory. He wrote his father:

"I hope you will not believe all that is said of 'Sully's successful expedition' against the Sioux. I don't think he aught to brag of it at all because it was what no decent man would have done. He pitched into their camp and just slaughtered them, worse a great deal than what Indians did in 1862, he killed very few men and took no hostile ones prisoners . . . and now he returns saying that we need fear no more, for he has 'wiped out all hostile Indians from Dakota.' If he had killed men instead of women and children, then it would have been a success, and the worse of it, they had no hostile intention whatever. The Second Nebraska pitched into them without orders, while the Sixth Iowa were shaking hands with them on one side, the soldiers even shot their own men."

Sam read the letter to Nathan. "Will you see that it gets posted?" he asked.

"Certainly. I was there, and your letter is correct. Some of us refused to fight, Sam. Solomon and Jesse left their weapons holstered."

Emily placed an arm around Nathan's waist as they watched a roomful of students scribbling on slates. "We have to take small steps to right wrongs, Nathan. In our own way, maybe we will make their future just a tiny bit better."

"But we can't replace what was, Emily. All we can do is try to make their new world less terrible. We'll just keep teaching."

That October, Will Duley helped to rebury the victims of the August 20, 1862, attack at Lake Shetek. The bones of fifteen—nine children and six adults—were removed from a grave near the slough where they died and reburied near Lake Shetek. Tom Ireland, Charlie Hatch, and H. Watson Smith returned to their former settlement to join Duley in the ceremony.

When the others departed, Will Duley stood alone beside the mass grave. His eyes misted over as he bowed his head and spoke softly. "My beloved little ones, you are greatly missed by me and your mother. You will be in our hearts forever."

His voice grew sharper as he finished. "But the man who killed you is dead. I avenged your murders with my own hand. Pawn will never kill another woman or child. I made sure of that. I did it for you."

The wagons of supplies from Minnesota finally reached Crow Creek in the first week of December. Much had been lost along the way, and the shipment was woefully inadequate. For the many who had already died from starvation, it was simply too late.

Standing Buffalo and his Sisseton journeyed to Canada. Medicine Bottle and Shakopee still lived near Fort Garry. They felt they were beyond the reach of Major Hatch and his battalion at Pembina.

∞49∞

THE ORDER HAD COME FROM WASHINGTON at the request of Minnesota politicians. Secretary of War Edwin Stanton authorized Major Edwin Hatch to raise a regiment of cavalry to protect the settlers on the frontier of northwest Minnesota and in the northeast Dakota Territory.

Secretary Stanton had listed two main objectives in his order. "You will seek to punish those Indians guilty of crimes against American citizens, and you will prevent persons in the vicinity of Pembina and across the Canadian border from furnishing Indians with firearms and ammunition to further carry on their warfare."

It was expected that the order would be carried out in the summer, but delay followed delay in arranging for supplies and transportation. The march to Pembina in the summer would have had favorable weather, abundant grazing and no need for a cumbersome forage train.

Delay meant that forage had to be supplied by contract at designated points along the way from Fort Snelling to the Canadian-Dakota border just west of Minnesota. Finally, on October 5, 1863, the 1,000-man army of Major Hatch struck its tents and began the march.

Edwin Hatch had been chosen for the assignment because of his life in the "far west" since early manhood. He had lived among the Sioux and was well-acquainted with their customs and characteristics. Major Charles Nash was the quartermaster in charge of equipping the force.

The first snow of the season slapped the faces of the regiment unseasonably early as it rode toward Sauk Centre on October 15. Hatch rode near the front with Nash and other officers. Farther out and nearing the stockade were the scouts, led by Joseph Brown, who had been transferred to Hatch from Sibley.

Captains Chamblin of Company A and George Whitcomb of Company B trotted alongside Hatch. The wind picked up and drove big white flakes at them.

"Sibley told me about a man in Sauk Centre," Hatch told his companions. "He scouted with the expedition all summer and just recently returned to Sauk Centre. His name is Foot. I'm advised to seek his help."

"I know him," Whitcomb commented. "I was at Forest City last year during the fighting. A woman brought him to us from the Kandiyohi lakes. He was all shot up after driving off a whole swarm of reds who attacked him and some others in a cabin. I didn't think he'd make it."

"Not only did he live, but a couple of weeks later he rode off to help a one-armed fella rescue four white women and kill their captors. He's quite a man, all right."

"Brown knows him, too," Hatch responded. "He's supposed to ask him to go to Pembina with us."

At the head of the scout party, Joe Brown rode through the gates into the Sauk Centre stockade. Two familiar faces greeted him. Walking toward the scouts were two men, one with a full-brimmed black slouch and knee-length black coat. The other wore the uniform and blue overcoat of an officer.

"Solomon, Jesse!" Brown called happily. "Good to see you!" He dismounted and shook their hands. "You remember Jim Atkinson," he gestured to their companion from the Sully campaign. "Sibley detached me and some other scouts to head up north with Hatch. We picked Jim up in Forest City. They want us to make sure that there are no attacks on the frontier. Hatch wants you, Solomon, and now that I know Jesse is here, I'd like him, too."

"I dunno, Joe," Solomon demurred, "it's been barely two weeks since I've been back here. Adaline and the little Foots will be a mite put out if I leave so soon."

"Just get us started. We're going to Pembina. Word is that we're going after some of Little Crow's chiefs that got away. Men like Medicine Bottle and Shakopee, two of the biggest murderers from last summer. We can use you."

"Now that intrigues me a little," Solomon responded. "Those two helped to start the war by convincing Little Crow to attack the Redwood Agency the day after the Acton massacre. I'd lay more of what happened on them than on Little Crow."

Brown continued, "They've been holed up in Canada ever since the war ended in Minnesota. Just over the border they are, mocking us, knowing that we can't do anything about them."

"We can't," Solomon questioned, "can we?"

"There's a plan. How about you, Jesse?"

"I guess you could say I'm at loose ends right now."

"I'm sorry about Miss Miller, Lieutenant."

"Thank you." Jesse fought through the painful memory that briefly flickered across his face. "I think they sent me out here to keep me busy. We ride the circuit of posts and rotate from stockade to stockade. We keep the mail route open between St. Cloud and Fort Abercrombie. It's better than sitting around. But if Major Hatch can get me released from my present duty, I'll go with you."

"Excellent. Consider it done."

Solomon had made up his mind, too. "Joe, I'll clear this with Addy, but I think you can count me in, too. At least one more time."

THE FOLLOWING DAY SOLOMON AND JESSE took their places with the scout detail as it forged a few miles ahead of the main column. For nearly the next month Hatch's battalion trudged over long, monotonous miles, covering ten to twenty each day. The travel was tedious with a heavily-loaded supply train pulled by oxen and mules.

The weather was horrible. Nearly every day some form of stormy conditions plagued them. Rain and snow alternately soaked and pelted the troopers. High winds from the northwest blew in their faces, blurring eyes and stinging cheeks red.

Each night they camped in small, drafty tents on the cold, bleak, desolate prairie. At Pomme de Terre, fifty miles east of Fort Abercrombie, the army camped at a small stockade that doubled as a station of the Minnesota Stage Company. There Hatch called his officers together.

"Gentlemen," he began, "from the beginning last summer we've suffered one delay after another. We shouldn't have to be dependent on having forage supplied to us. But we are and the suppliers are inconsistent at meeting us at the appointed times and places. We need supplies."

"What do you suggest?" Captain Whitcomb asked.

"I'm going to divide the command. The bulk of the army will continue on to Fort Abercrombie. There we'll obtain additional ordinance supplies. Lieutenant Mix, I want you to escort the supply train to Georgetown, that's about fifteen miles below a little village called Moorhead.

"That route should cut about thirty to forty miles off the march to Pembina. We'll meet up with you at Georgetown. Remember, you have most of the food. We're going for supplies in guns and powder."

The next day each detachment of men made its departure. Both marched through a snowstorm of twelve inches that bogged down the heavy wagons. Then the air turned bitter cold as high winds mercilessly whipped the snow into even higher drifts.

Next the days became warmer. But the warmth, while welcome to the frozen troopers, created another obstacle. The snow softened, and the wagons bogged down even more, making it impossible to progress. Lieutenant Mix decided that the column would travel at night when colder air froze and crusted over the snow, making travel possible.

The scouts led Hatch and the main body of troops into Georgetown on October 30. But concern grew when Mix and his force did not reach the rendezvous. Solomon and Jesse volunteered to search for the tardy soldiers.

The two scouts rode to the east searching for the missing detachment. The sun's bright reflection off the snow caused the men to squint and shade their eyes as they scanned the distant prairie. One day out, Mix with his men and wagons appeared on the horizon.

Jesse and Solomon trotted ahead to the missing soldiers. Jesse smiled broadly. "Well, Lieutenant, you are a sight for sore eyes. You had us worried."

"Couldn't move the wagons in this white stuff," Mix declared.

"Problem is," Solomon demurred, "you've got the rations for the main body. Luckily we managed to shoot a few elk, or the men would be mighty hungry. As it is, the men will be happy ta see you for more than one reason."

"We still don't have enough forage," Jesse explained. "Suppliers didn't come through again, and Major Hatch has ordered us to commandeer grain and hay from settlers. The government will compensate them later. But we can't have our animals die on us before we get to Pembina."

Hatch and his men were overjoyed when Mix rode into Georgetown with his command. They renewed their march north on November 5. The trail they followed was covered with snow. Occasionally they veered off and lost it in foot-deep snow and deeper drifts. Once again blizzards howled, blasting the men on the trail during the day and in their tents at night.

And once again animal forage ran short, and the exhausted, starving creatures pawed through the deep snow seeking grass. The trail became marked by the bodies of dead animals.

The Hatch Battalion finally ended its torturous journey when it reached Pembina on November 13. Camp was established on the north side of the Pembina River, where it joined the Red River of the North, just south of the Canadian border.

Hatch surveyed his new home. "Five miserable little log buildings," he complained to Whitcomb and Chamblin. "And here's a surprise," he said sarcastically, "the grain that was supposed to be here, isn't."

"I've got some good news for you," Whitcomb said. "Atkinson tells me that the scouts found a good supply of hay just a few miles from here. It'll get us by for a while."

"Good news! The animals will be seen to. Now, let's get the men taken care of. Get details working on buildings for the officers and men." He paused and then continued, "We need headquarters, a hospital, commissary and quartermaster's warehouse, guard house, barns, stockade and whatever else you see that we need."

It was fortunate that the men worked quickly to erect shelters. The weather grew even more severe. For one solid week the temperature lows ranged from twenty to forty degrees below zero. The soldiers brought in the new year of 1864 by celebrating sixty below.

In spite of the frigid temperatures, Hatch sent troops out to fulfill his mission. "Captain Chamblin," Hatch explained, "our scouts tell me that most of the Indians that were on this side of the border have moved up to Fort Garry. But they occasionally return. I'm told there's a camp of them on the American side near St. Joseph. In the cold weather they'll be holed up. They won't expect you. I want you to strike a decisive blow on them. Your success would minimize trouble with them in the future. We need to get them under control to fulfill our mission."

Solomon and Jesse rode out as scouts for Chamblin and his detachment of twenty men. A full moon shone in the brisk, frosty night, reflecting soft light off the snow. The horses' breaths formed little clouds around their snouts

The two scouts pulled their overcoats tight and rode forward of the troop. Not far from the little town of St. Joseph they encountered a small camp.

"We've gotta go tell the captain," Solomon said, "but I've got a bad feelin' 'bout this."

"What do you mean?" Jesse asked.

"This'll be the third defenseless village that I've been part of attacking."

"We're scouts, Solomon. We don't have to shoot."

At 3:00 that morning, Chamblin's detail surrounded the little village. The soldiers charged into the tipis, and in a heartbeat it was over. Three Indians were dead, a couple dozen captured and two soldiers were wounded. Solomon and Jesse watched from a distance.

A few days later word came from Governor Dallas at Fort Garry that a large number of Sioux had expressed a desire to surrender depending upon Hatch's conditions. He gave permission to the Americans to negotiate with the Dakota in Canada. "Major Hatch," Dallas wrote, "I have nearly 600 Indians flooding over the border. They're hungry and putting a strain on our resources. My citizenry is understandably nervous. I know that you seek Standing Buffalo, among others. It is a blessing for us that Standing Buffalo and his Sisseton have crossed back on your side of the border and, as I gather, have headed west to the Badlands. Others you seek are here— Shakopee, also known as Little Six, and Medicine Bottle are among them."

The major sent Joe Brown, along with George Whitcomb, Jesse, and Solomon, into Canada to meet with the Sioux.

At a camp outside Fort Garry the soldiers met with Santee leaders. Shakopee, Little Leaf, Medicine Bottle, and White Spider, Little Crow's half-brother, sat in a warm but smoky tipi. The Indians were slender, their faces worn and haggard. They were joined by Hatch's four negotiators as they formed a circle on buffalo robes around the fire.

"Are you hungry? Do you want to eat?" Shakopee asked. He was in his mid-fifties and the oldest of the Indian leaders. His sallow face reflected a recent illness.

The white men accepted buffalo jerky as an obligation to decorum. White Spider began the negotiations. "We will return with you to Minnesota, but we have one condition."

"What's that?" Joe Brown asked.

"We wish to be treated like the others, the ones you sent to Crow Creek. We fought a war, we lost. Treat us as defeated warriors and not criminals. We will surrender if you assure us that none of us will be punished."

Brown cleared his throat and contemplated before responding. Then he repeated what Major Hatch had told him to say. "There can be no conditions. You know that trials were held for those who killed defenseless farmers and women and children. Punishments were given out to them. I'm not authorized to guarantee pardons for those who escaped punishment by fleeing to Canada."

"We are not criminals!" Medicine Bottle proclaimed indignantly. "We are soldiers who tried to drive invaders from our land. I only fought soldiers. I never killed women and children." At thirty, the young leader had a pleasant, strong face.

Whitcomb asserted, "There are those in Meeker and Wright counties who believe that you did the killings of the Dustin family by Howard Lake. If that's not true, say so in court."

"Many of those hanged at Mankato did nothing. Chaska even protected whites, but you killed him, anyway," Shakopee countered.

"You may all surrender," Brown responded. "We will see that your bellies are full and that no starving time comes. We will keep you warm in the time of the tree-popping moon. Later a trial will decide who deserves punishment and who does not."

The Indians rose to their feet to dismiss the whites. "We will not surrender under your terms," Shakopee announced. "It would be death to us as certainly as the sun will rise tomorrow."

The white party returned empty-handed to report to Major Hatch. Brown and Whitcomb were in the process of explaining their failed negotiations when Solomon burst into the log headquarters building.

"Hold on, Joe," he interrupted Brown, "take a look outside."

Over 200 forlorn-looking Santee were assembled on the parade ground between the buildings. White Spider stepped out from the mass and declared, "You promised to care for these people. To feed them and keep them warm. We are here. Little Crow's wife is here and six children, his sister and her husband, his other half-brother and me, the other half-brother to Little Crow. We are here, and we place our lives at your mercy. If we must die, it is better to do so quickly and not starve or freeze to death."

Hatch strode over to White Spider and shook his hand. "We will see to your care. Major Nash," he called to his quartermaster, "see that these people are fed and are given shelter."

He turned back to White Spider. "Where are the others? Where's Shakopee and Medicine Bottle, and Little Leaf?"

"They stay near Fort Garry. They don't trust you. They know you will kill them."

Hatch drew his lips tight. "We just may yet."

❦ 50 ❧

A LIGHT SNOW FELL ON THE ICY NIGHT OF January 10, 1864. Major Edwin Hatch scraped frost from a window and looked out his head-quarters building. Two men cast shadowy images as they hurried along the pathway toward him. Their shoulders were hunched up against the cold as they sought to keep warm beneath heavy fur coats.

Without waiting for a knock, the major swung open the door. Pale yellow light from the room cast a glow on the visitors. The first to enter the building was a handsome man with a bushy mustache frosted white, a couple of small icicles frozen to it. He removed a round fur hat to reveal thick brown hair that dropped over the tops of his ears. His blue eyes were nearly as icy as the night air.

The man extended his hand to Hatch. "I'm John McKenzie, and this is my friend Onisime Giguere. I'm told you have need of us."

"Please, sit down by the fire." Hatch gestured to three chairs that rested before the fireplace. "Warm your bones." McKenzie's companion was older and of French ancestry. He opened his heavy coat and stood be-fore the blazing fire, extending his hands palms out to warm them before sitting down.

Hatch sat to the left of the other two and turned his chair so that he could see the men directly as he spoke to them. "You've told no one why you were sent for?" the officer inquired.

"No," McKenzie answered, "we're a little short of details ourselves. Seems you would like us to find some Indians for you."

"Yes, but before those details, and please keep your task a secret, I'd like to know more about you."

"Onisime and me, we came up to the Red River to trap. My friend here comes from a long line of trappers. We've been living in the Red River settlement for a few months."

"Where were you before, Mr. McKenzie?"

"Meeker County, most directly."

Hatch chuckled. "Meeker County, you say. Seems that my command is becoming a haven for Meeker County folks."

"Who else?" McKenzie wondered.

"Well, let me see, we've got a scout named Atkinson, my captain of Company B. George Whitcomb, another scout from the Kandiyohi lakes, Solomon Foot, who spent some time at Forest City, and now you. "

"I know Whitcomb, he was our county treasurer, and Atkinson was our first state representative from Meeker County. Foot, I've just heard of. Never met him."

Hatch paused a moment and then continued. "Well, let's get down to brass tacks. We want two men, both murderers, Shakopee and Medicine Bottle, taken back across the border to me. The State of Minnesota will pay you one thousand dollars bounty if you deliver them."

"Deed or alive?" Giguere asked in a heavy French accent.

"We want them alive. The people of Minnesota want them tried and then they want to watch them hang."

"That makes it a little trickier," McKenzie considered, "but I know Shakopee. He was a friend of mine."

"It is because of your friendship that you were suggested to me. You can get close to them."

McKenzie stared into the flickering yellow and red flames in the fireplace. Thoughtfully he turned to Giguere. "Well, I'm game. How about you?"

"I go weez you."

"Then it's a go. Major, when do you want us to begin? Does tomorrow suit you?"

"It suits me right down to the ground."

Hatch stood and shook their hands. "I'm told that they are camped between Pembina and Fort Garry on the Assinibone River. I'll see that our best horses are ready for you."

McKenzie hesitated. "No thanks on the horses, Major. We have our own transportation."

"What's that?"

"Dog sled."

The next morning the two set off, each man driving a sled of six dogs. With a sharp bark from the lead dog, they glided through thick snow toward the Canadian border.

McKenzie and Giguere found the Indian village on the Assinibone River on the night of January 16, six nights after their conversation with Major Hatch. Shakopee greeted his old friend warmly, believing he had nothing to fear. They were in Canada, free from American law, and these men were trappers, not soldiers.

"John," the old chief greeted, "come to my lodge. It is warm and the night wind will not reach you. Do you want to eat?"

Giguere and McKenzie entered the buffalo hide tipi and accepted a ladle each of dog stew. Medicine Bottle and Little Leaf joined them. They sat around the fire and smoked.

Shakopee opened the conversation. "I'm sorry the stew was thin. The dog was skinny. Why have you come to us?"

"Just doin' some trappin' 'round here. Do you have any furs you want to trade?"

"Some, maybe," Shakopee acknowledged.

After small talk about furs and the cold weather, McKenzie began to lay the groundwork for his mission. "I saw White Spider a bit ago. He looks good, getting some meat on his bones. I know his people were suffering here. Now they are well fed and warm. You should come to Pembina, too."

"They would kill us at Pembina!" Medicine Bottle snapped.

"I have it on good authority that no one intends to kill you at Pembina."

Giguere stifled a smile that played on his lips. *John speaks true*, he thought. *They want to kill you at Fort Snelling.*

The men bantered back and forth, but it soon became clear that the Indians were adamant in their refusal to go to Pembina.

McKenzie continued to cajole the Indians. "Look, we'll protect you. I've got some top notch firewater for you. Good stuff, ummm, not rot gut." He patted his stomach and winced.

"We will go with you and drink your firewater," Shakopee announced, "but not to Pembina. We know you have a cabin by Fort Garry. We will meet you there tomorrow."

"Fine," McKenzie winked at Giguere. "Tomorrow it is."

Late the next day Shakopee and Medicine Bottle entered John's cabin just west of Fort Garry. The white men had made preparations for their guests. The small cabin was warm and cheery. A lively fire danced in the stone fireplace, and a young mixed-blood man stood behind a wood-plank counter with liquor bottles resting on it.

"This is White Feather. He's Ojibway, and he will be our bartender tonight. What's your pleasure, my friends?" McKenzie asked warmly.

Shakopee pointed to a bottle of whiskey.

"Pour away, White Feather. Toddies for all," John commanded.

The Indians begin drinking strong whiskies. Their "bartender" served the two white men water disguised as toddies. The conversation was pleasant and centered around families and hunting as the four sat around a small wooden table.

As the night wore on and drink made his guests' tongues looser, John McKenzie began to ask more pointed questions.

"Why does the army want you so bad?" he asked Shakopee.

"They say I killed many whites, that I led the young men when many whites were killed at Beaver Creek. The white woman, Wakefield, claimed at Chaska's trial that I tried to kill her and that Chaska stopped me." He finished with a derisive snort.

"Is is true?"

Shakopee smiled a sloppy grin and held out his tin cup for more liquor. "I fought in a war. Some people died."

Giguere sidled over to White Feather and whispered as he reached into a coat pocket and handed over a small bottle. "Start slipping a shot of this in their drinks." It was laudanum.

"What about you, Medicine Bottle?" McKenzie asked.

"They say that I was with Shakopee and the others in Little Crow's house after the Acton killings. That I helped talk Little Crow into war. Some say I killed Philander Prescott at the agency the next day."

"Did you?"

Medicine Bottle's only response was to laugh long and loud. Then he held out a bare right arm covered by tattoos. "One mark for everyone I killed." He laughed again.

Through the night the men talked and drank. Slowly but surely the Indians began to slur their words and become more and more obviously intoxicated. But they remained upright, and the two whites dared not make a move.

Then Shakopee stood unsteadily from his chair. He removed a long knife from his belt. "This is my scalping knife!" he cried. "Many of your people felt it in Minnesota." The Indian rocked back and forth on trembling legs and then tumbled backward unconscious.

Medicine Bottle covered his mouth and laughed uproariously at his prostrate friend. McKenzie instantly snatched up Shakopee's knife. Tired of waiting for Medicine Bottle to pass out, he yelled, "Now!" to Giguere.

In his stupor, Medicine Bottle was too late to recognize the impending danger. In an instant the two white men were wrestling their drunken guest to the floor. Giguere placed a rag drenched with chloroform over the struggling Indian's nose and held tight as the man twisted beneath him. Soon Medicine Bottle's body went limp. Immediately each Indian was strapped to a board and placed on one of the dog sleds.

At daylight they set out for Pembina. The two sleds glided swiftly over the packed snow-covered trail. The two captives were securely bound with gags fitted over their mouths. Only hate filled eyes were visible between the restraints and fur hats pulled to just above each the Indian's eyebrows.

As they reached the border, McKenzie noticed two riders approaching. They looked like two black ink spots spreading against a stark white background, as the riders grew closer in the snow.

McKenzie pointed ahead signaling to Giguere. John's hand tensed on the stock of a rifle that rested in a scabbard tied to the sled. He relaxed when he recognized a wide brimmed black hat. It had to be Solomon Foot.

Solomon and Jesse trotted their horses down the trail toward the oncoming dog sleds. When they met, Foot greeted, "Hatch sent us out to guide you in." He gazed at the tethered bundles and observed, "Looks like you got yer limits."

"Who are they?" Jesse asked.

McKenzie grinned and proudly announced, "We have the notorious murderers who have eluded justice for almost two years, Medicine Bottle and Shakopee."

"Impressive" Solomon replied, "How'd you do it?"

"Brains and skill, old man," McKenzie chuckled, "with a little help from a jug. Now lead us on to Major Hatch. He's got a little something waitin' for us."

"Ees gotta lot of sometheen." Giguere laughed.

Shakopee and Medicine Bottle were delivered to Hatch. Within days over a hundred more Dakota people walked down the snowy path to Pembina and surrendered. Soon after, the Quartermaster, Major Nash, spoke urgently about the new situation with Hatch. "

We're getting too many people and too many horses," Nash explained, "we don't have the forage or the food to take care of the numbers we have here."

Hatch considered Nash's words and then offered, "Soon as it warms up a little, I'll send Brown and fifty men with the Indians to Fort Snelling. Can we make it to February?"

"Yes, but not much longer. What about the two outlaws?"

"Medicine Bottle and Shakopee? I'll wait a little longer, 'til spring and then send them to Abercrombie with Lieutenant Mix. I'm guessing that sometime, before long, they'll order me to leave here, too. Once things settle down there'll be no need for a fort at Pembina."

☙ 51 ❧

arly in the spring of 1864 General Pope ordered Sibley and Sully to join him in Milwaukee to plan the summer campaign against the Sioux. The three gathered around a small round table in Pope's brick headquarters building.

Pope greeted his two generals warmly. He brushed a lock of hair from his eyes and smiled. Pope was a self-assured man from Kentucky. He had a full, bushy beard and an ample head of dark hair that sometimes flopped over his right eye.

"Henry, Alfred, I've finally managed a rendezvous for you two, something we couldn't quite work out last summer." He chuckled as Sibley and Sully forced tight-lipped smiles. "I congratulate you both again on your magnificent victories last summer."

Sully grimaced slightly. "I'm not as jubilant as you, General Pope. I won't be satisfied until the Sioux are completely destroyed as a fighting force, or until they are driven so far away that they can't return to Minnesota or the Dakota Territory.

Pope spread a sheet of paper on the table. "General-in-Chief Hallack notes that the Sioux are still resisting along the Missouri. That's not new to you, Alfred. He tells me that there are no troops to spare because of the war in the South. Because of that shortage of manpower, Hallack urges me to seek peace with the Sioux."

"No! We must stop them now," Sully asserted. "Poverty will drive the Indians together. I warn you that tribes that have long been enemies will join together to fight us. They will rob or kill to get food when it's in short supply. When the grass is high in the spring and they have forage, they'll be at us again."

"I'm keeping the frontier patrolled," Sibley added. "We'll call Hatch back from Pembina soon and disperse his men on the western spaces in Minnesota."

Pope folded the paper and placed it in a pocket. "I agree with you both for the most part. General Sibley, you will order Hatch away from Pembina when practical and have troops continue to patrol western Minnesota. You, Henry, will go to Devils Lake and establish forts there and on the James River.

"General Sully, I have a more ambitious task in mind for you. First, there will be no rendezvous. You will establish a fort on the Missouri near where you and Sibley should have rendezvoused last summer. You will use that as a base of operations from which to drive all Sioux from the Dakotas. I don't care if you have to push them all the way to Yellowstone. Eliminate them from the Dakota Territory."

"General Pope," Sully replied, "this just might be the best order you've ever given me. I felt that my job was only half-finished last summer. I'll finish it for you this time. How many men will I have? I'd like eight or nine more cavalry companies."

"Not as many as I'd like to give you. I don't know about the cavalry increase, I think I can get you a battalion of the Seventh Iowa. Most of your men will be from Minnesota."

"I'd rather stay with my men in Minnesota," Sibley countered.

"Request noted," Pope replied, "but I want you to go to Devils Lake. When the forts are built, leave some troops and go home. Most of your available troops from Minnesota will be with Sully."

SULLY RETURNED TO THE DAKOTA TERRITORY eager to finish his plans for summer operations against the Sioux. Sibley reluctantly prepared for one more foray west.

Solomon and Jesse joined Joe Brown in the march with Indian prisoners to Fort Snelling. As they neared Sauk Centre, Solomon bade farewell to his friend.

"Take care, Jesse. I know it's been a tough winter for you. I'll spend some time here and then likely go west again. Either Sully or Sibley can use me, I think."

"I'm going the rest of the way to Fort Snelling. Atkinson is going to ride with us until he cuts off for Forest City. He'll probably be back with you for the summer campaign," Jesse said. "I'll meet with Colonel . . . er . . . Governor Miller in St. Paul. He wrote that he has an assignment for me that I might be interested in taking."

"JoAnna's death was very hard on him, too, wasn't it?"

Jesse swallowed. "He lost his wife a few years back, and now his only daughter. Yes, it's hard on Governor Miller, too."

The two men clasped in a firm handshake.

"Our paths will cross again," Solomon nodded. "Greet Nathan and Emily for me. Good luck to you, my friend."

Jesse injected a playful comment to ward off the choked-up feeling that threatened his composure. "Watch your top knot, old man, what's left of it."

Emily and Nathan Cates, along with John Williamson and Samuel Hinman, continued to teach and minister to the destitute Indians at Crow Creek.

In the cool stillness of an early spring night, Nathan threw another log into the stone fireplace of their small, snug cabin.

"Are you sure you want to spend another summer here?" he gently asked Emily.

She answered with no hesitation. "They need us, Nathan. Are you having second thoughts?"

He smiled, wrapped his arm around her and responded, "Not yet, but life is hard here. I just want you to be sure."

"Life is made bearable here by the knowledge that we are doing something worthwhile and that you are with me."

Nathan bent down and tenderly kissed his wife. He whispered into her ear, "And I always will be."

IN MAY, HATCH WAS ORDERED TO LEAVE Pembina. His men were detached to Abercrombie, Alexandria, and Pomme de Terre.

Back in Minnesota, Oscar Wall wrote a book about his experiences with the Sibley Expedition.

Medicine Bottle and Shakopee were taken to Fort Snelling and sentenced to death. As he mounted the gallows the whistle of the first steam locomotive to pass the fort echoed up the valley. Shakopee pointed to the train and cried, "As the white man comes in, the Indian goes out."

Standing Buffalo and his band continued to wander through the Dakotas, as Sitting Bull, joined by Inkpaduta, camped east of the Missouri River. The Teton chief cast a wary eye toward Minnesota. He knew that his encounter with white soldiers the previous summer was but a foretaste of what was to come. He vowed to be ready.

Inkpaduta's journey with Sitting Bull would eventually lead him to Little Big Horn and the fight against George Custer.

General Sully's half-Yankton daughter Mary, or "Akicita Win" (Soldier Woman), married Philip Deloria, an Episcopal priest. Among her descendants is author Vine Deloria, Jr.

Alfred Sully and Henry Hastings Sibley planned and prepared for the summer of 1864. Sully did so with relish, Sibley with trepidation. While the great war to save the Union was waged in the East, General Sully was determined to do his best with the hand dealt him. If he couldn't be in the midst of the biggest war ever fought in North America, he would become the greatest general ever to fight Indians.

Jesse Buchanen was melancholy as he approached the Miller home. Memories of happy times there with JoAnna came flooding back. But the governor of Minnesota, her father, wanted to see him. A new mission awaited.

❧ Sources ❧

Recollections of the Sioux Massarcre by Oscar G. Wall, 1909, Home Printery, Lake City, Minnesota.

Little Crow, Spokesman for the Sioux, Gary Clayton Anderson, 1986, Minnesota Historical Society Press, St. Paul, Minnesota.

Henry Hastings Sibley, Divided Heart, Rhoda R. Gilman, 2004, Minnesota Historical Society Press, St. Paul, Minnesota

The Dakota Indian Internment at Fort Snelling 1862-1864, Corinne L. Monjeau-Marz, 2006, Prairie Smoke Press, St. Paul, Minnesota.

The Dakota Uprising, A Pictorial History, Curtis A. Dahlin, 2009, Beavers Pond Press, Edina, Minnesota.

Ashes, John Koblas, 2006, North Star Press, St. Cloud, Minnesota.

No Tears for the General, the Life of Alfred Sully 1821-1879, Langdon Sully, 1974, Western Biography Series, American West Publishing Company, Palo Alto, California.

Over the Earth I Come, The Great Sioux Uprising of 1862, Duane Schultz, 1992, St. Martin's Press, New York, New York.

John P. Williamson, A Brother to the Sioux, Winifred W. Barton, 1919, Fleming H. Revell Company, New York, Chicago, London and Edinburgh.

The War of the Rebellion: A Compilation of the Official Records of the Union and Confederate Armies, Series 1-Volume 22, Part 1, United States War Department,1888, United States Printing Office, Washington, D.C.

North Dakota State Historical Society, T. Reed.

Minnesota State Historical Society, Patrick Coleman.

Elders of Crow Creek Reservation, Fort Thompson, South Dakota.

Whitestone Hill, Clair Jacobson, 1991, Pine Tree Publishing, La Crosse, Wisconsin.

The Dakota War, The United States Army Versus the Sioux, Michael Clodfelter, 1998, McFarland & Company, Inc., Jefferson, North Carolina and London.

The Sioux Uprising of 1862, Kenneth Carley, 1976, The Minnesota Historical Society, St. Paul, Minnesota.

The Death of John H. McKenzie, Litchfield Saturday Review, Wednesday, March 24, 1920.

Condensed History of Meeker County, Frank B. Lamson.

Narrative of Hatch's Independent Battalion of Cavalry by Major C.W. Nash.

"A New Look At the Elusive Inkpaduta," Peggy Rodina Larson, Spring 1982, *Minnesota History Magazine*, St. Paul, Minnesota.